Heart of the Wild Gods

Kendall Brooks

Published by Kendall Brooks, 2025.

This is a work of fiction. Similarities to real people, places, or events are entirely coincidental.

HEART OF THE WILD GODS

First edition. January 31, 2025.

Copyright © 2025 Kendall Brooks.

ISBN: 979-8218878757

Written by Kendall Brooks.

Table of Contents

Prologue 1
Weod-Monaþ ⚔ August 7
1 | Uht ⚔ Before Dawn 9
2 | Nīwe Dæg ⚔ New Day 19
3 | Norþmenn ⚔ Northmen 25
4 | ⚔ Wōdenléah ⚔ 35
5 | Burne ⚔ Stream 53
6 | Ġemōt ⚔ Meeting 61
7 | Lufiend ⚔ Lover 67
8 | Gewær ⚔ Watchful 77
9 | Cirice ⚔ Church 85
10 | Foresteall ⚔ Ambush 91
11 | Cheping ⚔ Marketplace 99
12 | Biscop ⚔ Bishop 107
13 | Sorg ⚔ Sorrow 111
Geol-Monaþ ⚔ December 125
14 | ⚔ Winter ⚔ 127
15 | Rīdan ⚔ Ride 133
16 | Læwa ⚔ Traitor 137
17 | Lænland ⚔ Loanland 149
18 | Ġestolen ⚔ Stolen 159
19 | Onræs ⚔ Attack 165
20 | Onfundennes ⚔ Finding Out 173
21 | Læderas ⚔ Leaders 193
22 | Sōcn ⚔ A Visit 207
23 | Fær ⚔ Journey 217
24 | Gæst ⚔ Visitor 229
25 | Hæftling ⚔ Captive 243
26 | Huntung ⚔ Hunting 255
27 | Wintanceaster ⚔ Winchester 265
28 | Þæc ⚔ Thatch 285

29	Hām ✕ Home	299
30	Géola ✕ Yule	305
31	Symbel ✕ Feast	319
32	Sēocness ✕ Sickness	337
33	Ærende ✕ Message	351
34	Æfter ✕ After	359
35	Horsern ✕ Stable	365
36	Ġeflit ✕ Argument	377
37	Wrecca ✕ Banish	381
38	Eode ✕ Travelled	393
39	Gield ✕ Tribute	399
40	Scidd ✕ Shed	403
41	Nīewe Þegn ✕ New Thegn	409
42	Ġetacen ✕ Taken	419
43	Cwepan ✕ Accused	425
44	Styrtan ✕ To Start	431
45	Gūþ ✕ Battle	439
46	Unwreoghen ✕ Revealed	455
47	Los ✕ Loss	465
48	Aesce ✕ Ashes	471
49	Cyre ✕ Choice	475
50	Langscip ✕ Longship	491
Epilogue	497
A (Ridiculously Brief) Note About History	499
Author's Notes	503

This story is woven from both actual historical events—its kings, its battles, its faiths—and the people, places and moments born of imagination.

Beyond the historical references, any likeness to real individuals, living or dead, is unintentional and coincidental.

This book is dedicated to my fellow daydreamers. The world needs us more than it might ever know.

— Kendall Brooks

"She is more dear to me than any maiden has ever been to a man, but no one among the gods or elves will let us be together."

— *Skírnismál, The Poetic Edda*

Prologue

The Burh of Wōdenléah ⚔ Kingdom of Wessex ⚔ 879 AD
It wasn't until Cenric had nearly caught the horse that he finally saw it.

Blood.

It soaked into the saddle and streaked down the horse's flank, all the way to its knee. The saddle had slid askew, and the stirrup leather was torn and dangled low on one side, striking the animal in the flank with each nervous movement.

Leofwynn!

That morning, he had saddled the chestnut gelding for Leofwynn, beloved wife of Osric, the newly appointed thegn.

He caught the reins with trembling hands and shouted.

"Alaric! Godwin! Everyone—leave your work—quickly! It's Leofwynn's horse!"

Billhooks and spades were instantly abandoned as soon as Cenric raised the alarm. Many of them knew well the paths the thegn's wife favored for her morning rides, so those who had been working at the far end of the field near the creek had arrived quickly.

By the time Cenric reached the creekside, a crowd was already gathering. Leofwynn's lifeless body lay beneath a tangle of snapped branches and disturbed earth, her riding cloak tangled in the brambles where the brittle undergrowth had claimed her.

She was already gone.

Ceorls and servants, friends and neighbors alike, stood in stunned silence, their hearts breaking as one was sent running to the hall, all of them dreading the moment her husband, Osric, the thegn of Wōdenléah, would arrive.

* * *

Cwenhild burst into tears as soon as Æfre opened the door, her words barely intelligible through her sobs as she stood trembling on the threshold of Æfre's hut, struggling to compose herself.

"It's Leofwynn," she managed, her voice cracking with anguish; "There's been an accident."

Cwenhild and her husband, Cenric, were steadfast pillars of the burh of Wōdenléah. The pair had always been a source of quiet strength and practical wisdom—Cwenhild in particular was the kind of woman who seemed to hold the answer to every crisis with the unshakable calm of experience.

Now, Æfre stood powerless as she watched that steady, unflappable presence crumble before her eyes.

"Leofwynn!" Æfre exclaimed, " Not gentle, kind-hearted Leofwynn!"

"They think her horse bolted after losing its footing on the sodden ground," Cwenhild said through a veil of tears. "Leofwynn's riding cloak got caught in the stirrup as they slid down the embankment!"

Æfre pressed a cup of ale into the distraught woman's hand, ushering her into a chair by the hearth.

She listened in horror as Cwenhild recounted how the horse must have dragged her behind it as it bolted, knocking her unconscious until, eventually, she succumbed to her injuries and the land claimed her.

"I swear on my good name," Cwenhild said, "this is a day that will deeply etch into the memory of every one of us in the burh. As long as I live, I will never forget the soul-bearing cries of our Lord Osric when he saw his Leofwynn lying there!" Cwenhild dissolved into a fresh flood of tears; "It tore the very soul from every one of us!"

For a long while, the two women sat in the weighted silence of grief, until the hour finally forced Cwenhild to rise from her chair.

HEART OF THE WILD GODS

"Æfre, I'm deeply concerned with how heavily this grief presses upon Lord Osric," she said. "The relentless demands of his position still bind him. His duties can be unforgiving, and of course Bishop Æthelwod will offer no reprieve!" Cwenhild looked at Æfre and pleaded, "I know well there is no herb or healing charm that can quickly mend such grief, but the man is truly lost! Will you call on him?"

Æfre did not hesitate. Whatever aid she could offer as a healer, she would call upon the thegn of Wōdenléah.

* * *

At first, Osric was distant—resistant to her presence. At times, he could be downright hostile, brusquely claiming to be buried in his work and abandoning her, leaving her no choice but to set down any remedies she'd brought and retreat.

In those early days, it was clear that duty kept Osric going. His thegnship made him an official servant of the Church and guardian of its lands, and true to Cwenhild's observations, the bishop granted him little rest from his endless stream of demands, even in the face of great personal tragedy.

Eventually, he began to open up to her. Often, he would speak of how the bishop was quick to demand loyalty and obedience, and even quicker to unleash disproportionately harsh punishments upon those who questioned his authority or failed to meet his lofty, often arbitrary expectations.

As the weeks turned into months, their interactions strengthened—hostility softened to reluctant acceptance, and that at last gave way to quiet companionship. Some days, they would walk together in silence, sharing the peace of the outdoors and the steady rhythm of their footsteps. On better days, Osric would accept her herbs to aid his sleep, talk about his duties, or reminisce about Leofwynn, his words slowly untangling the thick web of pain he wore like a mantle around his heart.

On his hardest days, days when he struggled with the weight of his grief, Æfre would sit with him, letting the silence between them hold space for his pain. When tears came, or his voice faltered with the raw edges of sorrow or rage, she would never push or rush, but simply guide him back to himself—offer a steadying touch, or simply remind him to breathe, to place one foot in front of the other.

As the months wore on, he was healing, moving through his grief. While the shadows of sadness still clung to him, they no longer defined him. There was something steadier in his presence—a quiet peace that hadn't been there before. It had taken the better part of a year, but her visits were no longer a necessity.

And that's when the man took her entirely by surprise.

* * *

In the blustery autumn, he stood at the threshold to her hut, holding out an offering of a small clay jug of herb-infused mead—just enough for a generous cup, or perhaps two smaller cups each—an unmistakable luxury, no doubt quietly lifted from the bishop's private stash.

Conversation began cautiously, words carefully chosen as they navigated the delicate terrain of his shared vulnerability. But as the moments passed and the mead flowed, the tension eased, and soon they were laughing like children—Osric even daring to give Æfre a glimpse of his impersonation of Bishop Æthelwod.

With the mead finished and both feeling the warm glow of the fire nudging them towards sleep, Osric stood to leave, and Æfre busied herself clearing the empty cups from the table.

Then Osric gently caught her by her upper arm.

"Æfre," he said softly, "forgive me. Speaking of this past year is no easy thing, but I've come to realize something. I'm fortunate to have had much support after Leofwynn's passing, yet in the past year, there was but one who called upon me without expectation or agenda, and that was you."

Still holding her by the arm, he said, "Thank you, Æfre," his gaze steady.

Æfre placed a hand over his, genuinely moved by his sincerity. "You are most welcome, Osric," she said, smiling warmly while returning his steadfast gaze and holding it for a moment before squeezing his hand and turning to continue clearing the cups from the table. But Osric didn't let go.

With a gentle hold on her upper arm, Osric eased Æfre towards him, his movements slow and unhurried, as if giving her time to pull away. Her breath caught as their faces grew closer, and his gaze softened, filled with a quiet intensity.

Stunned, she took a moment to take in what was happening, then looked up at him, as if seeing him for the first time.

"Do I overstep?" he asked softly, his voice barely audible, the words brushing her ear like a secret.

"No," Æfre whispered.

Osric smiled as he leaned in, his lips brushing past her ear, the nape of her neck, her cheek—until finally he found her lips with a tender, tentative kiss.

Weod-Monaþ ⚔ August

The Burh of Wōdenléah
Kingdom of Wessex
881 AD

1

Uht ✕ Before Dawn

The familiar voice boomed, cutting through the quiet of the hut.

"She stirs at last!"

Æfre groaned in faux protest. This was their game—she feigning a wish to languish in sleep, and he pressing her to observe his mischief before he slipped away in the discreet, pre-dawn hours, before the burh stirred and anyone marked the absence of the thegn of Wōdenléah.

She was secretly glad that today she'd awakened in time to enjoy it before he took his leave. Not that she planned on giving him the satisfaction of hearing her say it, mind you. That, too, was part of their game.

She blinked the sleep from her eyes, noting that the first light of dawn had not yet appeared at the edges of the hut's window coverings.

"By what sorcery are you awake, Osric?" She asked, yawning.

"A thegn such as I, Æfre," Osric bloviated, "is forged of hardier stuff than the mere sleep and softness of you floral-scented womenfolk."

He winked at her, shirtless and preening as he poked the previous night's embers, thoroughly amused with himself.

"Indeed, we are splendid specimens who sleep little and rise before the sun," he continued, enjoying his own theatrics, "yet we still look as if carved by the hand of the Almighty himself."

"Big words, my lord," Æfre snorted, rubbing her eyes and stretching as she rolled onto her back, "but I believe it is we, the 'floral scented-womenfolk' who are the ones to measure the truth of that claim."

Æfre grabbed the nearest weapon available to her—the pillow from his side of the bed. She hurled it, striking him squarely on the side of the head.

"How dare you?" Osric laughed, his voice heavy with mock indignation. "Such reckless behavior!" He leaned down and retrieved the pillow, dusting it off, "and such accuracy—"

Æfre squealed and hid under the coverlet as the pillow she'd thrown came sailing back at her, hitting its target with satisfying accuracy. For his benefit, she let out an exaggerated, battlefield-worthy groan which quickly dissolved into a fit of giggles.

Emerging from under the covers, Æfre yawned again—like a contented cat, then reached blindly towards the chest at her bedside. The familiar comfort of her leechbook[i] should have been there, but instead, her hand met nothing but cool, empty wood. She lifted her head off the pillow to check, even peered over the edge of the bed—certain she'd left it there—she'd been working with it just yesterday and had set it there to allow the ink to dry.

"Is it this you reach for?" Osric held something in the air.

Ah. My leechbook.

Propping herself up on her elbow, she narrowed her eyes, her voice warm with faux accusation as she raked her fingers through her hair.

"Lord Osric! Have I just caught the thegn in an act of thievery?"

He glanced up at her, unbothered and unrepentant. He tilted her leechbook slightly—showing it off before brazenly resuming paging through it.

"For mercy's sake, Osric, just don't set it alight!" Æfre laughed, unable to stop her own grin as she flopped back down onto the feather-filled mattress and snuggled in.

HEART OF THE WILD GODS

By the Gods, that is a beautiful man, she thought, taking full advantage of his distraction and allowing her gaze to linger on him, peering at him through a gap she had fashioned in the coverlet.

His tunic lay draped over his knee, as if forgotten halfway through the process of dressing. A pair of well-worn boots waited patiently at his feet, like two obedient little dogs lying in wait for their master. He looked like a man with no intention of leaving, which suited her just fine.

Her eyes traced the diagonal scar that wrapped around his left flank—a jagged reminder of the blade of a determined Northman, a near-miss during the Battle of Edington. He rarely spoke of it, deflecting her questions with a vague smile, but she knew the weight it carried. She'd felt it in the terrors that sometimes gripped him during the night, when his dreams dragged him back into the conflict. She was a witness to the price he'd paid for his distinction in battle, yet she knew it was something he would only ever speak of with a few of his closest brothers in arms.

Her gaze moved to the powerful lines of his jaw, the way his unruly, wavy hair always fell slightly out of place no matter what he did, and then down to his hands—rugged and calloused by work and battle. Yet those same hands had moved over her with such care the night before—she could still feel the lingering echoes of his touch.

The vividness of the recollection flooded her, bringing a bashful warmth to her cheeks and spreading like fire under her skin, her stomach fluttering with a mix of desire and amusement. A giggle escaped her before she could stop it—a quiet, breathy snort as she curled her toes reflexively under the coverlet.

"What's this laughter for then?" Osric asked dryly without looking up, the corner of his mouth quirking into a wary smile as he continued to study her leechbook.

Æfre pressed her hands to her flushed cheeks—a futile attempt to contain the blush. "The noise we made..." she managed, her voice trailing off into a sheepish laugh as the memory surged to the forefront of her mind. Her skin was still burning with the vividness of it.

Osric's brows arched in exaggerated innocence, though the glint in his eyes betrayed him. "I know not of what you speak," he replied, his tone thick with exaggerated solemnity as he casually flipped another page of the leechbook.

"Do you not?" Æfre mused, "Just as well, my lord, since it likely made its way into every ear between the burh and the trading camp!" Her laughter spilled over as she covered her face with her hands.

Setting the journal aside, Osric rose from his chair, shifting it slightly backwards and unsettling the rushes covering the earthen floor beneath him.

Æfre peeked at him from behind her fingers, her breath catching as she watched his every step.

When he reached her, he leaned down, his hands gently wrapping around hers, easing them away from her face. He kissed her deeply, lingering just long enough to completely melt any resolve she might have had left.

And just as quickly, it was over.

"Good," he declared, his voice definitive. "Let us hope they heard well."

Æfre blinked, reeling as he reached out and lightly ran the back of his fingers down her cheek. Before she could gather her thoughts or summon a witty retort, he was already walking back to his chair, where he plopped himself back down and reclaimed her leechbook.

She actually found it rather infuriating, perhaps even alarming, how easily he could disarm her.

Æfre pulled the coverlet back over her head and re-fashioned

HEART OF THE WILD GODS

the small opening to peer through. Cozy in its familiar, cavernous warmth, she allowed her gaze to drift around the hut, noting the scattered state of things. She sighed, vowing to herself to set aside time later that day to put things right.

The hut was a simple, one-room wattle-and-daub structure with a timber frame and a thatched roof, warmed by a raised hearth at its center. At the far end stood a stout hardwood table with two benches, and along the walls, shelves were cleverly fitted into the timber frame. Each shelf held rows of clay jars, packed with herbs, dried roots—nature's tools—remnants of the healing craft passed down through generations. Æfre's mother had used them, and her grandmother too. Now it was her turn, though often she still felt like a child playing at her mother's work.

The air inside was heavily scented with various herbs mingled with hearth smoke—ever present, always faintly clinging to Æfre's skin and hair. On this particular morning, it was a heady mixture of dried lavender and sage with an additional note of the previous night's stew, all rising gently to the rafters with the smoke and warmth from the hearth.

Everything in the hut was spare and serviceable.

With one exception—the bed.

It was a striking piece—a monument to Æfre's father's Danish heritage. It was a bed too large for the space and too fine for its surroundings. Her father had made and carved it himself as a gift for her mother.

A Dane by birth and a renowned craftsman and woodcarver by trade, he had shaped the thick wood into something fit for nobility; dragons coiled snarling along the headboard, and two curled at the tops of the bedposts. It was a piece drawn from his memory of the first longship he'd sailed on to cross the sea. It looked out of place in the modest hut, but it had always stood there, a quiet monument to something wilder than the life they all shared within the walls of the hut.

Both gone many winters now, Æfre thought as she snuggled herself deeper into the bed fit for a queen. She continued to gaze around the hut, pausing as her eyes again came to rest on the wooden table at the other end of the hearth.

That table.

That table had been their first time, she and Osric—over a year ago now. He'd lifted her tall frame up onto its wooden surface like it was nothing—an unrestrained wildness flowing through them both as bits of dried herbs tangled in her long, pale hair; a symphony of bowls and spoons clattering across the floor, displaced by their enthusiasm.

She wasn't sure how long she'd drifted in that memory when Osric's voice cut through the silence.

"Æfre—these pages in your leechbook...the script—this is Latin!" Osric rose from the bench, eyes alight with surprise and no small measure of wonder.

"You're learned in the language of scholars!?" He stepped closer, holding the leechbook as though it were some holy relic unearthed from the tomb of a saint. "Since when?" An incredulous smile spread across his face. "What else do you keep hidden behind that mischievous gaze? I know plenty of high-born nobles who couldn't do this," Osric marveled. "Truly—no one in Wōdenléah, save Bishop Æthelwod, could put their hand to such work!"

Osric continued to flip through the delicate pages of Æfre's leechbook with a heightened curiosity, tracing his finger lightly over her intricate drawings of the roots and herbs that were the backbone of her practice.

"It was my father," Æfre said, sitting up in bed as she gathered the surrounding coverlet. "He learned it during the summers he spent traveling for commissions."

She swung her legs over the side of the bed and stood, wrapping

HEART OF THE WILD GODS

herself in the coverlet. "He'd visit the monasteries—or at least try to—the ones willing to open their doors to a Dane."

She gathered up the coverlet so she could walk, then continued.

"I can imagine it was no small task, convincing the monks he wasn't a threat. But I guess his skill as an artisan won them over. He would trade craft for knowledge."

Æfre had never hidden her literacy or her heritage, but equally she had always kept these things in quiet reserve; a layer of protection against those who might judge her for not having adopted Christian beliefs, for being a woman, a half Dane, for possessing knowledge, or for any number of other reasons people found to castigate a woman for existing beyond expectation.

"Fair work for a *heathen*, don't you agree?" She smiled wryly.

"And a half-breed Dane at that!" Osric exclaimed, feigning horror.

Despite Osric's experiences with the fierce Danelaw occupiers on the battlefield, Æfre knew that Osric understood well enough that Saxon and Dane blood had become inextricably intertwined long ago, the moment the first longship had come ashore and onto their soil.

It was one of the things she admired most about him—his grasp of this often uneasy balance. Complicated and messy alliances with ever-changing boundaries called for the skillful navigation of a changing landscape. One moment, two people are enemies and invaders; the next, kin by marriage, partners in trade, and neighbors raising their children side by side.

As a product of one such complex alliance, Æfre deeply admired Osric's ability to hold two such truths in the same hand.

"Two worlds etched into me, yet I belong fully to neither," she mumbled.

The words slipped from her before she could stop them. She

hadn't meant to utter them aloud—she rarely let such things rise to the surface. When she glanced up, Osric was no longer reading. He had lowered the leechbook, his gaze steady, yet warm and thoughtful, as if seeing something he hadn't noticed before.

Barefoot and still haphazardly wrapped in the coverlet, Æfre shuffled closer, her pale, bed-rumpled hair tickling his nose as she pressed in closer, guiding his hands back up so she could see her leechbook.

"See the plants in these pages," she said, "the names in Latin—you know this, I suppose, but these are the names the learned men use—the true names, written as the monks do in their great books."

She tapped the margin with her fingertip, then pointed to the first image. "This here is Camemillan, see? There are two kinds."

Æfre pointed to a detailed drawing.

"This is *Anthemis nobilis*—that's the Roman sort, the kind in the garden. And this—"

Her finger moved across the page to a second drawing.

"*Matricaria chamomilla.*"

She glanced up at Osric, who stood listening, brows furrowed in interest. A small smile tugged at her lips as she continued.

"My father brought the seed from one of his summer journeys. There was a kind monk, fond of spreading knowledge—he gave him many cuttings, too. Said the garden is as important a place for study as any scriptorium."

She looked up to find Osric's eyes locked on her, filled with wonderment as if watching some rare specimen perform some unimaginable feat.

"Forgive me—I prattle like a hen in the thatch once I start speaking of plants..."

But she saw the look in his eyes before she could finish—how he listened intently. Osric's gaze was unwavering.

"Go on, Æfre," he said gently. "I'd hear the rest."

She hesitated, suddenly aware of the warmth in her cheeks. Then, with a shy smile, she reached over and guided Osric's hands to close the leechbook.

"That's all, really. These pages... they're plants I use—mostly for healing, although a few are there simply because they interest me; the way they grow, their scent, or their properties that I have yet to learn to make use of."

She paused, then looked him dead in the eyes.

"Of course, some may be turned to poison as well... so you'd best not anger me, *my lord.*"

Osric grinned widely, then dropped the leechbook and recoiled, clutching his chest as if stricken, staggering backwards with a gasp.

"I am undone!" he cried, and with a sudden motion grabbed Æfre by the waist and pulled her down with him into the chair by the hearth.

"It was the stew!" Æfre squealed.

"The stew!! Aiii!" Osric arched his back, sputtering. "My world grows dark!! Farewell!!"

Æfre dissolved into a fit of giggles as she struggled to keep the coverlet wrapped around her. She could tell that the warmth of her closeness was having an effect on him. She liked having that effect on him.

Yet as dawn closed in on them, so did the demands of Osric's station. The Bishop would come seeking him first thing, as he always did, before the first labors of the day began. Osric should have been gone already. But this morning, she was not ready to let him go. Not yet.

And by the look in his eyes—dark, fixed, and growing hungrier by the moment—she could clearly see that he wasn't ready either.

Osric suddenly rebounded from the throes of death and swept

her into his arms, moving towards the bed.

"Osric, we mustn't. Your time is short," she said, though she still tilted her head, baring the pale curve of her neck to him, knowing full well he needed no such encouragement.

He leaned in and kissed her, his beard prickling the exquisitely sensitive area as he murmured against her neck, "Just a moment longer."

Then his lips found the spot beneath her ear—that same spot that had rendered her helpless against his charms that very first time—and her fingers released the coverlet. It slipped to the floor, pooling at their feet like water from an overflowing basin.

"As you wish. Perhaps just a moment..." Æfre said, pretending to let go of a resolve to deny him that she'd never had to begin with.

2
Nīwe Dæg ⚔ New Day

The sun had already risen over the hills when Osric slipped out of the hut. He was late—too late—but still he paused at the door, casting a backward gaze at Æfre, who still lay peacefully in sleep, her hair a flaxen waterfall tumbling over the edge of the bed, illuminated by the light from the open door.

The sight pulled at him so strongly it nearly unraveled his resolve—leaving felt a bit like tearing a vital organ from his chest. Yet as much as he might have willed it, his duties were not going to simply disappear, and he swiftly headed towards the paddock near Æfre's livestock shelter to retrieve his horse.

It was a glorious late summer morning at Æfre's homestead. A fine mist still clung to the clearing behind the hut, but the sun, rising steadily, cut through it now, reaching fingers of light beyond the shadows of the surrounding hills. Osric could hear the creek that meandered through the far edge of the clearing, its usual babbling subdued and thirsty—its flow thinner than it ought to be.

The land has gone too long without proper rain, he thought, though casting an eye over Æfre's herb garden, one would certainly never have guessed it. The garden was flourishing despite the dry summer, and Osric smiled as he realized that over the last year his association with Æfre had earned him a newfound ability to identify several of the medicinal plants she cultivated; the yarrow stood tall, its flat clusters of pink and white flowers reaching skyward while the camemillan, the very one she'd shown him in her leechbook, crept low, sun-scorched but still thriving. He recognized feverfew, blooming at the edge of the garden in small groupings of small, pale flowers, and also the sage with its thick, silver-white leaves standing defiant against the rising heat. The garden breathed resilience—fragrant, buzzing, and bountiful.

He stretched and drew in a deep breath of morning air, silently acknowledging that sleep had been too short. It was early yet, but he could already tell the day was going to be stiflingly warm. No doubt the ceorls would grumble about it as they worked the fields, tirelessly preparing for the coming harvest.

A soft nickering from the paddock pulled Osric from his thoughts. Lēodlufu, his stout bay gelding affectionately known as "Leo", stood contentedly chewing a mouthful of hay beneath the lean-to that ran the length of the livestock shelter. Beside him, Æfre's dapple grey mare, Epona, nudged at his side as the two well-acquainted horses vied for the choicest mouthfuls of hay.

Osric retrieved his saddle and bridle, and soon the gelding was shifting with anticipation beneath the tack, stretching for one last bite of hay before setting off.

Osric gave Leo's neck a brief pat, then mounted, glancing wistfully one last time at the hut behind him as he guided the gelding onto the uphill path that led to the main road.

The track to Wōdenléah was well-worn, linking the fortified burh to the Norse traders' camp that had established itself along the Thames in the years following the Battle of Edington.

Æfre's homestead sat in a valley midway between the burgh and the camp. It was a location both close and far enough from the camp and the burh for her to feel both safe and vulnerable at the same time—depending on the rise and ebb of the political tide.

Once on the road, Osric gave Leo his head, and the gelding eagerly surged forward at a gallop, hooves striking the earth with a rhythm familiar to both horse and rider.

Osric knew he had overstayed this time. The sunlight was now breaking through the thinning mist, and the long shadows that had cast across the fields were disappearing altogether. He was in plain sight now. The burh would surely see him coming.

HEART OF THE WILD GODS

Yet in this moment, he couldn't quite bring himself to care. He was enjoying the rare sense of freedom that he always felt when traveling back from Æfre's, and he leaned low in the saddle, urging speed from the powerful gelding while his tunic snapped against the wind and the Earth flew past beneath them.

Let Bishop Æthelwod scowl. Let the people whisper. If I must bear wagging tongues as the price of a moment of unrestrained contentment, so be it.

* * *

Æfre awoke with a gasp, sitting bolt upright in bed. The sudden pounding at the hut's door dragged her from sleep and left her feeling raw and disoriented. She blinked hard and took a few deep breaths, noticing the warm slant of sunlight through the shutter cracks. The air inside the hut was already thick with heat.

"Hold just a moment!" She called to whoever was at the door, realizing that she'd slept later than she'd intended.

Flinging off the coverlet, she swung her legs to the floor, only then recalling she hadn't a stitch on—a reminder of the previous night's assignation.

Osric, she smiled as the memory flooded her thoughts.

They'd barely slept—the scent of him still clinging to her skin and hair.

She snatched her linen shift from a wooden peg and pulled it quickly over her head, fingers fumbling in her haste. The pounding came again.

"Æfre!" A girl's voice—young, familiar.

"Yes, yes! One moment, I'm just coming!"

Realizing she did not have time to get fully dressed, Æfre hastily looked about her for something to throw on over her underdress.

She spotted the crumpled coverlet at the foot of the bed,

snatched it up, and wrapped it about her like a cloak as she padded to the door.

"I am truly sorry for disturbing you," came the voice again, muffled through the timber, "Cwenhild sent me to fetch you."

Æfre unlatched the door and opened it to reveal Gytha, the young serving girl from the burh, standing fidgeting in the sun. Æfre could see her husband waiting for her in the cart, doing his best to idle the hot and impatient oxen.

"Gytha! Are you well?" Æfre smiled and gave a slight wave to the man beyond.

"Yes, Æfre, all is well," Gytha said, her eyes flicking over Æfre's tousled hair and makeshift attire, cheeks coloring. "Cwenhild bade me to come on our way to the trading camp with our cheese—Wynn, the thatcher's wife, she's gone to her childbed this morning."

"Aah—Gytha, you have my thanks. I knew this news would come soon," Æfre exclaimed; "I'll leave straightaway."

"Cwenhild reckons the babe could arrive by midday," Gytha said.

"Then let's hope that the little one agrees with Cwenhild's predictions. But just the same, I won't dawdle."

Æfre quickly bid Gytha farewell, suggesting that she and her husband visit her henhouse before continuing on to the camp—her birds had been laying as though bewitched of late, producing what seemed like an endless supply of eggs.

She pulled her blue summer apron dress over the shift, bound her hair back with a scrap of linen, and filled a small bronze cooking pot with water and set it on the hearth. From her shelf of clay jars, she decanted a shake of dried mint and a carefully measured spoon of pennyroyal, scattering them into the warming water. As the herbs steeped, their sharp, familiar scent filled the hut.

While the infusion steeped, she moved nimbly about, swiftly

gathering what she'd need for the birth: clean cloths, salve, clean linen wraps, a small bundle of protective herbs, and the amber amulet her mother had always brought to such labors.

When the infusion was finally ready, she poured herself a cup and sipped slowly, pausing for a moment while her mind mapped the day. She'd planned to muck out the paddock, collect firewood, groom Epona—the poor mare was in sore need of it—and check the fish traps along the tributary. With the water level running low lately, she suspected they could be a complete loss.

There was also small game—probably hares this time of year, coming to drink, so even if the fish traps had failed, there was always her bow. But of course, all that would have to wait.

Wynn's child would not.

Yet even as she hurried about the hut, her thoughts kept drifting back to Osric. The quiet moments they shared felt like a dangerous secret; a glowing ember fallen unseen into a haystack, its warmth threatening to consume everything around it.

The more time she spent with him, the more she looked forward to their moments together. She often wondered if it was turning into something more. There was something in his gaze when he looked at her now, an unspoken connection that she felt gripping her chest. They both knew well what that might mean—the complications it could bring—so neither of them dared speak it. But that didn't stop her heart from quickening at the thought of him.

That would have to be enough—for now.

She packed the last of her things and set them on the table, where her carved seax knife lay. Picking up the blade, she slid it into its sheath, which hung from her belt. The bone hilt bore a curling Norse dragon motif; the same one echoed in the carved headboard of the bed her father had made.

Draining the last of the herbal infusion from her cup, she

headed for the door, pausing only to sling her bow and quiver over her shoulder.

Perhaps I'll have time for this later, she thought as she headed out into the bright morning light towards the paddock.

3
Norþmenn ⚔ Northmen

Torvald Ironsight balanced his foot on the mossy stump while he carved neat slices from the apple in his hand, chewing each piece thoughtfully, deliberately as the edge of his seax flashed with the reflection of the morning light.

He ran a hand through his long dark hair and smoothed his silver-flecked beard, watching as the sun burned away the last wisps of mist clinging to the edge of the clearing where the trading camp stirred to life.

The clang of metal, crackle of fire, and the rising sounds of coarse laughter drifted up the hill to where Torvald perched, as still and silent as a wolf. The familiar cadence of Norse voices rang out, delivering the punchline of a bawdy joke that made him chuckle lightly to himself as the men below roared with unrestrained laughter.

He could see most of the camp from where he stood. The road to Wōdenléah cut through the woods to the east, while just beyond the embankment to the west, the Thames shimmered in the morning sun. Several wooden longships lined up along a wooden pier where a handful of warriors stood watch, leaning on their shields, scanning the forest and shoreline for signs of trouble. A few men unloaded piles of furs and textiles from one ship, their tunics already darkening with sweat under the rising sun.

At the heart of the camp sat the hall, the central gathering place, with Torvald's chieftain's quarters nestled at the back. Just behind the hall, merchants had set up their makeshift outdoor stalls; some of the more established ones even with woven or thatched awnings.

Torvald's gaze skimmed the traders as they haggled in a mixture of languages over everything from silk and amber to iron tools and blades. At the edge of the row of stalls, a smith worked at his forge, hammer ringing against iron as he shaped a gleaming axe head, sparks bursting into the air with each strike of the iron.

* * *

Torvald had begun his life in the hard-edged village of Úlfsnes in Hǫrðaland[ii], bouncing from household to household in a place where an orphan had to learn quickly if he was to survive.

Fascinated by the local warriors, the moment he had come of age, Torvald joined a local raiding party, eager to prove himself. He fought alongside seasoned warriors from many of the northern kingdoms, watching and absorbing their knowledge and tactics in everything from the way men moved and spoke to how they led. As he grew into a man, he gained a reputation; while others rushed towards the chaos and ferocity of battle, Torvald never did so without first calculating the angles.

It was this refined skill set that consistently led him to the best course of action amidst chaos. It also earned him unerring loyalty from his warriors and comrades, who bestowed upon him the moniker "Ironsight," and eventually positioned him to become one of the youngest chieftains to lead the settlement of Styrvik, which would subsequently become part of Danelaw East Anglia.

A few years after settling in Styrvik, tragedy struck. Just after the Battle of Edington, Torvald was away forging fragile trading relationships in Wessex when he received word that his wife and firstborn had died in childbirth. A man accustomed to predicting and controlling outcomes, the loss untethered him, and he buried his sorrow in purpose, turning his focus entirely to the advancement of his people.

Citing the untapped potential for prosperity through

commerce, Torvald exiled himself, his sorrow becoming his fuel as he threw his energy into forging trade relations with the Saxons of Wessex. He eventually took his leave from Styrvik entirely as he brought to life a vision of a trading party that could quickly transition into an army of warriors, his keen strategic mind blending seamlessly with a warrior's instinct to help realize a vision of a future where trade, diplomacy, and military strength coexisted side by side.

* * *

Footsteps crunched the tall, dry grass behind Torvald, pulling him from his reverie.

"Laughter like that," the familiar voice said, "they're speaking either of coin flowing or skirts lifting."

Still chewing while he smoothed the apple juice from his beard, Torvald turned to see Svend, the camp's affable overseer of trade. Tall, red-bearded, and smiling, he was Torvald's oldest friend and closest ally.

"This time, both." Torvald's eyes flashed with humor as he flicked the last of the apple core down the hill and wiped the blade on his trousers before sheathing it.

"Jarl," Svend began with a reluctant exhale, "we've a problem."

"Já?" Nonplussed, Torvald turned his head back towards the vista.

"It's Bjørn."

"Bjørn," Torvald echoed flatly, the name bringing an immediate frown to his face. He released a long exhale.

"Bjørn was to meet the textile shipment that arrived early this morning, but only moments ago, the goods were still aboard the ships, untouched. I had to pull Geir and Håkon to do it—Bjørn is nowhere to be found." Svend paused, looking at Torvald from under raised brows.

Torvald continued to look out over the horizon.

"Nobody has seen him since last night," continued Svend.

Torvald, still gazing at the vista, let out a deep breath before finally turning to Svend with a nod.

"Thank you," he said finally, clapping Svend on the shoulder. "I'll see to it. Geir and Håkon—make sure they're compensated."

"They'll see you by midday, Jarl."

"Good. Also, Svend, if you see the boy, send him to me, please."

Torvald turned back to face the vista once again.

"Of course."

Svend gave a respectful nod and made his way back toward the camp.

Torvald stood alone again.

Bjørn.

Bjørn was the son of a chieftain from Hǫrðaland—sent south to shed his sense of entitlement under Torvald's watchful guidance. The young man had been born to privilege, believing every clan resource to be his by right. But here, Bjørn was just like every other man in the camp, and Torvald had no intention of treating him otherwise. The young man would need to learn to be worthy of the blood he carried.

He'd learn it—or he'd fail.

As Torvald continued to gaze at the horizon, he felt a tug at his trouser leg.

The boy had found him.

He was small and wiry, even for a child, rendering his age indeterminate beyond a best guess. A displaced Saxon, they'd surmised, the boy moved with a quickness in his step that told a tale of survival. Shod in a gifted pair of too-big shoes, he slipped through the bustling Viking trading camp, too fast for his own shadow, a spark of sharp intelligence in his bright, watchful eyes. As far as anyone in the camp knew, he had no home and no name, but what the boy lacked in personal history, he made up for in usefulness.

He knew instinctively how to stay out of sight until needed, and seemed to hear every rumor, every whispered deal, and every grumble of discontent. Whatever utterances reverberated through the camp, in whatever languages they might have been uttered, the boy stored these tidbits away like treasures.

"Boy, do you know where Bjørn is?" Torvald asked.

The boy nodded quickly and pointed to a line of tents just beyond the camp, in a clearing near a creek.

Torvald followed the line of the boy's finger. He'd guessed as much.

"Have you eaten today?" Torvald asked the boy, studying his hollow eyes and reedy frame.

The boy shook his head, lowering his eyes in shame.

"Come," urged Torvald. "We'll fix that, then you will take me to Bjørn."

With his hand on his shoulder, Torvald steered the boy around, and together they started down the hill and into the sound, scent, and smoke of the camp.

* * *

Torvald parted the crowd as he strode through the camp, the boy trailing behind, his pockets now stuffed with dried meat, tearing into an apple like a starving cub as he struggled to keep pace while fiercely guarding each bite of his precious meal.

Torvald moved from stall to stall, speaking with merchants and warriors, every word, nod, and lighthearted quip measured and purposeful. More than just idle chatter, this was the chieftain's way of taking the camp's pulse. Today, trade was steady, blades sharp, and tempers low.

Good.

Satisfied, he turned to the boy. "Very well, boy, take me to Bjørn—lead the way!"

The boy, who had been chewing his meat with grim focus, quickly stuffed the unfinished food back into his pocket. With a brief upwards glance at Torvald, he trotted into the camp, disappearing like a shadow into the market stalls as Torvald strode behind him, awkwardly ducking under awnings and sidestepping ox-carts, the occasional apologetic grunt escaping him as he pushed through openings built for a smaller man.

They reached the far end of the camp, where a creek gurgled through the trees. A line of tents stood in a small clearing, their openings facing the creekside, and the remains of a smoldering fire still clung to life in a nearby fire pit. Torvald noticed more than a few empty jugs strewn about the ground.

The boy led them all the way to one of the last tents before the treeline when Torvald suddenly recognized the sounds of a rhythmic chorus of grunts and giggles coming from beyond the tent's woven entry—the unmistakable signature of a raucous and frantic coupling.

"Boy!" Torvald boomed, and the boy pulled up just short of the entrance.

"Thank you, I've got it from here." Torvald flipped the boy a silver coin.

"Go see Svend and tell him that Bjørn will join him on his journey into Wōdenléah."

The boy nodded, and in seconds, vanished back into the camp, instantly disappearing without a trace.

Torvald paused for a moment, looking around the clearing until he spotted a large bucket lying on its side at the creekside, abandoned by a careless owner. Torvald lifted the bucket, filling it nearly to spilling with creek water, and headed for the tent, splashing water over his boots with every step.

HEART OF THE WILD GODS

Approaching the tent, the sounds grew louder; a mixture of laughter and the raw, urgent sounds of ecstasy building, escalating with frantic intensity.

Perfect timing, thought Torvald as he entered the tent, walking directly into a dank, heavy cloud of stale ale and sweat, so thick it seemed almost alive as it took the wind out of him for a moment—a moment he used to allow his eyes to adjust.

The first thing that Torvald saw was an impressive set of floppy, oversized breasts bouncing up and down just feet from where he stood. Attached to those breasts, he recognized the plump, disheveled Saxon woman as one of Wōdenléah's serving girls, reverse-straddling Bjørn like she was breaking a stallion, mewling with the fervor of a trapped animal clawing for escape. Another woman, naked and snoring, lay crumpled at the foot of the bed, oblivious to the revelry inches from her face.

All of them blind to Torvald's presence.

The robust woman riding Bjørn began to cry out loudly now. Torvald stepped forward, raised the bucket, and with perfect calm, doused the three bedfellows.

"On your feet, Bjørn Ívarsson! Allow these poor women to flee now that you've finished disappointing them!" Torvald tossed the bucket out the tent's opening and stood like a fortress at its center.

The reaction was immediate, and chaos unfolded all around him.

The robust Saxon woman let out another, different type of shriek as she struggled to extricate herself from her predicament, awakening her sleeping companion, who joined in the shrieking to form a chorus of deafening caterwauling.

Bjørn jackknifed upright, tossing the robust woman off of him in a single motion, his eyes reddened and bleary with drink.

Torvald stood silently, rooted in place, while the drenched women scurried to collect their clothing and belongings, squinting against the daylight as they stumbled out of the tent, dropping and retrieving pieces of each other's clothing as they went.

Bjørn, unsteady on his feet, wobbled and clung to the tent's support pole as he hastily finished dressing himself, finally attempting to stand, swaying like a sapling, in front of the chieftain.

"Jarl Torvald..."

"Silence!" boomed Torvald.

Torvald stepped in, his face inches from Bjørn's, whose blonde hair stuck to his face, matted with bits of leaves and what appeared to be vomit.

"You've dishonored the trade, the men, and your birthright," Torvald said, his voice low and dangerous. "Over and over again, you shame yourself. You are a stinking drunk, stumbling around less gracefully than a pig in shit, yet you're too proud to lift your own weight. While the rest of us work, you sit idle and let others bear your burden. I've buried better men for less."

"Jarl, I..."

"You. Will. *Listen*! You will not speak, you will listen," commanded Torvald evenly, the still, focused anger in his voice reverberating all the way to the far corners of the camp.

"Do you think The Gods favor fools who leave their brothers to struggle while they waste themselves on drink? I tell you this, Bjørn Ivarsson, consider this your only chance. If I must speak to you again - if I see you in this state again while those around you are shouldering your work, you will leave this camp, and you will not find welcome on another ship."

Torvald stepped back.

"Dress. Now. You'll report to Svend and follow his instructions. You are assisting today in Wōdenléah."

"Assisting Svend!?" exclaimed Bjørn, unable to help himself. "But that is the role of a servant! He can take as many of them as he chooses!"

HEART OF THE WILD GODS

"Yes, he can." Torvald stated flatly, "But today, he is taking you. Straighten yourself, and meet me outside. You leave now."

Torvald strode out of the tent, squinting against the bright daylight, more appreciative than ever of the crisp, fresh afternoon air.

4
⚔ Wōdenléah ⚔

Osric urged the gelding through the timber palisade and into the burh of Wōdenléah, where the morning's activities were already well underway. The rising summer sun cast everything in a soft gold, and the air carried the steady rhythm of people setting about their daily routines.

Children darted across the damp green, their high-pitched squeals carrying over the thatched rooftops like birdsongs. Women passed each other carrying baskets of fresh bread and wool, their hemlines glancing against the dusty ground as they shared the latest gossip. The first scents of smoke and cooking were rising from the hearths, while in the distance, golden waves of barley and hops moved in the breeze like the mane of a great gilded horse.

The men had already gathered, sharpening tools, filling water bladders, and tucking cloth-wrapped bread and cheese into sacks for the day's labor; everyone's thoughts fixed on the upcoming harvest.

Clustered around a central green were many small homes—a mix of timber-plank and wattle-and-daub structures—their thatched roofs like a clutch of nests huddled at the very heart of the burh. At the far end of the green, Osric's eye fell on his destination—the livestock shelter and stable, where bleating goats shuffled in an outdoor enclosure, and several horses stood loosely tied, waiting patiently, sipping water from a wooden trough.

To one side rose the hall—a broad, rectangular structure of wattle and daub, its steep thatch roof darkened with age. A thin twist of smoke curled from the smoke-hole at its crown.

Across from the hall stood the church, older than the burh itself. A simple, narrow rectangular structure built of wattle and daub atop a stout stone foundation, its timber-shingled roof rose into the sky with a silent, stern demeanor.

Slightly offset from the church sat the Bishop's house, similarly built atop a stone foundation, like the church, more modest than the burh's hall, yet easily twice the size of any of the villagers' homes. It was a neatly kept home; the roof was well-tended, and a generous garden thrived behind its fence, with orderly rows of herbs and a few vegetables among the flowers. Tucked behind the residence was the burh's brew hut, a moderately sized thatched-roof hut where the Bishop personally oversaw the crafting of ale and mead.

Osric reined in near the stable and cast a quick glance towards the Bishop's residence. No smoke from the rooftop. No robe-clad figure in the doorway. The thegn allowed himself a flicker of hope that Bishop Æthelwold might, for once, have found reason to delay his usual intrusions.

Osric saw movement out of the corner of his eye and turned his gaze back towards the stable. Cenric had appeared, already busy at work tacking up one of the tied horses. At the sound of approaching hooves, he turned and smiled, nodding as he approached.

"Lord Osric! A fair morning... or near enough," Cenric said with a wink, the corner of his mouth twitching upward as he drew out the word *morning*.

Osric swung down from the saddle, unsuccessfully suppressing the grin that tugged at the corners of his mouth. The barb was gentle, but unmistakable—and very typically Cenric.

There was an unspoken understanding that both Cenric and his wife, Cwenhild, the eyes and ears of the burh, were aware of Osric's connection to Æfre. Osric suspected the pair even approved of it.

It was a point of pride for Osric, having the loyalty of Cenric and Cwenhild. Loyalty in the burh was earned; the kingdom was still reeling from the years leading up to the Battle of Edington. Yet, the harvest had flourished under Osric's leadership, the burh had prospered, and in a short time, the new thegn earned widespread trust by helping to shield the people from the harsher whims of Bishop Æthelwod, whose propensity for cruelty had long cast a shadow over their lives.

As Cenric took the reins of Osric's horse, he stepped in close, speaking low.

"Bishop Æthelwod awaits you, my lord," he said, holding Osric's gaze for a moment before coaxing his horse towards the stable.

A warning.

"In the hall," Cenric added over his shoulder.

"Thank you, Cenric."

Osric paused, his hands resting on his belt. He allowed himself to briefly close his eyes as the effects of his sleepless night settled over him. Finally drawing a long, steady breath, he willed his mind to clear before finally pushing himself forward, step by step.

* * *

The hall was dimly lit beneath the soot-blackened rafters, the air thick with the mingled scents of wood smoke cooking meat. Daylight crept in through the propped-open door, casting long shadows off the hanging dried herbs, smoked fish, and bundles of kindling that hung like offerings over the low-burning central hearth.

Osric squinted as he stepped inside, walking headlong into the warmth and the smell of the meat simmering over the low fire. His stomach tightened, grumbling a reminder of just how long it had been since he last ate. He also realized it was unlikely he'd get another chance until at least midday.

He hastened over to the hearth and peered into the pot.

Hare stew.

Osric took up the wooden spoon resting beside the hearth and stirred the pot, releasing the rich, savory scent of the slowly cooking meat. He dipped the spoon in, inspecting the readiness of the stew when a familiar voice startled him, sending the spoon clattering to the earthen floor.

"Ah! Lord Osric! There you are!"

Bishop Æthelwod stood at the end of the hall, a looming, dark shadow before the long wooden table that had witnessed countless meals and official dealings. Beside the table stood a large, carved chair—the thegn's chair. Osric noticed his wool cloak still draped over the back of it, abandoned there since the first warmth of spring. On this morning, it appeared as though both his cloak and the Bishop wore the same expression—one of disdain. They both waited in silent judgment of him, impatiently anticipating the commencement of the day's affairs.

Bishop Æthelwod was a striking creature. Unnaturally tall and reedy, his gaunt face was lined with equal measures of rigidity and a lifetime of stooping over sacred texts. His presence made all who encountered him uneasy, in no small part because he wielded his ecclesiastical power like a blade dishonorably slipped between the ribs of a sleeping king.

"At last," clipped Æthelwod again.

"Bishop Æthelwod, my lord."

Osric stooped and picked up the spoon, shaking it off, replacing it at the side of the hearth.

"A fine morning, is it not?" Osric asked, willing himself to keep his tone easy.

After a pause, the Bishop stepped from the shadows, his gaze sweeping over Osric with cold scrutiny. "A fine morning indeed," he said, voice dry. "Though I fear there's little of it left to enjoy, Lord

HEART OF THE WILD GODS

Osric."

The sting in Æthelwod's words was unmistakable, and Osric forced a smile and braced himself.

"I did not see you at morning prayers," the Bishop continued, his gaze hawkish.

"Indeed, Bishop," Osric replied with what he hoped appeared to be a deferential nod, "today I find myself rather behind the hour. I apologize, Lord Bishop, if I've kept you waiting overlong."

The Bishop sniffed, again looking Osric up and down. "You appear tired, my lord. Are you quite well?"

"I am Bishop. Very well indeed." Osric smiled briskly. "Bishop, are you joining me today to oversee morning's first labors?"

"Oh, goodness no," scoffed the Bishop.

Osric already knew that Æthelwod would refuse any offer that involved a journey out onto the land—exactly why he had offered it—any distance between himself and the Bishop was always a welcome relief.

"Well then, you'll forgive me, my lord, I'm afraid I mustn't delay..."

"There is...one matter that I should like to discuss with you, Lord Osric." Æthelwod interrupted, cutting him off.

"My lord?" Osric was sure everyone in the burh might have heard the air hiss audibly from his lungs.

"Lord Osric," Bishop Æthelwod fixed his gaze on Osric, his eyes narrow with disapproval, "I know I need not remind you of your duties, which you have always executed honorably, yet I am troubled by the company you keep. Whispers have reached my ear...a man of your station indulging in...unworthy entanglements."

Osric felt his gut drop to his ankles in anticipation of what he knew was coming.

"I will remind you that you serve not only this burh but Christendom itself, a responsibility that demands propriety and loyalty—a man set apart, with an unwavering commitment to God's order."

"Of course, my lord," began Osric, "might I..."

"And yet," the Bishop interrupted with a sharpened tone, "I hear tales that you keep company with one unsanctified by the Church."

"My lord, if you speak of Æfre, the healer..." Osric again tried to appeal to the Bishop.

"The heathen," spat Æthelwod, "and a half-breed Dane at that."

"Bishop," Osric softened his tone to something between pleading and exasperation, "Æfre is a valued member of this community. Her family has served Wōdenléah longer than any of us in the burh."

Including you, Osric thought, though he dared not speak it aloud. No sense in starting another war.

"Lord Osric, I shall speak plainly," Æthelwod cut him off, his tone impatient and sharp. "It has been well over a year now since the passing of your dear wife. It is time you sever whatever ties you may have with this woman, however it pains you, and take a Saxon wife of Christian virtue. A wife who will bring honor to the burh, and to God. One who is befitting of a thegn who has so distinguished himself."

Æthelwod stepped in a bit too close, the thin, painted-on smile on his face a stark contrast to his dark, unsmiling eyes. Osric could feel the hairs of his beard flutter with each of the Bishop's close-spoken words.

"Let us not forget where the true power lies in this land, my lord," Æthelwod said, "and that is with God himself."

Osric felt sick. Meeting the Bishop's gaze, he gave a slight nod. "Of course, my lord. Praise be to God Almighty."

"Indeed," Æthelwod sniffed, "may God guide us that the Lord's will be done."

HEART OF THE WILD GODS

Æthelwod turned on his heel and took a few steps towards the door. Pausing, he turned back around in what Osric could tell was a feeble attempt to be more accommodating towards his thegn—the man who not long ago had saved his life.

"Lord Osric, I acknowledge that your half-breed companion possesses skills of undeniable value—skills that indeed serve the good people of Wōdenléah. I have no wish to deprive this settlement of such a resource. However, if she is to continue her healing practices here, she would be wise to do so under the guidance of the one true God. This is more than just a matter of principle; it's a matter of salvation, and on that, there shall be no compromise."

Æthelwod again turned and strode towards the door, calling out to Osric without looking back.

"I shall see you for the afternoon administration. There is much to do."

Æthelwod disappeared out the door of the hall, his cloak fluttering behind him like a shadowy dog trailing its master.

Osric stood stunned and alone in the hall, feeling a bit sick, reeling from an encounter that was more threat than counsel, the hare stew all but forgotten.

* * *

"Wynn begged me not to speak of it," Æfre heard Aelf say.

Cwenhild had gone to answer the pounding on the hut's door while Æfre remained by Wynn's side as she labored.

"She made me swear to it—that I wouldn't make a fuss," Aelf said from the doorway, his voice bearing the unmistakable overtones of worry as the sounds of Wynn's cries rose to fill the hut.

Cwenhild nodded briskly as Aelf strained to see over her shoulder. "You did right to come, Aelf. Thank you for telling us—we'll see to her now," she said, before practically shoving him back out into the heat to wait in the hall with their young son and a handful of the burh's elders.

Æfre was pressing her weight against one of Wynn's legs as Cwenhild arrived back to join her, picking up the other leg.

"That was Aelf..." Cwenhild said quietly.

"I heard everything," Æfre said quietly, wanting to give her full attention back to Wynn as she labored.

"Good Wynn, well done—rest now."

Æfre had indeed overheard Aelf telling Cwenhild that his wife had actually been laboring since long before sunrise—he'd found her fighting the pain alone in the dark the night before when he'd arrived late home.

"She's weakening," Æfre murmured to Cwenhild, who knelt beside her. Æfre noted how Wynn's limbs shook with exhaustion; her cries had now become only breathy whimpers. Her reserves were low.

"We must change her course soon."

The air inside the hut was thick and stagnant, and sweat clung to all three of the women as the day grew hotter.

Wiping her brow, Æfre leaned close to Wynn's flushed face. "Wynn, come," she said gently but in a tone that brooked no argument. "It's time. You must rise. We'll bring this child into the world yet. On your knees now, dear—we need to create an easier path for this child—we'll use the earth to draw the babe down."

"I can't," Wynn cried, "it's too much. It's so hot..."

Æfre lifted her chin so their eyes met. "Yes, you can, just as you have done before with your first. You are not doing this alone, Wynn—we are with you, hand and heart."

Æfre knew that if progress slowed further, both mother and baby were going to be in serious trouble. She needed to encourage Wynn to tap into her inner strength—but without alarming her.

She reached into her satchel, which sat next to her, and pulled

HEART OF THE WILD GODS

out her mother's amber amulet, placing it around Wynn's neck. "This is the gift of Goddess Eorðe[iii]—she will lend you her strength, Wynn—but now we must act swiftly."

Without a word, Cwenhild hooked an arm beneath Wynn's shoulder, grunting with the effort as they shifted the woman up onto her knees. She wailed with exhaustion, but did as they bade her.

"Come on, child, up you get." Cwenhild huffed, casting Æfre a look as she did.

"Wynn, I'm going to check the position of the baby." Æfre moved behind Wynn and placed her hands carefully on her belly—one side, then the other. Then she gently slid two fingers inside, probing. She quickly bumped up against the baby's head, low and firm, but there was little progress since the last time. The baby was stuck.

She glanced up. Cwenhild's eyes locked with hers. Æfre tapped her own shoulder twice—the child's shoulder was caught, a dangerous predicament.

"Wynn, listen now." Æfre leaned in close and spoke low; "You must rock yourself, back and forth. Cwenhild will help you. Let the bones here part and your hips open wide," Æfre patted the young woman's hips, "We will need to show this stubborn babe a better way into the world."

Æfre took a deep breath to steel her nerves, which felt as frayed as rat-chewed thatch.

"Wynn," she said with firm, gentle authority, "now you must chant[iv] with me.

"This is my remedy for hateful, slow birth.
This is my remedy for heavy, dismal birth.
This is my remedy for loathsome, imperfect birth."

Cwenhild and Æfre guided Wynn as she rocked back and forth, sweat dripping, the amber amulet swinging around her neck as all three women chanted, focusing Wynn's energy. Æfre silently prayed for another birthing pain to help end this grueling labor and bring forth the child, before things were too far gone.

It needed to happen soon.

After what felt like an eternity, Wynn let out a deep, primal moan. Æfre's head snapped up. She knew that sound. This was the time.

"Now, Wynn. Now! Sink to the earth! Let Cwenhild bear your weight. You will feel my hands—push now! Push with all your might as I guide the babe—"

"That's the way, sweeting—grab hold of me now," Cwenhild urged. "Big breath, and push!"

Wynn emitted a deep, guttural cry and bore down, calling on every remaining shred of strength she had left. Æfre worked swiftly, pressing against the lodged shoulder to ease it free. But still it would not come.

She looked up—shook her head.

"One more, Wynn," she said. "One more push!"

Æfre withdrew her hands and wiped them on a cloth, trying not to reveal how much they were shaking. Wynn was tiring. Æfre could feel the strength ebbing from her.

That baby needs to come out now, Æfre thought, not wanting to dwell on what might come next if Wynn could not deliver.

"Come now, girl, one more." Cwenhild encouraged, "Let that babe slip like a greased sow through a narrow gate."

Again, Wynn emitted a feral keening sound as she bore down a second time. This time, Æfre put even more pressure on the baby's shoulder, and this time she felt the arm slip out from beneath Wynn's pelvic bone.

With one final push, the baby slid into Æfre's waiting hands.

But the child was blue.

"A girl," Æfre announced quickly, trying to keep her voice

steady. "You've a daughter, Wynn."

Cwenhild soothed an exhausted Wynn, murmuring soothing words and rubbing her back, but her eyes were fixed on Æfre.

Æfre took up a clean cloth and began stimulating the baby. "Come now, little one," she whispered. "Come to the world. Breathe."

She cleared the baby's mouth and nose, rubbed her chest, tapped her feet, then turned her over and patted her back. The child remained limp.

"Does she cry?" Wynn mumbled weakly, "Does my child draw breath?"

"Eorðe, grant her breath," Æfre pleaded softly.

Æfre continued to rub the baby vigorously, pausing to blow a gentle breath of air across her face.

"Come now, child, take the breath..."

Seconds stretched into an eternity as the women waited.

Then, the baby moved.

A little at first, just a twitch of her little fingers, then her little mouth moved, and her little nose scrunched.

"That's it, little one," Æfre said softly, giving the baby another few rubs with the cloth, "let us hear your little voice..."

The baby gurgled a few times, then scrunched up her eyes, opened her mouth, and let out an almighty wail. High-pitched and gurgly at first, then a gulp of air and louder. The baby turned from ashy blue to robust pink as she took another gulp of air, and wailed louder still.

Only then did she meet Cwenhild's eyes. The older woman closed hers briefly, whispering a silent thanks, before moving to help Wynn recline, brushing the sweat-soaked hair from the woman's brow.

Æfre looked over the baby girl as she pulled out another clean cloth and set her upon it.

Ten fingers. Ten toes.

The child's limbs were sound—save for one.

Æfre tied off the cord, watching the girl's right arm with sharp eyes. It hung slack. She pressed the tiny palm; the baby's little fingers curled weakly at first, then tightly around her thumb.

Good. This will probably improve.

"Is she..." Wynn's voice was barely audible.

"She's here," Æfre said gently. "And she's strong."

"She's beautiful," Cwenhild said, beaming.

Æfre laid the child in Wynn's arms. "Wynn, she had a hard time coming out, like her brother before her. Her arm was caught, and it is weakened and will need time. It may well recover in very short order. When you're rested, I'll show you how to help it along."

"Thank you, Æfre. Cwenhild—" Wynn burst into tears; "I'm sorry. Forgive me—I should have said—I was just so frightened after last time."

"You've nothing to be sorry for, Wynn," Æfre said. "And your daughter is alive and well."

"Godhild." Wynn sniffed, "She's to be called Godhild."

"Beautiful, Wynn. Hello, little Godhild." Æfre cooed.

"Shall I go fetch Aelf now, Æfre?" Cwenhild asked, heaving herself up off the earthen floor and straightening with a grunt.

"Oh, Yes, Cwenhild! But take your time, we'll just finish up here, and Wynn and I will see if this new little sweeting is hungry."

Cwenhild wiped her brow and offered her congratulations to the new mother once again before trundling off into the midday heat towards the hall.

The hut fell quiet, but for the soft sounds of the newborn, who was already suckling at her mother's breast.

"See? She knows the way." Wynn beamed, her exhaustion forgotten.

"She does indeed," Æfre observed, tucking the amber amulet

HEART OF THE WILD GODS

beneath Wynn's linen shift so it wouldn't press against the baby.

It took a few more moments before Æfre allowed herself to let go of the breath she'd been holding—hours of constant worry and critical action left her feeling as taut as her bowstring.

Yet as she watched mother and child nestled together, that tension slowly drained from her, replaced by a profound, deep-boned fatigue.

Sitting quietly, she allowed a feeling of quiet triumph to creep in, and for this moment at least, all was well.

* * *

Osric gripped his shield, gesturing with it as he shouted across the green at the sparring men.

"Alaric! Eyes on his hips, not his spear!" he barked. "Both the hand and the spear can be used to deceive you—to know your foe's next move—watch the hips!"

He struck the haft of the blunted practice spear against his belt for emphasis.

"Good! Now drive low—don't let your shield waver!"

Exhausted from lack of sleep and the unrelenting heat, Osric still felt more engaged here on the sparring green than he had all day. The fyrd never failed him. It wasn't only the exercises—it was the men. The bond forged with those who made up the heart and soul of the burgh.

And yet, even here, today, his thoughts would not stay focused on anything for long.

He'd left the hall that morning with the exchange with Bishop Æthelwod still running through his mind, and was left distracted.

Why has he waited until now to confront me about Æfre?

Osric had long suspected that his association with Æfre might one day clash with the expectations of his station, but now he began to harbor the worrying possibility that he'd underestimated the depth of Æthelwod's contempt—for Æfre's old Gods, for her heritage...

Surely not.

But it sat ill with him all the same.

"Lord Osric!"

The familiar voice broke through his daydreaming—calling from the edge of the green nearest the hall.

Osric turned to see Cwenhild standing just beyond the sparring field, and beside her, Æfre, leading a tacked-up Epona.

"If any of you still mean to eat, best you hurry!" Cwenhild called. "The stew's going fast!"

Seeing Æfre there, the sun in her pale, a quiet thrill shot through him.

"Men—enough!" he barked, eyes still fixed on her. "We've run long, the sun's near to cruel, and Cwenhild here warns me that the stew may not outlast you!"

Groans and laughter rippled across the field.

"Get yourselves fed and into the shade—we'll pick this up next time!"

As the men gathered their gear and wiped their brows with their tunics, Osric trotted to the green's edge. He grinned from ear to ear, his exhaustion momentarily forgotten.

"My lord," Cwenhild greeted him warmly. "Will you be joining us?"

"Cwenhild, I'd welcome it—but I've a few matters before the afternoon's duties."

"I thought you'd say as much," she said with a smile. "I left a trencher[v] in your quarters. And perhaps I'll return before the afternoon administration, to see you haven't buried yourself too deep in your work."

She stepped close, her voice low. "And I'll see the others leave you in peace."

HEART OF THE WILD GODS

"Thank you, Cwenhild. Truly."

"And Æfre, you did well today," she added, beaming.

"I did not do it alone," Æfre answered. "Thank *you*, Cwenhild."

"We'll speak soon, dear," Cwenhild said, giving Osric a fond squeeze on the shoulder before trundling off to join Cenric beneath the oak at the edge of the green.

Osric and Æfre stood watching one another, suppressing grins like a couple of adolescents until Æfre broke the silence.

"You've not slept, have you?"

"Not even for a moment," Osric grinned, stepping closer—too close for two not intimately bonded. "I didn't expect to see you here today."

"Wynn and Aelf had their baby this afternoon. Cwenhild and I attended," she said, smiling.

Her emerald gaze cast a spell. Osric had to will himself not to gather her into his arms right there.

"Ah! That explains Aelf's absence." He turned briefly to Epona, who recognized him and nudged his shoulder, lowering her head for a scratch. "Everything went well?"

"It was difficult. Worrisome, even—the babe was stubborn coming out, but I believe she'll come right and all will be well," Æfre said.

"Glad to hear it," he mumbled, stepping closer. "I need to come see you tonight."

They were close enough now to see the weariness etched on one another's faces, their clothes damp from heat and sweat, but their eyes smiled in a way they dared not show outright.

"You know the way, my lord," Æfre said, voice low. Then, after a pause, "all is well?"

"Yes," Osric replied. He hesitated. "Well... I believe so. I'll tell you all about it this evening."

"Mmm—very mysterious." Æfre laughed. "Now I've no choice

but to look forward to it."

She hiked up her skirts, placed a foot in the stirrup, and mounted Epona in one fluid swing of her leg.

He moved alongside her and slid a hand under the hem of her skirt, and let it rest gently on her ankle just above her boot. "What will you do with the rest of your day?"

"I'm headed to the river. I'll check the traps—though with this dry spell, I doubt much lives in them. But it's an excuse to cool off," Æfre said, smiling down at him.

"A perfect afternoon," he said, giving her leg a light squeeze. "Until tonight then."

"Good," Æfre whispered mischievously. She nudged Epona into a walk and glanced back with a wink. "I shall await it gladly."

Osric watched her ride toward the palisade gate, a smile on his face as she disappeared through it.

He turned towards the hall—and froze.

Bishop Æthelwod stood not ten feet away, hands folded before him, his expression icy.

"Good afternoon, Lord Bishop," Osric said evenly, nodding.

"Lord Osric."

Æthelwod stared as Osric retrieved his shield and spear and made for the hall.

Wā! That's unlikely to help matters any.

Inside, the hall sweltered with heat from the hearth and sun. Even with the door propped open, the air felt heavy and oppressive.

Osric dragged himself to the back of the hall and rounded the partition to his quarters, dropping his saddlebag, shield, and spear as he went. He stripped off his tunic and let it fall to the floor.

Cwenhild had indeed been in. On the small table lay a wooden trencher with bread, hard cheese, and dried fish. A freshly filled jug of water and a basin sat on the lone shelf beside the old, polished brass mirror left by his predecessor.

HEART OF THE WILD GODS

He collapsed face-first onto the feather mattress, his feet still in his boots as they hung over the edge of the bed.

For a breath, he tried to stay awake, thinking of Æfre—thinking that he likely was going to need a plan.

But sleep took him before he could finish the thought.

5

Burne ᛉ Stream

The thought of Osric brought a soft smile to Æfre's lips as she rode the well-travelled track between Wōdenléah and the trading camp. After the intensity of the birth, fatigue tugged at her, but she couldn't fathom how the thegn was managing the day's duties, given the previous night's lack of sleep. All things considered, Æfre felt better than she thought she deserved to.

A few minutes' ride outside the entrance to the trading camp, Æfre guided Epona down a narrow, well-concealed path that wound its way downhill to a small clearing. Next to the clearing, a meandering tributary fed into the Thames—her favorite spot. She dismounted, removing the saddle and bags before allowing the mare to graze freely in the slightly cooler shade of the surrounding trees.

Grabbing her bow and quiver, Æfre headed to the edge of the clearing and began searching for telltale signs of hares. She knew she'd missed the best time of day for their activity, and it was far too hot for them to be out, but with the shade of the forest, she remained hopeful that she might catch a curious straggler.

Besides, coming here wasn't really about the game. This was the place where Æfre felt the happiest—free, and entirely in harmony with her surroundings.

Still moving carefully through the clearing, a smile formed on her lips. This place had been her private sanctuary since childhood. She would sit here for hours, whispering to Gods, Goddesses, and whatever creatures might have dared cross her path. She used to lie on her back in the tall grass, looking up through the swaying tips of the trees, creating entire worlds from the swaying branches and clouds drifting by. Once, after her father's sharp Norse scolding for letting loose an arrow inside the hut, she had even run away to this spot, vowing to make the clearing her new home. It was a grand adventure that had ended sooner than she'd planned. Her father had found her fast asleep beneath her half-finished shelter of driftwood, hazel, and woven grass—another proud rebellion undone by lack of sleep.

At the clearing's edge, she found a hare form[vi] in the tall grass. *Perfect.*

Pausing at the edge of the treeline, she knelt with respect and mumbled a quick prayer, her hands resting on the Earth.

"Goddess Eorðe, I humbly seek your blessing to take one of your creatures, with my promise to honor its spirit and give thanks for its sacrifice."

Æfre rose and moved silently closer to the tall grass at the treeline.

Her steps were slow, deliberate—her bow at the ready, her breath steady. She moved through the silence like a shadow, every muscle tensed in anticipation. For what seemed like an eternity she stood as still as the grave before a slight, subtle movement came from the ground. She stilled her breathing, doing her best to blend into the stillness of the woods, her presence no more than the wind in the trees that surrounded her.

Again, a flicker of movement caught her eye. She waited again—yet another eternity—until a hare finally appeared, its cautious nose exploring the edge of its form, twitching against the breeze, straining to pick up the scent of danger.

Æfre took a deep breath and drew back the bowstring, feeling the familiar press of the arrow against her knuckle.

The hare began to emerge from the form, stretching a little at first, then a bit more. Æfre took aim.

The hare finally stepped further from the form, exposing its vulnerable side. Æfre exhaled slowly, loosing a single arrow with a sharp whistle. The arrow landed true, striking behind the hare's shoulder and sinking deep into its heart. A humane and instant kill.

Æfre knelt again, placing her hand on the small animal, which was warm and lifeless. She thanked it for its sacrifice, promising to honor it and the Goddess Eorðe by wasting none of it.

With a quiet reverence, she removed her arrow and dipped her finger in the animal's blood before marking her forehead with it—a silent gesture of respect. Unsheathing her seax knife, she began the careful work of gutting the animal, each movement made with purpose and gratitude.

* * *

Torvald Ironsight sat leaning against a tree just beyond the bank of the tributary, the tall, grassy embankment concealing him from view. The bread and meat he'd brought for his quiet meal away from the bustle of the camp sat forgotten in his lap, his attention entirely consumed by the sight before him.

A woman.

She was tall and strong, her frame graceful yet commanding, with a shock of windswept, pale blonde hair that seemed to catch the sunlight in a way that made her appear to glow from within. She could easily have been mistaken for a Norse woman had it not been for her Saxon attire. Yet, there was something distinctly different about her, an untamed quality that set her apart from the other Saxon women he'd known.

He'd watched in awe as she'd taken down a hare—at least he thought it was a hare...he couldn't quite see—she'd taken something down with a single arrow, shot from her bow, then knelt, momentarily disappearing from sight.

He strained to sit up a bit higher without giving away his position and saw that it was indeed a hare. Now, the woman knelt in quiet reverence, appearing to give thanks for the life she had taken, her forehead marked with the animal's blood.

I would remember having met this woman, he thought, sifting through his memories in vain for any moment when their paths might have crossed.

Then suddenly, he remembered—*the healer*.

He remembered catching sight of her once. It was only very briefly, on a market day in the burh back in the early days of the camp. She'd been far off, moving quickly through the crowd. Svend had nudged him then, nodding toward her with a quiet sort of acknowledgment. He'd told him her name was Æfre and described her as a 'healer of considerable skill', noting that she lived like a völva[vii], in the valley between the burh and the camp."

I hadn't fully appreciated her beauty that day. Hadn't even really seen it, he thought, gazing at the woman by the river's edge.

He chuckled to himself, realizing it was his habit of avoiding crowds—preferring solitary hunting trips over visits to the burh—that was likely what kept her from his sight all this time.

The men spoke of her occasionally—he remembered laughter in the hall over stories about how a few had tried to win her favor with feigned injuries and fabricated ailments. She'd seen through them immediately, of course. Sent them on their way with little more than a kind word and a fresh case of mortally wounded pride.

Watching her now, Torvald couldn't help but think of how his young self might have handled this moment—and the thought made him grimace. Back then, he would've tried to take her without a second thought. A brash, horrific act meant only to gain favor with the raiding party and feed his own pride.

But he was a different man now. Older, more measured—he knew what real loss was, in a way he could not have back then. No, this wasn't a woman to be conquered, and after witnessing the accuracy of her bow, the notion of someone 'claiming' her seemed all the more absurd.

HEART OF THE WILD GODS

Torvald watched, entranced, as she worked intently just beyond the edge of the tall grass, her form only half-visible. Then, rising to her full height, she held up a freshly gutted hare, its entrails left as an offering to the forest floor. She hung the animal from a nearby branch, then pulled a threadbare blanket from her saddlebag and spread it on the ground.

To his utter delight, she suddenly lifted her skirt—revealing a pair of worn, practical boots like those worn by Saxon men, and the sight made him smile. She loosened and kicked them off, removed her belt, set aside her seax, and slipped off her overdress. With a quick tug, she knotted her linen chemise underdress to just above her knees, allowing herself to move more freely.

Torvald sat in awe of the stunning vision before him—assured, unfazed in her solitude, the blood of her kill still streaked across her hands and face—it stirred something within him. He couldn't look away.

He watched as she waded into the tributary, staying close to shore. She moved slowly, methodically, feeling her way along the riverbed with her bare feet. Her gaze remained downcast as her toes worked the silt below. Torvald followed her progress with sharp focus, his presence still unnoticed.

As she drew closer, he had a moment of panic as he realized he needed to change position or risk being seen. As silently as he was able, he slid himself down the tree trunk until he lay almost flat against the ground, concealed by the tall grass.

She was close enough now to hear even the slightest rustle, and he dared not breathe too deeply, let alone move. Her back was to him, and she was knee-deep in the water, still probing with her feet.

Suddenly, she paused, leaned forward until her chin nearly touched the surface, her arms feeling about beneath the water. She rose again with a wicker fish trap clutched to her chest.

She turned towards the shore, water from the trap streaming

down the front of her chemise, soaking it to transparency as she lifted and shook the trap to inspect its contents. Grinning ear to ear, she opened it and counted her catch—four respectably sized perch, and one minuscule one.

Without hesitation, she reached in and grabbed the smallest fish, tossing it back into the river, then gathered the others in her skirt, holding them securely as she prepared to make her way back.

As she turned, Torvald couldn't help but lift himself slightly for a better look at the final act of what had become the most riveting scene he'd stumbled upon in some time. Her delight with her catch was infectious. He caught himself grinning just as wide as she was.

Torvald pressed his elbow into the ground to lift himself just a bit more, when a sudden, silence-slicing crack rang out.

He'd snapped a dry branch beneath him. It was the kind of sound that could have only been made by a man, and he froze.

She spun towards the sound, and Torvald instantly flattened himself onto the sandy ground, holding his breath while biting insects instantly found their way into his beard, ears, and nose.

He peered through the tall grass, watching as the woman's eyes scanned the shoreline, sharp and quick. Her hand reached for the place her seax would be—but came up empty. He watched her expression cloud with frustration as she realized her blade was still ashore on the blanket, far out of reach.

Her soaked chemise, clinging to her form, left absolutely nothing to the imagination, betraying every curve as her chest rose and fell with the heightened breath of someone on sudden alert. Torvald felt she was looking straight at him—through him—and yet she hadn't seen him. He stayed still as a stone, transfixed not just by the sight of her body, but by the force of her presence. Unarmed, alone, yet utterly undaunted, she was clad only in transparent, drenched linen and unflinching resolve, every inch of her focused and unyielding.

HEART OF THE WILD GODS

At last, she turned, fish bundled in her skirt, and walked briskly back toward the riverbank. Then she was gone.

Torvald continued to lie still for a while after, knowing he was well past the time when it was safe to move, yet not yet ready to do so. Instead, he rolled over and watched the white clouds drift across the clear blue sky while the memory of what he'd just witnessed took hold, lingering like a spell.

6

Ġemōt ✕ Meeting

Osric barely stirred as a hand gripped his shoulder.

"My lord... Lord Osric," Cwenhild murmured, voice low but urgent.

The thegn of Wōdenléah lay face-down on his bed, boots still on—exactly as he had collapsed an hour earlier. A muffled groan now escaped him, his face buried in the bedcover.

"Lord Osric!" she tried again, this time shaking him firmly. At last, he stirred, lids heavy, slowly coming to the world like a bear after a winter's sleep.

"It's time, my lord. The afternoon administration awaits. You must arise."

Osric blinked, dazed, and struggled upright, rubbing his eyes as though the daylight pained him. "Cwenhild... thank you," he mumbled, his voice thick with sleep, as he tried to gather himself.

"My lord, you've been buried in your work," Cwenhild said with a grin, leaning close and meeting his gaze with a warm, knowing wink. She handed him a cup of small ale[viii] she'd brought, her eyes flickering with a touch of humor.

"Indeed, I have," Osric replied with a weary smile and a soft laugh. No secret in Wessex could be kept from Cwenhild, who saw everything precisely as it was.

"Mmm." She smiled, then swatted the side of his head lightly. "Water's drawn. Refresh yourself. Your things are laid out."

Osric glanced toward the table. His cloak, which had been draped over a hall chair for weeks, if not months, was now neatly folded, his saddlebag slung over the back. She'd tidied while he slept.

"There's bread and cheese. Eat something," Cwenhild added

briskly. "Now up with you. They'll be arriving soon."

With that, Cwenhild swept out, deftly scooping up a wicker basket of washing under one arm.

Osric drained the cup, grimaced, and stood—unsteady, half-blind with weariness. He staggered to the basin, splashing cold water onto his face until he gasped. It shocked him to the bone, but chased the fog. With wet fingers, he raked back his unruly hair and glanced at his reflection in the polished bronze mirror.

"He still looks like death," he muttered.

Snatching a slice of bread and a wedge of cheese, he quickly stuffed them into his mouth and chewed, grabbed his bag, and headed out around the partition and into the passage that led to the great hall.

***

With the afternoon administration underway, Osric finally set aside the worries pressing on his mind, determined to be fully present in his duties to the burh he was sworn to serve.

Though the late sun had cooled the day, the air in the hall still hung thick and close. Osric, seated in the thegn's seat, found himself grateful that the day's business mainly was routine: harvest estimates, craftsmen's needs, and updates on burh inspections were all on the agenda, as well as a disciplinary complaint that had been requested at the last minute.

Svend, the trade overseer from the Viking camp, was there to discuss projected barley and oat requirements for overwintering at the camp, and he had another Northman with him that Osric did not recognize. The man was a giant, blonde and imposing, and looked every bit as exhausted as Osric felt.

After a few minor disputes among the people had been swiftly resolved without tension, there was only a disciplinary matter left to contend with, brought forth by Edwin, the tanner.

HEART OF THE WILD GODS

As Osric prepared to begin the proceedings, he noticed Bishop Æthelwod slip quietly into the back of the hall, accompanied by an older woman he recognized as Wynnflæd of Aldhem, the widow of the neighboring landowner whose village bordered Wōdenléah. Osric gave them a respectful nod before calling the hall to order.

"Good people of Wōdenléah," he called, projecting his voice through the hall. "Before me stands Edwin, who brings a complaint against his sister, Ardith, for unseemly conduct and dishonor to their household."

Osric felt his ears burn as he read out these accusations, and felt the cold, unyielding gaze of Æthelwod fixed firmly upon him. He despised disciplinary proceedings, and this one in particular made the hairs on the back of his neck stand up.

Unseemly conduct and bringing dishonor upon her family.

It was an accusation that, considering his activities the previous night, might just as easily have been laid at *his* feet.

He looked out at those gathered and took a breath.

"As the lord and keeper of this burh, I call this hall to order. All who speak shall do so truthfully, that justice may be served before God and man. Let Edwin and Ardith step forward, as well as any who might bear witness to this matter, or wish to speak in her defense—if they will swear to the truth."

The crowd shifted. Ardith stumbled forward, shoved from behind by her brother. Osric recognized the robust, ample-bosomed serving woman at once—a kind soul, cheerful and chatty—perhaps more heart than wit, but good enough at her job and always smiling.

As she emerged, the blonde Northman by Svend straightened, eyes narrowing with sudden amusement. Osric noted the change at once.

He continued. "Ardith, your brother claims you failed to return home last night, and by this he accuses you of unseemly behavior and of shame brought upon your family."

The irony struck him like a blow—words that more or less described his own morning perfectly.

He cleared his throat. "You may answer the complaint."

"Ġēa, my lord," replied Ardith, the accused, her tone nonplussed. "We were drinkin' at the market at close when a few of the Northmen asked if we wanted to see the camp."

"That weren't all ye did, Ardith," interjected her brother Edwin, giving his sister a little shove, his voice tight with irritation. "Sun was well up by the time we caught sight of ye, sneaking into the hut."

Osric tried not to wince overtly.

Ardith shot her brother a look. "I was gettin' to that," Ardith snapped back at her brother. "Like I said, we was drinkin' and... well, I wore out my welcome a bit too well, my lord." She shot a bold glance at the towering Northman beside Svend, who let out a booming laugh, and a ripple of shock and laughter spread through the crowd.

"We were talkin' is all," Ardith added, eyes twinkling.

Osric resisted the urge to sigh aloud. *God Almighty, strike me down.*

Osric rapped the table with his hand, his patience wearing thin. "Enough, enough. Is there anyone here who would offer a witness account?"

Dear God, I hope not.

A pall fell over the room. Not a single person had the appetite for speaking.

"No witnesses?" Osric asked, scanning the room, his eyes resting momentarily on the giant blonde Dane, who returned and held his gaze, a look of menacing amusement in his eyes. Osric was now certain that there was, in fact, at least one witness present in the hall.

Osric tried again. "No one here who can speak to harm done or peace unsettled by this matter?"

Still nothing.

Thank God Almighty.

The hall remained silent, giving Osric a welcome opportunity to draw a swift conclusion.

"I ask a final time, is there anyone here who can bear witness to this complaint? I ask that you speak now, if you hold truth in your heart and honor in your word." Osric felt his stomach churn at the taste of his own hypocrisy.

Nothing.

He turned to Edwin. "With no corroboration, we cannot take the complaint forward. But the matter is not without weight."

He paused in thought for a moment, then faced the hall. "Despite a lack of witness, this cannot go entirely unanswered. Ardith, your actions carry with them the risk of unsettling the hard-won truce and flourishing trade between the burh and our Norse neighbors, however unintentionally."

Osric swallowed and thought for a moment, steadying himself as he pressed on. "A fine of two silver pennies shall be paid to the church. Let it remind us all—the peace we keep here is sacred. Let no folly endanger it. As to penance, two days under the spiritual guidance of Bishop Æthelwod."

The nature of Æthelwod's penance did make Osric wary, but he knew he had little choice but to give his patron his due.

"I believe this to have been an isolated event," Osric continued, his gaze sweeping across the hall before meeting Svend's gaze, "but I must warn you all that if this happens a second time, curfews between the trading camp and our burh shall be reinstated." Svend nodded his head in quiet approval while Bjørn glowered.

Osric paused, letting his words settle over the crowd, relieved at having arrived at a fair and measured conclusion.

Thank God.

Making his way to the front of the hall, Svend, who approached with a warm smile intercepted Osric.

"Lord Osric," Svend greeted, open-faced.

"Svend." Osric nodded.

Svend gestured to the giant Northman. "This is Bjørn," he said.

Bjørn gave the faintest of nods, his gaze lingering on Ardith.

"I trust you're satisfied the curfew stands lifted?" Osric asked.

"I came to say exactly that," Svend replied, smiling. "Jarl Torvald has granted me authority. Peace is our highest aim. What you did here—fair and fitting."

"Excellent," Osric said. "May your road back be uneventful," he added with a nod, eager to make his escape and step outside for a breath of air.

He turned toward the door, barely resisting the urge to run.

7
Lufiend ᚷ Lover

"Whatever you've got on that hearth fire, it smells fit for a feast," came a voice from the doorway.

Æfre smiled without looking over her shoulder—he'd made it, just in time.

She had debated starting the fish without him—Osric was forever being caught up in the business of the burh. If it wasn't questions, counsel, the fyrd—there was always some last-minute crisis—it came with the position, with being the one they all looked to. But tonight, she'd taken a chance, propped open the door, and gutted and cleaned every fish from her trap before laying them over the hearth on her hanging griddle with some herbs and salt.

"Osric! You've arrived at the perfect time! I only just set the fish on moments ago!"

"Good," he said as he crossed the hut in three strides. "I'm starved."

He slipped an arm around her waist and kissed the nape of her neck, causing little thrills to run down her spine.

"Careful, Lord," she teased, pressing into his embrace, "keep on like that and we'll both miss dinner."

"Mmm. Then we'd waste this," Osric's other arm came around, revealing a small clay jug, which he passed to her.

She held it up, eyebrows lifting. "Is this—?"

"Æthelwod's elderflower mead."

She gasped, grinning as she inspected the jug. "Osric! What a treat!"

He murmured something unintelligible, his lips still grazing her neck.

She suddenly stopped, tilting her head. "Osric..."

"Mmm?"

"You stole this, didn't you?"

"How dare you?" Osric declared with a grin, plucking the jug back and rummaging through a shelf near the hearth until he found two earthenware cups.

"I merely reallocated surplus goods. Æthelwod keeps more of his special mead in storage than he'd ever be able to use in his lifetime. And the good folk who keep the burh running—they get to have some once a year, at Yule."

"So... you stole it," she grinned.

"I liberated it." He poured the mead, passing her a cup, his eyes raking over her now with renewed interest.

Æfre snorted dismissively, chuckled, gladly accepting the cup of mead.

"Æfre, what are you wearing?" His voice suddenly lowered.

Æfre looked at him, confused for a moment before she remembered she was wearing her mother's faded old green linen dress, loosely belted with a cord at the waist—the dress was loose and threadbare, the top constantly sliding off one shoulder, making clear to Osric that she had absolutely nothing on underneath.

"What? Oh—this," she laughed, "I soaked my chemise checking my traps, got hare's blood on my dress hanging it in the livestock shed, and by he time I arrived back here, everything smelled of fish. I'm actually not that long back from the creek. Everything is drying by the hearth."

Osric looked where she had indicated and spotted her dress and chemise hanging there. He raised his cup of mead.

"Then I shall raise a glass to the hare and the fish both." Osric raised his glass and, without taking his eyes off of Æfre, took a long sip of mead.

"My lord," Æfre laughed, "if you think you can summon the

strength to tear your eyes from this threadbare sack I'm wearing long enough to clear a space on the table, we might eat. The fish is ready."

They ate in near silence, both ravenous after the long, sweltering day. The heat still hung heavily in the hut, and for several minutes the only sounds were the scrape of their knives and the soft clunk of wood and earthenware. Most of the fish was gone before either spoke again.

Osric poured the last of the mead into their cups, then reached across the table to take Æfre's hand in his.

"Æfre," he said, "I need to tell you what passed between me and Æthelwod today."

"By your tone, I might guess it was nothing good."

"No, it was not." He hesitated. "Æfre, he named you."

Her brows lifted. "What do you mean, named me?"

"He wanted me to know that he knows. About us."

"Ah." She let out a short, dry laugh. "And he expressed his disapproval, did he?"

"He called it an 'unworthy entanglement with one unsanctified by the Church.'"

Æfre snorted. "That's actually a fair bit more poetic than I'm used to, Osric! In the past, when someone wanted to take issue, they would just call us "filthy heathens," though it certainly never stopped them when their children burned with fever or something hurt." She rose and took her empty cup with her. "Osric, my family has endured this type of nonsense my entire life! This shall pass. It always does."

She stood, clearing the table, stacking the trenchers and cutlery. At the hearth, she scraped the scraps and fish bones into a bucket for the compost, then rinsed the utensils and earthenware in a basin of water she'd drawn from the creek earlier.

"I want to believe that's all there is to it," Osric said. "And of course, Æthelwod was trying to intimidate me. But there was something about it…it felt different. Why would he feel the need to take an interest now? He warned me quite plainly that if I don't sever my ties with you, he would see to it you would be unable to continue your practice unless…"

Æfre turned slightly, speaking over her shoulder. "Unless what? And how would he manage that, I wonder? The folk of the burh come to me of their own free will, Osric—I do not force it upon them."

"His words were that he did not want to rob the burh of its healer, so long as you healed in the name of the one true God. Else not at all."

"Ah, of course. Æthelwod wants me to become Christian."

She dried her hands, then came to sit beside him, backwards on the bench, leaning back against the table to look him in the face.

"This is not new, Osric," she breathed, exasperated. "They rail, threaten, and in time, they'll simply move on—find some new thing to upset them." She reached out and stroked his beard. "All will be well."

"I do hope you're right," he said as he leaned in slowly and kissed her—softly at first. Then again, with a growing intensity. He reached over and slowly pulled the cord that cinched the threadbare linen dress around Æfre's waist until it unfastened, and it slipped quietly to the floor.

Æfre stood from the table and faced him, slipping an arm out of the dress and allowing it to flutter silently to the floor, leaving her completely uncovered, vulnerable, and glowing.

"Enough talk of Æthelwod, Osric. Come to bed."

Æfre watched Osric's gaze intensify as he rose and stood in front of her, his eyes sweeping hungrily over every inch of her exposed body. The deliciously familiar ache of longing was building rapidly within her, and her breath quickened in anticipation of his touch.

Æfre saw how the linen of Osric's trousers was stretched tight, incapable of obscuring his desire as he stood facing her, and she bit her lip with anticipation as she looked at him.

Moving closer to her, he gave her a playful little shove. "As you wish, my...what was it you said they called you?"

"Filthy heathen," Æfre said playfully as she took a few backward steps towards the bed.

He slowly moved in and gently pushed her again. "That's it. As you wish, my filthy little heathen."

Æfre giggled and took a few steps more. With one final gentle shove from Osric, she fell back onto the bed with a bounce and a laugh.

Arching her back, she tossed her pale locks out of her face, her eyes fixed on him, and a wry smile of anticipation spreading across her face, daring him to take it further.

Osric stood beside the bed, drinking in the wild, unguarded splendor of her naked form. She stretched out one leg and teased him with her toes, gently tracing the inside of his thigh—light, lingering touches that tested and invited. His body responded instantly. She felt him stiffen and curled her heel behind his leg, trying to draw him closer.

He swatted her gently.

"Wait," he commanded teasingly—the soldier's edge slipping into his tone. He reached for her leechbook from atop the small chest by the bed.

A grin spread across Æfre's face as she watched him. "Not my leechbook again, Osric," she laughed. Ignoring his command to wait, she traced gently up his inner thigh with her foot, glancing against his manhood through his trousers as she slowly massaged it while looking up at him.

"Close your eyes," ordered Osric, as he playfully swatted her foot away again. "Lie back."

With a mischievous giggle, Æfre did as she was told with a sarcastic "yes, Lord," and adjusted her position in the bed, once again leaving her smooth, flawless body on total display in front of Osric. She closed her eyes and raised her arms up to adjust the pillow, then arched her back slightly, allowing the deep, delicious ache to flow freely and have more control.

"Keep your eyes closed," said Osric, gazing appreciatively at her beauty. "You have quite a lot of knowledge recorded in this leechbook, and I'm going to see if you recognize it with your eyes closed."

Osric climbed on top of Æfre, straddling her, his trousers bulging, the leechbook still in hand. Flipping through it, he said, "Tell me what I'm drawing. You have to describe it, and tell me its meaning. Understand?"

"Yes, Lord," purred Æfre, the fire in her voice betraying the combination of amusement, longing, and impatience that flooded her.

Osric continued to flip through the leechbook until he came to rest on a page towards the back—a beautifully illustrated page that featured the Elder Futhark runic alphabet.

"Good. Now close your eyes and tell me what I'm drawing."

Using his index finger, Osric traced over Æfre's left breast - slowly dragging his finger from the upper left corner to the lower right. Osric teased her with a feather-light touch, slowing down only briefly over her nipple, the electric sensation making her draw in a sharp breath followed by a soft moan as she bit her lip and writhed.

He then repeated the same tracing, but this time from the upper right corner of her breast to the lower left, ultimately creating the shape of an X.

Æfre writhed beneath him. Her breasts heaved upwards as she

arched her back, trying desperately to meet his touch.

Osric leaned down over her, and Æfre felt the firmness of him pressing against her most intimate silken warmth, straining at the seam of his trousers. Unable to resist, she reached out and cupped her hand around it, rubbing it a few times before Osric playfully swatted her hand away.

"No! First, you have to pass my test. What is it? It's from your book—what did I draw?" Osric asked insistently. He once again traced the shape of an X over Æfre's left breast, once again slowing down when he got to Æfre's nipple, which was now standing like a soldier at attention.

"The gebo rune." Æfre breathed. "Gebo—a gift."

"Gebo," Osric repeated as he traced the X across her left breast for the third time, causing another surge of aching pleasure. Æfre again arched her back, enjoying his delicious touch, not wanting it to stop.

Osric sat up once more, studying the journal before fixing his attention on Æfre's right breast. She was breathing more heavily now, no longer able to resist the urge to move beneath him as he straddled her.

With his free hand, he traced one vertical line down the center of her right breast, again slowing over the bead of her nipple before continuing down. He then drew a smaller, nearly perpendicular line through it.

"Naudiz... that's naudiz," sighed Æfre, recognizing the rune. "The symbol of *need*."

"Need, you say?" asked Osric, the sly smile evident in his voice. "That's excellent work, Æfre—well done. Let's just review that once more, shall we?" He then positioned himself over her right breast, and this time, with his tongue, traced the symbol for naudiz, giving her nipple a little extra flick.

Æfre moaned again, her hips instinctively rising as she arched her back and thrust her aching core against Osric's trousers, again trying to extend the duration of his touch. She felt as if she were on fire, the blaze sending thousands of little sparks of electricity running through her. She tried to reach for Osric's waistband, but he pulled back.

"Wait," he commanded. "One more."

Osric swung a leg over Æfre, temporarily dismounting her so he could shake a leg out of his trousers, kicking them off in a smooth motion as they fluttered to a heap on the floor.

Through her half-closed eyes, Æfre could see that he was fully ready, his need extending out in front of him like a divining rod, athletic warrior's body prepared for conquest. Her arousal grew as she watched him take in the sight of her unadorned body lying before him, vulnerable and receptive. She loved that it electrified him, the way he was taking it all in—as if making a mental etching of the moment.

She moved her hands to his upper thighs as he straddled her and began to caress them in an upward motion.

"You're cheating," scolded Osric softly, mockingly.

"Yes," giggled Æfre, "I am."

She arched her back and wriggled a bit in an attempt to guide Osric closer to her entrance - her desire to feel him inside her overruling her patience.

Osric once again leaned down and whispered in Æfre's ear.

"Wait."

His breath was coming faster and harder now. "Here is the last one."

He took his time with the final rune, drawing a straight line from just beneath her navel to the soft, sensitive swell below. Æfre gasped, pressing up into his finger as he moved. When he circled lightly over her most sensitive nexus, she bit her lip, too breathless to speak.

HEART OF THE WILD GODS

"What is it?" he asked softly, fingers circling, coaxing more.

She writhed beneath him, the tension building so fast it was almost unbearable.

"What did I draw?" he repeated, his finger now slick with her desire, moving in slow, knowing strokes.

"Isa!" Æfre rasped, "The symbol for ice!" She moved her hips in time to his rhythm, driven by instinct and need.

"Isa," Osric repeated, positioning himself between her thighs. He took her breasts into his mouth, flicking and nibbling until she moaned his name again, writhing to guide him deeper.

"Osric, enough, I need you," she whispered, clinging to him like someone afraid to let go or be drowned.

But he resisted. He kissed his way down her stomach, tongue flicking, teeth grazing just enough to make her cry out. At last, he reached her silken heat, pressing a single kiss against her core.

Æfre whimpered, grabbing fistfuls of his hair.

Osric worked his tongue in a rhythm she immediately matched, hips moving, breath ragged. Her cries grew louder, sensation overtaking her, climbing to a fever pitch as she surrendered to the rhythm of his mouth. She was spiraling, the peak building with every flick, every stroke, every breath.

Sensing her release was near, Osric shifted quickly, positioning himself at her entrance. He kept his thumb moving, teasing her just long enough for the fire to overtake her.

She cried his name as her climax broke, his name spilling through the hut as if she wanted to paint it onto every beam until he became a part of the walls themselves.

He thrust deeply into her, and they moved together again and again, lost in one another until he too shattered the quiet of the hut like a dropped bead of crystal splintering into a million shimmering stars.

They lay there for an amount of time neither could have

guessed—limbs entwined, neither daring to break the spell.

In the stillness that followed, Æfre knew that they both felt the shift that was happening. Whatever boundaries had once defined them were slipping. What had begun as something unsaid, a quiet understanding that their connection existed only within the walls of her hut—it now felt much more complex, more entwined.

They didn't speak of it, but she knew he felt it too.

For now, they lingered in the perfect stillness of moments such as this, where the world beyond her door didn't exist.

8

Gewær ✕ Watchful

Torvald stood motionless, leaning against the hall's doorframe, his sharp gaze fixed on the setting sun as the merchants packed up their wares, but his thoughts overtaken by the image of the woman he'd seen earlier by the river. No matter how he tried to distract himself, his mind found its way back to her. He rubbed his eyes and shook his head—he needed focus, he needed clarity. Instead, there she was again—her pale hair catching the sun, and a gaze as steady as her bow. It was a gaze that had fixed directly upon him—unflinching, yet thankfully, unseeing.

It was becoming clear to him that the sight of this woman had ripped something open within him, something that for whatever reason, he was now unable to put back in its container. It was a part of himself that he thought was forever lost after losing his wife and child, and the sudden emergence of these feelings he thought were long buried unsettled him.

It wasn't just that the woman was beautiful, which she undeniably was—it was something more elusive than that. The sight of her hunting alone, standing in a river completely unafraid—it made him feel something that felt natural and unrestrained—almost wild. It reminded him of a life that existed outside of the constant control and carefully cultivated relationships he surrounded himself with, and it had captivated him completely.

Still, he knew better than to let the camp see him distracted. For a man in his position, the low hum of dissent was never far away, even at the best of times. A gathering of warriors-turned merchants might trade blades one day and sharpen grudges the next, and any perceived weakness on his part was a spark that could easily ignite a cataclysm of unrest.

The sound of a wagon brought Torvald back to the present. Svend and Bjørn had returned from Wōdenléah. Svend caught sight of him and waved him over.

"Jarl Torvald!" Svend called, his voice carrying over the sounds coming from the hall.

Torvald strolled over, returning the greeting with a nod.

"All went well, did it?" Torvald asked, his gaze briefly shifting to Bjørn, who had just hopped down from the wagon and was unloading several bags of grain. Bjørn gave Torvald a subtle nod, a silent, conciliatory gesture, which Torvald mirrored with a brief acknowledgment.

"It did," Svend replied, his voice light. "Come, let's get some ale and I'll tell you."

Svend turned to Bjørn, but before he could speak, Bjørn cut him off.

"I've got it, Svend. You go." Bjørn's tone was deferential—as if it belonged to an entirely different man than the one Torvald had confronted earlier that morning.

Svend raised his eyebrows, a light smile crossing his face. He exchanged a brief look with Torvald, winked, then motioned for Torvald to follow. The two men made their way toward the hall.

As they entered the hall, the atmosphere shifted immediately. The men inside stood with deference, some even vacating their seats to make room for the two of them. Torvald encouraged them to stay seated and chose a spot near the entrance, allowing him a clear line of sight to Bjørn, who was still unloading the wagon outside.

Svend began recounting the events of the day, his tone animated as he spoke of the disciplinary hearing of the young woman Torvald had seen that morning with Bjørn. Svend recounted every detail of the proceeding, even affecting an impressive falsetto voice to act out the part of the young woman, contrasting it with the observable exasperation of Osric, the thegn. The men began to gather as Svend spun his tale, and before long, a crowd formed around them, laughing heartily at the absurdity of the story, a welcome diversion from the routine of daily camp life.

"I'll have to remember that one," a rough-looking trader slurred, making a crude thrusting motion with his hips. "Let me show you the camp, dear lady!"

The men roared with laughter. Another called out, "Jarl Torvald, when was the last time *you* showed a lady the camp?"

The men roared, and Torvald grinned, knowing they were waiting for a reply to fuel their revelry. Allowing a wry smile to spread across his face, Torvald gave them the response he knew they wanted to hear. "Men," he declared, "in my experience, the Saxons are best suited for two essential functions: fighting..." He paused, an eyebrow raised for effect, "and fucking!"

The men roared once again, ale splashing all around them. Torvald looked at Svend, and they exchanged a knowing smile.

If they only knew, Torvald thought. Despite all of this grand talk, his mind darted straight back to his strange afternoon; bugs crawling in his beard, lying as still as a stone on the ground—hiding in the tall grass from one such beautiful Saxon who still occupied his thoughts.

Torvald continued to listen to their banter with half a smile. However, his attention split between their tales and the actions of Bjørn outside, nodding in agreement as Svend recounted how Wōdenléah's thegn had stopped short of reinstating the trading hours curfew.

Torvald had never had cause to sit down with the thegn in person, but his name, Osric, was known to him. He was a man spoken of with respect in the streets of the burh, both for his skill as a warrior and his leadership. From what Svend had told him, Osric was the type of leader skilled in bringing out the best in those who served under him.

Torvald knew enough about Osric's patron, Bishop Æthelwod, to understand that the thegn would need all of those skills, and more. Æthelwod was little more than a rat in a robe; he was sanctimonious, grasping, and lacking the nuance and charisma that authentic leadership demanded. Torvald often wondered how such a man had ever risen to spiritual authority—but of course, power frequently did favor the cunning over the worthy.

Bishop Æthelwod's simmering hatred for the "heathen Danes," as he never tired of calling them, was well-known in the camp, although the moniker was a hostility he generally extended to all non-Christians. To Æthelwod, they were not merely outsiders, but a disease upon Wōdenléah—a blight that needed eradication in the name of the one true Christian God. But the chieftain wasn't fooled. All one had to do was look deeper to see that Æthelwod's relentless campaign to "purify" the region was as much about consolidating power as it was about faith.

Torvald's gaze shifted toward the entrance of the hall, where he could now see Bjørn standing in hushed conversation with three other men. Two were traders Torvald recognized, both relatively new arrivals—but the third was unfamiliar. The group huddled together, speaking in low tones, their eyes darting around them as they conversed. The way they gestured sharply and leaned in close suggested this was no casual discussion.

Torvald narrowed his eyes, studying the unfamiliar man. He was leading the conversation, his tone and body language hinting at persuasion, or even instruction. One by one, the others nodded, their faces etched with an intensity Torvald recognized—the quiet urgency of men preparing for something beyond routine.

"What distracts you, Jarl?" Svend asked, his earlier laughter fading as he followed Torvald's gaze. He finished his ale, signaling

HEART OF THE WILD GODS

for another round.

Torvald leaned in, keeping his voice low. "Something is stirring, Svend." Torvald nodded subtly toward the men outside. "Look at them. That isn't idle talk. And there have been other signs—I've heard whispers from a few of the merchants. Something is taking shape in the shadows, Svend."

Svend frowned, folding his arms and lowering his voice as he leaned in. "You think they're planning to rise against us? Or perhaps the Saxons are?"

Torvald shook his head thoughtfully and took a breath while he considered the idea. "Not the people of the burh, no. They have nothing to gain."

Svend nodded. "And Osric wouldn't start something without cause. He's loyal to his king's treaty and clever enough to keep Æthelwod in check..."

"The Bishop Æthelwod," Torvald sighed. "Those who knew the thegn's predecessor would talk of how he used to speak of the Bishop's desire to take over this camp. If he were to clear us out, he would gain control of one of the most lucrative trading routes in Wessex."

Svend leaned back, exhaling a held breath, his expression grim. "The people... the fyrd...would they follow him?"

"The people are mostly afraid of him. And his talk of heathens, of cleansing the land...he doesn't need to convince them, all he needs to do is feed their fears in the name of their God." Torvald replied, and the two men looked at each other knowingly for a moment,

"Keep your ears open, Svend. Currently, this is nothing more than a theory, and it should remain between the two of us—nobody else. We can't get ahead of ourselves, but we need to find out what's truly happening."

Svend leaned in. "Jarl Torvald, I agree. Which brings us to

Bjørn."

Torvald looked at Svend. "What of him?" Torvald asked. Bjørn had been a consistent pain in his ass, but he was still the firstborn son of a chieftain and a warrior with the strength of an ox. He just also happened to have the mating habits of a stray dog.

Svend leaned in, "He's restless. You know the sort. Thinks he's being left out, untested, wants a chance to lead—to prove himself to you, Jarl. He knows he made a mistake, and he knows he's a selfish bastard that won't get another chance. He wanted to come apologize—it was I who told him to wait until we first spoke."

"That may be," Torvald replied cautiously, "but I've no interest in handing a man a sword if it's unclear he won't just turn around and fall on top of it."

"That is why," Svend chuckled, "we must guide him. I spent a fair bit of time with him today, and I believe now is the time to pull him back from the brink. It was you who told me that the best way to bind a man is to make him part of something he can't afford to lose."

Torvald smiled at Svend's cleverness, throwing his own strategy back at him. "Bjørn's pride makes him reckless, Svend," Torvald said, doubting Bjørn's fealty to anyone but himself.

"Yes, Jarl, but it also makes him predictable." Svend sat back and drained the last of his ale.

Torvald exhaled slowly. Like the timber frame of a longship, the skeletal foundation of a plan was forming in his mind.

Bjørn needed to be handled carefully, but Svend was right—leaving him rudderless, potentially stewing in resentment, felt like dereliction.

"Svend," Torvald said at last. "You constantly remind me why you are my closest ally—few see the long game as well as you. We will bring him in, possibly even let him lead, but he carries out any task under my command. As it happens, I have a few ideas." Torvald gave a knowing grin to Svend before draining his ale horn.

Svend smiled, satisfied, before signaling for a third round of ale.

Torvald turned his gaze back to the entrance, his mind already working on the next steps.

"Bjørn," he called out the door of the hall, "come inside and get yourself some ale!"

9
Cirice ⚔ Church

Osric slipped in through the back entrance of Wōdenléah's hall just as the dawn began to break, grateful for what Æfre referred to as his 'affliction' for rising early. As much as he hoped that yesterday's late arrival and subsequent confrontation with Æthelwod had been an isolated event, he had no intention of tempting the man's wrath again—especially when he knew Æfre would likely be caught in the crossfire.

He quickly refreshed himself and straightened his tunic. An appearance at morning prayers was unavoidable, though at the moment, he could think of nothing he'd rather do less. It was market day in the burh, which meant endless questions, disputes, and decisions that would pull him in every direction—likely until the sun went down. He couldn't help but think how he would have much preferred to begin the day with his usual quiet ride out to the fields. Or better still, with Æfre, tucked beneath the coverlet, her head cradled against his chest. But such mornings were rare.

Through the partition, he could already hear the daily bustle of the burh—footsteps, cookware, low voices, the crackle of the hearth. There was no avoiding it now. He rolled the kinks out of his neck and stepped around the partition and into the main hall, where Cwenhild was at the fire, stirring a large pot of porridge.

"Lord Osric! Good morning to you," she called brightly, tapping the wooden spoon against the side of the pot. "Off to morning prayers?"

"A very good morning to you, Cwenhild," he said, "just making my way there now. Will you be joining me?"

"I'll be along just as soon as my gallant husband ends his heroic standoff with the goats—he was losing ground when last I checked," she said wryly.

"Then I'll see you both there," he grinned, "provided your husband survives the siege."

He turned to leave, shielding her from seeing his great disappointment at having to go forth and face Æthelwod alone.

"Don't miss the morning meal, my lord. We've got blackberries this morning, and fresh honey! I'll set some aside in your quarters so you don't miss out."

He turned back with a slight bow. "Cwenhild, the burh would be lost without you."

"That's the truth of it, my lord," she called to him over her shoulder, "although it's difficult to get too puffed-up with pride when you awaken each morning smelling of goat."

* * *

Æthelwod stood preening at the entrance to the church, greeting some and holding court with others as the people of the burh filed in. Osric saw no evidence of the cold and manipulative man he'd encountered the day before. But then, that was Æthelwod—a man capable of shifting skins in an instant. One never truly knew which version of Wōdenléah's bishop you would get.

"Ah, Lord Osric! There you are. A fine morning to you," Æthelwod called out, his smile bright, even warm—his whole bearing transformed from the dour, judgemental man Osric had dealt with the day before. Today, he was the affable clergyman.

"Lord Bishop, good morning." Osric strained to match the warmth in the bishop's voice.

"I hoped we might speak after today's service," Æthelwod said, his voice light and smiling. "Just a small matter. Shall we say—at the residence, once the last of today's worshippers have departed?"

"Of course, Lord Bishop. I'll come by once prayers are done."

"Very good. Excellent, in fact. And may the Lord Almighty

bless and keep you, Lord Osric," Æthelwod said, placing a hand, meant to reassure, on Osric's shoulder before once again turning his full attention to the next parishioner.

"Thank you, Bishop." Osric nodded his recognition, but his resolve faltered. The sudden cordiality was unsettling.

Could this be a bit of remorse for yesterday?

After all, he had risked his life for this man and, in a relatively short amount of time, brought these church-held lands back into prosperity.

But no. Remorse was far too simple an answer for a man like Æthelwod.

Osric crossed the threshold of the church into the nave, where the smell of tallow clung to the thick, still air. The people of the burh found their places—the thegn in the back of the nave, ceorls standing beside servants, men beside women. The bishop didn't seem to mind this casual mixing at these early services, all being equal in the eyes of God. Or perhaps more likely, because it suited the image of the humble shepherd he wished to project.

Osric lingered at the back, letting the burh folk fill the space in front of him. He spotted Cwenhild, and Cenric offered a quick nod. A moment later, Aelf the thatcher and his wife, Wynn, arrived, their newborn, Godhild, cradled in her arms, asleep.

When the last of the congregation had arrived, Æthelwod strode through the nave and into the chancel, cradling his Vulgate [ix] like a relic.

"Brothers and sisters," he began, "it gladdens my heart to see so many present. And the heat shall surely become intolerable quite quickly, so I'll keep today's service short. Let us begin with a blessing. And please, kneel if that suits you better."

There was a soft scuffle of leather shoes against stone as heads bowed and knees bent against the cool floor.

"Lord Almighty, you who are our shepherd, lead us not by rod but by mercy. We walk in remembrance of Christ's sacrifice, and strive to follow in His name. As we guard against wolves in our fields, let us also guard against wolves among us—those who would spread discord among Christian folk. It is by your Godly light that we shall go forth in unity and fellowship. Amen."

And there he is again, Osric thought. *That sounds more like the Æthelwod I know.*

He knelt with the others, his head bowed as Æthelwod opened the Vulgate and carefully removed the leather cord he used as a marker.

"For this morning's reading, we shall hear Deuteronomy, chapter eighteen."

The bishop cleared his throat, squared his shoulders, and began in Latin:

"Nec inveniatur in te qui lustret filium suum, aut filiam, ducens per ignem: aut qui ariolos sciscitetur, et observet somnia atque auguria, nec sit maleficus..."

As usual, Osric let his mind drift during the Latin, as most of the congregation likely did. While it indeed cultivated an atmosphere of ecclesiastical wonder, it meant little to those who did not understand it. Of course, for Æthelwod, this was all part of the performance—a reminder of who held the power of knowledge and the keys to the scripture. Ironically, Osric supposed the only other soul in Wōdenléah who might truly understand these words the bishop spoke was Æfre.

Finally, Æthelwod began the translation.

"Let no one be found among you who walks their son or daughter through the fire, who practices divination, interprets omens, engages in witchcraft, or speaks charms or spells. She who does these things is detestable to the Lord."

The translation grabbed Osric's attention like a signal horn in the fog.

HEART OF THE WILD GODS

She?

He glanced left through the crowd. No reaction. All eyes were forward. Blank. Then he looked right—and found Cenric staring straight back at him. An acknowledgement of what he'd just heard.

Æthelwod's voice went on, measured and calm.

"The love and acceptance of our one true God," Æthelwod continued, "requires so little of us—only that we walk humbly in his name, our eyes watchful to what might walk beside us. Gēa, all may bask in the light that is God's love, yet we must mind how easily his blessings may be revoked when we allow ourselves to be touched by that which he has forbidden."

After an intentional pause, the bishop's gaze again found Osric at the back of the crowd.

Osric lifted his eyes, his thoughts sharpening. The bishop's look had cooled—gone was the pleasant mask. The warmth had drained away, leaving something hollow behind.

"When what God forbids is allowed to grow roots and flourish," Æthelwod continued, "it brings ruin in its wake. Crops fail. Households fall ill. And children... children struggle mightily to come into the world unafflicted."

Then Æthelwod looked directly at Aelf the thatcher, whose wife still held their sleeping infant.

Osric's stomach dropped.

You filthy bastard. You're actually doing this.

Osric looked over at Aelf and Wynn. Wynn was gently rocking the baby, frowning, looking confused and unsettled by the bishop's words. But Aelf—he was rapt. He hung on Æthelwod's every word.

Then the bishop changed his tone again, this time sounding softer, more conciliatory—a father offering comfort.

"The wolf may cover herself in a sheep's wool of spoken kindness." Æthelwod gave a soft smile, "and she may never show her teeth."

Again. She.

"But do not mistake me, good people of Wōdenléah, She has already begun to gnaw at the very fabric of what is sacred."

A soft, uneasy murmur rippled through the congregation.

Suddenly, Æthelwod's warm smile returned—his entire demeanor snapping back to the affable, smiling bishop he had been at the start of the sermon.

"I say this to you, brothers and sisters, not to strike fear into your hearts, but to remind you that the blessings of the Almighty are not to be taken for granted. Now please, let us all bow our heads and pray..."

10

Foresteall ✕ Ambush

"My lord!"

Osric heard the footsteps behind him, coming fast.

"My lord! Lord Osric—wait!"

Cenric's voice. Getting closer.

Osric didn't slow. He'd been the first one out of the church and was halfway up the path to the bishop's residence, his fists clenched at his sides, blind with rage and intent on waiting there for Æthelwod to arrive for their meeting. The bishop had turned a holy space into his personal stage, spinning a tale to the congregation like a scop around the hearth—and Æfre was to play the part of the loathsome, scary witch.

Osric felt a hand suddenly grab his arm, ushering him forcefully off the path. Looking up, he saw that it was Cenric who had intercepted him.

"Come, Lord, just a moment—this way now." Cenric's bulk herded him toward the brew hut as he looked left and right over his shoulder. The door to the brew hut was wedged open to bleed off the day's heat, and Cenric pushed him over the threshold.

"Christ's nails, Cenric!" Osric said testily, rubbing his arm as he stumbled and sat down heavily onto a stack of wooden boxes.

The thick brew hut air hit him at once—oppressive, yeasty, and rank with the bitterness of fermentation.

Cenric raised his hands. "Lord, I'm sorry—I shouldn't have laid hands on you like that—but I couldn't let you storm in there hotter that a blade fresh out the forge."

"You heard him!" Osric sprung to his feet and began pacing. "That sermon was a blade all right—a blade wrapped in Scripture! And he leveled it at Æfre—even if he didn't say it...he didn't need to! He meant for me to bear witness to that!"

"Yes, Lord. He did," Cenric said coolly, crossing his arms and blocking the door. "And you stormin' in now, crippled with rage? That's what he's hopin' for."

Osric froze. Cenric's words settled over him like a yoke as the message sank in—the effectiveness of Æthelwod's poison relied on the target running in unprepared and swinging wild.

"I'm sorry for layin' hands on you, Lord, truly I am." Cenric's tone gentled. "But I saw it in your face—the way I once saw it in your predecessor's. You're ten times the man he was, but all the same, rage'll get you killed. And Æthelwod? He feeds on it."

Osric let out a deep, shaky breath and sank back onto the boxes. The heat and fermentation sourness in the hut was stifling. Osric's tunic clung to his back, and he ran a hand over his face, sweat stinging his eyes.

"I should thank you," he muttered. "You're right."

"This isn't swordwork, or even the shield wall, Lord," Cenric continued, his voice low. "In the fyrd, sure—you sometimes let anger drive your blade. But this?" He shook his head. "This is a longer game—the blade gets weakened by a thousand little nicks, until eventually it breaks in the hand."

Osric nodded, but said nothing for a moment, his mind already trying to work the puzzle of what exactly Æthelwod might want.

"What do you reckon he's after?"

"What he's always after," Cenric answered flatly. "Power. Influence. Silver, maybe. It's not the *what* that matters, it's *how* he means to get it."

Osric stared at the packed earth floor, sweat dripping from his brow. "We'll need to watch Æfre. She and I spoke briefly of this, and she was certain that it would pass."

"Right, Lord. You did say he was circlin' her." Cenric pulled a cloth from his belt and wiped his forehead. "She may be right, though. Might blow over. Might not."

Osric gave a grunt and ran his hand over his face again—not yet midday and already his head was throbbing.

Cenric extended a hand. "Come, Lord. Let's take the air before your meet. We're boilin' in our own broth in here."

* * *

"Lord Osric, come!" Osric heard Æthelwod's voice call to him, his tone unusually cheerful.

As Osric entered the dimly lit receiving hall of Bishop Æthelwod's residence, he paused, allowing his eyes to adjust. Heavy tapestries hung along the walls, muting any light that seeped in, and shelves displayed various religious relics and artifacts that cast strange shadows across the room when any light did manage to seep in. There was a partition on the left side of the hall that led to a small room that served as Æthelwod's private library, and beyond that were his private quarters.

Looking to the back of the hall, he saw them at once—three figures. Æthelwod wasn't alone. Osric suddenly felt the airlessness of the room close in on him.

What am I walking into?

"How good of you to join us, Lord Osric," Æthelwod said, his voice cold and smooth like a slithering eel. "You left the service quite sharply. I'd expected you sooner."

"Apologies, Lord Bishop." Osric fought to keep his tone even. "Cenric and I walked a bit—an attempt to take the edge off this wretched heat."

"Yes, of course. But you are here now." Æthelwod turned, gesturing grandly. "You already know Lady Wynnflæd of Aldhem. But perhaps you do not remember her daughter—the maiden Eadlin."

Osric stood stunned for a moment, absorbing the realization of what was happening.

"Eadlin," Æthelwod said, his voice overly ceremonious, "allow me to present Lord Osric, thegn of Wōdenléah."

Osric couldn't deny Eadlin's beauty. She appeared very young, slight and fine-boned, with lustrous auburn hair and large, deep brown eyes. She looked at Osric with a soft gaze, her head dipped modestly as she offered a demure nod.

"Lord Osric, I hope this day finds you well."

If by 'well' you mean standing in an ill-wrought snare, Osric thought.

His stomach twisted as he crossed the room. In an instant, the arrangement unfolding before him had become clear. Eadlin was being presented to him, unmistakably intended as his match. It could only be a move designed to unite the lands of Aldhem and Wōdenléah. Such a union would consolidate power, serving the interests of both houses—and all under the watchful eye of Æthelwod and the church.

In an instant, Osric's confrontation with Æthelwod the previous morning made sense. It had been more than a warning, more than the bishop's disingenuous prattling about duty and station. No, it had actually been the first step in a carefully laid scheme. Osric swallowed hard as yet another wave of rage surged through him.

"Eadlin," Osric replied, straining himself to maintain decorum, "it's a pleasure to properly meet you." He dipped his head. As he did, his eyes caught it—a shared glance between Æthelwod and Lady Wynnflæd. Cenric's words echoed in his mind.

"The blade gets weakened by a thousand little nicks."

He had surely just collected one more such nick, and he felt a fool for not having seen it coming—for having allowed himself to become a pawn in a game he might have anticipated, but was wholly unprepared for, instead allowing himself to be cornered like a whelp.

"Perhaps, Lord Osric," Lady Wynnflæd said with the barbed, uneasy sweetness of those born to privilege, "you might show Eadlin the garden."

Both Æthelwod and Lady Wynnflæd looked at Osric expectantly, their gazes heavy with unspoken judgment. Osric fought the instinct to turn and flee, instead forcing a smile.

"Eadlin," he said evenly, "it is indeed an oppressive day. The garden may offer a touch of relief."

"Of course, my lord."

"Please," Osric gestured to the door and followed Eadlin out, hands folded behind his back, casting a hollow smile at Æthelwod and Lady Wynnflæd as he did. He would let them see what they wanted.

For now.

After a pause, Lady Wynnflæd spoke. "Bishop Æthelwod, I do hope that you will be able to bring your thegn to heel for the sake of my daughter," she said. "It's clear to anyone in possession of their eyesight that his affections lie elsewhere."

Æthelwod dismissed her observation, stating smoothly "My dear Wynnflæd, even the hardest iron does eventually bend beneath the hammer of time."

* * *

The garden was deafeningly quiet, and Osric struggled to fill the void with anything that didn't make him appear more on edge than he already was. Eadlin watched with quiet interest, her hands clasped demurely before her as they strolled around the small enclosure.

"The fields will yield well this year," said Osric, the words coming out more stiffly than he'd intended.

Eadlin inclined her head. "Yes, my lord. They'll bring blessings come harvest." She paused, "and may that blessing find its way to your table, as well."

She'd left him an opportunity after her response—a cavernous gap just waiting for him to step into. But Osric just didn't have it in him, simply nodding instead, wishing the breeze would do the speaking for him, as it did for the leaves on the trees around them.

"Your family's lands," he said after a pause. "They border Wōdenléah, do they not?"

He cursed himself the moment the words left him. Of course, the lands bordered the burh. He knew they did. Eadlin knew he knew they did.

"They do, my lord. Wōdenléah shares a border with our own Aldhem," she replied, attempting a small step closer. "My mother spoke highly of Wōdenléah—and of you."

Osric turned his eyes away, fixing them on an unruly patch of rosemary that crept stealthily near the path, managing only a curt nod. "I'm glad to hear it," he muttered distractedly.

As soon as he'd said it, he could see the light of Eadlin's hopefulness drain from her face.

"My lord," She said, her tone unadorned and honest, "I know this meet was not of your choosing. But I had hoped that, perhaps, you might find favor in it." She looked at him, her gaze almost pleading.

Osric turned to her, a wave of guilt washing over him for his awkwardness, which hung between them like a wet blanket. None of this was her fault—God only knows what they had told the poor woman before parading her in front of him like one of Cenric's prized goats.

He offered a weak, apologetic smile, his voice gentling.

"Eadlin, forgive me. I ask your pardon for giving little in return." He met her gaze earnestly. "I am not easy company today. But trust that I can see that you are a woman of patience and kindness, and I would never wish to slight that."

A flicker of relief crossed her face, then a faint smile. "Thank you, Lord Osric. Patience has long been my practice—you've met my mother." She raised an eyebrow and waited for the jest to land.

Osric paused, then blinked, uncertain at first—then saw her raised brow, and let out a sudden, honest laugh.

They finished their exploration of the garden in silence, a newfound comfort between them.

As they arrived back at the entrance to Æthelwod's residence, Osric steadied himself with a deep breath, gesturing with his arm. "After you."

Eadlin gave a grateful nod, walking ahead as Osric trailed after, a mounting sense of dread and sadness settling over him.

11

Cheping ⚔ Marketplace

Æfre dismounted and removed her saddlebag, passing Epona's reins to Cenric.

"Thank you, Cenric," she said. "There's no need to untack her, I'll not be long."

"You've a place for her here with us whenever you like," Cenric replied, patting Epona's neck. "I'll trim her feet while you're gone. She'll be the queen of the paddock by the time you're back."

He hesitated.

"But—Æfre—before you go... Have you spoken to Lord Osric since the morning prayer service?"

Æfre hesitated, sensing that there was more behind his question. "No. I haven't seen him."

"I figured it." Cenric gave Epona a gentle tug toward the paddock. "Well... he'll want a word. It's not my place to say more."

Æfre exhaled slowly. "Cenric, I can probably guess—does it concern a certain bishop?"

Cenric offered a faint smile. "Nothing ever sneaks past you—but I'll let Osric tell it." He looked over his shoulder, lowering his voice. "Just keep your eyes open, dear one."

"I will, Cenric. Thank you. It's certainly not the first time my kin have been the topic of the burh's whispers."

"I hope that's all it is," Cenric murmured, leading Epona away. "You be safe, Æfre."

Æfre slung the bag over her shoulder and headed for Aelf and Wynns' hut, anxious to check on little Godhild after her difficult entry into the world.

When she arrived at the hut, like most of the burh, Wynn and Aelf had the door propped open to help offset the summer heat.

"Wynn?" Æfre called gently into the dim interior. "It's Æfre."

There was stirring behind the partition at the back of the hut, and then Wynn appeared, babe in arms.

"On my way," she called. But halfway across the hut, she stopped short, recognition flashing across her face.

"Æfre," she said, blinking with uncertainty. "I didn't know you were coming."

"You look well," Æfre said with a warm smile. "And the little one? Is she nursing? I came to check her arm. I've a few exercises to help it heal."

Wynn's face softened, and she stepped forward, pulling back the blanket to reveal the baby's face.

"She feeds near-constant," Wynn said, keeping her voice low. "I've become a milk cow."

They shared a brief, hushed laugh, then a voice rose from beyond the partition.

"Wynn! Who is it? Who calls!?"

Aelf.

Wynn's expression changed.

"Æfre, I'm so sorry, perhaps not just now—"

Æfre marked the change immediately. She had been in and out of enough homes over the years to know how situations such as the birth of a child could sometimes fuel other, more sinister disturbances at home.

"Wynn is all well here? Truly?"

"Yes, Æfre!" Wynn smiled weakly, still speaking softly. "It's nothing like that, I swear it. Aelf—he's not unkind. But after what Æthelwod said this morning, he's gotten it into his head that—"

"Who calls, Wynn?" Aelf appeared, smiling, from around the partition—until he saw Æfre. Then the smile died.

"Æfre," he said. "I see." He came to stand directly behind Wynn and put a protective arm around her.

HEART OF THE WILD GODS

"Aelf...hello," Æfre said, "I was just hoping to—"

"We're grateful for everything Æfre, but we'll be able to tend Godhild from here."

"Of course, Aelf," Æfre said gently, "I'm only—."

Before Æfre could finish her sentence, the door had closed firmly in front of her.

She stood stunned for a moment, fighting the individual emotions that rose within her—the hot burn of anger, the ache of sadness, and the sting of exclusion all mingling bitterly at the back of her throat. This was Æthelwod, pulling the strings. Wynn had said as much before Aelf interrupted.

But the question was why?

Æfre took a deep breath and prepared to turn and head back towards the market when the door opened once more. Wynn stood there, Godhild tucked against her shoulder.

"I'm sorry," she whispered, then slipped something into Æfre's hand and disappeared inside, closing the door once again.

Æfre looked down at the object in her hand. It was her mother's amber birthing amulet—the one she'd placed around Wynn's neck during her labor.

The sight of it chilled her. Whatever was happening here, it was more than mere gossip or discomfort. This was a sudden act of rejection, interwoven with fear. Something had shifted.

Still standing at the door to the hut, she opened her bag and drew out a large linen head covering.

Better to meet the gaze of the burh with modesty and concealment, she thought, tucking her hair away and drawing it loosely over her head.

As she turned to leave, she saw three women watching from a distance. They said nothing, and at her glance, they averted their eyes.

Æfre moved towards the market. For the first time, she felt

doubt coiling in her chest as she realized that whatever Æthelwod's motive, she had unwittingly become the burh's very own monster, gnawing on a bone in the shadows while the villagers cowered in fear.

* * *

Torvald leaned one shoulder against the grain barrel, his eyes scanning the bustle of Wōdenléah's market. All around him, merchants shouted prices, children ran underfoot, and the scent of meat smoke rose with the summer heat. He watched, amused and smirking, as Svend stood mid-stall, turning a clay jug in the light.

"It's a sturdy piece," the potter said, puffing his chest, "shaped by these very hands."

"It is a fine piece–" Svend held up the jug and inspected it in the light, "but seven coins!?"

"As I said, thrown by these very hands," the merchant repeated.

"Svend—by the Gods, man, are you buying that thing or courting it!?" Torvald quipped in Norse before taking a bite out of the savory hearth cake he'd purchased from a ruddy-faced woman at a nearby stall.

"It *is* quite shapely, who would blame me?" Svend shot back at Torvald in Norse before turning back to the merchant.

"How about I give you 10 coins and I take two of them."

Torvald chuckled, glad that Svend had talked him into accompanying him to the burh's market. He'd resisted at first, citing his dislike of crowds and the summer heat, but Svend had persisted, expertly appealing to his oldest friend's ego by telling him with a wink that 'a wise Jarl would want to watch for himself what coin moves where.'

So now here he stood, sweating like a smith at the forge and watching Svend flirt with pottery.

He dusted the crumbs from his tunic and pushed himself off

the grain barrel, turning his attention back to his friend.

"Svend! Are you and that jug planning on starting a family? Come on, man! Finish this business alre—"

Torvald took a step forward, his shoulder unwittingly making hard contact with a passing market goer, who uttered a muffled "Oof!"

"Fyrirgef mik [*forgive me*]," he said instinctively as his hand reached out to steady the person he'd nearly just run over.

It was a woman, and the contact had been just enough to dislodge her head covering, revealing a flash of pale blonde hair and a pair of emerald eyes that, for a brief moment, met his—and then they dropped.

"I'm sorry, forgive me, my attention was elsewhere," the woman murmured with a slight smile, reaching out and placing an apologetic hand on his arm, a gesture of reassurance, before tucking her hair back into place, pulling her head covering back up, smiling and ducking away, leaving him momentarily stunned.

That's her. That's the healer, Æfre.

Torvald stood rooted to the spot, his mind racing, the ghost of her touch lingering on his arm. He was still standing there watching her walk away when he suddenly marked Svend calling his name. Signaling to Svend to give him a moment, Torvald moved to follow Æfre.

He moved swiftly, keeping his distance as he watched her navigate the market, going about her routine with the same efficiency of movement he remembered from the afternoon at the river.

Her presence seemed to command respect from some in the burh—some gave her space, some bowed their heads respectfully, or smiled and said hello. But there was something else as well—something unspoken in others. With them, her presence seemed to generate a sense of unease, almost suspicion. At times, hushed conversations even stopped abruptly when she passed, replaced by sidelong looks and even a few murmurs just loud enough to be heard. It wasn't outright hostility, but it was pretty clear to Torvald that something was amiss—that a seed of discontent had sprouted between the healer and the people of the burh.

She stopped in front of a market stall that sold produce and chatted with the merchant for a while before purchasing a small parcel of mixed vegetables. Then she moved on to the grain stall, waiting patiently while all the others waiting were all served before her. Torvald watched as, over and over again, she tried to gain the merchant's attention, only for him to studiously ignore her. More people would arrive, and they would be served while she stood ignored.

Torvald watched her for quite some time, until it had become clear to her that she would not be served. He watched her shoulders slump—at first clearly out of frustration, then perhaps ultimately out of defeat as she retreated from the stall with no grain or flour. Even without fully understanding what he was witnessing, he bristled at the wrongness of it.

He watched as she yanked her head covering further down, further obscuring her face, and left the stall, stomping off in frustration. She weaved a path through the stalls, moving swiftly and steadily, stopping to purchase a few odds and ends from friendlier merchants, until she reached the stable. There, she approached a large, dapple-grey mare tied to the paddock fence. He'd seen that horse before, in that paddock in the valley—the hut he now knew to be hers.

A large and impressive mare, he thought, *excellent confirmation, of good stock, and very obviously well-kept.*

Torvald watched as her entire demeanor softened as she pulled a single carrot from her bag. She offered it to the horse with a murmured word and a gentle pat—the affectionate gesture made him smile as he recalled all the times he'd done exactly the same.

Finally, she hoisted and secured her saddlebags, hiked up her skirts, and mounted.

As she turned the grey mare towards the gate, he saw her hesitate—a small group of people stood staring at her. No words were exchanged, and when she returned their gaze, they averted their eyes and scattered.

Æfre secured her head covering and rode off at a brisk trot, her posture upright and commanding. Once she'd passed through the timber palisade and out the main gate, he watched as she removed the linen covering, shaking free her cascade of pale hair. Urging the mare into a canter, she'd disappeared over the rise.

Torvald lingered a moment longer, letting the image of her settle deep into his mind, as if needing a moment to fully absorb. Then, with a slow exhale, he turned back toward the market square.

Svend stood just behind him, looking directly at him with a smug grin on his face, his two pottery jugs nestled in a wooden box under one arm.

Torvald halted mid-step, startled by his friend's proximity, then composed himself and walked on, his voice even.

"Don't say it, Svend."

"I'm saying nothing, brother," Svend said, falling into step with him. "If Freyja chooses to place a charm into a man's hearth cake, that's nothing to do with me; that is entirely her mischief."

"Þegi þú. [*Shut up*]," Torvald said stoically.

Svend burst out laughing, clapping him hard on the shoulder. "It's always you quiet ones," he said, still chuckling.

Torvald shot him a look, but the corner of his mouth twitched. "You'd have asked that jug to marry you, had it smiled back."

"Why do you think I bought two of them?" Svend grinned.

12

Biscop ✕ Bishop

"Ah! Gytha, there you are," Æthelwod said, the words snapping from his mouth with a touch too much impatience. "I cannot imagine what could delay a simple plate of food—I'm half-starved!"

"Apologies, Lord Bishop," the serving girl murmured, eyes downcast. "There was a—"

"Never mind," he cut her off, already losing interest in the conversation. Then, remembering himself, he softened.

"Patience is the path to righteousness," he added in a forced tone, "even when that path is painfully slow. Set it down and be off with you, girl."

She did as instructed, setting the tray on the table before hastily slipping from the chamber.

Æthelwod leaned back in his high-backed chair, sighing. The day was ebbing away, yet there was still much to do. He'd chosen to take his meal in his library, surrounded by sacred artifacts and texts—objects of power, and reminders of the sacred duty of his station. It was here, among these holy objects, that his mind began to fully coil around the scheme he was weaving.

The meeting between Osric and Eadlin had gone precisely as planned. It was his masterstroke, this union between Wōdenléah's thegn and the house of Aldhem. It wasn't merely political—it was providence, guided by his hand. Land, influence, and loyalty would be yoked together under the eyes of God... and of course, carried out under his own careful gaze.

He broke a crust of bread and dipped it into the thick stew Gytha had left. Chewing slowly, he reviewed the players. Osric was dutiful, brooding, perhaps even noble in his own dull sort of way.

And of course he was a tragic widower with a strong sword arm and an even stronger sense of duty. He wouldn't have called him clever, but he was definitely competent enough to be a helpful instrument in the scheme. Osric's role would be to act as a blunt sword—strong and serviceable, yet only as sharp as the hand that wielded it.

Yet, as he chewed, he could not entirely quell a flicker of unease. There was something in Osric's eyes—a look that was too steady, too knowing. Osric had always carried out his duties meticulously, had always done what was asked of him—but today Æthelwod had seen a flash of steel beneath the surface.

Today's introduction had been a test as much as a trap. He had wanted Osric to flinch. He had hoped the sight of Eadlin, so young and demure, would provoke something in him. Or perhaps it was the absence of what he desired that would catch him out—how Eadlin stood where Æfre might have, were things different. It was, after all, his knowledge of the thegn's affection for this pagan woman that had shaped this entire day. It was a move that should have chastised him, even humiliated him. If he had lashed out, even slightly, Æthelwod could have seized on it—used it as leverage, as penance owed to the Church.

Yet, instead of faltering, Osric had stood unshaken, radiating the same infuriating fairness and measured calm that had always marked him.

His reaction was infuriating, the bishop thought, as he swigged from his cup of mead. Yet he knew he'd touched a nerve. He'd seen it in the church. The memory of it caused him to sniff in disdain. He lifted his goblet and drained the last of his mead, then poured another cup.

A man like Osric—burdened by both principle and power—a man like that could be troublesome if not carefully hemmed in.

Eadlin, however, was another matter entirely. She was young, eager to please, and her doe eyes had betrayed her naiveté the moment she set foot inside his hall. She could be molded. Through her, Osric could be bound.

Wynnflæd, Eadlin's indomitable mother, had been embarrassingly simple to manipulate. The woman's pride was her failing. She had long sought greater standing, and Æthelwod had dangled it before her like bait, promising an enduring legacy, Church favor, position, protection, and prestige. She had swallowed it all like sacrament, blind to the strings being tied to her consent.

In exchange for the alliance, Wynnflæd of Aldhem had agreed to turn a discreet eye away from the bishop's dealings. Whether it was alliances forged in shadow, indulgences better left unspoken, or interventions in burh affairs, she acquiesced without resistance.

Æthelwod chuckled to himself and dipped another piece of bread in the bowl. The camp, too, had a role to play. His plans for the greedy, heathen Northmen were already in motion. They would succumb to their own savage nature, the inevitable chaos and infighting brought by heathens was the perfect pretext for a swift and righteous purge under the banner of restoring order. He needed only to wait for the moment to present itself.

Æthelwod was scraping the last of the stew out of his bowl when he heard the murmur of voices outside, followed by the steady clip-clop of hooves. Pulling back a small corner of the woolen window covering, he peered out the narrow window opening.

Osric.

There he was, standing with Cenric, who busied himself saddling Osric's favorite gelding. The two spoke in low tones, their words muffled by the crisp evening air. Æthelwod didn't need to strain to hear; he already knew. After today's events, there was but one destination for Lord Osric—to her. To Æfre, his heathen whore.

The bishop's lips thinned as his gaze lingered on the two of them talking. So predictable. So foolishly steadfast. Æthelwod gazed at the crucifix mounted on the wall. Let him go to her. Even the thegn of Wōdenléah would be powerless to stop what was coming.

13

Sorg ⋇ Sorrow

The familiar road stretched ahead, yet it felt strange and foreign, as though a hundred years had passed since he last rode it. Yet it had been just that morning that he had taken this same horse down this same road. But that was a different man who had ridden it then. That man had been light-hearted, hopeful, and blind to the storm that was already gathering behind him.

He could not tear his thoughts from Æfre—from what he knew might lie in store for her, and the guilt was suffocating. This was his doing. He had placed her squarely in the path of Bishop Æthelwod.

By the time Osric turned the gelding onto the narrow path that dipped toward Æfre's homestead, his hands were numb on the reins—he was unaware that he'd been gripping them so tightly.

A thin plume of smoke coiled from the thatched roof, and the warm glow of the hearth seeped through the half-open door, casting faint golden pools on the earth outside. The sight, so familiar and serene, caused a wave of dread to rise in his chest.

He had yet to work out what he would say.

He dismounted at the paddock, removing the saddle and bridle and hanging them over the fence. He gave Leo a pat on the hindquarters, and the gelding trotted into the enclosure where Epona grazed, their noses touching in greeting.

Æfre's figure suddenly appeared in the doorway, framed by the light behind her. Seeing Osric, her face lit up instantly.

"Osric!" Her voice was warm with delight. "I wasn't expecting you!"

She rushed to greet him, but as the distance between them closed, her smile faltered. She saw the look on his face.

"What's wrong?"

Osric stopped and looked at her. He tried to find the right words, but they were trapped—caught on something deep in his chest. Every part of him longed to hold her as he always had, to act as though the day had never happened.

"Osric, what's wrong? What is it?"

She reached out, closing the gap, and gently placed her hands on either side of his face, her touch warm and grounding.

"Osric, you're frightening me. Please, speak. What has happened?"

He met her gaze. The worry in her eyes undid him.

"Come," he said at last, voice hoarse. "We must go inside. There's much to tell."

Inside, she poured him a generous cup of ale. He could feel her eyes darting to his face as she set it before him. He knew he probably looked ghastly, and he felt utterly drained.

"Osric," she said softly, "have you eaten? I've got a hare stew on the fire."

He hesitated, brow knitting as he tried to recall.

He blinked, tried to remember. "I think so... perhaps. I don't know." He rubbed his brow. "Maybe not."

Æfre scowled, then dragged a chair close to his, taking his hands in hers.

"Osric, you must tell me now. Whatever it is." She said, her voice steady but laced with dread.

Her words were gentle, but Osric could see that the look in her eyes betrayed her growing fear of what might come next. In the silence that hung between them, the crackle of the hearth seemed deafening. Osric squeezed her hands, bracing himself to shatter the fragile peace that, until this moment, had always surrounded them whenever they were together in this space.

"The bishop," he began, "turned the sermon today. Sharpened

HEART OF THE WILD GODS

it like a blade. He wasted no time twisting sacred texts to imply your healing practices are somehow offensive to God. He didn't name you outright, but Æfre, he didn't have to. His meaning was clear enough."

Osric's voice darkened as he recounted the bishop's words, how he had insinuated that Æfre's very existence within the community was a situation that jeopardized the natural order.

Æfre's stomach tightened, and she sat up, folding her hands tightly in her lap and adjusting in her chair.

"But worse yet," Osric continued, "The bishop wove the thatcher's wife into it. He spoke of 'babes who struggle to come into the world,' and he looked directly at the thatcher's wife."

Æfre's face drained of color. "He looked at Wynn?"

"He did."

She exhaled, leaned back, eyes unfocused.

"That explains it," she said quietly.

"Explains what?"

Æfre took a deep breath and sat back in her chair.

"Osric, I went to the burh late this morning," she said, "to see Wynn and Aelf. Godhild's arm needs tending. They... they would not let me in."

"What!?" Osric balked.

"No—Aelf wouldn't permit it. Wynn looked torn, but her fear won her over."

Osric let his head drop into his hands and groaned.

"They gave my mother's amber birthing amulet back to me as I left—Aelf probably would have thrown it at me had Wynn not been there." She closed her eyes and let out a long exhale as she pieced it all together. "And the market. Of course."

"The market?" Osric asked, not lifting his head from his hands.

"At the market... they stared. I wore a head covering just to disappear. Beorthulf wouldn't even sell any grain to me. Wouldn't even meet my eye."

"You never wear a head covering." Osric said softly, "I don't think I've ever seen you wear one."

"No. But today was the day, Osric." Her voice cracked. "Three hens are gone. Vanished when I returned. I thought it was a fox. But there's no blood. No feathers."

Osric's head snapped up.

"Gone?"

"Yes. No sign they were ever there."

Osric leaned back in his chair, rubbed his hands against his face, and took a deep breath. He started to say something, then stopped. Æfre could see there was more.

"There's more," he said unsteadily, his voice heavy with fatigue.

Æfre stared at him, bracing for yet another blow.

Osric reached for her hand, his grip firm, his voice heavy. "The bishop," he began, "he's done more than issue threats. He's made plans, Æfre. He's set things in motion, things that..." He stopped, his throat catching as his words faltered.

Her heart plummeted as his silence filled the space between them. Whatever it was he was about to tell her, she knew instinctively that it would change everything. It was likely to have already changed everything.

"What things, Osric?" Æfre asked, her voice beginning to fray around the edges.

He squeezed her hand. "He summoned me. The bishop did, after the sermon. I was about to go in there with steel drawn—I was so angry at how he manipulated that sermon—thankfully Cenric saw me and tethered my temper, because when I did go to the meet, it wasn't just Æthelwod who was there. It was the bishop, the Lady Wynnflæd of Aldhem, and her daughter Eadlin. It was an ambush, Æfre and an unwilled introduction to Eadlin."

He paused. Æfre's face had gone pale, her hands resting over her stomach as if she'd just taken a blade. He pushed on, knowing she needed to hear it all.

"This is about land, Æfre. As you know, Aldhem borders Wōdenléah. A marriage between the two would ensure Æthelwod has control of both. I'm certain he has made this plan with the full participation of Wynnflæd of Aldhem—and I am the tool by which it can be achieved."

He let the silence settle around them. They had both always been keenly aware that their association came with risk, but both assumed they would always have ample time to figure it out.

"If I defy him," Osric said, "he'll strike. But he won't strike at me. He needs me. Æfre, he'll strike at you."

Æfre's eyes flared.

"He's already begun. Look at what he has managed in only one day. He'll break you—break *us*. I am nothing but a tool to him, a means to an end."

She stared into the hearth. Her voice, when it came, was shaky.

"We must stop, then. You and I."

Osric closed his eyes.

"Osric?"

He raised his head. "Neither of us wants that, Æfre."

"No," she whispered. "But this could cost you your position. I'll endure. I'm accustomed to fending for myself. But you, Osric, you're duty-bound—you belong to Crown and Church."

"There might be a way," he said slowly, growing quiet as he lost himself in thought. "Remember, I told you that Æthelwod said that unless you came under the Church's authority, your ability to practice your healing would be taken from you. And he didn't just threaten your work, Æfre, he threatened your place here—your ability to exist in Wōdenléah."

"If you were to... renounce the old ways. Just in name. Receive the sacrament. Be sealed in Christ. I might persuade him to allow you to live and practice unhindered."

Her hand recoiled.

"To *allow* me?"

"You know what I mean. It would be only—"

"Is that what you want for me, Osric?" she asked softly, her voice suddenly low, charged. "You want me to become a Christian? For me to lie? To become what I am not?" The pain in her eyes cut him more deeply than any blade he'd ever known.

"No, Æfre," Osric said, his voice thick with pleading. "No...no... It's not what I want, but I—" He stood abruptly, running his hands through his hair. "I want to keep you safe! That's all I want."

Æfre rose too, stepping away. Her face flushed, her voice hardening. "Osric, I cannot. You know I cannot. And you know Æthelwod, you're savvy enough to know what this is. The moment you give that man what he wants, there will be another demand. Another ultimatum. That's not survival, Osric. That's submission, and I will not submit."

"Æfre, please," Osric said, his voice steadily rising, his desperation palpable. "Think of what's at stake! This is a dangerous man, and you are now his target! Do you think I can just stand by and do nothing while he threatens you? Surely you cannot refuse to at least consider any measure necessary to ensure your safety!"

"Osric, do not raise your voice to me." Her tone was measured, but searing. She took a step toward him, her anger white-hot and blazing. "You're not asking me to choose safety, but to surrender the very essence of who I am! And for what!? So that I may survive long enough to watch you live out your days with your new wife!?"

"Æfre, please!" Osric interjected, his voice louder and more urgent, but she cut him off, her own voice rising above his.

"What you're talking about is my freedom, and it is the only thing I have!"

"What I am trying to tell you is that I cannot lose you!" Osric thundered back, his voice raw with emotion as he made a sweeping gesture, catching the near-full ale cup on the table and sending it crashing against the wall.

Æfre flinched, and the silence that followed was absolute.

Osric ran a hand through his hair, a tidal wave of realization and sorrow instantly washing over him for his actions. He threw his hands up in surrender and took a step back, his voice softening to a whisper.

"I'm so sorry," he said, his shoulders sagging under the weight of his exhaustion. "Æfre, forgive me. That was unintentional, I...forgive me." He hesitated, his voice breaking. "I need a moment. I'll get some air, then I'll come clear up."

He turned toward the door, pausing at the threshold—hoping she might stop him. When she didn't, he stepped outside into the night, the late summer air feeling cool as it hit his face. He leaned against the side of the hut, trying to steady himself, listening to the cavernous silence between them.

Inside, Æfre had sunk to her knees, palms braced against the earthen floor as if the world was spinning. She made no move to wipe the tears streaming unchecked down her cheeks as she crawled over to the wall where the ale cup had shattered and began gathering the broken pottery in trembling hands.

Minutes that felt like hours passed before Osric stepped back inside, his footsteps tentative as he approached her. He knelt beside her, his presence warm and solid in the wake of the storm generated by all the emotions that had passed through the walls of the hut. Gently, he placed a hand under her chin, tilting her face upward until their eyes met.

Æfre closed her eyes, her pale blonde hair clinging damply to her tear-streaked cheeks. Osric's heart twisted at the sight of this fierce, headstrong woman reduced to a state of raw, unguarded pain. He had done this.

Carefully and without a word, he took the pottery shards from her and laid them aside before cupping her face in his hands, brushing her tear-soaked hair out of her face.

"I'm sorry," he whispered, his voice thick with regret. He leaned forward, planting a lingering kiss on her forehead. "I'm so sorry," he murmured again, his lips brushing against her closed eyes as he kissed away the traces of her tears. "Æfre, I am so sorry," he repeated once more, his voice breaking as he kissed her trembling lips, the gesture both an apology and a plea for forgiveness.

"I have brought this on you." Osric agonized. "

"Æthelwod will use you, if he thinks it'll bend me to his will. He'll hurt you, Æfre. Because he knows."

He faltered. The words sat heavy on his tongue, unspoken until now. But they had known for a while now, hadn't they? Yet until this moment, naming the truth was a line they dared not cross.

It was in her gaze that he saw it—reflected and returned. The truth neither of them had dared give breath.

"He knows... my heart is yours," Osric said, the words hoarse but certain. "He knows I love you."

There. It had been said.

Æfre leaned forward into him, her hands clutching at his tunic as if anchoring herself. Their foreheads met, the closeness a fragile shelter from the invisible storm gathering around them—reality forcing its way in.

They stayed as they were, kneeling on the floor of the hut, time seemingly standing still, until Osric finally spoke.

"Come, Æfre," he said softly. "Let us get up off this floor."

Getting to his feet, Osric guided her gently up by the arms, brushing the ale and pottery dust off her skirts and smoothing her hair away from her face, as if gently trying to glue the parts of a precious broken artifact back together.

She looked up at him, face streaked with tears, eyes heavy with

HEART OF THE WILD GODS

sorrow. He pulled her close and kissed the crown of her head.

"Please don't cry, Æfre, my love. I cannot bear it."

They stood a while, resting against each other, until Æfre pulled away slightly, allowing Osric to take her face in his hands once again and kiss her.

Æfre kissed him back, and the two locked in a passionate sealing of unspoken truths.

Then Æfre stepped back. She wiped her tears with the back of her hand, her gaze still locked on his. Without a word, she slipped off her shoes and undid her belt, letting it drop. Her shoulder brooches followed, and then her overdress, drawn up and over her head in one motion. The linen fell to the floor in a heap, and she stood before him in nothing but her chemise—thin, clinging, translucent in the light of the hearth.

She stood there, her hair wild and unbound, a windstorm wrapping itself around her tear-streaked cheeks. Her eyes burned with raw, untamed emotion—vulnerable and fierce.

She stepped towards him again, and in that moment, Osric felt as though she were the only thing keeping him tethered to the earth. She kissed him with a slow certainty and whispered, "Come to bed, my love," in his ear, taking his hand.

Time seemed to stretch, each second drawn out as he watched her turn and walk to the bed, the flicker of the hearth outlining her form beneath the linen, her movements deliberate as she walked with a slow, almost ritualistic grace. As she passed the length of his arm, his hand dropped, a soft emptiness left in its wake. Pausing halfway there, she turned to face him.

He stepped out of his boots and undid his belt. His seax and pouch clattered to the floor. As he moved toward her, he pulled his tunic off in one swift motion, never looking away. Every step, every breath he took yearned towards her with a consuming hunger.

When he finally stood before her, she reached for the cords that fastened his trousers and braies, slowly loosening them, allowing everything to fall effortlessly to the floor—his desire on full display as he stepped out of his shed clothing.

Osric placed his hands on Æfre's waist—she felt alive and reverberating with the tenderness that pulsed between them. Slowly, he knelt, his hands trailing down the curve of her sides while she ran her hand slowly through his thick, wavy hair, sighing softly, almost sadly as she did.

Their eyes remained locked, each trying to etch the other's body into memory, as if a single glance in another direction might whisk one or the other away forever.

Osric found the hem of her chemise and slowly rose, each movement of his hands revealing another curve, another delicate contour of her form to remember. Æfre raised her arms and he slid the chemise off, letting it flutter to the floor.

Osric paused for a moment, taking in her raw beauty, at once feral and ethereal, as if light and energy were pulsating through her as she stood before him, neither of them daring to break their locked gaze.

Osric leaned down and kissed her hungrily, running a hand up her back and into her thick, pale mane before bending at the knees once more and scooping her up off the ground entirely. He wanted to dive into her, to be wholly absorbed until every barrier that existed between them was forever demolished.

Osric placed Æfre gently on the bed and kissed her again as he positioned himself on top of her, feeling the familiar arch of her body beneath him as she rose to meet his touch. He took one of her hands in his and kissed it before locking their fingers together, each entwined digit weaving a thread in a bond he could never truly break.

He kissed her while slowly, reverently entering her, both of them gasping like a wound freshly opened, their bodies as close as possible for fear of bleeding their longing into the space between them.

They moved slowly, their movements deliberate, knowing that every second spent together now was a moment they would never get back.

Æfre wound herself around him as they moved, her breath warm against his skin as she whispered his name into the nape of his neck over and over again.

It broke him.

A surge of desire shot through him, and he hoisted her up, sitting back until she was astride him, their faces touching. Æfre's untamed hair cascaded over both of them as they moved as one amidst a tangle of bed linens that seemed to mimic, or even mock, their own knot of tangled emotions.

Osric moaned as her pace quickened, his hands gripping her hips, his voice caught in his throat.

"Æfre," he whispered hoarsely. "Look at me. I want to see you."

Æfre sat up, breathless and near ecstasy, cradled Osric's face in her hands, and kissed him like she was trying to pour a lifetime's worth of stolen love into a single moment.

"Osric..." she whispered his name again.

"Yes," he murmured. "Don't look away."

Osric wanted an eternal imprint of this moment—one he might replay at will. He was desperate to remember everything about it, the smell of her hair, the way she looked and felt as she came—he wanted every detail.

He felt her tense, her fingers curling into his hair, and he pulled her closer to him until their foreheads touched.

Æfre cried his name as her face twisted in a fierce and beautiful release, her muscles tensing rhythmically as tears streamed down her cheeks.

He held her face in his hands and kissed her as he followed her over the edge, his release overtaking him in waves—each sensation a slow unraveling of the quiet world they'd created together.

"I love you, Æfre," he whispered into her ear, voice ragged.

"I love you, Osric," Æfre whispered back through a veil of tears and ecstasy.

They remained there, clinging to each other in an agonizing, silent embrace until Æfre finally stirred.

Osric watched as she shuffled towards the hearth, pausing to pick up his discarded tunic and slip it over her head—a temporary suit of armor against the world. The sight made him grin with affection—he could never grow tired of it.

Æfre grabbed a bowl and scraped the last of the stew into it, stealing the serving spoon from the pot and carrying it with her back to the bed.

"Osric, you must eat," Æfre said gently.

They sat facing each other on the bed, sharing the last of the stew with the big wooden serving spoon.

Osric closed his eyes as he savored the richly seasoned stew. "Æfre, that's delicious," he murmured with his mouth full. He actually couldn't remember the last time he ate. Æfre pushed the bowl with the remaining stew into his hands, and he polished it off without hesitation.

As she rose to take the bowl and spoon from him, he caught her by the arm.

"Æfre," he said quietly, "promise me you'll stay out of sight for now. I'll have Cwenhild bring whatever you need. Just give me a little time—I need to find out exactly what Æthelwod is planning. Let me try to protect you from this. That's all I ask."

She leaned down and kissed him, whispering in his ear, "Very well, Osric."

* * *

HEART OF THE WILD GODS

Æfre and Osric walked to the paddock in silence, arm-in-arm. Neither dared speak the truth aloud—that they couldn't be certain when they would see each other again.

The night was crisp and well-lit with the light of the moon. Epona, munching hay, nickered at Æfre from the paddock as Osric saddled Leo under the moonlight.

"Æfre," he said at last, tightening the girth strap, his voice low. "Keep out of Æthelwod's sight, I beg you. Let me buy some time to let reason do its work." He trailed off, no longer able to find the right words. They all tasted hollow, and this felt too much like a death—an oath he could very well fail to keep. He closed his eyes and drew a slow breath through his nose.

Æfre stepped close and straightened the neck of his tunic, her hands trembling. "And in return, I ask that you ride safely, Osric. The night is dark." Æfre's voice cracked as she forced herself to let go.

Osric looked at Æfre, lit by the moonlight, her face streaming tears, wanting to freeze the timeline they were in and go no further. He pulled Æfre to him and kissed her under the moonlight, a kiss that held all the weight of the goodbyes they refused to say.

With one last look, he mounted his gelding and turned up the path.

As he climbed the hill, he watched as Æfre stood rooted to the spot, her arms wrapped around herself as if to hold on to his warmth. He allowed the gelding to pick his way up the path as he fixed his gaze over his shoulder, watching her until she disappeared behind the crest of the hillside.

Geol-Monaþ ⚔ December

Wōdenléah
Kingdom of Wessex
881 AD

14
⚔ Winter ⚔

"Bjørn! Toss the augers and mallets down—get your carcasses inside!" Torvald bellowed from the edge of the roof as he shook sleet from the ladder. "This wind is colder than a draugr's[x] clutch, and we've got more weather coming! Time to see to the hearth and horn!"

Torvald hopped down from the ladder, landing with a splat in the half-frozen muck just as a gust of icy wind bit through the layers of his wool tunic and cloak. He looked at the darkening sky. They were losing the light, and a freeze was coming—sure as Skaði[xi] walks, the snow soon follows.

Repairs to the hall had taken longer than expected, the days grew shorter, and the weather had turned sharply. The landscape surrounding the camp had transformed from a rich display of autumnal reds, yellows, and oranges to a far more somber palette of muted gray and brown. The trees looked skeletal, leaves long dead, their limbs rattling in the wet, icy gusts like angry ghosts.

Torvald rounded the side of the hall just as sleet began to hammer down, freezing in the men's beards like pale winter jewels—he was more than happy to see this job come to an end. He stepped against the side of the longhouse just as Bjørn shouted for an end to the work—tools rained down, the men above eager to abandon the cold roof for the promise of warmth and ale.

He didn't need to be up on that roof with them, but even as Jarl, he had always preferred to work alongside his men—sharing the toil, especially now that the camp's numbers had dwindled for the winter. Many merchant-warriors had gone, some back to the Danelaw or even further north and eastward. Those left had spent weeks tarring longships and rationing food stores, though Torvald still occasionally led hunting parties into the forest to add fresh game to their stores. Plus, it was another opportunity for him to possibly catch a glimpse of *her*.

He entered the hall, shaking bits of sleet and the beginnings of the first snow of the season from his cloak, instantly grateful for the warmth of the hearth as it radiated its glowing orange heat. Gradually, the men all filed in, laughter already chasing the cold from their bones. Some got up and offered the Jarl their seats next to the fire, but Torvald refused.

"Stay where you are, men," he said, waving off their offers of a seat.

He instead chose a bench at the side of the hall behind the men. He sat and leaned back against the timber wall, pulling up another bench for his feet.

Before long, the men were telling stories, laughing, and sharing the latest news from Wōdenléah, The Danelaw, and beyond. Torvald drank deep, letting the warmth settle into his bones.

At some point, he must have closed his eyes because he startled back to the present when someone kicked his foot, knocking it off the bench and causing ale to slosh from his horn. Blinking and momentarily disoriented, he finally recognized the familiar voice.

"Jarl, you alive?"

It was Svend, grinning as he stood over him, sleet glistening in his beard, fresh from his return from Wōdenléah.

"Can a man not die in peace in his own hall?" Torvald chided.

"Not when he's chieftain, he can't," laughed Svend, as he accepted a horn full of ale from Bjørn. "It's an oath to be paid in blood and bone."

"Fair. Come, sit." Torvald chuckled, patting the empty space on the bench beside him, gesturing for Svend to lean back against the wall as he did. "What news do you bring me, then? Anything worth

HEART OF THE WILD GODS

the frigid journey?"

Svend dropped down beside him, stretched out his legs, and let out a long sigh. "There is some—perhaps a bit of a twisted tale, but já, worth it." Svend took a long, dramatic pull from his ale horn, watching the men converse by the hearth for a while before continuing.

Torvald grinned—Svend always dragged things out just to annoy him and test his patience.

"Well?" Torvald finally asked.

"It's being said," Svend began, wiping his beard, "that Lord Osric, the young thegn of Wōdenléah is to wed."

Torvald lifted a brow. "That so?" he muttered, swirling the dregs in his horn. "Man's a widower, isn't he? Hardly strange for a Saxon lord to seek out a warm bed and a new line of sons."

"Já," Svend agreed. "They're also saying that he's to marry a woman called Eadlin... of Aldhem."

Torvald's hand stilled. Aldhem. Now that *was* an interesting development. "Aldhem—the lands that touch Wōdenléah's border." His voice sharpened with interest.

"They do, Jarl," Svend confirmed, his tone growing more conspiratorial. "And word is, this match was not the thegn's wish. Folk say his heart belongs to another." Svend took another long draught of ale.

Torvald simply stared blankly at Svend, waiting.

"To a pagan healer," Svend added, voice quieter now, a knowing look in his eyes. "A woman called Æfre."

Torvald's grip on his horn tightened, and he froze, his ale horn halfway to his lips. The name hit him like a blow to the chest, robbing him of breath.

Æfre. Of course, it would be her.

But it wasn't just the words—it was the way Svend delivered the news, gently yet laced with intrigue. His old friend Svend knew him too well. Knew that name would land hard.

Torvald cleared his throat and recovered himself, taking another draught of ale as if the news meant nothing. "And who is it who says these things?"

"The kind of people who love to talk, Jarl." Svend said, a bit more softly as he sat back, "particularly when the ale flows."

"Indeed, Svend," Torvald chuckled, though at this point his heart was well lodged somewhere in his throat. His mind buzzing, he kept his face steady, but damn the Gods—this was ridiculous! He was heartsick and filled with self-reproach at his own pathetic yearning for a woman he had never really met, and did not know. How does one go from being a feared warrior to this!? It was foolish, perhaps even dangerous, to be so distracted.

"The question remains, Jarl," Svend pressed, bringing him back to the present as he leaned in to shield their words from curious ears, "if Lord Osric didn't want the match, who did?"

Torvald didn't hesitate. "Æthelwod."

"That shitwolf has likely been scheming for months. A marriage between Wōdenléah and Aldhem binds Aldhem's land and coin to the church's hand."

Svend frowned. "But why would the thegn agree? He's not like Æthelwod. I've spoken to him, had dealings—he's fair, steady, respected. He's not ruthlessly ambitious like the bishop."

Torvald met his gaze. "You sure of that? I know few men without ambition in their blood."

"Já, I think so. Oric acts from duty, not greed. So why go along with this? Unless…"

"Unless he isn't being given a choice," Torvald said flatly.

Torvald's jaw tightened as he mulled over the possibility.

"If Æthelwod becomes the custodian of both Aldhem and Wōdenléah's lands, that would make him the most powerful land owner in Wessex, this side of Wintanceaster," Torvald said, keeping his voice low. "Trade would certainly be the first thing to suffer with Æthelwod at the helm."

Torvald tipped his ale horn back and drained it in a single, impressive motion.

"Svend, I'll need to speak with this Saxon thegn. Likely very soon."

He set the empty horn into Svend's hands, his expression a mix of resolve and weariness.

"But not yet. I have a few matters to attend to—and some thinking to do. I'll take my leave before any more ale falls into my hands."

Svend chuckled and gave him a knowing look but said nothing.

Torvald rose purposefully from the bench, giving Svend a brisk nod as he strode out of the hall.

As the frigid air hit his face, he knew he would get little done that evening. Thoughts of what he'd just learned were invading his peace, and with Æfre's name still ringing in his ears, would likely be stuck in his own head for a long while yet.

15

Rīdan ✕ Ride

"Easy girl, you'll get your chance to run."

Æfre chuckled as Epona pranced sideways up the path, snorting and tossing her head with the playful exuberance of a horse in need of a good run. The mare danced beneath her, hooves crunching the crust of the previous night's freeze.

Epona had grown slightly plump and fuzzy with the winter cold and a few long months of idle grazing. They weren't making nearly as many trips to the burh now, and horse and owner alike felt a need to get out of the hut and stretch their legs. Now, the mare's playful energy bubbled over into a series of mock bucks and high steps that made her seem more like a feisty stallion than the steady companion she was.

Once they reached the level ground of the road, Æfre loosened her hold and Epona surged forward, finding her gait. The steady beat of the mare's hooves gave Æfre space to think as the tension that had coiled so tightly in her shoulders over the past months began to unravel.

She had not seen or heard from Osric since *that* night.

With each passing day, the void yawned wider. On some days, despite her best efforts, it threatened to consume her entirely.

At first, it had been sorrow—waves of it she'd fought to keep from dragging her under. They'd never gone more than a few days without seeing each other, but as the days turned into weeks and there was no contact, her sadness calcified into anger.

She was angry at Osric for coming to her that first night, for igniting something in her only to suddenly vanish. She was furious with Bishop Æthelwod, for his false piety, perversion of the new faith, and his venomous determination to bend the world to his will. She even found herself resenting poor Eadlin, who she knew asked for none of this, yet whose existence served as a reminder that nothing about this was simple.

And yet, when she forced herself to take an honest look inward, it wasn't Æthelwod, or Osric, or even fate itself that stoked her anger—she was first and foremost, angry with herself.

She had let herself be led astray, swayed by feelings that now seemed fragile and uncertain in the cold, harsh light of Osric's absence.

Was any of it even real?

But now, the cold, crisp air filled her lungs, and it was clearing the fog of worry that had settled in her mind. *I should have done this weeks ago,* she thought, smiling at the realization as she leaned forward in the saddle. She couldn't hide in her hut forever, but she also knew she couldn't confront Æthelwod's rising influence head-on.

The bishop's poison words were seeds scattered in rich ground, and every day she was experiencing how they'd taken root in the burh. The last few times she'd tried to go to the market, she left practically empty-handed. People she'd known her entire life—people she'd seen and helped through some of their most vulnerable times—they were turning their backs on her. Hissing *wicce*[xii] as she passed them in the road.

She'd bargained with one of the ceorls in the burh for a goat to keep Epona company, but when she went to collect the animal, the man had refused to part with it. At the time, she had been heartbroken, yet in hindsight, Æfre realized it was likely for the better. In the weeks that followed, her hens had disappeared entirely, one by one, vanishing from their enclosure in the dead of night.

Several times, she'd had to rely on Cwenhild for bread and grains. It was at the point where she wondered if that was indeed the plan all along—a siege to starve out the witch.

She urged Epona into a gallop, giving the mare her head and complete freedom to run. The exhilaration of the ride filled her chest, sweeping away the stagnant despair that had clung to her, even if only temporarily. For the first time in far too long, she actually felt free.

Let them see me, she thought fiercely. *Let them know I'm still here.*

She resolved not to shrink into a shadow of herself based on the threat of what might be. She was still Æfre, still a healer, still a part of this land—whether they liked it or not. If Osric had truly abandoned her—no, she stopped herself there, not allowing herself to linger on his silence. The way forward, as it always had been, would have to be under her own power.

She reined in Epona at the crest of the hill overlooking Wōdenléah, which lay spread out like a winter tableau, wrapped in muted December light. Smoke rose in thin tendrils from hearth fires, curling upward into the pale sky, and the faint hum of life drifted on the cold air—voices mixed with the occasional clatter of wood or tools. The preparations for Yule were already underway.

She told herself she wasn't riding down towards the burh to confront anyone. Then again, before she'd set off, she'd said to herself that she wasn't going anywhere near the burh at all. But fresh air and time in the saddle, surrounded by the land she'd always known, had emboldened her. She knew that being seen—the act of simply existing in defiance of the whispers—that was in its own way a quiet rebellion.

If she timed it right, she could slip through the edge of the palisade, circling around to the back of the stables, where she might find Cwenhild and Cenric. A quiet visit, no more.

Æfre tucked her hair back up and secured her hood and scarf. With a cluck of her tongue, she urged Epona down the path to the burh. As the horse's hooves crunched against the frozen ground, Æfre's thoughts quieted, her resolve hardening like the frost underfoot. She was determined not to let anyone steal her place in the only land she'd ever known.

16

Læwa ✠ Traitor

"Oh, Mercy, Eadlin!" Cwenhild exclaimed, her voice laced with concern. "What have you done!?"

"Oof! How could that have happened?" Eadlin winced, her tone a mix of disbelief and amusement as she carefully plucked at the tip of the bone pin beater[xiii] she'd been using on the tapestry—now deeply embedded in her upper thigh. "I don't think I could drop it in such a manner again if I tried!" She chuckled, rubbing the sore spot gingerly while the two women crouched before the two-beam vertical loom in the weaving hut.

"Gracious me, and a freshly sharpened one at that!" Cwenhild fretted. "I had Cenric sharpen all our tools earlier this week! Let me fetch you some salve, dear, before it festers." She rose, scanning the room for the hut's healing basket.

"Cwenhild, truly, you're too kind, but it's nothing," Eadlin insisted, lifting her skirts to inspect the small puncture—it was actually deeper than she had initially thought, but thankfully not bleeding much. She could deal with it later. She'd have hated to have made a mess of the tapestry now that it was well on its way to completion—it had taken them most of the fall to get as far as they had. "See? It's hardly bleeding. Just a poke. It'll heal well, leaving no trace for a spring wedding." She smirked, casting a sly glance at Cwenhild, her eyes sparkling with mischief.

"You mischievous thing!" Cwenhild sputtered, her cheeks reddening as she caught the implication. With a soft laugh, she elbowed Eadlin playfully, causing her to giggle in return.

"You're blushing!" Eadlin teased, her grin widening.

"You are a mischief-maker!" Cwenhild shot back, and the two women tittered away like a couple of market gossips over a basket of apples.

"Who's a mischief-maker!?" boomed a familiar voice as the door to the hut swung open, ushering in a rush of cold winter air and pale morning light. Osric strode in with purpose, grinning roguishly, his heavy woolen cloak trailing in his wake.

"Lord Osric!" Cwenhild exclaimed, moving to greet him.

"Good morning, Cwenhild. And... Eadlin!" His gaze shifted to her, "What luck! I had hoped to see you here this morning." His smile was warm but fleeting as he continued, "I can't stay, unfortunately. There are a few matters I need to ride out and attend to with the morning's labors—but Mistress Eadlin...perhaps we could meet in the hall for the midday meal?"

"Of course, my lord," Eadlin replied softly, her lips curving into a subtle smile. "Cwenhild and I thought it best to spend the morning making better progress on the textile." She cast her eyes downward demurely but glanced back up at him through her lashes, noting the circles under his eyes—the man was clearly not getting enough sleep, that much was evident.

"Very good, I'll leave you two to your work then." Osric smiled at the women, indicating the tapestry with a quick "nice work," before turning and heading back out the door.

Eadlin smiled weakly—she remembered those tired eyes. They were etched into her memory after their last attempt at a midday meal together on an unseasonably warm autumn day.

* * *

Eadlin had ridden out to meet him, her saddle laden with a basket filled with bread, meat, honey, cheese, and apples. They'd spread a blanket under a canopy of golden leaves and shared a meal in what had felt to her, at least for a while, like a moment of pure tranquility.

The afternoon had started well enough. She and Osric had

talked easily—a pleasant, unremarkable conversation that allowed Eadlin a rare sense of hope. When the food was gone, they had stretched out, side by side on the blanket, gazing up at the slow-drifting clouds. It was then, buoyed by the peaceful intimacy of the moment, that Eadlin had finally found the courage to speak to him about her anxieties over their potential nuptials.

But just as she took the leap and really opened her heart, she was interrupted—by the distinct, steady rhythm of Osric snoring.

The thegn of Wōdenléah had fallen asleep.

She'd turned and sat up to look at him, sprawled out on the blanket, his face softened by sleep. For a fleeting moment, he looked completely at peace—more so than she had ever seen him. And that was when the sadness crept in—a sadness that settled into her bones. She felt sadness for his loss of Leofwynn, for his being seemingly inextricably tethered to a man like Bishop Æthelwod. She even reserved a bit of sadness for Æfre, though she tried to push that thought away the moment it crept in.

But most of all, Eadlin reserved most of her sadness for herself.

She hadn't wanted to cry, but tears threatened to spill over as she sat there, her reality quietly settling around her like falling ash—Osric would never love her the way she had so desperately hoped.

She had wanted to reach out, to run her fingers through his hair, to press her lips to his—but she didn't. She couldn't. Deep down, she knew that this man, whom she hoped would soon be her husband, would never truly be hers.

Eadlin had let him sleep for as long as she dared. She studied the contours of his face for a while, but the quiet of the afternoon soon shifted, and the distant sounds of the burh stirred to life again. She knew he would be needed elsewhere, so she leaned over him.

"Lord Osric," she'd whispered, giving his shoulder a gentle

shake.

He didn't stir.

"My lord," she tried again, a little louder this time.

Still nothing—then a faint shift as Osric moved to turn onto his side.

He turned, still in the throes of sleep, and murmured drowsily, "Don't cry, Æfre, my love. I cannot bear it," before falling off to sleep again. He reached out in his sleep, his arm trying to draw someone closer to him—someone who wasn't there.

Eadlin's breath caught in her chest as if struck-through with an arrow.

Eadlin sat frozen, her throat tightening as tears blurred her vision. She didn't need him to say anything else; confirmation of the bitter truth had already been laid bare. No matter what good days they might someday share, no matter how much kindness or effort she offered, the name that this man whispered in his dreams would never be hers.

She swallowed hard, forcing the tears back, and cleared her throat.

"My lord," she said sternly, this time with her whole chest, her voice steady and projecting despite the ache coming from the deep chasm where her heart had been only moments before.

Osric jolted awake, inhaling sharply as he sat upright, his eyes darting around to reorient himself. He blinked at her, disoriented for a moment, then offered an apologetic smile.

"Eadlin. Forgive me," he said, his voice hoarse with fatigue as he rubbed his face with his hands. "Ugh, I'm so sorry... I haven't been sleeping."

He reached out then, placing a hand on her shoulder—a gesture meant to both steady himself and reassure her. He clearly had no memory of the words he had just uttered.

Eadlin had managed a soft, understanding smile in return,

though she knew her smile had likely been anything but convincing.

The remainder of their outing had been polite but distant—clipped and awkward in a way that left Eadlin feeling as though they were speaking over a high fence. Osric had excused himself, citing the afternoon's administrative duties back at the hall. She had waved him off with a weak smile, insisting that she would pack everything up herself and follow shortly.

Before departing, he had leaned down and kissed the top of her head as she knelt to gather the remains of their meal.

As one would to a child, she'd thought to herself.

Eadlin had watched him ride away, his cloak trailing behind him as his silhouette grew smaller and smaller along the road. When he finally disappeared, she allowed herself to collapse onto the blanket, burying her face in her hands.

The tears came in an overwhelming surge, sobs wracking her chest as she let go of everything she had been holding back.

But even in the wake of that experience, the flutter of affection she held for him refused to die. Eadlin still found herself drawn to him, still wanted to turn his head her way, even if only for a fleeting moment now and again.

It wasn't much, and she knew better than to hope for more. But if that was all she could ask for, then she would set her expectations accordingly. It wasn't resignation—not entirely, anyway—it was survival, a matter of realigning her hopes with something she could hold onto without breaking under its weight.

No, not all was lost.

She would carve out her place. It wouldn't be the grand love she'd hoped for, but it would be something—a life she could build and a purpose she could claim.

She could live with that.

What choice did she have?

***

"Cwenhild!" The sudden sound of Cenric's voice echoed through the door of the weaving hut, his shout breaking Eadlin's reverie at the loom. The familiarity of his tone tugged a smile from Eadlin's lips before he continued, stepping into view. "Cwenhild, my love, could you spare me just a moment of your labors? Ah, good morning, Eadlin! My apologies for interrupting—this won't take long."

"Good morning, Cenric!" Eadlin called back with a cheerful lilt. She didn't mind the intrusion; her hands paused mid-weave, being careful to retain her grip on the pin beater this time.

Cwenhild, sighing with performative exasperation, rose heavily from the chair where she was spinning wool. "Oh, what is it now, husband?" she teased, rolling her eyes as she made her way across the hall with a knowing smirk. She glanced back over her shoulder at Eadlin. "Will you manage without me for a bit, dear? I'd hate for you to impale yourself again—you're already down a leg as it is!" She finished with a playful wink.

"Don't trouble yourself over me, Cwenhild," Eadlin replied, laughing. "I still have one good leg and two arms, that should keep me in good stead at least until midday!"

Cwenhild chuckled, patting Eadlin's shoulder as she passed. "I'll return shortly, dear."

Once alone, Eadlin sighed, relishing the quiet as she turned her attention back to the loom. The faint hum of activity from outside drifted into the hut, but for now, she relished the rare, peaceful moment to herself.

***

As Osric moved through the biting morning air, the chill seeped into his bones. He always felt pulled in too many directions at once,

HEART OF THE WILD GODS

his obligations seemingly mounting with each gust of frosty wind that billowed at his cloak.

He owed Eadlin his attention—it was actually long overdue, especially after their last attempt at sharing a meal had ended with him falling sound asleep.

He chuckled bitterly at the memory, more out of disbelief than anything—there was no real humor in it, particularly for her. In fact, he was in worse shape now than he was then—more distracted, more exhausted—his thoughts were constantly circling back to Æfre and her safety; it consumed him from the moment he opened his eyes to the second he collapsed into restless and fleeting sleep.

He heard the whispers in the burh, was usually present when Æthelwod would twist the scripture during a sermon, and saw firsthand the corrosive effect it had on the people—poisoning some of the more impressionable minds with utterly predictable stories of heresy and witchcraft. It was a move men of Æthelwod's vocation always seemed to rely on when they needed leverage and there were women involved.

They weren't just words, of course. Osric knew precisely what they were—they were weapons, expertly sharpened to sow fear and distrust, to turn the people of Wōdenléah against their neighbors and trading partners. The bishop had made a grand show of his concern for their souls, drawing lines in the soil, ensuring Æfre, the Northmen with whom they traded, and any other he deemed "non-sanctified", would remain firmly on the side of *other*.

A grim-faced Cenric had come to him one morning to recount Cwenhild's distress. She had returned from the market in floods of tears after seeing Æfre there. Hood drawn low, Æfre had tried to move discreetly through the market to do her shopping, but she left with little to show for it. Most vendors now refused to serve her, and those who did cast furtive glances over their shoulders, terrified of being seen. When she finally rode out of the burh, children threw stones, their cruel laughter echoing as they tried to spook her horse.

Osric had felt physically ill at this news, and that was the day he'd asked Cwenhild to set aside extra loaves of bread, sacks of grain, and whatever odds and ends they could spare for Æfre, enlisting Cenric to find clever ways of getting these things to her. If he was seen doing so himself, he knew Æthelwod would only escalate his tactics. The bishop was showing him that he would at every turn.

And now Osric was heading up the path to meet with the man responsible for all of this—to meet with him about some banal administrative matter, as if none of these other, darker things existed between them. The thought sickened him.

His steps slowed as he crossed the empty market square, his gaze lifting toward the church and Æthelwod's residence. Every fiber of his being begged him to find some other task to busy himself with—anything but this.

He stopped in his tracks, the church's dark wooden door just ahead. His gaze lingered a moment on the weathered threshold—perhaps he'd first have a quiet moment in the church, light a candle for Leofwynn, and sit in much-needed silence for a few moments. Maybe there, in the stillness of a sacred space, he could gather his thoughts and summon the strategy he needed to face the man who seemed determined to single-handedly plunge Wōdenléah into mistrust and conflict.

The church door hung slightly ajar as Osric approached, granting him a sliver of sight into the dimly lit interior. Just as he reached out to push it open, a flicker of movement—a dark cloak brushing past the narrow gap—caught his eye. Someone was inside. The low murmur of voices drifted through the gap, and Osric hesitated, pressing himself against the outside wall just out of

HEART OF THE WILD GODS

sight.

"...and in the camp?"

The voice was Æthelwod's, speaking in hushed tones to someone he couldn't see.

"You must ensure these whispers of rebellion burn hot enough to catch fire. The fyrd will only march with ample justification."

Another voice, quieter, answered—a man with an unmistakable Norse accent.

"The whispers spread, Bishop. The big one—the Chieftain's son—likes to drink and is quick to anger. I believe he grows impatient with Torvald Ironsight's leadership. He might be encouraged."

Osric's brow furrowed.

A Northman? Here, speaking with Æthelwod?

He edged closer to the door, straining to catch every word.

"Jarl Torvald is no fool," the Northman continued cautiously. "He knows his men well. If he suspects that a hand is guiding this rebellion..."

"I will remind you," Æthelwod interrupted sharply, his nasal voice cutting the man off, "that you are being paid handsomely to serve me, not Torvald Ironsight. You are a tool, Northman, nothing more. If your nerve fails you, I'll find another with the stomach for the task."

"Bishop, I ask only that you consider your strategy! The routes will appear compromised; you have my assurance on that. But I am only one man, and these are warriors we're talking about! These men do not trust easily!"

"Then give them something else to think about." Æthelwod enunciated each word with the deliberate precision of a man speaking to a dim-witted child.

Osric held his breath, his freezing fingers digging shallow little grooves in the exterior wall of the church as Æthelwod's voice rose, a mockery of slow, measured reasoning.

"Burn something. Rape, pillage, raid—do the things you heathens excel at! Saxon or Norse, it hardly matters! Any perceived activity on either side can be bent to stoke the natural overabundance of heathen anger in the camp. Men are wolves—they will tear each other apart when the scent of blood is strong enough. And when the dust settles, when the fyrd has marched and peace is restored, it will be my standard—and that of Christendom—that rises above their shallow, heathen graves."

Osric realized he'd been holding his breath, his entire focus locked on the conversation inside while the two men argued on.

He took a step back, eager to slip away before he was discovered, and a sharp *crunch* rang out.

Osric looked down.

He'd stepped directly onto a frozen puddle—the grinding ice shattering the stillness.

Inside, both voices stopped instantly.

"Go and see," Æthelwod commanded, his voice low.

The sound of movement followed—boots scuffing against stone, getting closer. Osric ducked around the side of the church as one of the men moved towards the open door.

Osric moved farther back down the side of the church and pressed himself against the side of the building, his hand brushing the hilt of his seax as the heavy footsteps of what he assumed was the Northman approached the doorway.

"Nothing," the man muttered.

Osric heard him step back from the doorway. His voice carried a flicker of unease as he addressed Æthelwod again.

"Look, I'll do what I can, but I need assurances. What will become of me once you're successful?"

"Ah, yes." Æthelwod's voice dripped with scorn. "What's in it for me?" he mocked. "The eternal question of a coward."

Æthelwod's tone shifted to one of exaggerated indulgence.

"Do you have any notion of how much wealth flows through that camp? The furs of the North, the amber of the Baltic, the iron... when the fyrd restores peace and the burh claims the camp and its routes, there will be a place for you. There will be wealth, safety... who knows, perhaps even a plump little Saxon wife to warm your bed."

There was a momentary pause before the Northman spoke again.

"And if you're not successful?"

Æthelwod's tone turned instantly, giving way to a flat, deadly calm.

"If this effort fails, Northman, then your life becomes a cautionary tale told around the hearth."

There was a pause before Osric heard Northman's voice again—full of disdain. "The same fate that befell your last thegn, from what I understand."

"Watch yourself, heathen." Æthelwod spat. "The former thegn was the author of his own undoing, and a lazy coin grubber at that. Now leave me. I must pray before my meet with the current thegn."

Osric pressed himself tighter against the church wall as the Northman swept past the door, the dark hood of his cloak pulled low, concealing his face entirely. His boots crunched softly against the frost as he disappeared down the path and into the burh.

Osric waited, heart pounding in his chest, not daring to breathe for fear he might exhale too loudly. He remained concealed for a while, his mind processing what he'd just witnessed.

And yet he knew he had no choice but to go in there—to attend to the day's business with the bishop. The absurdity of it gnawed at him, but dealing with what he'd just seen and heard would have to wait until later.

With one last glance toward the empty path where the

Northman had vanished, Osric squared his shoulders, muttered a curse under his breath, and moved towards the door.

17

Lænland ✕ Loanland

"She's just on her way, Æfre dear," Cenric said, his tone deliberately light.

Æfre was grateful that Cenric had been working behind the stable, just as she'd hoped. She'd ridden straight to him, whispered his name, and the moment he recognized Epona, his eyes had grown as big as the moon.

He motioned for her to dismount quickly and ushered her into the stable, leading Epona in behind her before vanishing to fetch Cwenhild.

When he returned, he carried a sack of barley and a basket packed with hard cheese, dried meats, and smoked fish—each parcel wrapped neatly in linen.

"These are for you," he said, setting them down. "We've been putting some by, waiting for the right time."

Then he knelt next to Epona, running a hand down her leg to inspect her overgrown hooves. "Now, Epona, let's have a look at those tattered feet."

"Thank you, Cenric. Truly." Æfre's words came out softer than she'd intended, the sadness she'd been trying to bury bubbling up.

Cenric glanced up sharply, his brow knitting.

Æfre could clearly see the kindness in his gaze, but also a searching weight that made her wish she could shrink into herself until nothing was visible. She busied herself plucking a piece of invisible lint from her cloak, willing back the tears stinging her eyes.

She hated this—hated the overwhelming feeling of helplessness that came with accepting charity from those she'd known all her life. But she could no longer avoid the truth of her situation. The burh had grown colder with each passing week—the hostility generated by Æthelwod's strategically venomous sermons continued to fester. Few merchants would sell to her now, no matter how much coin she offered.

"Epona will be good as new after this," Cenric's words pulled her out of her spiraling thoughts. His tone was stoic, as though he hadn't just witnessed the unspoken weight of her struggles.

Æfre gave him a tight smile, forcing herself to meet his kind eyes. "Thank you, Cenric. You and Cwenhild have both done so much for me."

"We look after our own," he said simply, his steady hands still at work on Epona's hooves. "No need to thank us for that."

The sincerity of Cenric's words hit Æfre deeply, and she was struggling to maintain her composure when Cwenhild burst through the stable door.

"So what is it then, Cenric? I'm meant to be at the l—" Cwenhild spotted Æfre standing just out of view.

"Oh! Æfre!" Cwenhild flew across the stable, engulfing her in a tight embrace. "Oh, dear Æfre—what a blessing to see you! Are you well? Too thin, I think. Did Cenric give you the food we put aside?"

"Cwenhild, for mercy's sake, let the woman breathe," Cenric chided.

"You, husband, can keep your own nose in your own ale cup," Cwenhild shot back, waving him off. Cenric grinned, surrendering instantly to his wife with his hands upraised before going back to Epona's hooves.

"Come," Cwenhild urged, leading Æfre to a stack of wooden storage boxes in the corner. They sat, and Cwenhild clasped both of Æfre's hands in hers, her eyes intent.

"My dear, I see how they treat you, and it isn't right. In fact, it is downright ungodly! You and your kin have always served this burh well." She kissed Æfre's hand and squeezed it. "Many here—many more than I would ever have believed, are easily swayed."

"Swayed by Æthelwod," Æfre stated plainly.

"Yes." Cwenhild looked Æfre in the eyes as she confirmed it, "Æthelwod has poisoned them, has planted stories—lies! Lately, any time some misfortune befalls anyone, the bishop is right there in their ear, whispering of heresy."

Æfre's chest tightened with frustration. "But for what purpose?" she demanded, exasperated. "My craft has always been a tool used to serve this burh. My mother and grandmother before me healed these people, birthed their children, and buried their dead. I have no power worth scheming over. And goodness knows the bishop's disdain is nothing new. What has changed?"

"My dear, that's the thing." Cwenhild took a deep breath, "It's Lord Osric."

At the mention of his name, Æfre felt a deep ache in her chest.

"Æthelwod announced Lord Osric's betrothal to Eadlin last night—he did so without Osric's leave. He's pressing the match." Cwenhild paused as she watched Æfre take in the news, before continuing softly. "The bishop has ambitions—for which he needs Osric bound to him."

Æfre's thoughts whirled. Months ago, Osric had warned her of this. "He told me once," she murmured, her voice hollow, "that Æthelwod might use me to bend him to his will."

"That is exactly what he means to do," Cwenhild said, her voice grim. "Do not mistake me—Eadlin is a sweet girl, innocent in all this, but this is no marriage match forged from love. This is about power and land—the marriage is a chain, meant to bind Osric to Æthelwod by his sense of duty."

"But such a marriage," Æfre asked hesitantly, trying to focus. "Surely a union between Wōdenléah and Aldhem strengthens Osric's position, not Æthelwod's. Wouldn't the land and power pass to Osric, not the bishop? What does Æthelwod gain from all this?"

Cwenhild glanced at her husband, who was still working on Epona's hooves—and clearly listening to their conversation. "Cenric?" She passed the question to him.

Cenric stood and leaned against a timber beam, his face darkening with thought as he wiped a large metal rasp with a cloth.

"Ah, well, that's the thing," he said. "As you may remember, after Edington, King Alfred made some broad strokes in the way lands are granted—service and loyalty in exchange for the land and title."

"I remember," Æfre said, "I always assumed it was meant to rid us of the dead wood—keep a tighter rein on lords who sat idle and got fat by the fire." Æfre thought instantly of the old thegn. A soft, doughy-looking man who looked like he'd never seen a day's work in his life, let alone any military service. The rumor at the time was that he'd been caught taking Danish silver in exchange for information on the movements of the fyrd—a claim that was never verified, as the man had disappeared without a trace just after the fighting came to an end.

"That's true, Æfre, but there's more," Cenric continued. "Land grants like Lord Osric's are now mostly benefices, often granted to a military man or handed over to the church. In our case here in Wōdenléah, both of these things are true. Regardless, if the conditions for service set forth by the charter are not met..."

"Ownership of the land goes back to either the Church or the Crown," Cewnhild interjected flatly.

"Does that mean—" Æfre trailed off, the implications of Osric's situation sinking in.

"No matter how many seasons Osric tills this soil," Cenric said, "it is not truly his land while conditions of the charter name the church as his overseer. And may the Lord Almighty forgive me for saying so, but if something were ever to happen to Lord Osric, upon his death—"

"It returns to the Church," Cwenhild finished her husband's sentence while making the sign of the cross over herself.

Æfre sat stunned for a moment, a surge of guilt running through her. Her mind shot back to that awful night in the hut, both of them shouting at each other, falling completely apart—how she'd railed about her freedom. The memory of that moment made her stomach churn now—how selfish that declaration seemed in light of what she had just learned. Osric was every bit as trapped as she was—perhaps even more so.

Æfre took a deep breath and pressed on.

"So—the land reverts if the conditions of the charter for service and loyalty aren't met, but who judges whether these terms have been broken?"

Cenric and Cwenhild both looked at Æfre, their silence in perfect unison.

"Æthelwod." Æfre realized aloud.

The realization sat like a cold fist in her chest. "And once the marriage is made, what's to stop the bishop from just—"

"From ridding himself of me and taking it all?" A deep voice interjected, coming from the doorway.

Æfre's head snapped toward the sound.

Osric.

His frame filled the doorway like a monument in silhouette. Æfre felt a strange mix of relief and dread as his gaze bore into her, like he already knew exactly what had been said.

* * *

Osric stood frozen in place, his breath caught in his chest. Æfre stood before him at the far end of the stable. His heart twisted—a tangled knot of relief, fear, and longing.

"Cwenhild, my dear," Cenric's steady voice cut the silence, "let's give these two a moment. I can finish Epona's hooves outside." He turned toward Osric. "Lord—shall I saddle the gelding for you?"

"Please, Cenric," Osric replied, his voice tight, his eyes never leaving Æfre.

Cwenhild embraced Æfre, kissing her on the cheek with a gentle, sisterly warmth that made Osric's chest ache. As she passed Osric in the doorway, she gave his arm a brief but knowing squeeze—a silent acknowledgment of the things she dared not say.

Cenric hefted his tools and Æfre's provisions before leading Epona from the stall. The mare's hooves thumped against the earthen floor, her tail swishing as Cenric led her through the stable door. "I'll tie her out of sight, just round the corner, Æfre." Cenric's voice was calm, even, as though this were just another day. He nodded once at Osric before vanishing.

"Thank you, Cenric," Æfre said softly.

And then they were alone.

The silence hung heavily between them. Osric's thoughts churned; shock at seeing her, panic at the danger she risked simply by being there, and a pull to take her into his arms so strong he thought it might break him.

"I wasn't expecting you," he managed at last, his tone unsteady. Inside, he was at war with himself. He wanted to scold Æfre for her recklessness, but also pull her to him and never let go.

"I was out riding," Æfre replied, her tone softly defiant. "I decided I'd like to see Cwenhild."

Osric nodded, finding the silence between them unbearable.

"I didn't think you'd be here," she added. "I thought you'd be in the fields. I needed to get out—get some air."

"You shouldn't be here," he blurted abruptly. The words came too quickly, much more sharply than he'd intended. "Do you have any idea what might happen if someone saw you? If Æthelwod saw you?"

Æfre flinched, her jaw tightening, her eyes narrowing. He could see the hurt flare up behind her eyes, but her voice remained steady.

"What do you mean, *what might happen*? It *is* happening, Osric. It has *been* happening." Her voice cracked, her composure splintering. "It has been nearly four months. *Four months.*"

The weight of her words crashed over him, and an unrelenting guilt clawed at his chest. He opened his mouth, fumbling for an explanation, but she wasn't finished.

"I was waiting." She said softly, "Perhaps foolishly, but I waited—never for a minute thinking that the night I watched you ride over the crest of the hill would be the last time we would speak."

"Æfre, I stayed away to protect you—" Osric felt the bitter aftertaste of his excuse even as the words left his mouth. He'd been telling himself he was operating strategically—lying in wait for some battle that he knew could never be fought.

"Protect me?" Æfre scoffed. "Osric, please. I know you to be a more intelligent man than this. What peace did you think I'd find in your silence? Am I safer left alone to wonder if you're still alive, or to suppose you've just already moved on? How did you think I might fare when news of your betrothal reached me and I had not yet heard from you?

Osric felt the energy drain from him as he stood there, suddenly stricken by the truth—his careful reasoning had been nothing but folly. He had told himself that distance might act as a shield, that keeping away would somehow guard her from danger. Yet all he had delivered was abandonment—that much was evident as Æfre stood before him, her voice laying bare the wound he had carved. He could no longer pretend otherwise. He had hurt her deeply.

"Æfre, no," he began, voice breaking. "I didn't know what else to do. Everything is spinning out of control. I cannot bear the thought of harm coming to you—"

"And do you think I could bear the thought of harm coming to you?" Her voice softened but didn't lose its edge. "This is impossible, Osric, and your silence changes nothing. Æthelwod's ambition will not falter; your duty makes it plain that you have no choice but to go through with this marriage, and your silence will not protect me from any of it!"

"Æfre—"

"All it has done is leave me feeling utterly alone."

Osric felt his heart throb under the weight of her words. The saddlebag over his shoulder suddenly seemed impossibly heavy, and he let it slip to the ground with a dull thud.

"I rode out today because I needed to remember that I belong here too," Æfre said, her voice steady, though her eyes were red-rimmed and betraying her. "Yet I am the one expected to vanish while you share meals with your newly betrothed. I know that you and I together may be beyond what's possible, but what have I done, Osric, other than drawing breath, that deserves this treatment!?"

Her words seared him to his core, and he took a step toward her. He felt sick with the truth he found himself confronted with—he had let Æfre carry the full burden of Æthelwod's schemes alone while he buried himself in duty and silence—an act of utter cowardice disguised as protection, and as she stood so tall through her pain, he was deeply ashamed of how he had handled himself.

"Æfre, stop, please." His voice was raw. "I thought I was protecting you. I—"

"Osric," she interrupted him, "we are powerless here. Do you not see that?"

The hopelessness of her resignation was so painfully out of

character that it was more than he could endure. Osric crossed the space between them in four strides. "Please, stop," he implored softly.

But Æfre held her ground—he could see both fire and sorrow in her eyes as she faced him down. "Why, Osric!? Why must I stop? I'm the one who has to navigate an entirely new reality! I'm the one who suddenly finds herself relying on the charity of others *to eat*!"

"Enough!"

Breath ragged, he seized her shoulders, pressing her back against the stable wall, and kissed her like it was the only way to silence the chaos inside of him. She kissed him back, fierce and hungry, and for a moment the two of them were back in the hut—everything else forgotten.

"No," Æfre said softly, her voice trembling as she remembered herself and gently tried to push him away. "Please, stop. We must stop."

Her words cut through the moment, forcing them both back to reality. Breathless, Osric let his hand fall from the wall where he'd braced himself, standing frozen as she slipped out of his embrace. He could still feel the warm signature of her on his skin—another aching reminder of her absence.

"It's just too painful when it ends," she said quietly, her hands shaking as she straightened her skirts and tugged her cloak into place. "I can't relive that."

Osric watched as she quickly wiped a fresh batch of tears from her cheeks, as if to wipe away her vulnerability before it could betray her any further.

Her eyes met his for a moment, her lips parting as if to say something, but the words faltered and died. She turned quickly, drawing her hood over her head as she walked away, her steps brisk.

Osric didn't follow, though every part of him screamed to do so.

He heard a soft, stifled sob as her footsteps grew softer, then the clatter of hooves from outside as she mounted Epona. Finally, hoofbeats becoming increasingly distant, until they finally disappeared altogether, and he knew she was gone.

He sank heavily onto a nearby wooden storage box, his strength giving way as the brittle tension of the moment collapsed around him, the weight of his regret pressing down like a yoke. He had told himself he was protecting her, but had only given her another wound to carry.

He knew he was needed in the fields, yet he was unable to move. Within him, a storm raged, churning with the opposing forces of duty, exhaustion, longing, and the bitter sting of knowing he had failed at the one thing that mattered to him most.

18

Ġestolen ✕ Stolen

Torvald and Svend sat in the hall, the air thick with the smell of hearth smoke and damp wool.

"The Saxons won't wait forever, Torvald," Svend said, breaking the silence.

Between them, Torvald had scratched a rough rendering of the trade routes into the packed earth floor with a stick—a series of jagged lines and circles for the Thames and surrounding burhs, peppered by crude marks where deals had soured and shipments gone missing.

Torvald stared at his creation in silence, his jaw set. Each mark was more than a loss of coin; it was a potential fracture in the fragile post-conflict ecosystem he'd been instrumental in creating. No accident could explain it. The pattern was too sudden, too intentional.

"Every time a shipment turns up with missing goods, we lose a bit of ground with them," Svend said. "There's only so much trust they'll extend before they decide we're more trouble than we're worth."

Torvald's brow furrowed deeply as he leaned forward, the stick tapping at the earthen floor. Svend rarely pressed him, but Torvald understood why—he could hardly hold it against him. It was Svend whose face the Saxons saw when deals were made. It was Svend who bore the brunt of their frustration, and Svend who was ferrying messages to and from the burh and standing face-to-face with men like Osric, who no doubt had their own issues to contend with.

Torvald let out a slow exhale, his eyes fixed on the map. "This is deliberate," he muttered. Someone is trying to disrupt the trade, trying to unravel what we've built. This—" he struck the earth with his stick over the burh of Wōdenléah. "This is the sort of disruption that breaks down treaties. Someone means for that to happen."

Svend studied the chieftain for a moment. "You're thinking of appealing to the Saxon thegn."

Torvald straightened, his gaze sharpening. Osric had been on his mind more than he cared to admit, but not just for reasons of trade. It was Æfre. All these months later, the memory of her at the river, golden hair in the light, eyes unflinching—he couldn't shake that image, which clung to him like wood smoke to a wool cloak. Of course, it didn't help that it was also whispered that she was romantically tied to the Saxon thegn. This jealous thought left him feeling utterly ridiculous, as if he were still a lovesick young warrior struggling to prove himself.

Nevertheless, things appeared to be escalating now, and he had no choice but to handle it.

"I think it's time," Torvald said finally. "If there's any hope of untangling this mess, I'll need to speak with the thegn. The man may work for Æthelwod, but as you've said yourself, he's certainly no fool. I'm guessing he, too, sees the bigger picture here."

Svend studied him, waiting.

Torvald raked a hand through his hair. "It's a risk. Yet this treachery cuts across both our people. Between the stolen goods and this marriage being forged between Wōdenléah and Aldhem, if the thegn is not involved in any of this, I have a feeling we will soon need each other—whether we wish it or not."

Svend nodded, a flicker of approval behind his eyes. "I agree, Jarl. I'll make arrangements. I'm seeing him tomorrow and can set it up."

Torvald hesitated, then gave a short nod. "Very well. And Svend, let him choose the time and place. This meeting needs to happen."

Torvald saw Svend's eyebrows rise slightly at the

concession—he was rarely one to let the other side dictate terms, even for something as minor as the location of a meeting. But Svend knew better than to question him openly, simply replying, "Understood. I'll handle it, Jarl. You'd like me to send Bjørn in?"

"Please, Svend, thank you."

As Svend left the hall, Torvald heard him shouting for Bjørn, who was loading one of the wagons outside. Torvald remained deep in thought, the stick in his hand still tracing over the markings on the packed earth floor. There was a pattern emerging that gnawed at him—an unseen force mobilizing against them.

His thoughts veered again as Æfre's face came unbidden into his mind once again. Her quiet strength, her piercing gaze—how much did she know of Osric's dealings? Could she, too, be a thread in this increasingly tangled web?

He cursed under his breath as he tried to clear his mind. Thoughts of Æfre would have to wait—whoever was working to disrupt the trade likely would not.

* * *

Torvald sat as still as stone, watching Bjørn pace before him. He'd noticed that the younger man had taken to choosing his words more deliberately of late, though this day, they were laced with urgency.

The talk from across the camp in the past months spoke well of Bjørn's sincerity and dedication, and the chieftain was more than happy to have been wrong about the young man. Yet with each passing day, rumors of unease grew, and Torvald wondered whether Bjørn might come to regret his choice of taking on more responsibility.

"It's moved along more quickly than expected since we last spoke," Bjørn said, keeping his voice low. "It isn't just idle grumbling anymore."

Torvald leaned back in his chair, forcing his face to remain expressionless even as his mind was running in circles.

"Go on," Torvald said, his voice measured, "Tell me what you know."

Bjørn stopped pacing, his hand resting on the hilt of his seax, as though anchoring himself. "It feels forced—like it's being guided by someone, Jarl. What's being whispered all seems to focus on a sense of anger and mistreatment—that the Saxons are robbing us, that they are purposely compromising the shipments, that we've grown weak in our dealings with them..." Bjørn glanced up, cautiously reading the chieftain's reaction before continuing.

Torvald nodded faintly for him to continue.

"There's one tale in particular," Bjørn went on, his voice reluctant, "You're too lenient. That..." He faltered.

Torvald arched a brow, waiting.

"They say you've forgotten what it is to be a warrior," Bjørn blurted, then visibly braced for the storm of the chieftain's reaction. Torvald's jaw tightened, the words cutting deep, but he did not react.

Úff, that one stung. Someone is trying to bait me into a fight. To rattle me in front of my men.

Torvald simply nodded, raising an open palm for Bjørn to continue.

"There's also talk of preparation. Possibly armed. No solid plan—yet. Just the younger men—those easily led—told to keep themselves ready for when the time comes".

Torvald's fist curled at his side, but his tone remained even. "You have names?"

"Yes, Jarl," Bjørn nodded, "I can name everyone. And I fear there may be more."

Torvald exhaled slowly through his nose. This wasn't just a petty merchant squabble or a drunken spat after too much ale. This looked increasingly like a coordinated effort to undermine him as chieftain, to fracture his camp, and perhaps even disrupt the fragile peace of the treaty agreement.

"You said 'someone', Torvald's eyes narrowed. "You believe this is the work of one man?"

Bjørn hesitated for a moment before nodding. "The whispers, they're similar."

"As if they sprang from the same tongue?" Torvald asked.

"Yes. But I don't know who yet."

Torvald's gaze fell to the floor, his mind again turning to the Saxon thegn, Osric. No step could be taken until they spoke, though the thought made Torvald's chest tighten with unease.

If he can be trusted.

"Bjørn, keep close watch on the names you've gathered. Everyone. Listen, and stay calm. We will approach them when the moment is right, but for now, let them believe you share their feelings. I have matters tomorrow, but after that, you'll hear from Svend and me."

"And this supposed threat from the Saxons?" Bjørn asked, observing his chieftain carefully.

"Bjørn, whoever is behind this is trying to destroy what little peace we've built with the Saxons. This time, the Saxons have as much to lose as we do."

Bjørn inclined his head in agreement.

Torvald tapped a finger against the table. "Continue gathering what you can, but be subtle. If whomever this rat is senses we're onto him, he'll either go to ground or force his hand before we're ready."

Bjørn nodded, though the flicker of unease in his eyes did not escape Torvald.

The chieftain leaned forward, his voice lowering. "This stays between us for now—you, me, and Svend. Continue with your work as if nothing has changed. Gather the names of those involved, and pass them to me. And Bjørn," he locked eyes with the younger man, "you've done well. Stay sharp."

Bjørn gave a brisk, curt nod, a fleeting flash of pride and warmth in his eyes. "I'll be careful, Jarl."

19

Onræs ⚔ Attack

The tears on Æfre's cheeks froze in the biting wind as she urged Epona into a canter, a storm raging inside of her. The steady, familiar rhythm of the mare's hooves against the frost-hardened ground was the only thing keeping her loosely tethered in the present as she replayed the confrontation with Osric again and again.

She hadn't meant to be so harsh with him—she hadn't planned to speak her mind in that way at all. But everything she was holding inside had been so raw, so close to breaking, that the smallest little thing had threatened to tip the balance and spill it all over.

And it had indeed spilled over.

She replayed every heated word she'd hurled at him, words that were meant as a plea for understanding but ended up being wielded as a weapon. He had hurt her, and she had struck back. But shame pressed in now—she wished she had been kinder—or maybe just more controlled, or softer...she honestly didn't know, exactly. All she knew was that right now, her cheeks burned—in no small part from the memory of how he had kissed her.

That kiss.

It was haunting her already. That kiss would be the thing she saw every time she closed her eyes—the desperate look in Osric's eyes, the warmth of his hands as he pushed her against the stable wall, his lips crushing hers with a ferocity that instantly shattered every defensive barrier she had carefully constructed around herself in the months of his absence.

It had felt like returning home, like the two of them were the unshakable pair they had once been, and it had undone her completely.

Epona instinctively slowed to a trot as they reached the narrow path descending towards her homestead. Æfre drew in the reins, guiding the mare carefully down the familiar slope. But as her hut came into view, her pulse quickened. A horse she didn't recognize was tied to the fence at the far end of the paddock.

She hadn't been expecting anyone. It had been weeks since anyone from the burh had dared to risk being seen coming to her for healing. Likely, there was some harmless explanation—but a sense of unease crept into her gut. Something felt off.

Dismounting by the paddock, she tied Epona a short distance from the unfamiliar horse and swiftly pulled her bow and quiver from the saddle pack, their weight steadying her as she crept towards the livestock shed. As she drew closer, she noticed a flicker of light filtering through the gaps in the timber slats.

And then she saw the smoke.

The inside of the shed was on fire.

Æfre sprinted to the shed's entrance, her heart pounding in her chest. Covering her hand with her cloak, she yanked the weathered door open, only to be met by a billowing plume that stung her eyes and blackened her view. Coughing, she squinted through the haze to assess the situation.

The fire hadn't been burning long, thank the gods, but it was hot. The source was unmistakable—a deliberate pile of loose straw that had been placed at the shed's center. The flames were already beginning to leap greedily onto the aged timber beams above, their orange tips reaching for the thatched roof. If they caught, the entire shed—and possibly even her hut if the wind carried it—all of it could be lost.

There was no time.

Æfre dropped her bow and quiver and shrugged off her thick woolen cloak. Squinting against the thick, black smoke, she rushed into the shed and flung the cloak over the flames, its heavy weight enveloping the blaze with a sizzling sound. Her eyes stung, and her throat tightened as smoke wound its way into her lungs. The searing heat bit through the fabric of the cloak, scorching her hands and singeing her eyelashes when she ventured too close. Desperation fuelled her efforts as she moved around the fire, adjusting the cloak, pressing down on the flames where she could, fighting to smother them before they could burst back to life and consume anything further.

The acrid smell of charred wool and fur filled her nostrils, but she persevered. The fire hissed and sputtered beneath her cloak, embers glowing angrily around the edges. Æfre finally was able to stand on the cloak, feeling the heat rise through the soles of her boots while she stamped at the sparks until they finally began to die down.

Her good winter cloak lay in tatters, still glowing faintly at the edges. Her hands throbbed with the rawness of heat, the skin reddened and tender, but she barely registered the discomfort.

Her gaze shot upward to the rafters, where the beginnings of the flames had given way to smoldering, darkened wood—a visual reminder of how close the fire had come to growing out of control. Several sections of thatch were charred beyond saving, brittle, and blackened. She would have to patch the roof before the next rain or snowfall. She exhaled a shaky breath, half relief, half exhaustion, then was wracked by a coughing fit brought on by the thick, foul air, which sent her staggering out of the shed.

As she stepped back into the cold, clean outside air, she swept at her cheeks with her raw, painful hands, smearing away stinging, smoke-streaked tears. As her vision and lungs cleared, she rounded the side of the shed and glanced toward the paddock. The unfamiliar horse was still there.

The person who did this is still here.

Her breath halted in her chest as she cast her gaze towards the hut and froze. Carved deep into the wood of her door, the word *wicce* glared back at her.

Witch.

My bow, she thought, remembering that she'd dropped it by the shed.

Æfre spun towards the shed, but in her path, less than ten feet in front of her, stood a man—a tall, hulking figure in a dark cloak, hood up, a dark cloth obscuring his face, leaving only his long dark hair and beard visible.

Æfre's instinct was to make a dash for the hut and slam the door behind her, but she'd barely moved before the man lunged. He was fast—trained, and he instantly closed the gap between them. The force of his body colliding with hers sent her sprawling to the ground, the impact driving the air from her lungs and her face into the hardened earth. Panic surged, cold and choking, as he flipped her over onto her back and pinned her arms with a grip that felt like an iron clamp. This man was heavy—efficient in his movements. She was in trouble, and she knew it.

I need to fight, right now.

The cloaked man tore at the neckline of her dress as Æfre thrashed wildly against him, her kicks destabilizing him enough to make him grunt in irritation, but it didn't dislodge him. Desperation surged through her as she somehow managed to twist her body, freeing her right side just enough to lift herself partially off the ground.

With a growl of defiance, she raised her head and sank her teeth into his ear, biting down hard until the metallic tang of blood filled her mouth. The man howled in pain, jerking back and shoving her off him with brutal force, causing his hood to fall away, exposing the long, brown hair with shaved sides—a style worn by many of the Northmen.

A Northman! Æfre thought. *But why!?*

HEART OF THE WILD GODS

Suddenly, the back of the man's open hand cracked across her face, sending a sharp jolt of pain through her skull, the coppery taste of blood spilling onto her tongue

"Heimskr lítil píka! [*Stupid little bitch!*]" The man cursed as he tore Æfre's dress further, exposing the pale curve of her shoulder. His eyes flicked to it, and Æfre's chest filled with an icy dread of what was about to happen.

"Ljótr skítkarl! [*Ugly bastard!*]" Æfre spat a mouthful of blood directly into the man's face, the language of her father instinctively rolling off her tongue, her eyes blazing fire.

The man faltered at hearing his own language thrown back at him—the look in his eyes changed for a moment to one of confusion, and he frowned and sat back slightly, trying to get a better look at his prey.

It was just enough to allow Æfre to free her right arm and unsheathe her seax.

She plunged the seax into the man's side, aiming for the vulnerable space beneath his arm. But he was well-armored—he wore a hardened leather vest beneath his thick wool cloak. The blade slowed as it met the vest, but still skittered across his ribcage, slicing him well but failing to incapacitate him.

The man roared in pain and rage, recoiling slightly as his hand flew to his side where her blade had struck. When he pulled it away, it glistened with fresh blood. For a moment, his face twisted with surprise, as if he had not expected a fight. Then, a shadow of pure rage descended over his eyes.

Æfre's blood went cold as she realized she was now in even more danger—there would be no more hesitating. Again she struck, this time some blood splattered down, landing hot against her dress and collarbone, but the wounds were shallow, and his rage only grew.

His expression darkened further, and his hand clamped around her throat. She slashed a third time, fighting through the terror.

The third strike was enough to weaken the man's grip, and he backed off, clutching at his torso where she had cut him.

Æfre seized the opportunity, twisting and wriggling free. She rolled out from under him, seax in hand, her muscles burning with effort, and scrambled to her feet, her skirts tangling around her legs as she struggled. She managed to get herself clear—his hands clawing at her heels and pulling at her skirts, but with a frantic final kick, she dislodged him. Without looking back, she bolted toward where she'd dropped her bow and quiver.

Her heart thundered in her chest as she reached the spot, her knees hitting the dirt hard as she grabbed the bow and clutched it to her chest. The pounding of boots behind her warned that he was close. In a single motion, she rolled onto her back, grabbing an arrow from her quiver. Her fingers found the shaft, readied the arrow, and drew, aiming just as the man lunged toward her.

Æfre loosed the arrow, a sharp whistle cutting through the air. The man turned, trying to shield himself, but the arrow struck, burying itself deeply in his left shoulder. The man's roar of pain echoed across the clearing, his body jerking back from the force of the hit.

Æfre could hear Epona nearby, whinnying and snorting at the threat in her midst, pulling at her reins that were tied to the fence.

The man staggered, clutching at the arrow embedded in his shoulder. His furious eyes flicked between Æfre and the wound. With a grimace, he reached up and snapped the fletching off the arrow, leaving the shaft lodged in his flesh. Blood trickled out of the sleeve of his tunic and darkened his chest, but his expression remained hard.

For a long, tense moment, his gaze met Æfre's, a silent promise of unfinished business. Then, without a word, he turned and bolted—towards Epona.

HEART OF THE WILD GODS

"Nei!...NEI!" Æfre shouted at him, scrambling to her feet—panic in her voice. She readied another arrow as she moved towards him, watching him grab the mare's reins—he was going to take Epona!

Æfre angled her shot and loosed the arrow, hitting the man again in the left shoulder, this time diagonally from the back.

Gripping Epona's mane with his uninjured hand, the man struggled to lift himself into the saddle as Epona sidestepped and kicked out. The man's movements were clumsy and uncoordinated, his wounded arm betraying him. Instead of mounting the mare, he stumbled and fell heavily against her, driving the arrows deeper into his shoulder while smearing blood across Epona's chest, mane, and shoulder.

Epona let out a sharp snort and bucked violently, her eyes rolling with panic. Her ears pinned flat against her head as she pulled back, snapping her bridle and rearing, hooves pawing at the air.

The man's cloak had caught on the saddle as he'd attempted to mount, now causing the fabric to tear loose with a harsh rip. Driven by terror, the mare twisted sharply and bolted, her powerful strides thundering up the path towards the road.

The man stumbled backwards and collapsed into a heap on the ground, his movements strained as he pushed himself up. He turned towards his own horse, the creature standing calm and steady amidst the turmoil, its unflinching demeanor betraying a life accustomed to chaos.

Æfre followed, bow drawn and pointed directly at him. "Fara frá! [Leave!]"

The man glowered at Æfre one last time before awkwardly mounting and turning his horse up the path, urging it on until he disappeared over the hill at a full gallop.

Æfre sank down hard onto the ground, her legs refusing to

hold her any longer. She didn't know how long she sat there, resisting the impulse to vomit while her mind whirled. She felt oddly disconnected—as if she were watching herself from some high above place.

Epona. I need to find Epona.

Her heart clenched at the thought of the mare out there—lost, frightened, or even worse, becoming injured as she ran through the forest in a panic. She pressed her hands to her temples, breathing deeply, trying to calm the torrent of emotions surging through her. Her mind was cycling through too many things, too quickly. She was frozen in place, yet at the same time overwhelmed with the urge to move, to run.

She needed to get up and get moving. She needed to find Epona. By the might of the Gods, it was cold out. But right now, she just needed to sit, just for another minute.

20

Onfundennes ⚔ Finding Out

It was well past the time when any good steward of the land should have already been in the fields, but Osric had only just gathered himself enough to ride out. His unexpected meeting with Æfre had left him raw. If only he could wind back time—he would jump at the chance to undo the last four months. The idea that she thought he'd abandoned her sickened him to his core. No, he couldn't go back in time, but he could yet do right by her. He swore he would. He owed her that much and more.

As he reached the edge of the fields, a cluster of ceorls stood waiting, their talk low and wary. He dismounted quickly, offering them a brief apology for his tardiness, when a voice broke through.

"Lord Osric, you'll want to see this," came Godwin's voice, cutting through the hum of idle chatter.

Godwin, one of the most experienced and trusted ceorls in Wōdenléah, stood at the center of a group of men gathered near one of the large tool storage sheds that sat at the edge of the fields.

Osric brushed past the workers with a nod as Godwin led him towards the shed.

The shed would usually have held little more than farm tools—billhooks, spades, rakes for the harvest, perhaps a stack of wooden boxes for storage. Instead, the dim shed interior revealed a surprising hoard: crates brimming with woven silks, silver jewelry gleaming in the half-light, and, in the shadows at the back, a chest heavy with ornate weapons—swords, axes, daggers, each clearly forged with skill and bound with carved hilts.

A slow breath escaped Osric. "Lord preserve us.... Godwin, where did this come from?"

"No telling, Lord," Godwin said quietly. "I can tell you it was not here two days past."

"You and Albert were last in here?"

"Gēa, my lord. And I swear it on my life, none of our folk would dream of risking such treachery."

Osric studied him, then gave a firm nod. "Don't worry yourself, Godwin, I believe you." And he did. Godwin had weathered too many winters in the burh to suddenly stoop to something as base as theft—and Osric was sure that what he was looking at was theft. These goods were Norse—from the camp.

No, the source of this theft lay elsewhere, and after what he'd witnessed earlier that day, Osric was fairly certain he knew exactly who the driving force was. He had witnessed Svend's frustration over the past weeks, as shipments had gone astray and deals had gone bad. These were Norse goods, and their sudden appearance here could well disrupt their trading relationships, perhaps even unravel the hard-won peace between their people.

With a nod to Godwin, Osric said, "I have a few ideas about this. Please reassure your people that they are not under any suspicion. What I need from you is a full accounting of everything in those crates that doesn't belong to us. I want every item counted and set down. Get it to me as soon as possible...have you someone who can write?"

"Gēa, Lord," Godwin responded quickly. "Alaric's wife can set the numbers in order and such."

"That's excellent, Godwin." Osric paused, his mind already turning toward his next move as he drew a hand across his mouth. "I'm going to have to pay our Norse neighbors a visit."

"It will be done, Lord."

Before Osric could respond, they heard a disturbance coming from outside the cellar—shouting, and the sound of hooves approaching quickly. The noise grew louder until, moments later, Osric recognized Alaric's voice, urgent and sharp, just outside the shed door.

"My lord! Come quickly! Something has happened—you're needed in the burh straight away!"

What now!?

For a moment, Osric froze as he locked eyes with Godwin—his face a mix of disbelief and dread. Without a word, he turned and hurried toward the door.

* * *

Osric urged the gelding into a full gallop, his stomach tightening with each powerful stride. *What now!?* What could have sparked such panic? The last time he had seen anyone in the burh react with such fear had been that awful day, when Leofwynn...

He wouldn't allow himself to finish the thought.

As he rounded the corner past the stable, he had to pull the horse up sharply. There, in the middle of the road, stood Cenric. The pallor of his face, grim and drawn, made it clear something was terribly wrong.

Osric barely came to a complete stop before he dismounted, his boots hitting the ground hard as he strode toward Cenric. The man looked pale, his expression twisted with dread, as though he could barely bring himself to speak.

"Lord Osric," Cenric began weakly, his voice trembling, "I don't even know how to begin to tell you this—"

"What is it, Cenric?" Osric demanded, his tone sharp, fear already clawing at his chest.

"It's Æfre." Cenric swallowed hard. "Epona appeared in the market square not long ago."

Osric froze, the world narrowing around him. "What?" The word escaped him in a hoarse whisper.

"Lord, please—come." Cenric grabbed Osric's arm with one hand, gripping the gelding's reins with the other, and pulled them both around the side of the building toward the stable green.

Once they rounded the corner, Osric immediately saw a small crowd gathered near the stable. They stood hushed and still like mourners at a funeral, their silence heavy with tension. Cwenhild was there, pale as death, tears streaking her face. Eadlin lingered in the doorway of the hall, her expression unreadable as she silently observed. Even Æthelwod was present, unusually still and grim, standing beside Eadlin.

Then Osric saw Epona.

The mare trembled, flanks heaving, nostrils flared, sweat slick on her hide. A burh boy held her, looking as though he'd have preferred to be anywhere other than where he was.

The saddle still clung to Epona's back, the bridle hung half-broken, the bit dangling loose. The basket of provisions was askew, most of its contents long gone—likely scattered across the hills.

But it was the blood that froze Osric where he stood.

Epona's left shoulder and neck were drenched in blood that ran dark down her side. The sight struck Osric like a hammer to the chest. Had Cenric not had a hold of his arm, he might have crumpled to the earth then and there.

No. Not again. By God, not again.

"How long ago did she arrive?" Osric rasped, his voice hoarse with the urgency of his growing panic.

"My lord, I've got men searching the hillsides as we spea—"

"How long!?" Osric cut him off, his voice sharp.

"Just under an hour, Lord," Cenric answered, his tone low, cautious.

Osric stepped back, his eyes locked on Epona, his mind both racing and stalling at the same time. He dragged his hands through his hair, struggling to pull his thoughts into order.

Then, suddenly, he turned and mounted the gelding in one

HEART OF THE WILD GODS

fluid motion.

"My lord, take men with you!" Cenric called after him, his voice imploring.

But Osric was already thundering towards the gate.

He urged the gelding to gallop hard, hooves hammering the earth in rhythm with his own frantic heartbeat. But as the palisade fell behind him, his soldier's clarity cut through the panic—at this pace, he might ride straight past her—or miss some vital clue that could lead him to her.

Osric pulled back the horse into a steadier gait, his eyes scouring every frost-covered field, every row of forest. From time to time, he called Æfre's name, but there was no answer.

When Osric finally reached the path leading down to Æfre's homestead, he pulled the gelding to a halt at the crest of the hill. His eyes swept the landscape, searching hungrily for any sign that might point him in the right direction.

The view below was heartbreakingly peaceful—almost mockingly so—the rolling fields stiff with frost, the trees standing silent under the pale sky. On any other day, this scene would have brought him comfort, perhaps even a fleeting sense of peace. But today, it filled him with dread.

He nudged the gelding forward to begin his descent to the hut. Partway down, something dark in the frozen grass caught his eye. Osric pulled the horse to a stop and slid off, his boots crunching beneath him as he landed on the frosty ground.

There, tangled in a mix of earth and frost, was a charcoal-colored woolen cloak, torn and partially soaked with frozen blood. A silver brooch dangled from the end of a broken chain with the likeness of a wolf on it.

Osric recognized the trinket at once—Fenrir, a wolf from a Norse tale—the harbinger of chaos. He had seen that beast's likeness often enough—etched into shields and hanging from the necks of warriors he had faced in raids and battle.

Osric's pulse quickened, and he recalled the cloaked Northman he'd overheard with Æthelwod that morning. His chest tightened, his mind forming a picture he didn't want to see—panic swelling within him.

He stuffed the bloodied cloak and brooch into his saddlebag, hands trembling with urgency. Then, mounting the gelding, he urged the horse onward down the path.

"Æfre!" he shouted, his voice echoing through the stillness.

Only silence.

He called again, louder this time, straining to hear even the faintest response. The quiet pressed in around him, offering no answers.

Osric's eyes caught a patch of disturbed earth near the paddock—hoof marks, as though a horse had been pawing the ground anxiously. He swung down from his gelding, tying the reins to the paddock gate. Kneeling, he inspected the area more closely. His stomach tightened as he noticed a dark stain against the frozen soil. Blood—and not just a trace either.

No, don't think about that now.

Straightening, he started toward the hut's door—then stopped dead in his tracks.

The word *"wicce"* cut deeply into the wood of Æfre's door, the gouged letters raw and crude against the grain. His stomach lurched, and guilt washed over him in a suffocating wave. He knew he would never escape it—the part he had played in Æfre's casting out, in the whispers and barely-hidden threats that now followed her like a curse.

With a hand resting on the hilt of his seax, Osric approached the hut and pushed the door open, stepping cautiously inside. "Æfre?" he called, his voice echoing in the stillness.

Empty.

HEART OF THE WILD GODS

The hut felt both hauntingly abandoned yet familiar—so far removed from him, as if it were a scene stolen from a dream. He stood in the doorway, scanning the interior. The small table was cluttered with a scattering of dried herbs, as it always was. The hearth had nearly gone cold—that was certainly unusual. The chair he had once claimed as his own sat untouched by the fire—its presence felt almost accusatory.

The air still had that faint, comforting scent it always did—a mixture of herbs and something distinctly *her*.

His gaze shifted to the bed, which was neatly made but empty, and a sudden pang of guilt and sadness washed over him. Memories flooded back—nights spent by the fire, watching Æfre sleep, and the quiet conversations that had once filled this space. He took a deep breath and swallowed hard, forcing himself back to the present.

Osric stepped out of the hut, pulling the door shut behind him. His eyes scanned his surroundings, taking in every detail, every mark on the earth, as if the ground itself might tell him what had happened. Near the paddock, he spotted another area of disrupted earth showing clear signs of a scuffle—another set of hoof prints mingled with dark patches of blood. Then, just beyond, something caught his eye.

A broken arrow lay discarded on the ground, its shaft splintered and bloody, the fletching ragged, and the tip missing. Osric's chest tightened, and he called out again, "Æfre!" His voice cracked against the frozen air, his panic reverberating through the hills.

The scent of old smoke reached him as he neared the livestock shed. He pushed the door and stopped cold.

He instantly recognized Æfre's winter cloak lying crumpled on the dirt floor, charred and ruined, its fur lining curled and blackened.

Osric knelt, hands unsteady as he gathered the garment. The fabric was stiff, almost crispy with ash, and heavy with the stink of fire. He was sure it had been used against the flames.

His gaze swept the shed, mind racing. He noticed the timber walls streaked with soot, the thatch above was blackened in patches, and several beams scorched. Fire had clawed its way through here, stopped only by desperate hands.

Æfre's hands.

A chill cut through him. There had been trouble here—of that there was no doubt.

But where was she?

"Æfre!" he shouted again as he left the shed, his voice rising to the edge of despair, the sick feeling in his stomach growing more intense with every new discovery.

Mounting the gelding in a blur, he shouted her name again as he guided the horse back to the path leading to the road.

The climb up the hill felt endless, the dread in his bones spreading with every step. He was unsure of just how long ago this trouble might have found Æfre , and it was such a cold, windy day—was she out in it? Reaching the crest, he reined in the gelding, his ears straining against the stillness of the road.

Then, faintly, he heard it—a high, distant sound, sharp and distinct.

A bird?

No—his heart stopped as the sound came again, clearer this time.

"Epona!"

That time, he heard it more clearly. It was still a fair distance away, but it was by far the most beautiful sound he'd ever heard.

It was Æfre.

The sound of her voice was like salvation! His breath caught, tears stinging his eyes as relief warred with the urgency still pounding through him. It was her. Æfre's voice. He didn't dare move, holding his breath as he strained to pinpoint the direction.

"Epona!" she called again, the sound faint but unmistakable, carrying from somewhere to his right.

Without hesitation, Osric urged the gelding off the road, heading down a wooded embankment. Branches scraped against him as he pushed through the forest, every beat of his heart driving him forward. He heard her a third time—the sound was growing louder. He was close.

"Æfre!" he shouted, his voice raw. "Where are you?"

An agonizing pause stretched before her voice called back to him, closer now. "Osric!?"

He turned the gelding sharply toward her voice, urging the horse faster. "I'm here! Keep calling out!"

"Osric! I'm here!" she cried.

He spotted the light filtering through the trees ahead and pushed the gelding onward, his focus narrowing to that opening in the forest. The moment he broke into the clearing, his wild eyes scanned frantically, searching.

"Osric!" Æfre's voice rang out, and he finally saw her—a speck standing at the far edge of the clearing. Relief surged through him, and he drove the gelding into a gallop, covering the distance between them as fast as the horse would carry him.

Æfre stood at the edge of the clearing, pale and hollow-eyed, clutching a braided leather halter draped over one shoulder, the rope dangling limply against her side. A thin shawl, barely more than a scrap of fabric, clung to her nearly bare shoulders, futile against the biting cold, as if she'd grabbed it as an afterthought after her cloak had burned.

Osric slowed the gelding to a trot, dismounting battlefield style in one single motion while the horse was still moving. He hit the ground running, closing the distance between them in seconds.

When he reached her, he wrapped her in his arms, still trying to shield her from a danger that had already come and gone.

"Oh my dear God, Æfre!" His voice cracked with relief and anguish as he buried his face in her shoulder, his body trembling. "I thought—I thought the worst had happened."

"Osric!" Æfre sobbed, clutching at him as tears spilled down her cheeks. "I've lost Epona! She spooked and bolted when the man tried to take her, and I followed her tracks down here—"

"Æfre, listen to me," Osric interrupted, pulling back just enough to look into her eyes. "Epona is safe. Cenric has her. She's safe. She's found."

Her face crumpled with relief, but before she could speak, Osric's gaze swept over her, and his expression darkened. His eyes locked onto the blood staining her hair, her face, her dress. She was awash with soot, but not so much that he couldn't see the bruise blooming on her cheek, the split in her lip, the angry marks encircling her neck. His hands began to shake.

"Æfre, are you hurt?" His voice was tight with panic as his fingers moved to her shoulders, then down her arms, searching for injuries. "My God, where is all this blood from!? Tell me!"

"Osric, I'm—" she began, but he wasn't listening. He spun her around, his eyes and hands darting over her body, scanning her for wounds as if she were a soldier on the battlefield.

"Æfre, for God's sake, where are you bleeding from?" he demanded, his voice rising in desperation.

"Osric!" Her voice was firm this time, cutting through his panic. She spun back around and grabbed his face between her hands, forcing him to meet her eyes. "Stop! Osric, listen to me—it's not mine! It's not my blood!"

Her words finally pierced the storm in his mind, and he froze. The tension drained from his body in a sudden, overwhelming wave. He staggered, his legs buckling beneath him as he sank to his knees at her feet. He clung to her skirts, his breathing ragged and uneven, his entire body numb.

For a moment, he couldn't speak. The weight of everything—the fear, the relief, the sheer enormity of what had just happened—crashed over him all at once. All the trauma, the memory of what happened to Leofwynn and seeing the horse covered in blood—his chest heaved, his breath coming in short, sharp bursts, as if he were drowning and couldn't quite reach the surface.

Æfre knelt beside him, her arms wrapping around his shoulders as she whispered soothingly, her own voice shaky but steady enough to anchor him. "Osric.... I'm unharmed... I'm *unharmed.*"

Osric finally lifted his head, his breath shaky as his gaze locked with Æfre's. Without hesitation, he cradled her face in his hands and kissed her with all the desperation and relief that had been building inside him. *Good God, her face was as cold as ice.*

Æfre winced, her split lip pulsating as if to remind her of its presence. The slight flinch cut through Osric's racing thoughts, dragging him back to the present. Despite her insistence she was unharmed, the truth stood plain before him, and it told a different tale.

His brow furrowed as he pulled back slightly, taking in Æfre's appearance with sharper clarity. She was shivering violently, her lips tinged blue, and her eyes distant and glassy.

"You're in shock," he said, his voice soft but resolute. Rising to his feet, he supported her as she swayed slightly while he helped her up. The moment she was standing, he unclasped his cloak and wrapped it around her shoulders, tucking it snugly around her. "Here. This will have to do for now."

Æfre's murmur of gratitude tugged at something within him. She needed warmth and safety—both of which were sorely lacking in the clearing.

"I think there's still a woodcutter's shelter near the clearing," he said, "We need to get a fire lit. You need warmth."

Osric found the shelter near where he'd remembered it to be, at the edge of the forest clearing, nestled near a winding creek. It was nothing more than a crude structure, but it had four walls and would break the wind, keeping out the worst of the biting cold.

Just outside the entrance, a small stone fire pit held the remains of charred wood, frozen and blackened from the last occupant's fire. Inside, the shed was sparse but serviceable. A stack of kindling, a cooking pot, a few straw mats, and a bundle of char cloth sat ready for use. Enough to make a start.

He worked quickly, laying one of the mats down for Æfre. She dropped onto it heavily, curling in on herself and hugging her legs to her chest.

"I should be helping you," she murmured. Even as she said it, her body sagged with exhaustion. The soldier in Osric knew that the energy from the fight had likely sustained her through the attack, and now it was ebbing away, leaving her hollow and spent.

Osric crouched beside her and managed soft smile. "Æfre, you've done more than enough. I'll take care of this."

She smiled faintly as she leaned her head back against the wooden wall. Her eyes were heavy, her breathing shallow. Osric's stomach twisted at how pale she had become, her usual vibrancy dulled by shock and the cold.

He turned to the fire pit, working quickly to get a fire started so that he could bring some warmth back to her. Using the flint and steel from his pouch, he set about sending sparks flying. It took more effort than he liked—his hands shook, both from the cold and the fear gnawing at his insides. Finally, the char cloth caught, and he nurtured it until flames were spreading hungrily over the kindling. Osric fed the fire, and it roared to life, its heat licking at the icy air. He filled the cooking pot with creek water and set it over the flames to boil.

"Æfre," he said, shaking her shoulder gently. Her eyelids fluttered, her gaze unfocused. "Mmm. Hello, Osric," she mumbled, her voice thick and slurred.

"Æfre, stay with me," he urged, his tone sharper now. Fear crept into his chest. "You've gotten too cold. We need to warm you."

She gave no response beyond a faint hum, closing her eyes again and letting her head fall back against the shed wall.

Panic sharpened Osric's focus. Scooping her up, he carried her closer to the fire and set her down just inside the doorway, where the warmth would reach her best without exposing her to the wind. He knelt beside her, unclasping his cloak and shrugging out of his tunic, woolen underlayer, and trousers until he was in nothing but his wool braies. The cold bit at him, but he ignored it, draping his cloak over her before he turned his attention to her sodden clothing.

"Help me, Æfre," he said softly near her ear, coaxing her to respond. "We need to get these wet things off you."

Her movements were sluggish, her limbs like lead, but she complied, weakly raising her hips and arms so he could peel the bloodied, torn overdress away. He spread it out over a pile of logs to dry. Her underlayer was in slightly better condition but still damp and torn down the front.

"Lift your arms again," Osric instructed, and she complied, slipping them out of the sleeves with what little strength she had left. He rolled the garment down to her waist, exposing her chest and arms to the warmth of the fire. Pressing a hand to her chest, he exhaled briskly at the frigid temperature of her skin. She was dangerously cold.

Osric pulled her to him, wrapping his cloak tightly around them both, then settled back against the doorway. He held her close, her head resting against his shoulder, his body heat mingling with the fire's radiant warmth to warm her. His arms encircled her protectively, his grip firm, as though holding the many pieces of her together.

"Stay with me, Æfre," he murmured into her hair, his voice trembling. He pressed a kiss to her temple, his breath warm against her skin, his heart pounding with the fear of what might have happened if he hadn't found her in time, or if the attack had occurred in the dead of night.

All he could do now was hold her and pray she would come back to him.

* * *

At first, Æfre was unsure how long they'd lain by the fire—nor could she even recall where they were or how they'd come to be there in the first place. But when she shifted, trying to slip free of Osric's protective embrace and sit up a bit, her body reminded her all at once. Every movement ached with stiffness, every muscle protested. And if the angle of the late-afternoon sun was anything to go by, they'd been there at least a few hours.

Æfre adjusted Osric's cloak around her shoulders, its warmth and smell a familiar comfort, and looked over at the man whose legs were still tangled with her own. As she did, the day's events began to emerge with more clarity, and she realized that the man attached to that tangle of legs had very likely just saved her life.

She knew the signs well enough. Her mother had called it 'frost-cold sickness', and Æfre had seen it claim a few unfortunate souls in her time. Now, she realized it had nearly claimed her, too. The cold and shock from the attack had stripped her of her ability to process simple things—to make sound decisions. It was like she'd been swimming in a giant lake of honey, her movements and thoughts sluggish and incomplete.

HEART OF THE WILD GODS

Some healer I am, she thought, chiding herself silently.

Osric stirred beside her, sensing her movement, and his eyes fluttered open. As his gaze focused on her, realization dawned. "Oh, thank God," he exhaled, before pulling her into a crushing embrace, his arms wrapping tightly around her as he kissed her hair, her forehead, her cheeks, and anywhere else he could reach.

"You know, Lord," she said between kisses, her voice weak but tinged with mischief, "if your desire was to see me naked in a forest, it would have been far easier for you to simply ask."

Osric paused mid-kiss while he let her quip sink in, then threw his head back and laughed from deep within his chest. Æfre couldn't help but smile wider at the sight of it.

By the Gods, it's good to hear that laugh again.

She reached across his lap for a log and tossed it onto the fire, only to wince as pain flared sharply across her bruised back. The pot still simmered on the stones, half its water lost to evaporation. Her throat felt like sand. She used the cloak to cover the pot handle and removed the pot from the fire, allowing it to cool in the frosty air. As she did, the cloak fell from her shoulder, exposing her bare upper torso, and she felt Osric's eyes on her.

Before she even had a chance to readjust the cloak, Osric gathered her in his arms and pulled her back onto his lap, protectively re-wrapping her in his cloak. She was sitting astride him now, with him leaning up against the shed door, very little between them other than his thin wool braies—and she could feel that she was stoking his desire.

"Sorry," He grinned, wriggling a bit underneath her, "old habits."

Æfre giggled and leaned in, snuggling against his warmth. "I've missed you," she breathed. "And I'm sorry for my angry words in the stable." She nuzzled his neck, aching to draw him nearer still.

"You've no need to be sorry," Osric whispered back, his arms crushing her to him in a fierce embrace. You were right."

He held her tightly for a moment longer before releasing her. Then, he studied her, still covered in bruises, blood, and soot.

"We haven't spoken of what happened," he said quietly.

He held her face in his hands, gently turning her head from side to side before gently running his fingers over the marks on her neck and over the dried, matted blood in her hair, his jaw hardening at the sight of her injuries.

"We will," Æfre answered. "I'll tell you everything before we return to the burh. But now..." She sat straighter, stretching her back and gingerly rolling her neck. "Now I'd like only to sit a little longer. Everything hurts."

They remained entwined in each other's arms, the silence between them feeling almost sacred. But Æfre felt the truth press against her heart—that every move they made from this point on would likely pull them steadily apart.

As the sun dipped towards the treeline, reality called them back. Osric helped steady Æfre as she slipped back into her torn and bloodstained garments, handling them gingerly as though they might spring to life and lash out at her one last time.

They shared the last of the boiled creek water in silence before Osric stepped forward to help her mount. Her body ached from the ordeal, and she winced as she settled into the saddle. Without a word, Osric climbed up behind her, enveloping them both in his cloak. One hand held the reins, while the other rested firmly around her waist, steadying her.

As the gelding began its slow, careful walk through the forest, Æfre leaned back into him, finding comfort in his steady warmth. The quiet of the woods surrounded them like a cocoon.

"I'm ready to tell you what happened."

HEART OF THE WILD GODS

* * *

Osric walked Leo through the palisade gate just as the pale winter light was dimming over the frost-covered fields and thatched roofs. The quiet hum of the settlement was first broken by Cwenhild, who'd emerged from the hall carrying a basket of bread. She froze mid-step when she spotted Osric and Æfre approaching, her basket hitting the ground as she broke into a run, voice ringing out through the cold air.

"Cenric! She's been found! Lord Osric is back! She's been found!"

Cenric, who had kept vigil all afternoon, snapped his gaze toward the gates. He'd spent hours scanning the hills and conferring with the men who had been searching. Now, as he moved quickly towards the approaching pair, the relief on his face was palpable.

Relief soon turned to alarm as the couple drew nearer to Osric and Æfre and saw what a sorry state the healer was in.

"Æfre!" Cwenhild's voice cracked as she reached up and placed a hand on her leg.

Æfre's eyelids fluttered open. Her lips curved into a faint, weary smile. "All is well, Cwenhild," she murmured, "I promise you it's not as bad as it seems", her hoarse voice betraying her exhaustion.

Cwenhild's eyes brimmed with tears. "We thought—we thought..." The words faltered, her voice breaking entirely as she quickly brushed away her tears.

"She needs rest, warmth, and food," Osric said firmly, his voice low and commanding.

Cwenhild snapped back into action, wiping her eyes as she gestured toward her hut. "This way. Quickly. We'll take care of her."

Osric dismounted, his arm steady around Æfre as he helped

her down. She stumbled, a sharp wince crossing her face, but Osric caught her easily. As he handed the reins to Cenric, Æthelwod seemed to materialize in the doorway of the hall, his sharp gaze fixed on the scene unfolding on the green.

"I'll take him in," Cenric said, nodding toward the stable, his expression tight.

Æfre attempted to reassure them, her words soft but determined. "I'll heal soon enough, really. Just a little battle-worn."

"Don't argue," Osric replied gently, his eyes locking onto hers. "Let them look after you."

The murmurs rippled through the burh as more faces emerged from their homes, alerted by Cwenhild's shouts and captivated by the sight of Æfre's appearance and the protective tension that radiated off of their thegn.

Osric helped Æfre cut through the crowd slowly, with Cwenhild leading the way towards her hut.

Once they crossed the threshold, Osric allowed Cwenhild to take over. "You'll be well looked-after here," he told Æfre, though the weight of his tone revealed his deeper worry.

Cwenhild nodded, managing a faint smile. "Don't worry, Lord. We'll have her back keeping your nonsense in check soon enough."

Osric knelt by Æfre one last time, brushing her hand with his fingertips. "I'll be back in a while. Do as Cwenhild says." He held her gaze, a flicker of worry flashing behind his eyes as he stood to leave.

Outside, he rejoined Cenric near the stable. Æthelwod was still watching, his posture tense. Osric offered him nothing more than a curt nod before turning back to Cenric.

"What happened?" Cenric demanded, his voice low and strained as they walked.

"An attacker," Osric said grimly. "Outside her own hut." His jaw hardened, the anger from earlier again flaring to the surface. "I'll explain everything once we're inside."

As they reached the stable doors, Osric cast one final glance toward Æthelwod, who stood unmoving in the distance. Then he stepped inside, leaving the burh's stares behind.

21

Læderas ✗ Leaders

Cwenhild could hardly believe her eyes. "She ate enough venison stew last night to feed the fyrd for a month," she whispered, trying not to wake Æfre as she shuffled about the hut. "She's like a sack with a hole in it, the way I just kept pouring it in—I've never seen the like!"

Osric chuckled—he'd absolutely seen the like. Æfre's appetite had always been a legend unto itself—impressive for someone so slender, the woman could eat like a farmhand twice her size.

Cenric had taken himself to the hall for the night, leaving Æfre in Cwenhild's capable care. She'd warmed pots of water on the hearth to help Æfre bathe, and assisted her in coaxing the soot and dried blood from her tangled hair. By the time Osric had arrived back at the hut, he'd been relieved to find Æfre sound asleep, her face finally free of the strain and exhaustion that had marked it earlier.

Osric had settled into the chair beside her bed, her hand in his, his thumb brushing absently over her fingers as he watched her breathing deepen in sleep. Weariness must have claimed him then and there—the last thing he recalled was resting his head on the edge of the bed, still holding Æfre's hand.

Cwenhild, who herself had fallen asleep in her chair spinning wool, later told him she hadn't the heart to wake him, and he'd slept right there where he sat. At some point, Æfre must have turned towards him in her sleep—when Cwenhild had finally woken him, Æfre's free hand was resting on his head, her fingers unconsciously threading through his hair.

"Can I fix you something to take with you, Lord?" Cwenhild whispered, handing him a cup of small ale, which he gladly accepted.

"No, thank you, Cwenhild, I'll get something in a while," Osric murmured. Rubbing a hand over his face, he drained the ale in a single swallow and handed back the cup.

"She'll be well, Lord. We'll look after her."

"Of that I have no doubt, Cwenhild." Osric said, "I am more grateful than you know."

"Good. Now up with you—get yourself moving, Lord. And if you would send that husband of mine back here as well."

"Of course, Cwenhild."

She's right, Osric thought, *I need to get moving.*

There would be no room for quiet reflection today. He quickly gathered himself, cast a final glance at Æfre, who still slept soundly, and stepped out into the cold, pale morning.

* * *

True to his word, Godwin had presented a complete inventory of the misplaced goods discovered in the shed. Alaric's wife had etched it onto a wax tablet, which Cenric placed in Osric's hands once he'd reached the hall. His plan was to ride out to the trading camp, hoping to secure an audience with the Jarl, Torvald Ironsight. He would have preferred a more formal, measured approach, but the events of the past day had stripped away that luxury. This meeting needed to take place as soon as possible, preferably with as few witnesses as possible, given the circumstances.

Shrugging on his winter cloak and gathering his saddlebag, Osric stepped back out into the morning air. He had just rounded the side of the stable when he nearly collided with Bishop Æthelwod.

"Ah, Lord Osric—there you are! Good morning!"

The bishop's nasal, clipped voice was the very last thing Osric wanted to hear that morning—the very sound of it grated on his ears.

"Lord Bishop," Osric replied, his jaw tightening, worrying for a moment he might have actually said his last thought out loud.

"I thought to let you know," Æthelwod bloviated, "that I am bound for Aldhem this morning," Æthelwod drew out his pronunciation of Aldhem into *'Aaaaldhem'*, as if he were dangling bait, eager for Osric to inquire after his business.

"Very good, my lord," Osric said briskly, sidestepping slightly to indicate his intention to continue on his way to retrieve his horse.

Æthelwod paused, clearly waiting for a follow-up question that never came. "Yes..." he said, more invitation than affirmation.

"Well. I must be about the day's duties," Osric said, hoping to steer the conversation to a natural conclusion.

"Indeed," Æthelwod replied, his voice suddenly laden with suspicion.

"So, I shall bid you good morning for now, my lord, and perhaps we can catch up later." Osric offered a frosty smile, his hand reaching for the door.

Æthelwod wasn't finished, calling out to Osric as he attempted to leave, "I trust your friend the healer is recovering well from her ordeal yesterday, Lord Osric."

Osric froze, his hand still reaching for the door. Slowly, he turned to meet the bishop's gaze. "Yes, Bishop. She appears to have endured it well," he said evenly, albeit not entirely truthfully.

"How admirable that she yet endures," Æthelwod said smoothly, his voice dripping with falsity. "Let us hope that such an enduring nature will continue to serve her well, once her situation becomes more... complex."

The insinuation hung in the air like rotting meat. Osric spun on his heel and closed the distance between them in a heartbeat, the air from his wake still circulating around him as he stood just a little too close and addressed Æthelwod directly, looking him dead in the eyes.

"Do give my very best to Mistress Eadlin this morning," Osric said coldly, his voice both accommodating yet incendiary, glinting with a razor's edge of tempered steel.

Æthelwod's expression flickered briefly. He nodded, his voice remaining steady, yet betraying just the slightest undertone of unease. "Indeed, I will, Lord Osric."

Osric held him there for longer than was comfortable—long enough to see the bishop's confidence falter ever so slightly.

Today is the day the balance shifts, Osric thought, certain he'd just witnessed the bishop subtly, almost imperceptibly flinch—acknowledgment of a loss of control over the man he relied on to do his official bidding.

* * *

Torvald strode into the camp's hall at first light, looking for Svend. He was keen to organize the day and set the camp in motion. But his mind wasn't entirely on any of the tasks ahead—he was still thinking about the news from the previous evening.

Svend's attempt to secure a meeting with Wōdenléah's thegn had fallen short, though not for lack of effort. Almost as soon as Svend had arrived in the burh, they'd received word that Æfre, the healer, had vanished. They found the grey horse in the hills, bloodied and wild-eyed, its reins trailing as if it had fled something terrible. Osric, the thegn, had gone to search for her as soon as the news reached him.

The news of Æfre's disappearance jarred Torvald like an axe to a shield wall, leaving his thoughts scattered for the rest of the night. He had hoped it was only a rumor—the Saxons did seem to enjoy the dramatic, but no word had come since. The silence gnawed at him like a burr caught in a cloak, and he'd hardly slept.

HEART OF THE WILD GODS

By the time Svend entered the hall, Torvald had already settled at the long table, tearing away at a hunk of bread with some cheese. The Jarl glanced up at his second, offering a grunt and a nod of acknowledgment.

"Morning, Jarl. Sleep well?" Svend's voice was casual, but Torvald knew he wasn't expecting an answer.

Torvald waved the question away, his mouth too full to speak, but the meaning was clear enough.

Of course not.

Before either man could speak further, a warrior's voice rang sharp from the doorway.

"Jarl Torvald! The thegn of Wōdenléah is here. He asks for a private word!"

Torvald froze mid-bite, locking eyes with Svend in disbelief.

By Odin's favor, Torvald thought. Something had actually gone right this morning.

Torvald swallowed his mouthful of bread and barked, "Já! Let him in!"

Svend was already on his feet, quickly gathering his plate and cup. "We'll clear the hall for you, Jarl," he said, "I'll see you after."

On his way out, Svend turned to the handful of men scattered throughout the hall. "Jarl needs the hall! Everyone—out! Let's go!" he bellowed.

The men responded without hesitation, wordlessly grabbing what they could of their meals and belongings. Within moments, the hall emptied, the scrape of benches and muffled footsteps fading into silence.

Torvald gave a curt nod to Svend, his thoughts already shifting to the unexpected visitor. As Svend slipped out, the warrior guarding the door stepped aside, allowing Osric to enter.

Osric appeared in the doorway, pausing just long enough to exchange a brief but warm greeting with Svend as they passed.

With a warrior's stride, he approached the table where Torvald stood waiting. Osric's expression was calm and measured, but there was no mistaking the urgency in his step.

"Jarl Torvald," Osric began, inclining his head in a respectful nod. "I apologize for approaching you in this manner. It was my intention to arrange a more mutually convenient time and place for us to speak."

Torvald stepped forward, extending his arm. The two clasped forearms in a firm, warrior's greeting.

"It seems circumstances are outpacing my intentions," Osric added, his voice carrying a note of weary resignation.

Torvald studied Osric as they exchanged greetings. He had prepared himself to dislike the man rumored to share a bed with the woman who haunted his thoughts. He had dealt with plenty of Saxon noblemen over the years, many of them born into their titles—men who preened like peacocks and hid behind layers of aristocratic airs, leaving the actual labor of leadership to others. Yet Osric was not soft like those Saxon lords. He was a striking-looking man, although seemingly unaware of it; instead, he carried himself in a way that Torvald recognized—he was a man who knew the burden of command. Worse still, Torvald thought grimly, he struck him as the type who, under different circumstances, he might even come to like and respect, which really only served to make the situation all the more maddening.

"Lord Osric," Torvald replied, his deep voice steady, "it is good that we finally meet." He gestured towards the table, where the food was laid out. "Sit. Eat. And if you spare me a moment, I can provision us properly."

Torvald disappeared briefly into his accommodation at the back of the hall, and the sounds of shuffling and clattering objects rose from the beyond the partition. He suddenly reemerged, carrying a trencher laden with a fresh loaf of bread, salted butter, hard cheese, and smoked fish. In his other hand, he balanced a pitcher of ale and two drinking horns. Without a word, he poured the ale, handing one of the horns to Osric before settling back into his seat.

"The good stuff."

They ate in silence, the quiet thick with thought, until Osric lowered his horn and began.

"Jarl, I know I don't need to tell you there's an undercurrent of discord being sown here—both in the camp and in the burh." Osric's gaze held steady, watching for Torvald's reaction.

Torvald kept his expression impassive, though inwardly he was bursting to ask about Æfre. The whispers of her disappearance had gnawed at him since he'd first heard, but there was no chance he would let that slip now—certainly not in present company. He merely nodded, gesturing for Osric to continue.

"I also recognize," Osric said, "that apart from our trade relationship, we have no real reason to trust each other, particularly when you consider who it is that I serve. I've come here today to offer you everything I know, as a gesture of goodwill. There are many things seemingly all happening at once, and I believe time is running short. My hope is that we can work together to preserve peace and prevent unnecessary injury and loss—for both of our people."

Torvald simply nodded.

Acknowledging the rat Æthelwod straight away—a promising start, Torvald thought. He reached for more smoked fish, his appetite persistent despite the gravity of the conversation.

Osric didn't hesitate. "Over these last many weeks, I've witnessed dealings that have shown me that Bishop Æthelwod fully intends to instigate an uprising in your camp."

Osric paused for a moment here, as if to allow the revelation the appropriate gravitas while attempting to read the chieftain's expression, which remained neutral.

"His ultimate aim," Osric continued, "I believe, is to rally the burh to raise the fyrd against you—not just against the camp, mind you, but against the very presence of your people here in greater Wōdenléah."

Torvald stopped mid-chew, his eyebrows raised in surprise at having just heard the thegn speak aloud what he too suspected. If true, this was a bold stroke, and the chieftain allowed himself some expression for the first time since they sat down.

"This is against the wishes of your King Alfred, is it not?" Torvald asked, taking a sip of ale. "It risks plunging us back into conflict. It seems a breach of our treaty."

"It most definitely would be Jarl. I believe that Æthelwod's desire to drive out Norse influence entirely from the region is about control of the camp's trade operations. The bishop will, of course, make the claim of preserving law, order, and the purity of Christendom from heathen influence," Osric smirked, "but his interest is, as always, entirely self-serving."

Torvald felt his gut clench at the audacity of the revelation, and took another, longer draught of ale before responding.

"And you know this how?" he asked, his tone studiously neutral as he reached for another piece of fish, though with the new information, the thought of eating it now seemed less appealing. The scheme the thegn had supposedly uncovered aligned far too neatly with his own suspicions, though he wasn't about to reveal that just yet.

Osric explained how he'd overheard the cloaked man with a Norse accent in secret counsel with the bishop, discussing their plans to pillage and stage it to sow discord, as well as shipments being interrupted to stir suspicion.

He then paused and rummaged through his bag, producing the wax tablet with the rough inventory Godwin had prepared, scrawled in Saxon hand.

"Do you read writing in a Saxon hand, Jarl?"

"I do."

Osric slid the inventory across the table to the chieftain, whose eyes soon narrowed at the familiar items listed.

"These were all discovered yesterday in one of our tool sheds. My workers strongly deny any knowledge of the goods or how they arrived there," Osric explained. "And I believe them. They've never given me cause to doubt their loyalty. The timing of this is suspicious. Our most senior ceorl had been in there less than two days before the discovery. The goods must have been placed there within the last two days."

Torvald studied the list in silence, his anger rising as he recognized many of the items. If what the thegn was saying was true, the situation was far more urgent than he'd anticipated.

"There are connections here," Torvald said after a long pause, giving Osric some acknowledgment while still keeping a neutral tone.

Osric's expression remained composed. He clearly knew the game he and the chieftain were playing, and he'd come prepared.

"I understand all of this raises more questions than answers, so I'm going to give you more, Jarl."

Torvald raised a hand, stopping Osric before he could continue. Scooping up the empty jug, he disappeared briefly and returned with another full one. He poured them each another cup. "Seems to me we're going to need this," he said dryly, gesturing for Osric to continue.

Osric smiled and gratefully accepted the cup and began again, laying out the whole story—his arrival in Wōdenléah after the battle of Edington, the land grant contingent upon Æthelwod's oversight, and the bishop's machinations to force a marriage alliance solidifying his control in Wōdenléah while increasing his holdings with Aldhem."

Torvald listened, his interest sharpening.

"Of all of Æthelwod's skills, what he is best at is exploiting weakness," Osric continued. "Æthelwod knows of my...affections for someone other than the intended betrothed. He sees this person as an obstacle to his plans and has thus become a man determined to either lean on this obstacle to manipulate me or to remove the obstacle entirely."

Torvald's stomach tightened. "And who is this...obstacle?" he asked, hoping he did so with enough neutrality to mask the fact that he knew the answer already.

Osric took a deep breath before answering. "Æfre, the burh healer," he said, looking directly at Torvald. "We're familiar. For over a year now."

Torvald raised an eyebrow, meeting the thegn's confession with a flat stare. "Familiar. Are you lovers?"

"Yes," Osric said evenly, without flinching.

He'd looked Torvald directly in the eye as he said it. The truth of it was, the admission stung—sharper than Torvald expected. He had expected to get a bit of satisfaction out of watching the man squirm a bit, yet the Saxon thegn's candor, his laying-bare of pride and weakness alike—there was a strange honor to it. A warrior's gesture, like a blade to one's own chest, and the man was currently bleeding openly across the table from him.

"Æthelwod has known about us for some time," Osric continued. "He's been using that knowledge to poison the burh against Æfre with accusations of heresy, witchcraft—the usual nonsense—and I'm afraid to say it has worked. Most everyone in the burh has either witnessed her mistreatment or participated in it."

Torvald nodded grimly, having himself witnessed it firsthand.

Osric's voice dropped, anger simmering just beneath the

HEART OF THE WILD GODS

surface. "Lately, every time Æthelwod feels the need to remind me of his authority, he does something to Æfre. It started small, but yesterday, everything changed. Yesterday, she was attacked, brutally, at her own homestead. Her horse spooked and bolted. A boy from the burh found it wandering the hills, covered in blood."

Torvald leaned forward sharply. "Blood!? Is she alive?"

"She is," Osric answered, weariness etched deep. "Only because I found her, wandering, injured, and in shock. She fought hard—cut him with her seax, nearly bit his ear off, and put two arrows through his shoulder. The blood on the horse was his."

Torvald's anger flared, but it was tempered with an odd pride, and he fought the urge to smile.

Fierce as a shieldmaiden.

"He's escalating, Jarl, and she is in danger."

"As are you, by the sound of it," Torvald replied, leaning in slightly. The thegn was circling the point, and Torvald could sense where this was leading. Yet, he refrained from steering the conversation, waiting to see if Osric would make the ask on his own terms.

Osric waved off the implication of danger to himself with a dismissive gesture. "This is entirely my fault. I brought it to her doorstep. It was I who pursued her, and it was I who was entirely naive about Æthelwod's true capabilities..." He allowed the thought to trail off, gathering himself again before continuing, his voice lowering.

"But there's a reason I bring this up. Æfre saw him—the attacker. Shoulder-length dark brown hair, shorn at the sides. A full beard. Spoke your language."

"You just described most of the men in the camp," Torvald said dryly.

Osric half-smiled as he reached into his saddlebag and pulled out the torn, bloodied cloak and broken Fenrir brooch, placing them on the table.

Torvald's eye instantly snapped to the items, "These are his?"

"They are, Jarl. I found them myself while searching for her."

Torvald's jaw tightened as he turned the brooch in his hand. It was unmistakably Norse. One of his men had indeed done this.

"May I keep these?"

"Please," Osric replied, gesturing for him to take them.

Torvald's mind worked furiously. Æfre was attacked mere miles from where he and his men sat, oblivious. He now felt like this was deeply personal. This was no longer just a matter of trade agreements or inter-community discord—and the timing was certainly no coincidence either. He set the brooch down and leaned back in his chair, the quiet weight of the moment settling heavily between them.

Torvald knew it was time to give the thegn something back. "Lord Osric," he began, "You have given much. In return, I'll give you this—the healer will not be harmed again. She's close by—it will be no trouble for us to ensure her safety. My most trusted men will take care of it. I will select them myself."

Relief flickered across Osric's face. "You have my thanks, Jarl. I recognize too well that my efforts to shield her from this have fallen short."

Torvald waved off Osric's self-reproach, although he agreed with it internally. He paused a moment before continuing.

"I will share with you and you alone that we have known for a while that there is at least one who has been whispering dissent into our ranks over the past few months. We have not yet identified this person, but we will. I have always suspected Æthelwod to be at the root of it, but it has been difficult to prove. I also believe that an alliance between us is not only beneficial but necessary."

Osric nodded. "Agreed, Jarl."

"Because of what you've shared," Torvald continued, "we

should be able to identify the man on our end swiftly. I suspect the one who attacked Æfre is the same man you overheard with Æthelwod—and it is not a stretch to guess perhaps he's the one sowing whispers in my camp."

"Agreed," Osric said again, reaching for a handful of fish.

"So that leaves us really with what we plan on doing about it." The chieftain shifted in his chair and focused on a spot on the wall, deep in thought. The two men sat for a moment, each winding their thoughts around the situation they found themselves in, drinking their ale in silence.

"Shutting down a movement gradually sown from whispers could prove difficult," Osric said. "That damage is done—there are those who will choose to follow Æthelwod, no matter what. He has his true believers."

"And we can't be certain when he might act," Torvald said, nodding in recognition of the situation's complexity. The two men sat in silence for a moment, contemplating each other and their predicament, each searching for the loose thread that might unravel Æthelwod's scheme.

Finally, Osric spoke, his voice low and thoughtful. "Æthelwod needs me," he said. "I train the men. I command the fyrd. He holds ultimate authority, and he knows me well enough to understand that I would never raise the fyrd under false pretenses. He also needs me to make this marriage match with Aldhem." Osric trailed off, the beginnings of a strategy forming as he spoke.

"So killing you is not an option—at least, not at this moment," Torvald said bluntly.

Osric gave a bitter chuckle, "No, not at *this* moment anyway." He drained what remained in his drinking horn. "But, he would send me away—temporarily replace me with someone he felt less likely to question his authority."

"And this is your way in," Torvald said.

"*Our* way in," Osric corrected. "Yes. You know as well as I, Jarl, battles are never fought by one man alone. I fought with several men elevated to similar positions as myself after Edington. I would need to obtain the blessing of our king, but I believe we might use old alliances to steer this rebellion. Perhaps even rid ourselves of...a larger problem."

Torvald met Osric's steady gaze, resisting the grin that threatened to curl at the edges of his mouth. An unspoken plan was crystallizing between them. One tactician to another, both recognized the audacity of the gamble laid before them, and it was going to require every ounce of trust they could muster.

"So, we let the rebellion happen," Torvald said, his tone edged with wry amusement.

Osric met the chieftain's gaze, his tone calm and resolute.

"Yes. We let it happen."

22

Sōcn ✕ A Visit

Bishop Æthelwod reined in his horse sharply in front of the hall at Aldhem, the animal tossing its head in protest at the taught reins and the abrupt pinch of the bit. The bishop muttered unintelligibly under his breath as the horse jolted him to an abrupt stop.

The summons from Wynnflæd, matriarch of Aldhem, had left him little choice but to endure this indignity. He detested riding—horses were filthy creatures, leaving hair and dust on his fine robes and the smell of animal tainting his skin. Æthelwod much preferred the wagon, where he could ride apart from the filthy creatures. But that morning, Cenric had been repairing the wagon's wheel, leaving him no choice but to straddle the snorting brute like a common soldier.

He slid off the horse awkwardly—more awkwardly than he would have liked— and thrust the reins into the hands of an amused ceorl standing nearby. Without so much as a glance at the man, the bishop smoothed his robes and cloak, ignoring the trail of horsehair clinging stubbornly to the hem. There was no point delaying further; he knew precisely why Wynnflæd had called for him.

The tale of what had transpired the previous day—the attack involving Æfre and her subsequent rescue by Osric—was already making its rounds through the hearth fires of Wōdenléah, if not all of northeastern Wessex by now, undoubtedly growing more fantastical with each breathless retelling. Æthelwod had little doubt Lady Wynnflæd would want to discuss how the incident might affect Aldhem's precarious position, particularly with the announced betrothal of Osric and Eadlin on the horizon. A scandal now could unravel months of careful planning, and he had no intention of letting that happen.

He took a moment to look around him, taking in the details of his surroundings. Aldhem was a study in mediocrity; a tableau of deferred maintenance and quiet decay. Indeed, it had potential—rich soil, sprawling fields, but a lack of leadership was reflected in every sagging roof and overgrown path. Unlike Wōdenléah, which had flourished under the leadership of their new thegn, Aldhem had clung to outdated ideals of the past and had become trapped in the self-made mire of stagnation after the fighting at Edington had ended.

Æthelwod allowed himself a private sneer. The blame for Aldhem's decline was easy to place. The noble departed Lord Aldhem, may he rest in peace, had been a man who clung to the hierarchy of the past like a barnacle, sharply resisting change at every turn, even while the village crumbled around him. His refusal to accept Osric's offers of assistance, whether it be workers, defense training, or anything else, had begun as a source of mild frustration, and later turned into a tragic misjudgment for his family.

Æthelwod sneered again as he recalled Lord Aldhem's final act of obstinacy; the blade of a Northman at his throat during a summer raid, his wife pleading for reason, and the fool refused to part with a few pieces of silver. The owner of the blade was thusly inspired to take Lord Aldhem's head instead.

A *poor trade, by any estimation*, thought Æthelwod.

Now, his widow, Wynnflæd, presided over the ruins of his gross mismanagement. Æthelwod suspected she was no more capable than her late husband, and she was most definitely equally proud. But the critical difference was that where Lord Aldhem had been proud and inert, Lady Wynnflæd was proud and desperate. And desperation, Æthelwod mused, was something he could work with.

He took a deep breath, steeling himself for his performance ahead. The church, by which he really only ever meant *he himself,* would soon be in a position to offer Aldhem some very much-needed, very mandatory guidance. Aldhem was like unformed clay, and he, the potter, was ready to form it into his preferred shape. But first, everything had to fall into place without delay.

Pushing open the heavy doors of the hall, Æthelwod glided in like a serpent. The smell of wood smoke and damp met him—the distinct undercurrent of disrepair. Wynnflæd stood waiting in the center of the room, her hands clasped tightly before her, her expression a mask of impatience barely concealing her anxiety. Behind her, seated next to the fire, was a pale and uncomfortable-looking Eadlin.

"Ah, Lady Wynnflæd! The very vision of dignity, if ever there was one!" Æthelwod swept into the room with expertly timed grace—a man skillfully playing his role. "Your strength, dear lady, is the pillar upon which this noble house stands."

His hawkish gaze flitted across the room, landing on Eadlin, who sat by the fire, looking unnaturally pale against the heavy, dark wood of the chair she sat in.

"And Eadlin, the heart of this blessed alliance between Aldhem and Wōdenléah," Æthelwod continued, his tone obsequious. "What an absolute joy to find you here!"

Eadlin offered a thin smile, one that barely touched her lips, and nodded, shifting uncomfortably in her seat. Æthelwod's sharp eye did not miss the stiffness in her movement, but he filed the observation away.

Wynnflæd, never one for subtlety, dove straight to the matter at hand. "Bishop Æthelwod, I shall not waste words this morning. As you might imagine, recent events have given me much to think about—the complexities of the upcoming union between my daughter and Lord Osric weigh heavily on a mother's mind, and it would be no exaggeration to say that certain recent developments out of Wōdenléah have cast a shadow over the joy of our preparations."

Æthelwod inclined his head solemnly, his expression a careful blend of sympathy and assurance, but before he could reply, Eadlin's voice cut through the tension.

"Bishop Æthelwod, won't you please come sit by the fire?" Her tone was light, overly so, an exaggerated politeness that did not escape him. Æthelwod recognized it for what it was—an attempt to undercut her mother's brusque approach.

"Indeed, I would, Eadlin. Thank you." He moved swiftly to take the offered seat, positioning himself directly across from her, allowing himself to study her further. Yes, it was as he suspected. Eadlin appeared to be unwell—her pallor too ashen for the glow of youth, her movements hesitant.

Wynnflæd, however, seemed oblivious to her daughter's discomfort. "Of course, Lord Bishop, your presence is always welcome. You must forgive me my directness," she said, pulling up a chair of her own and folding herself into it, sighing deeply with the choreographed poise of a woman accustomed to public performance. "Outwith this betrothal, I find myself forever beset by an endless stream of sudden winter repairs to the hall."

Æthelwod dipped his head graciously, his voice becoming more saccharine with each word. "My dear Wynnflæd, there is nothing to forgive. We are all as God has made us. The season's demands weigh heavily on every household, and none more so than this one. It is a fact not lost on me. Why, it is nothing short of miraculous that one so burdened with the trials of such a significant holding and the demands of an impending union could retain any semblance of composure—let alone embody it so gracefully."

The bishop's honeyed words earned a demure flutter of Lady Wynnflæd's lashes. Still, across the fire, Eadlin let out a sharp and

HEART OF THE WILD GODS

inadvertent scoff before immediately turning it into a cough. The sound caught Æthelwod's attention, and his gaze turned hawkish, fixing on her momentarily before catching himself and returning his attention back to Aldhem's matriarch.

"My Lord Bishop, however pleasant, your flattery is unnecessary," Wynnflæd said, her words accompanied by a smile as she turned to her daughter. "Eadlin, will you not offer Bishop Æthelwod some refreshment?"

For a fraction of a second, darkness crossed Eadlin's expression, her politeness faltering ever so briefly, making it abundantly clear to Æthelwod that she wanted nothing less than to rise from her chair. Yet she pushed herself up, her movements stilted. "Lord Bishop, may I offer you some refreshment? A small glass of mead, perhaps?"

Æthelwod immediately brightened at the mention of mead. "Well, certainly as long as it is indeed a small glass, I can find no harm in refreshment. In fact, to decline such a thing as a small glass of mead—not *too* small a glass, mind you—such a thing could be considered a slight to the generosity of the Lord God Almighty, for mead is not merely for refreshment, but a golden hymn of praise to His abundant gifts."

The bishop paused for effect and, in doing so, noticed that Eadlin was struggling. Before she had fully risen from her chair, she'd faltered, her hand darting out to grip the chair, her lips tightening as she forced herself to stand straight once more before walking stiffly away to fetch the mead.

"Eadlin," Æthelwod said, leaning forward slightly, his tone tinged with the perfect balance of concern and authority. "You seem to be in some distress. Is all well? Something you have not told us?"

"It's nothing," Eadlin replied softly, returning to the hearth with a small pitcher of mead and two glasses in hand, her movements sluggish and tentative. "Only a very minor injury—I was clumsy at the loom. It will heal." She poured the mead carefully, as though she felt the eyes of the room upon her.

"Really, Eadlin," Wynnflæd interjected with a dismissive wave of her hand, "these dramatics will do you no good. As you told me yourself this very morning, it was but a small thing, and you will recover soon enough. Unless of course you have misled me as to the nature of your injury..."

"An injury?" Æthelwod pressed, his brows furrowing in a rare moment of actual concern. "Have you summoned a healer? Injuries can fester, my dear. Even the smallest wound may grow into something grievous if neglected."

"It is nothing," Eadlin repeated as she set the pitcher down, leaning on it for a moment to steady herself. "Some proper rest and I will be fine."

"Precisely," Wynnflæd echoed briskly. "There is no cause for panic."

Æthelwod hesitated, then leaned back in his chair with a sigh, adopting the expression of a man reluctant to press a point but compelled to do just that. "Lady Wynnflæd, Eadlin," he began, his voice solemn, "as much as it pains me to keep saying so, any such wound that causes visible discomfort must be tended to at once. Eadlin's health must be preserved! The Yule feast is nearly upon us—mere days away now—and it will be a most joyous occasion! A celebration not only of the season but of the imminent union of Aldhem and Wōdenléah!"

Wynnflæd's expression tightened, her cool gaze meeting Æthelwod's. "My Lord Bishop, you aren't suggesting that I summon the healer Æfre, surely. That is simply out of the question."

Æthelwod inclined his head, his tone measured, yet insistent. "Dear Wynnflæd, the eyes of the region will be upon us. Even the simplest details must reflect strength in our alliance. I understand your hesitation, given the sensitivity surrounding the

HEART OF THE WILD GODS

healer's...*friendship* with Lord Osric. However, I can assure you that Æfre's remaining time in Wōdenléah is limited, and she will pose no threat to this union. Surely her skills could be employed discreetly—perhaps under the cover of night, if that would ease your concerns."

At that, Eadlin looked up, her pale face creasing with confusion. "Lord Bishop, what do you mean when you say Æfre's remaining time in Wōdenléah is limited? Is she planning to leave?"

"She will be leaving, yes," Æthelwod stated flatly, realizing he'd already said too much and offering no further explanation.

"No matter," Wynnflæd's voice cut defiantly through the room. "Bringing Æfre here would invite scandal and fuel the very gossip we seek to avoid. There are other ways."

Æthelwod opened his mouth to reply, but Wynnflæd pressed on, her tone sharpening with every word. "I do not argue your point that strength in our unity is of the utmost importance, Lord Bishop, but I must remind you that the cost of this alliance falls heaviest upon my daughter. With the landscape of this agreement ever-changing, I now see that I must insist that the terms of our arrangement reflect the totality of that sacrifice."

God Almighty preserve me, this woman is shameless, Æthelwod thought, suppressing the momentary flash of anger rising within him, though truthfully he wasn't exactly sure whether to be appalled by Wynnflæd's audacity or impressed by it. Deciding on the latter, he masked his distaste with a faint, approving smile.

"Your shrewdness does you credit, my lady," Æthelwod said smoothly. "Perhaps there is room to discuss additional...assurances. But let us not lose sight of the larger picture. This union is not merely a marriage; it is a cornerstone of stability for the region."

Eadlin stirred in her chair, her voice soft but resolute. "These are grand claims indeed, Lord Bishop. As for the affections of my betrothed, I have no illusions—I have made peace with that. I am prepared to do my duty for my family and our house. But I would ask you both plainly, how does one expect stability from a union where the foundation is cobbled from mollified appearances?"

Wynnflæd's patience snapped. "Eadlin, enough of this. Such matters cannot change what must be. Our family cannot risk any more scandals or societal whispering. A broken betrothal would be ruinous. This marriage must proceed, and with dignity. People do not measure a union by divine covenants, regardless of what the Lord Bishop might say—and forgive me my impetuousness, Lord Bishop Æthelwod—but it is true. People judge first and foremost by appearances. And if this alliance falters, for any reason, our family will face ruin."

"My dear Wynnflæd, Eadlin–" Æthelwod expertly steered the conversation back to Eadlin's mysterious injury. "Your daughter's well-being is of the highest importance. I trust you will see to this with the same wisdom and fortitude you have displayed so admirably throughout these delicate proceedings."

"It will be handled, Lord Bishop. You have my word," Wynnflæd replied, her tone clipped but composed.

"Excellent," Æthelwod conceded, his expression grave yet faintly approving, "and perhaps we can discuss the finer details of our arrangement after tomorrow's service. There is always room for refinement in such matters, after all."

Satisfied that his message had landed, Æthelwod drained the rest of his mead and turned his attention to Eadlin, his gaze softening with an air of paternal care that he absolutely did not feel. "My dear Eadlin, please do take care. You are, after all, the very heart of this noble endeavor. Worry not, for a bond such as this, though forged in duty, will only strengthen with time. Together, you and Lord Osric shall bring honor to your families and to the Almighty Himself. Trust in this, my child: the Lord sees the fortitude with which we bear our burdens, and He shall bless your steadfastness in due course."

Eadlin's lips pressed into a thin line, her reply cool and flat. "Indeed, Lord Bishop. Would that it were so."

Æthelwod did not falter at her doubt-laden response. Instead, he allowed himself a thin, knowing smile, the kind that suggested patience with those yet to see the larger picture.

Rising at last from his chair, he decided to end his visit with the final word of a prayer. "May the peace of the Lord dwell within this house, and may His guidance light your path."

Without waiting for a reply, Æthelwod swept from the room, his robes and cloak billowing behind him like a cloud of smoke as he strode purposefully towards the door, away to collect the detestable beast who'd brought him there.

His thoughts, however, did not linger on the well-being of those in the house, or even on the undignified ride back to Wōdenléah. His mind was fixed only on the many delicate threads of influence he was weaving. The seemingly failing health of Eadlin was certainly an unwelcome development—a snag in the woven fabric of his design. If left unchecked, it could unravel his carefully laid plans. He would have to remain vigilant.

23

Fær ✕ Journey

"Everything's ready, Lord Osric," Cenric said, his voice soft but steady. "The gelding's tacked, provisions bagged, and Svend will meet you just outside the gate after the evening meal. Word from Beornwic is that Lord Wulfric will join you on the road as you pass by."

Osric felt a familiar warmth at the mention of Wulfric's name. A steadfast brother-in-arms, Wulfric and Osric had fought side by side on the bloody fields at the Battle of Edington. Unlike so many others who had inherited their positions and titles by birthright, Wulfric was among the few families with hereditary holdings along the Thames who still held their ancestral lands.

The aftermath of Edington had been unforgiving. Many noble families broke under its weight—their members perished either in war or the ensuing raids that followed. In many cases, their lands were confiscated by King Alfred and granted to men who were more loyal or capable. Such had been the fate of Osric's noble-born predecessor—ultimately, his treachery had sealed his disgrace for eternity.

When Guthrum's army was finally defeated and driven back into what became the Danelaw, Wulfric's father handed the thegnship to his son, confident in the younger man's strength and integrity. Wulfric had more than lived up to that legacy, his unwavering commitment to the realm securing both his place and the continued trust of the king.

"Thank you, Cenric, my friend," Osric said sincerely. "Again, if you do run up against any issues, send a messenger to Beornwic. The ealdorman will assist."

Leaving the burh in such a stealthy manner had meant Osric

couldn't cover his own absence, and the thought of it, even for such a short time, left him deeply unsettled. It was, however, the only way forward.

"It's my privilege, Lord," Cenric replied, "Don't you worry about us. We've got tomorrow's hunt split into staggered parties, so we will not leave the burh too depleted of fighting men—just in case. Now you go and enjoy your meal. You'll see me in the hall once Svend arrives and we've adequately diverted the bishop—he'll not notice you leave, Lord. You have my word."

"Cenric, may you receive the Good Lord's bounty for the next few days' hunting. I'm sorry to miss it."

"Thank you, Lord, but no need to involve the Almighty when you'll be right there by my side the entire time," Cenric winked.

"How right you are," mused Osric. "Then I suppose there's no need for me to remind you to make sure you bring back enough game for a Yule feast fit for a road-weary thegn, a few of his men, and an entire burh, since, as you say, I'll be right there with you the entire time."

Osric gave Cenric a good-natured slap on the shoulder and started off towards the hall.

"That's right, Lord Osric," Cenric boomed, more loudly than necessary, making sure that any and all within earshot might hear him. "I'll be seeing you tomorrow morning for the beginning of the hunt. Got a feast to prepare for! May the night hold you safe, and sleep come easy, Lord!"

Osric chuckled softly, shaking his head as he raised a hand in farewell without turning back.

"See you in the morning, Lord!" Cenric shouted.

Still grinning, Osric made his way towards the hall, his mind already consumed by the trip ahead of him.

He'd known going into his meeting with Torvald Ironsight that he was going to need an audience with the King. The alliance with

HEART OF THE WILD GODS

the Norse chieftain provided the unified front required to stand against a man as powerful as Æthelwod, whose plot seemed darker to him with every passing day.

The audacity of it filled him with a quiet, simmering rage. That a man who claimed to serve God and kingdom—whose very life Osric and Wulfric and the rest of their men had saved on the battlefield at significant cost—how this man could brazenly threaten the kingdom they had fought for was beyond his comprehension. Such actions risked the security of the entire realm, all for personal gain. There was no other word for it. This was treason.

The journey to Wintanceaster would take just under a day's hard ride. With the Yule feast only a handful of days away, and Æthelwod ever watchful, time was of the essence—they needed to move swiftly, under the cover of night.

Traveling after dark was always a risk—the roads were fraught with danger, from opportunistic bandits to the treacherous terrain—but Osric trusted the men accompanying him. Each was a seasoned warrior, and together they could face whatever the journey might bring.

Now, there was little else to do but wait.

Osric stepped into the warm glow of the hall, the scent of roasted meat wafting to meet him. He would take his meal, perhaps exchange a word or two with some of the people, and then await Cenric's signal. Soon, they would ride for Wintanceaster—and it most certainly was going to be a long night.

* * *

"Svend!"

Bjørn's voice rang out, urgent and clear, cutting across the camp as he jogged from the hall to catch him before he reached the gate.

Svend drew on the reins, his horse shifting beneath him. He

turned in the saddle, brows raised.

"I'm glad I caught you," Bjørn panted. "Svend—I think I found him!"

Adjusting himself in the saddle, Svend nodded at Bjørn. "That is excellent news, Bjørn. But—" his eyes narrowed, "you think? Or you know?"

Bjørn dipped his head in acknowledgment, his expression serious. "I think," he said. "Not verified yet, but I believe it's the Dane who calls himself Leif, if that is in fact his true name. I've been watching the men, like you said. He is one of two who have bought a new cloak from Old Inga today, and I think he's hiding injuries like those you described."

The smile faded from Svend's face as his brows knit together.

Leif.

How have we overlooked him?

"Jarl Torvald should be back any time now," Svend said, "he'll be pleased to hear this news—as will the thegn." Svend paused, taking up the reins. "For now, do nothing. Just your normal routine. Jarl Torvald will decide how he wants to handle this."

Bjørn nodded briskly. "Understood. Go under Thor's protection, Svend," he said as he turned back towards the hall to await the chieftain's return.

Svend gave Bjørn a final nod before pressing his heels into the horse's flanks, and the animal moved into a steady trot, its hooves striking the packed earth in a slow, rhythmic clop that carried into the cold evening air.

The news had come none too soon. Knowing the man who had harmed Æfre—and who had likely tied himself to Æthelwod's dark scheme—had been among their ranks this whole time gnawed at Svend, and it was clear it weighed every bit as heavily on Torvald.

As if in answer to his thoughts, a rider appeared in the distance—the great black horse unmistakable.

HEART OF THE WILD GODS

Torvald.

"Jarl Torvald," Svend called, a sly smile spreading across his face. "A restful late afternoon?"

Torvald shot him a wry look, shrugged, then held up a stringer of three very small fish—his expression a combination of exasperation and amusement.

"It did give me time to think."

Svend's grin widened. "That's quite the hoard! You'll have to share the harrowing tale of how you managed to wrestle them from the river when I return."

Torvald let out a low huff.

"Jarl," Svend let the humor fade from his tone, "Bjørn thinks he has identified the attacker. The chieftain's head snapped to attention at the news. "He believes it was Leif."

Torvald was silent for a moment, weighing the name. "Leif," he muttered. "Fairly new to us. How did we not see this?"

"I've been asking myself that same thing, Jarl."

"And Bjørn—he's certain?" Torvald asked.

"Fairly," Svend admitted, "he'll come to you as soon as he hears you're back."

Torvald's gaze grew distant, his mind already moving ahead. Then he fixed on Svend once more and gave a single sharp nod. "Good. Travel safe under the Gods' care, brother. We'll drink together when you return."

"Indeed, Jarl."

The two men shared a final nod before urging their horses in opposite directions, the rhythmic clatter of hooves echoing along the ever-darkening road.

* * *

Osric rounded the palisade, the night air sharp in his lungs. He wore his cloak hood pulled low, the heavy wool masking the quilted tunic and sword hidden beneath. Beyond the gate, just out of sight, Svend waited astride his horse. The animal shifted restlessly, its breath puffing small clouds into the cold night.

Osric gave him a curt nod—a silent summons. Without a word, Svend touched his heels to his horse's flanks and fell in behind him. They rode in silence until the last light from the burh flickered out of sight. Once the shadows of the forest wrapped snugly around them, Osric finally drew back his hood and slowed his pace, allowing Svend to ride up beside him.

"Svend, good evening," he said with a grin, his tone warm despite the gravity of their mission. "You have my thanks for joining us and representing the camp, and my apologies for all the secrecy. Considering who we're dealing with, I thought it best to move with as few eyes on us as possible."

"Lord Osric, I'm glad to be of service," the Northman replied, a glint of amusement in his eye. "I won't lie—there's a certain satisfaction in knowing this alliance might finally give us the strength needed to pry out this rotten plank for good." He chuckled lightly. "The secrecy only makes things more interesting—a welcome change from camp routines."

Osric nodded, his smile tinged with understanding. He knew that restlessness well. Both of them—like so many of their kind—had once defined themselves in the clash of shields. Now their changing world demanded diplomacy, stratagems, and an endless supply of patience. Every bit as necessary, but rarely as satisfying.

"Well said, Svend," Osric grinned. "Then let's not waste any time. If we ride steadily, we'll meet the road from Beornwic within the hour. Wulfric will be waiting."

With that, they urged their horses onward, the rhythmic cadence of hooves blending into the quiet murmur of the night as they disappeared into the dark.

HEART OF THE WILD GODS

* * *

As promised, Wulfric was waiting at the junction. At first, Osric and Svend didn't spot him; he had dismounted and settled against the broad trunk of an oak, hidden in the seam where the moonlight met the shadow of the forest. His horse was tethered and obliviously grazing nearby.

Osric and Svend slowed their mounts to a walk as they approached the junction, their eyes scanning the dim road ahead. Suddenly, out of the silence, a creaking, troll-like voice rose from the darkness.

"Answer true, or turn away—three riddles guard this road today!"

Svend turned his head sharply, hand on the hilt of his sword, his expression a mix of confusion and alarm. He glanced over at Osric, unsure whether to laugh, bare his blade, or flee.

But Osric only threw his head back and let out a full-throated laugh.

"Hello, Wulfric," Osric called into the void, his voice thick with amusement. "I see the wait hasn't dulled your wit."

"I must be losing my flair," came the reply as Wulfric stepped out of the shadows, a sly grin lighting his face. "Although the riddle is usually most effective when I can utter it from under a bridge."

Wulfric looked every bit the Saxon nobleman he was. His dark blonde hair and beard were neatly trimmed, and a finely woven cloak hung from his shoulders, fastened with a brooch bearing his family's insignia—a match to the ring he wore on his right hand.

Osric swung down from his mount, and the two men embraced like warriors, gripping shoulders and clapping each other's backs.

"It's good to see you, Wulf," Osric said sincerely. "I'm grateful for your help."

"Come now, Osric," Wulfric replied, his voice warm as he

stepped back to clasp his old friend's shoulders. "That never needs saying. Of course, I'll help. And besides, it's been too long for two sworn brothers living a mere ride apart." He studied Osric for a moment, his grin softening. "You look well, Os. I'm glad to see it."

"I am well, Wulf," Osric replied, then gestured to Svend, who had dismounted and was watching the reunion with quiet curiosity. "Lord Wulfric, meet Svend, overseer of trade at the camp at Wōdenléah, our trusted trading partner."

Wulfric turned to Svend with an outstretched hand, clasping his forearm in a firm grip. "Of course! It's an honor to meet you, Svend. A friend of Osric's is a friend of mine."

"The honor is mine, Lord Wulfric."

"Well then," Wulfric said with a playful smirk as he stepped back into the shadows to retrieve his horse. "Shall we waste no time? The sooner we start, the sooner we accuse a bishop of treason."

Svend chuckled in approval of Wulfric's irreverence.

Osric groaned good-naturedly as Wulfric reappeared on horseback, leading his stallion onto the road.

"Said as plainly as that," Osric muttered, "the full weight of it feels somehow heavier."

"Then let us lighten the burden by doing the deed," Wulfric said, his grin undeterred. "Come, friends. The road awaits, and the King must hear what you have to say."

***

The heavy doors of the hall groaned open as Torvald stepped inside, the brittle night air rushing in behind him, curling around him like the fingers of a frigid phantom. He shook off the cold, eyes sweeping the smoky warmth within. The hearth blazed, casting writhing shadows on the timbered walls. Men crowded near the fire, horns of ale in hand, their laughter rising above the low murmur of voices.

Bjørn was already watching him. The young warrior slipped through the throng and handed him a full ale horn.

"Evening, Jarl Torvald," he said, voice dropping low. "I—"

"It's all well, Bjørn," Torvald cut in, firm but quiet. He lifted the ale, wetting his lips before continuing, "I met Svend on the road. He told me. Was it the brooch that gave him away?"

Bjørn nodded, relief flickering over his features. "Já. Not many like it in camp. Folk notice such things. He's there now—blue tunic." His eyes flicked toward the hearth, where Leif sat laughing with a group of merchants, his long dark hair half-pulled back but spilling enough to mask his ears. His left arm lay tucked in his lap, his horn raised in his right.

"Have you seen any wounds?" Torvald asked

"No, Jarl, I've had no reason to get close enough."

Torvald nodded, taking another sip while he studied Leif from afar. The man had similar hair to his own, though he was shorter and slighter in stature.

A bold choice, to be hiding in plain sight like this.

"Good work," Torvald said quietly to Bjørn, while his gaze swept the hall. "Does anyone else know?"

"Just you, me, and Svend."

"Good. Keep it that way." Torvald drank deep, eyes once again narrowing on Leif. "Tomorrow morning, we take a hunting party. Select men only. All of those you've marked—none you haven't. Leave him," he jerked his chin subtly toward Leif.

"Understood, Jarl."

"Good. I still have a few things to attend to tonight, so let's get started. Keep sharp, be ready to follow my lead."

"Yes, Jarl."

Satisfied, Torvald handed Bjørn his empty ale horn and moved in the direction of the hearth, where the men greeted him with cheers and offers of their seats, which he declined with a wave of his hand. "I'll stand," he said, moving among them with casual authority. He grabbed a large jug of ale and poured refills, laughing at their jokes, sharing a few hearty slaps on the back, slowly working his way closer to Leif.

After the contents of his ale jug were spent, Torvald sent one of the men off to fill it before shouting over his shoulder.

"Bjørn!" What's this I hear about you torturing these good men with Saxon riddles!?"

Torvald caught Bjørn's eye and saw the instant flash of understanding he was hoping for.

Grinning broadly and raising his ale horn, Bjørn called out, "Aaah! Very well, everyone, you heard it! The Jarl wants a Saxon riddle!"

The hall erupted in groans and protest, but Bjørn pressed on, undeterred.

"No! Listen! Listen! You'll like this one, I swear! A new one! I just learned it!

The room went quiet as Bjørn launched into his riddle.[xiv]

> A curiosity hangs by the thigh of a man, under its master's cloak.
> It has a hole in the front.
> It is stiff and hard and it has a good standing-place.

The hall erupted—men swatted each other, some jeered, and others thrusted their hips obscenely. Ale sloshed as Torvald wove among them, his jug replenished, clapping shoulders, refilling horns, his path leading him to a spot directly behind Leif as Bjørn continued dramatically.

> When the man pulls up his own robe above his knee,
> he means to poke with the head of his hanging thing,

that familiar hole of matching length which he has often filled before.

"What am I?"

Ale was splashing everywhere as the men, now well-lubricated with drink, shouted out their guesses.

"A dagger!"

"A jug!"

"Bjørn's tiny cock!"

The hall erupted in laughter, and Bjørn milked the moment, holding up his hands dramatically before delivering the punchline, watching and waiting until Torvald was standing directly behind Leif.

"The answer," Bjørn finally shouted, "It's a key! It's a key, you filthy bastards!"

The men groaned, pelting him with bread crusts, ale, and insults.

Torvald's laughter boomed above them all. "Bjørn, that was the worst one yet!"

Seizing his moment, Torvald clapped Leif on the back—firmly, just over the man's left shoulder. His hand lingered, pressing down subtly, just long enough to feel Leif's muscles tense as he fought against a noticeable surge of pain. As he did, his hair moved away from his left ear, revealing an inflamed and swollen injury.

"Am I wrong, men?" Torvald shouted, giving Leif another squeeze, then a firm slap this time feeling the stiff press of bandages beneath wool. Leif recoiled with a sharp breath, his skin paling, sweat beading along his brow.

Torvald's face never betrayed the discovery; his laughter rolled on with the others. But his eyes locked across the hall with Bjørn's.

The message passed without words.

Yes. We have our man.

Torvald lingered in the hall among the men a while longer, enjoying the laughter and another horn of ale before rising to his feet. The night was still young, but a task remained—one that had been crowding his thoughts since midday. Catching Bjørn's eye just as the younger man launched into another of his ribald riddles, Torvald gave him a brief nod, then turned and exited the hall. The hall's warmth and noise gradually fell away as he stepped into the cold, heading for the paddock where he'd left his horse.

24

Gæst ⚔ Visitor

The better part of the day had evaporated before Æfre finally found the will to rise. A familiar calm settled over her as her eyes scanned her disheveled hut. She was glad to be home again, free from the weight of others' stares when they saw her in her current state.

The hearth fire had gone cold in her absence, and even with it roaring again, it had taken most of the day to chase the chill from the walls of the hut.

Cenric had driven her home in the wagon with Epona in tow, trotting lightly behind them and tossing her head as they jostled down the frosty road. As uncomfortable as the journey was, Æfre was grateful for the wagon—spared having to sit Epona's brisk and bouncy trot with a chest full of bruised and cracked ribs.

She smiled faintly as she recalled Cenric telling her, with no small amount of glee, how he and a stable hand had sabotaged the wagon that morning to keep Æthelwod from claiming it for his journey to Aldhem. They had removed a wheel and made a great show of repairing it. Æthelwod was a notoriously poor horseman, so every chance Cenric got, he enjoyed forcing him into the saddle.

Despite his stoic exterior, Cenric harbored a mischievous streak that had been the source of some of the most ingenious pranks Æfre had ever witnessed. Today of all days, she was profoundly grateful that he had unleashed his hidden talent to her advantage.

Even so, his concern for her had been unmistakable. Though he tried to hide it, the worry etched onto his face as he drove her home was impossible to miss, and it hardened into anger as he pulled up to her hut and saw the remnants of the attack. The blood on the ground beside the paddock. The word *wicce* carved into her door. True to form, Cenric said nothing, but his hands were tense and his jaw set as he untethered Epona and led her to the paddock—no words were needed.

Æfre was thankful that he hadn't needed to go into the burnt-out livestock shed—she thought that he might have just bundled her back into the wagon and taken her back to the burh if he'd seen anything more that had unsettled him. Quite frankly, she was more than ready for a bit of solitude.

Cenric had also surprised her with another basket of provisions, tucked under a blanket in the wagon's bed. She knew it was Cwenhild's doing—a gesture meant to bypass her pride.

Æfre felt a pang of guilt as she thought about the first basket, likely strewn across the hillside after Epona had spooked. She couldn't keep relying on their generosity, especially knowing that at least some of the items in that basket were likely from the burh's overwintering provisions.

They'd found her hut in a sorry state—broken clay jars strewn over the floor, most of her ale poured out, and her leechbook had been left lying face down on the earthen floor, missing a few pages.

She cleaned the mess while Cenric secured Epona in the paddock, but the moment he'd finished and saw the wreckage for himself, he'd ordered her to sit and rest herself while he took the broom from her hands, efficiently completing the job himself.

Now she lay stretched out on her bed, studying the beams of the ceiling as she waited for the hearth to heat the water she'd set to boil. She had finally seen her reflection in that pot of water, and it had shocked her to her core. Her eye, though less swollen than before thanks to Cwenhild's careful ministrations, was a livid, angry reddish-purple, the bruise now creeping down her cheek—as if someone had overturned an inkpot onto her face. Her split lip throbbed with a dull, persistent ache that made eating and drinking a trial, and every breath she took made her chest feel as if it were pressed between a smith's tongs.

Worse still were the marks she hadn't been aware of—the ones she kept discovering. She had menacing bruises on her neck, perfectly matching each finger of the hands that had gripped her, and tender, mottled patches across her ribs and back after being slammed down onto the frozen, rock-strewn ground. She now understood why Cwenhild had flatly refused to allow her to see her reflection or describe her injuries to her—seeing herself in this state was like adding another wound to an already overabundant supply.

Æfre could hear the water in the pot boiling, and she forced herself upright so that she could gather her ingredients for the salve she planned on making to help soothe and heal her bruised and aching body. An involuntary *'oof'* escaped her as she hoisted herself up, her body objecting to the activity, ribs seizing and back spasming in protest as she shuffled stiffly over to the shelves that housed her herbs.

The familiar activity steadied her. Here, among the tools of her craft, she was in control. Here, she could focus on the work of mending herself, one simple step at a time.

As she worked, heard Epona in the paddock, pacing back and forth and snorting—Cenric had tossed a generous amount of hay into the paddock before he left, so she wasn't hungry—something else was agitating her. Removing the pot from the fire, Æfre cracked the wooden window covering, then immediately froze, gripping the wall to steady herself.

The Northman.

The man in the dark cloak.

He stood just outside the paddock, not far from her door. He stood at an angle to her, his head looking towards Epona. He hadn't spotted her—yet.

His hood was raised, concealing most of his face, but the tip of a dark beard and a few strands of hair peeked out from beneath the fabric.

For a moment, Æfre couldn't move. Her ears rang with the deafening roar of her rushing blood, feeling every bit of the raw aftermath of yesterday's attack in every part of her body.

He'd come back.

Her mind flashed to the look he'd given her as he'd staggered away—a look that carried a dark, unspoken promise to return and do worse. A shiver ran through her as she realized with sickening certainty that she would likely not survive a second encounter with this towering warrior, a man whose skills were undeniably forged by raids and battle.

Breathe Æfre, breathe.

Her hands shaking, she drew several deep breaths, fighting for control. She would have to act quickly if she were to stand a chance.

A few more breaths, and she felt her panic give way to something deeper, more rage-fuelled.

Enough of this.

Adrenaline dulled the ache of her battered body, allowing her to forget it at least temporarily as she reached for her bow. Quiver slung across her back, she readied an arrow and moved to the door, threw it open, and stepped out into the icy air.

Æfre aimed low and loosed an arrow, which just whizzed past the man, narrowly missing his groin before embedding itself into the paddock fence post with a *thwack*.

"Þú!" Æfre screamed in Norse, advancing with another arrow ready. "Why have you come back here!? Leave! If you mean to kill me, know I will adorn you with more arrows before you're through!"

The man froze, his head now angled down towards the arrow embedded in the post, his face still obscured by his hood. Slowly, he raised his hands in surrender, still staring at the arrow.

HEART OF THE WILD GODS

"Are you alone!?" Æfre demanded, looking over her shoulder, hoping she wasn't being drawn out into a trap.

The man was silent for a moment, still staring incredulously at the arrow that had come a hair's breadth from his manhood.

"I ask again, Northman, are you alone!?" Æfre demanded.

"Æfre, I am not here to harm you." A deep voice with a Norse accent resonated from under the black hood.

Æfre stood stunned for a moment, her bow still at the ready.

"Who are you?" This was not a voice she recognized, and she hesitated, not yet prepared to lower her bow.

"Æfre, I am Torvald Ironsight, from the trading camp. I'm going to take off my hood now. Just, don't shoot me...again."

Torvald stepped forward slowly, pulling back the hood to reveal a rugged, angular face framed by dark hair and a trimmed beard. His eyes, a startling hazel, met hers with a steady intensity.

Æfre's grip faltered slightly on the bowstring as her mind worked to reconcile what she was seeing. This wasn't the man who had attacked her. He was taller, broader, and carried himself with confidence, not malice. He was also absurdly handsome, a ridiculous thought she immediately cursed herself inwardly for—so utterly pointless and infuriating that her mind would even notice such a thing at a time like this.

Æfre lowered her bow slightly so that it was no longer pointing directly at Torvald's chest.

"I've seen you before. Wait...*Jarl* Torvald Ironsight? The chieftain?" She asked.

"Já."

The adrenaline that had propelled her drained away, leaving her trembling and lightheaded. She finally allowed the bowstring to slacken and lowered the weapon completely, though now annoyance flared to fill the void left by fear.

"You're dressed exactly like him," she said curtly, her annoyance plain as she chucked the unspent arrow back into the quiver with a resounding *thunk*.

"Like who?"

"You're dressed exactly like the man who attacked me yesterday." She enunciated impatiently, as if she were speaking to a petulant toddler. "I could have shot you!"

"You *did* shoot me!" Torvald shot back, gesturing indignantly to the arrow embedded in the fence post. "What if you hadn't missed!?"

"I didn't miss. That was a warning shot," Æfre snapped, limping past him to retrieve the arrow from the post.

Torvald stared at her, incredulous, but whatever retort he was about to make died on his lips as she stepped into his view and he finally got a better look at her face. His expression shifted from one of annoyance to something softer—concern, perhaps even regret.

"A splendid sight, is it not?" She said quietly, noticing the change in his expression and not wanting to meet his gaze. She tried to melt into the frozen soil beneath her.

"Lord Osric has clearly been to see you, Jarl. Why don't we talk inside?" Æfre straightened her dress around her shoulders, as much to cover her bruises as to keep out the cold.

Torvald hesitated, then gestured toward the paddock. "Æfre, if you're up to it, I'd like you to walk me through what happened out here first—before it gets any colder."

"Of course. Let me fetch a shawl and put up my bow." Æfre said.

"Of course," Torvald gestured, "especially the bow."

Æfre finally forced herself to meet his gaze, a mischievous glint flaring behind his eyes that unsettled her in a way she was not expecting. She turned stiffly to walk back into the hut, stifling the smirk that threatened to form as she spoke over her shoulder to him. "Don't let yourself get too comfortable, Jarl. I still have my seax."

"That is marked," he said wryly.

* * *

"How do you speak my language?" Torvald asked as they walked towards the bloodied patch of ground near the paddock where she'd fought off her attacker. His voice was calm, almost conversational, but there was a sharpness in his gaze as he studied the scene.

"My father was a Dane. From Jelling," Æfre replied simply. "I speak your language poorly, I fear."

"Not so poorly, I think," he said, stealing a brief glance at her.

She didn't reply, but instead began recounting the events of the attack, starting with the moment she'd first spotted the man's horse tied to her fence. Her words came haltingly at first, but as she went on, the story poured out with unsettling clarity.

She described the encounter in painstaking detail—more detail than she'd even given to Osric. Perhaps it was because Torvald wasn't a lover, someone whom she might feel compelled to shield from the rawness of the truth. There was no need to temper her words, no need to consider how they might spark some rash, misguided act of vengeance.

No, the Jarl was more than capable of handling the full weight of the story, and that inspired her to keep talking. When she reached the part where the man had ripped her dress, Torvald abruptly stopped and faced her. His expression darkened, his jaw tightened as his eyes locked onto hers with an intensity that made her pulse quicken.

"Did he...were you..." His voice was low, but he faltered, as though the words themselves were too vile to speak.

"If what you're trying to ask is if I was violated Jarl Torvald, the answer is no," Æfre said plainly, meeting his gaze, "but only because

I surprised him when I cut him with my blade." Her tone was flat, pragmatic, though her trembling hands betrayed her as she spoke the words aloud for the first time. "It was a narrow escape," she said, unsteadily. She looked away for a moment, trying to regain control.

Torvald exhaled the breath he's been holding, the tension in his shoulders easing slightly. He marked her struggling, closing his eyes for a moment, dipping his head as if to give her a moment of privacy while she collected herself.

As she finished telling her story, Torvald listened to her intently, missing absolutely nothing as she walked him step by step through what had happened. His sharp eyes missed nothing—not a splatter of blood in the frozen grass, the fletching from the broken arrow, or the scuff marks in the hard-packed ground where she'd struggled. He knelt at one point, tracing a deep groove in the ground with his fingers, as though the story of her fight were a part of the earth itself.

Æfre felt exposed under his scrutiny, as if he could see straight through her words and into the dark places inside her soul where even she herself rarely dared to look.

They were leaning against the paddock fence when Æfre finally finished recounting the events. Epona, ever the opportunist, bobbed her head between them, shamelessly nibbling at the chieftain's cloak and nudging his shoulder for scratches.

"She likes you," Æfre noted, amused by her mare, who typically completely ignored strangers, yet was now lavishing attention on the man who had been the source of her great alarm less than an hour ago.

"I like her too," Torvald replied, his large hand rubbing behind Epona's ears, "She seems a steady beast."

"She is indeed." Æfre smiled faintly, watching as Epona leaned into his touch, thoroughly ignoring her in favor of this new, apparently irresistible friend.

HEART OF THE WILD GODS

Torvald's tone shifted. "What about the fire? Can you show me the livestock shelter?"

"Of course. It's just here." Æfre pushed herself off the fence, momentarily forgetting about her injuries. Her ribs suddenly sent a jolt of pain through her upper body and back, taking the wind out of her, and she stumbled.

A powerful arm caught her around the waist, steadying her before she could hit the ground.

"Careful," Torvald said softly, his voice a mix of concern and restraint. His arm remained firm around her as he watched her face, his brow furrowed. He gave her a moment to allow the pain to pass.

"Oof, thank you. I'm sorry, I keep forgetting—it's this way." Æfre smiled sheepishly at him and led the way to the front of the livestock shelter. As she moved away from him, she felt his hand linger on her lower back, steadying her.

"I actually haven't been in here since it happened," Æfre said softly as she reached the shed door. She yanked open the door, which cracked and groaned loudly on its hinges, releasing a plume of straw dust, ash, and the overpowering, acrid smell of old fire.

They stepped into the shed, their eyes adjusting to the dark interior. Torvald immediately noticed her charred winter cloak at its center.

"What is this?" Torvald indicated the cloak, crouching down to inspect it.

"That is—*was*, my winter cloak. I was wearing it and used it to smother the flames when I discovered the fire. It was burning too fast and too hot to get to the creek for water."

Torvald picked up the scorched fabric, rolling it between his fingers. The scent of singed wool lingered in the air as he studied the extensive char marks on the walls, rafters, and the thatch of the roof. His fingers brushed the grit of ash embedded in the fur lining.

"This would not have been an easy fire to put out like this." He observed, casting her a sidelong glance.

"No, it was not."

"Are you burned?" He asked, still holding the cloak and looking up at the ceiling.

"No. Well, maybe—in a few places but not badly." Æfre looked at her hands and arms—she honestly hadn't even given it a thought until now. Sure enough, she had a few burns here and there, and she vaguely remembered Cwenhild dabbing honey on bits of her arm and hands, but it was certainly nothing like what could have happened.

"Must have been a good cloak." Torvald mused, a faint smile at the corner of his mouth as he stood again, leaning on one of the charred support beams, drumming his fingers in thought.

"It was," Æfre said, almost wistfully. She'd loved that cloak.

They were quiet for a moment, save for the chieftain's drumming fingers, when a faint rustling sound came from the rafters directly above him and a bit of stray dust floated down, settling on Torvald's cloak—though he didn't seem to notice. It was followed closely by another, slightly louder rustle, and then a falling handful of dust and ash, and then a larger chunk of thatch.

Æfre looked up and realized that the rafter beams they were standing directly under sagged precipitously, one of them actually was completely split where it had been charred, and the thatch was drooping in a way that she couldn't recall seeing before. It appeared to be getting lower as they stood there, with bits of thatch now raining down consistently in larger and larger clumps.

"Jarl Torvald..." she started

"Hmm?" Torvald had been deep in thought; hearing his name had brought him out of it.

A fair amount of thatch once again rained down upon them, causing Torvald to look up this time, just as a loud cracking sound cut through the shed.

HEART OF THE WILD GODS

"Jarl! The roof!"

The fire-damaged section of the roof gave way with a deafening crack, sending a cascade of thatch, splintered beams, and debris tumbling down. Torvald moved instinctively, twisting mid-leap and hooking Æfre by the waist, shielding her with his body. They hit the ground hard, crashing into the straw near the shed's wall, with him lying on top of her.

Dust and straw mushroomed around them in a choking cloud as Torvald braced himself, trying to hold his weight off Æfre as best he could while struggling to free his trapped foot from a heavy clump of debris.

"Æfre," he asked urgently, "are you hurt?"

She coughed, feeling every battered and bruised part of her body all at once, fighting to regain the breath knocked out of her. She waved away the straw tickling her nose and squinted up at him. His face was so close she could see the smudges of soot on his cheek, little bits of ash sticking to each individual beard hair. She noticed he smelled faintly of juniper.

"No, I don't think so. Well, no more than I already was. Are you?"

"No."

For a moment, they just lay there, inches apart, face to face, frozen in the absurdity of their predicament.

Torvald shifted his weight and a large clump of thatch fell off of him and onto Æfre's forehead, which he gently brushed off.

"Sorry," he said, then awkwardly wriggled his foot free. Æfre watched as his hazel eyes lingered on hers, as if he were about to say something—but then he seemed to think better of it, eased himself off of her and collapsed into the straw beside her with a groan.

They both lay in silence, staring up at the jagged hole now gaping in the roof, coughing and catching their breath as the dust settled. They could hear Epona's whinnies at the sudden noise, the crunch of her hooves resonating against the frosty ground. Through the gap in the roof, the sky came into sharp focus; a vast expanse of inky black-blue dotted with stars. Wispy clouds drifted by like fleeting thoughts, illuminated by moonlight, barely forming before they dissolved again.

Torvald finally broke the silence, his voice deadpan. "Your Saxon hospitality is truly unmatched."

For a moment, Æfre said nothing, still processing everything that had just happened. The absurdity of it all—the collapsing roof, her shooting an arrow at his groin, and now the two of them sprawled out in the straw, stargazing through a giant hole in what was her shed roof—it hit her all at once. She let out a sharp snort of a chuckle, and they both soon dissolved into fits of laughter.

"Ow—ow! Stop!" Æfre pleaded while clutching her ribs. "My ribs—I can't! Please stop!" But her pleas only made them laugh harder. They lay there, side by side, giggling like two children who'd tumbled into mischief.

When the laughter had finally settled, they once again lay there, taking in the night sky through the gap in the roof.

"It's really kind of nice," Æfre said.

"Já," Torvald agreed, his voice low and calm. "Peaceful."

"Perhaps I should leave it be." Æfre mused.

He turned his head to look at her and frowned slightly, reaching out to touch her exposed collarbone with the tips of his fingers. "You're bleeding."

"Am I?" Æfre brushed her fingers across the spot he'd indicated, frowning at the streak of bright red that came away on her hand. "Just a scratch, I think. I'll live."

They remained where they were for a moment longer, silent, as if the night itself had granted them a temporary truce from the chaos. But eventually, Torvald pushed himself up with a groan, shook himself off, and extended a hand toward her.

"Come. We should move."

Æfre waved him off with a wry smile. "I think I'm better off right here. Just throw some straw over me—I should keep till morning. Surely, to be felled like this twice in as many days—"

Before she could finish her jest, Torvald bent down and, without hesitation, scooped her up as though she weighed nothing. "Up," he said firmly as she let out a pained groan. He set her lightly on her feet and steadied her as she swayed. A hand remained at her waist until she found her footing.

"I'll have some of my men attend to this roof before the weather changes," he said, his tone brooking no argument.

"Thank you, Jarl. Truly," Æfre replied, her voice softer now, the gratitude genuine. She gestured toward the house. "Come, let's finish this talk by the hearth."

She limped stiffly toward the door, without turning, and said to him, "I hear the ale calling, Jarl. I think I might still have an unbroken jug. Don't make me drink your share."

Torvald followed, his eyes fixed on her as they made their way back to the hut.

25
Hæftling ⚔ Captive

"Not far now, men," Osric said to the group, "Best we find a place to stop and rest the horses—try to catch a few hours of sleep before making the final push with the sun."

"A wise move, my friend," Wulfric said, and Svend readily agreed.

The road to Wintanceaster was unnervingly still—oddly so. Even the sound of the horses' hooves seemed muffled by the frost. Each of them had remarked on it in turn as the darkness pressed in around them like a suspicious stranger who stands just a bit too close.

Soon, the road opened alongside a broad, flat field with a creek cutting through it. Osric drew up, and the others followed, sighing with relief as they slid from their saddles. They set to work in silence, removing tack and hobbling the horses so that they could graze and water.

Svend produced his flint and steel, and without a word, built the fire. Soon the fire blazed and the three of them were warming themselves under a crisp, clear night sky—a spray of stars dotted around a silent, frosted landscape.

The provisions came out next, and despite what Wulfric referred to as "the ungodly hour," the three of them ate heartily as if they were at a high feast: dried venison, hard cheese, a bladder of ale, and a small clay pot of butter to accompany a dense barley loaf that Cwenhild had baked especially for the road. Within moments, the only sounds to hear were the crackle of flames and the quiet sound of chewing as each man disappeared into his inner world.

When they had nearly finished, Osric reached into his bag and produced a cloth-wrapped bundle, presenting it to his companions with dramatic flair. Within the folds of the linen lay three generous slabs of Cwenhild's famed Yule honey cake.

The sight of the cake caused Wulfric to throw his hands in the air in celebration.

"Osric, you always had a gift for boosting morale!" Wulfric declared as he wasted no time in reaching across both men to scoop up his share, abandoning his noble-born manners as he stuffed half of the massive, sticky chunk into his mouth.

"Thven, haff you hadth thith!?" Wulfric was barely intelligible as he tried to speak to Svend with his mouth full of cake, eyes rolling back with delight.

Osric chuckled, shaking his head at his friend while Svend wasted no time eagerly licking the butter off his fingers and claiming his own slice of cake, taking a bite big enough to rival Wulfric's.

"By the Gods," the Norseman groaned, eyes rolling with pleasure as he swallowed his first bite, "they'll be serving this in Valhalla, I swear it! Perhaps I need to take a Saxon wife!" He laughed as he took another massive bite.

Osric laughed outright at the sight of them: two warriors, fierce battle-hardened men, undone by a hunk of cake. He made a note to remember to tell Cwenhild of her triumph over both Saxon and Norse warriors with a single slice of cake.

"A wife!" Wulfric exclaimed in mock horror, "Good God, Svend, no need to do anything so rash as that!" An exclamation that set Svend sputtering, nearly choking on his cake.

"You see, Svend," Osric began, himself speaking through a massive bite of cake and gesturing with the remains of it, "Wulfric here was ever the champion of the unwed."

"It's true," Wulfric agreed, swallowing his last mouthful with a grin.

"*Was?*" Svend's sharp eyes glinted as he licked honey from his fingers.

"Ah, very astute, Svend. He *was*." Osric laughed, then turned to Wulfric with an arched brow and a sly glance at Sven, relishing calling out his friend's lighthearted matrimonial hypocrisy.

"Tell me, my brother-in-arms, how does dear Edrys keep?"

Wulfric groaned good-naturedly. "Ah, Osric, how quickly you betray the reputation I've so carefully cultivated over the years." He chuckled, shaking his head. "But since you've asked, she is well. *We* are well. And, as it happens, we are quite with child."

"You devil!" Osric roared, clapping his old friend on the back, his laughter cutting through the night air. "Congratulations to you both! Hours into the journey, and only now do you speak of this!?" He beamed at Wulfric, then gave him a shove.

"Congratulations, my new friend," Svend added, raising his ale horn with a wide grin. "May the Gods bless you with many sons."

"Like I said," Wulfric replied with a smirk, "I have my reputation for wīf-gemædla, or I'd have mentioned it sooner." He winked and drained a long pull from his horn, a wide grin etched across his face.

"Wīf-gemædla," Osric said to Svend, "that's our way of saying—"

"For inspiring the wrath of a woman," Svend interjected with a knowing grin, "a noble pastime indeed."

Ale splashed out of horns as all three men erupted in laughter.

As the laughter ebbed, Svend gazed thoughtfully into the fire. "I was once betrothed," he began, his voice softening. "Aina—a shieldmaiden. Beautiful—and deadly. I used to make her *furious*, and I loved every moment of it."

Osric felt a quiet pang in his chest as Svend's mood softened. The Norseman's wistfulness struck a chord that resonated deep within Osric's buried grief.

"She was lost at sea," Svend continued, his gaze distant. "On a trading journey from Staraya Ladoga. She was not originally supposed to come—a handful of the shieldmaidens came along at the last moment to assist the trading party, mostly wives, partners. Three ships set out, only one returned."

"A storm?" Wulfric asked, his voice soft yet heavy.

Svend nodded. "Violent, sudden. Out of nowhere. I would have gone over myself, but Torvald—Jarl Torvald now, as you know—he caught my leg. But Aina..." He exhaled, shaking his head, "I never even saw her go over."

Osric stared into the fire, which popped little plumes of sparks into the night sky. None of them spoke for a while. Osric felt the familiar ache stir in his chest—Leofwynn's memory pressing close. He saw in Svend's eyes the same hollow absence he carried within himself.

"We all have lost something in all this," Svend murmured at last.

Osric nodded slowly. "Indeed," he murmured. "Apparently, God has other plans."

The silence deepened as the three men sat listening to the fire crackling until Wulfric cleared his throat. "Osric," he said insistently, "Since we're speaking of betrothals, I've held my tongue long enough. I'm afraid I can no longer bear the suspense. What's this I hear about a betrothal to Aldhem?"

Osric groaned, leaning back as if the weight of the question had physically struck him in the chest. He let out a long exhale before explaining. "It's true, my friend," he sighed. "I find myself in the most intricate mess—entangled in a snare set in part by my own hand."

"Surely not, Osric." Wulfric scoffed as Svend leaned in with interest.

"Get comfortable," Osric said, "I see no rest for any of us until I've told the tale."

HEART OF THE WILD GODS

At their urging, Osric told them everything: of Æfre, of her beauty and wit, her skill as a healer, how she had attended him after the death of Leofwynn, and of her family's resistance to be brought into the Church. He recounted the snares laid by Bishop Æthelwod; whispers of heresy, the forced betrothal, the cruel attack upon her only days past. His voice became raw with anger, then leaden with guilt.

"This sounds to me more like a love story than a mess," Svend said.

"I agree, Svend," Wulfric said, "Osric, do you love this woman?"

"Yes." Osric didn't hesitate. "But I'm afraid it's not that simple. Æthelwod has turned much of the burh against her," Osric said, voice low with bitterness. "I see now she may never be free in Wōdenléah—nor safe." He dropped his head, guilt darkening his features as he stirred the fire with a stick, sending sparks hissing into the night sky. "Each day she suffers some new slight—even from those whose lives she and her kin have saved, whose children she's brought into the world…" He faltered, his words trailing off into the crackle of the fire.

"Oh, my brother," Wulfric said, rubbing his eyes, "this is indeed a mess. What will you do?"

Osric let out a lengthy exhale before answering. "Old friend, I don't honestly know. For my part, my fate is sealed—I have a sworn duty to the crown and, of course, the church, but Æfre asked for none of this. It was I who brought all this to her doorstep, yet I see no way to truly ensure her safety where she can live free."

There was a silence as the men all sat, considering Osric's dilemma. Finally, Svend broke the silence.

"The Gods do not rush, my friend," Svend said. "When the time is right, they will set your path before you. Until then, all we can do is prepare." Svend stood from the fire and reached out to collect the empty ale horns.

"The day will come fast. You two thegns sleep first." Svend said in a tone that brooked no argument. "You stand before your king tomorrow. I take the first watch."

Osric opened his mouth to object, but Wulfric cut him off. "No, he's right, Os. Tomorrow's too important for anyone to fall on his sword." He turned to Svend. "Thank you, Svend, we will."

* * *

Svend crouched by the campfire, feeding it a few small sticks to keep the flames alive without creating too much smoke or light. His eyes narrowed, focusing on the treeline, trying to pierce the darkness beyond the flickering glow of the fire. Every rustle and snap seemed amplified, and he strained to pick out anything that felt out of place—each instance measured for threat.

When he'd sent the two thegns off to sleep, Svend had already decided he wouldn't wake them until dawn. The two Saxons had the more challenging task the following day, and Svend saw his role clearly—to guard the camp while they slept. They'd need their wits sharp when they made their case to their King, and a few hours of deep, uninterrupted sleep could mean the difference between success and failure.

The two of them had slipped quickly into a deep sleep, their soft snores rising into the night with the embers of the fire like an offering to the night sky.

Svend listened to the sounds of the night for a while before shifting his attention to his weapons. Pulling a whetstone from his bag, he splashed a bit of water onto it, soaking it before pressing it to his sword's edge. He worked methodically, dragging the stone along the steel with careful, measured strokes. Each pass was quiet enough not to disturb the others, though rhythmic enough to fill the stillness with peaceful purpose.

Svend's thoughts drifted again to Aina—they always did when

he was tending his weapons. He could almost see her again, lit by the firelight, her sword in her lap, sharpening her blade more swiftly and efficiently than he ever could. She would always finish first—a point of pride—then she'd grin and down the last mouthful of the ale in *his* horn before dragging him off to bed. She loved to irritate him by denying him the day's last mouthful of ale.

Always in a hurry, my Aina, he thought. *What I would give to scold her for it again.*

A breeze rolled lazily across the clearing, stirring the dead, frosty grasses and sparse branches before ebbing away again. It carried with it the faint rustle of movement—a small animal, perhaps a hare or fox, scurrying through last season's underbrush.

A sharp crack in the distance, too weighty to be a hare, suddenly made Svend's fingers tighten around the whetstone. For a long moment, it felt like the nearby forest held its breath with him.

He slipped his sword back into its scabbard and tucked the whetstone back into his bag. Rising, Svend stretched his arms and back, the quiet stiffness of a long night on watch settling into his muscles. The horizon lightened in earnest now, the faintest hues of pink and orange creeping into the sky like strokes off of an artist's brush.

Then he saw it.

A shadow hovering near the treeline caught his attention. It was out of place—darker, denser than it should have been.

Svend stopped mid-stride, breath hitching as his warrior's instincts sprang to life. He focused on the shadow, holding his breath entirely as if the noise of breathing might somehow interfere with his ability to see what was in front of him. The shadow seemed almost to watch him back, and Svend reflexively dropped his hand to the hilt of his freshly sharpened sword.

Silently and deliberately, he moved closer, each step calculated. But the shadow refused to resolve itself. It seemed to wait, watching him as much as he watched it.

Then, it moved.

It was subtle at first, an almost imperceptible shift, like a held breath released. Svend's grip on his sword tightened. He glanced quickly around, scanning the clearing for signs of movement, an accomplice perhaps, maybe even an ambush, but there was nothing else. Just the shadow.

It moved again, this time unmistakably.

A man.

The gait was deliberate, purposeful, closing the distance with a quiet confidence that set Svend's teeth on edge.

"Hold there!" Svend unsheathed his sword in one smooth motion. "Name yourself!"

The shadow continued to advance silently, details beginning to emerge in the soft glow of dawn. The shape of a cloak, a hint of a face—but there was still too much shadow to see clearly.

Unwilling to let the figure come any closer unchecked, Svend raised his voice.

"I said hold, you! Osric! Wulfric! Up!"

He needed the two of them to awaken, *now*.

"Here, Svend." Osric's voice was calm and measured, coming from just behind him. The thegn had awakened instantly at the sound of steel being drawn.

"What's this?" Wulfric uttered at Svend's other side. Like Osric, he too had awakened instantly, still rough from sleep but alert, sword already in hand.

The three of them instinctively spread out, forming a crescent perimeter in front of their camp.

"Identify yourself, man!" Wulfric barked, his tone carrying the edge of command.

The shadowy man finally halted and raised his hands, one gripping a heavy sack.

"Drop the sack!" Svend barked.

The man complied without argument, letting the sack thud onto the ground.

"Now kick it to me!"

Again, the man obeyed, nudging the sack forward.

"Remove your sword," Svend ordered.

The man exhaled audibly, as though this was all a minor inconvenience. With a deliberate slowness, he unbuckled his belt and slipped the sheathed sword from his side, tossing it toward Svend, who kicked it over to Osric.

"I am but a fellow traveler," the man said, his low voice smooth but unconvincing. He took another step forward, finally stepping close enough for them to make out his features.

"I said hold there!" Svend barked. He studied the man for a moment, noting the contradictions in his appearance. He was massive—a giant of a man with shoulders that looked like two boulders. His hair hung dirty and ragged, his beard patchy, and his cloak and tunic filthy and worn, the hem darkened with stains that Svend was certain were blood.

"What business have you here, hiding in the shadows?" Svend demanded, his eyes narrowing as he pieced together the puzzle of the man before him.

"As I said, Northman," the man replied, voice even, "I am but a weary traveler. I've run out of food and hoped for your kindness—a morsel by your fire, a cup of ale, perhaps." He spoke smoothly, but his slow, deliberate steps forward betrayed his intent. His unblinking gaze locked onto Svend like a predator circling its prey.

"Not another step!" Svend barked, raising his sword a fraction. "One more, and we make you food for the ravens!"

"There are weapons in the bag!" Osric called, his voice sharp. He had overturned the sack, revealing its contents. "Two seaxes, a hatchet...also a pair of coin pouches, and a gold ring and silver brooch!"

"Where did these items come from?" Wulfric demanded, looking at the man.

The man said nothing, his eerie calm unbroken. His slow advance continued, his cold, unfeeling smile unnerving.

"Wulf, look at this!" Osric said, kneeling to retrieve the man's sword without taking his eyes or his blade off of him. He tossed the sword to Wulfric, who caught it in one hand. "That's King's Guard."

Wulfric's gaze darted to the sword, its intricate hilt confirming Osric's observation.

"Look at his ankle," Osric said grimly.

All three of them saw it at once—a chain. Its links were bent and battered, and the jagged end spoke of a forced escape. The man had stuffed the chain into his shoe, but it had slipped free, glinting faintly in the morning light.

"A prisoner," Svend said, his voice low and firm.

The man's lips curled into a cold smile, his eyes darkening further—a gathering storm cloud ready to burst.

"Steady men," Osric said cautiously, "We need to do this without spilling blood. We don't know who he is or what—"

Osric's word were still on his tongue as the giant man lunged.

Svend reacted instinctively, in a flash of steel, sidestepping and slashing with his freshly sharpened blade. His sword's edge sliced through the man's tunic and bit into his flank, drawing blood but leaving only a shallow wound.

The man staggered slightly, but his cold grin only widened, a chilling expression that seemed to mock their efforts and almost beg for their blades. He spun on his heels, squaring up with Svend again, his eyes glinting with a dangerous, unhinged energy.

"What is this madness!?" Svend barked, his voice sharp with both anger and disbelief. "You're unarmed and outnumbered!

HEART OF THE WILD GODS

Stop, man!"

But the giant ignored him, lunging forward like a man possessed. Svend sidestepped again, pulling back just in time to prevent the man from impaling himself on his blade.

Osric seized the opening, stepping in swiftly and connecting the hilt of his sword with the top of the man's head. The blow landed with a crack, enough to fell most men instantly.

But not this man.

The feral giant barely wavered, his movements deliberate as he turned to face Osric. Blood trickled down his forehead, streaming into his eyes, but the man only laughed—a low, guttural sound that sent a chill straight to the bottom of Svend's spine.

The man lunged again, this time at Osric, his massive frame barreling forward with the force of an ox. This time, it was Osric's turn to leap to the side, narrowly avoiding being crushed under the weight of the man.

As Osric darted clear, Wulfric acted. With a running start, he launched himself forward, sliding boots-first into the man's legs. The impact sent the giant's hulking form toppling forward, his momentum working against him as he crashed heavily to the ground.

Before the man could rise, Svend was on him, delivering a second, punishing blow with the hilt of his sword. This strike hit true, the force reverberating through the man's skull. His body stiffened, then slackened, collapsing onto the ground unconscious.

The three men gathered around the sleeping giant, their breath ragged as they all looked at each other, their expressions incredulous.

"How long do you suppose he'll stay down?" muttered Osric, looking at his travel companions, their unease palpable.

Svend was already moving for the horses. "Long enough to bind him. Ropes are with my saddle."

"I've a feeling we'll come across his captors—or what's left of them—somewhere along this road," Wulfric muttered grimly.

Svend glanced back at Wulfric and nodded as he unfastened a coil of rope from his saddle, his thoughts aligning with the prediction.

"I think you're right, Wulfric," Osric said, his voice steady but tense. He knelt by the unconscious man, inspecting the crude chain on his ankle. "Let's get him secured. Whatever crimes this one's committed, we can't in good conscience leave him to roam Wessex unchecked. We'll have to take him with us."

"Hurry, then," Svend called back, tossing the rope toward Wulfric before turning to retrieve the horses' tack. "The sooner we're moving, the less time we spend tempting fate."

26

Huntung ⚔ Hunting

"Very well, men, let's pause for something to eat before we get them dressed!" Cenric shouted triumphantly to the hunting party, casting a satisfied eye over the two stags and the growing pile of hares and pheasants already brought in. "A truly incredible start to the first day!" he bellowed, his voice carrying through the crisp winter air.

Cenric's enthusiasm for the hunt radiated off of him like heat from a forge. Leading the Yule hunting party in the forest bordering Wōdenléah and Aldhem had become as much a tradition for him as the feast itself; it was a role he had relished every year since he and Cwenhild first came to Wōdenléah. It was, without a doubt, his favorite time of year.

By now, the winter sun had climbed high, and it was well past time for the midday meal. The hungry hunting party was more than ready for a rest—they'd been out since the first light of dawn, having barely stepped into the forest clearing when a stag had appeared, grazing at the edge of the treeline. The party had diverted all their energy into taking down the animal, and their focus had been unbroken since. Now, their stomachs were letting them know of their neglect.

"Grab yourselves something to eat and settle in, men," Cenric called, gesturing towards the fire Godwin was feeding with the wood they'd gathered. "I've got something every man here needs to hear."

The party gathered their provisions and sat around the fire, sharing loaves of bread and passing around the ale. Cenric stood at the center, his spear planted firmly into the frosty ground, the glint of determination in his eyes reflecting the firelight under a flat winter sky.

He took a deep breath and began.

"Again, we find ourselves gathered for the hunt that holds us close. Every year, we take from this land not out of greed, but with our deepest thanks—so our hearths stay warm, our bellies full, and our kin know the bounty that comes from our hard toil and fellowship, and of course the good favor of Almighty God."

He paused, looking around at the faces of the men. Some he had known since they were boys; others were battle-hardened comrades, their loyalty proven over years of shared struggle.

"This Yule, however, brings with it more than just our yearly feasting and kinship," Cenric continued, his tone deepening. "You all will have noticed by now—our lord, Osric, is absent today."

A murmur spread through the group. Men exchanged glances, nodding.

"There is good reason for this," Cenric said, raising his voice over the murmur. "Lord Osric has entrusted me to speak on his behalf, because at this very moment, he is likely arriving in Wintanceaster. His intentions are to stand before our king, Alfred."

The murmuring grew louder, but Cenric held up his hands for silence.

"All of you stand here for a reason," he said, his gaze steady. "You are all valued members of the fyrd—not just for how you bear a spear, but for the kind of men you are, having shown your worth in the shield-wall and in daily life. Osric believes, as I do, that God has laid a hard task in our hands, one that calls for our courage and complete trust in one another."

Cenric took a moment to pause while the men quieted down, anticipating the direction of his words.

"There is not a man here today who has not felt the weight of our Bishop Æthelwod's hand." Cenric paused for a moment while a silence instantly fell over the men at the mention of Æthelwod's name.

"It feels wrong to say it, especially about a man of the cloth, yet you all know it to be true. The bishop is no shepherd with a staff in hand, as he would have us all believe. To him, his station is merely a weapon. He speaks of good works, every so often he even does them—yet what comes of it in the end? Naught but grief—harsh punishment for our folk, and ill-fortune for those we trade with."

The men sat in heavy silence, transfixed—some even shocked—by Cenric's words. The sounds of the forest seemed to fall away as they listened to Cenric finally put words to the experiences so many of them had at the hand of the bishop.

"Æthelwod spits venom when he speaks of the Norse, calls 'em raiders and heathens. And on that, he's not wrong! Many of us have felt the bite of their steel—God Almighty knows I have, and of course, our Lord Osric nearly lost his life to a Northman's blade.

"And yes, it feels strange, backwards even—this trading with old foes. But mark me—you know as well as I that these times are shifting, and it is the wish of our king that we honor our treaty and turn from the endless bloodshed of the past to build a new Wessex—one built from peace, learning, and fair trade."

Cenric looked around at the faces of the men—all listening attentively.

Good. I still have their ear, he thought, pausing for another breath before continuing.

"To say it straight, it is the king's wisdom that the trade we do with these Northmen helps put food on our tables and keeps the wolf of war from our doors. Yet these past days, Lord Osric stumbled upon a scheme that laid bare how Bishop Æthelwod has no mind for our king's wisdom!

"Lord Osric, these past days witnessed dealings—secret work by the bishop, meant to stir an uprising against the Norse traders and justify using the fyrd to wage war on them. To speak it bare,

Æthelwod wants to drive the Northmen out, seize their camp and goods, and take over their trading routes."

A ripple of chatter zipped through the party, and Cenric paused while he allowed the weight of his words to settle upon them.

"I know I don't need to tell you men that greed is what drives him. It is clear the bishop cares naught for your safety or mine when you think on how such a scheme would violate our treaty and endanger the kingdom—every one of us has seen firsthand how quickly conflict with these Northmen spreads."

Cenric's tone was resolute, and he once again let his gaze sweep over their faces, their expressions a mix of anger and unease.

"Thanks be, we are not so easily fooled. Nor are we pawns to be used for one man's misguided game—a man who it seems has strayed from his oath of service and lost his way.

"Lord Osric and the Norse Jarl Torvald Ironsight have together forged a plan that, God willing, will put an end to this. It is a plan to preserve the king's peace and spare Wessex from the true cost of Æthelwod's ambition."

Cenric paused again, his words hanging heavy in the chilled air, allowing the significance of the moment to settle into the hearts of the men.

"But," he continued, his tone grave, "this plan does not rest on them alone. It begins here, with us. Every man present has a role to play—a vital role—and the first is this. What is spoken here today must go no further than this forest clearing. Speak not a word to your friends, your kin—not even your wives."

Cenric's eyes searched the faces of the men, looking for any sign that they had erred in their selection of who was present.

Thankfully, he saw none.

"You have all been chosen for this task because Lord Osric trusts each and every one of you, as do I. Our lord recognizes that this will not be easy, but that it is necessary to prevent a larger conflict that could risk pulling Wessex—even all of England—back into war.

"Lord Osric will return tomorrow, and be assured, we will meet again soon to answer your questions. But for now, know that this is a stand for the good of our burh, our families, and the peace of our kingdom that our king is fighting so hard to rebuild."

The men sat in silence, their breath rising into the frosty winter air, eyes fixed on Cenric. Nods of resolve moved across the group, rising and coalescing like a shield wall, unified in their agreement.

"Good." Cenric clasped his hands together. "Now—I need you to listen well to the details of the plan," Cenric said as the men leaned in, "and together, we'll set ourselves to the task."

* * *

A mile outside of the gate to the camp, Torvald Ironsight sat on a weathered log in a forest clearing, lost in thought while spinning his axe idly by the haft. The faint glimmer of the Thames shimmered through the barren, skeletal trees, a quiet backdrop to the low murmur of his men's voices.

The men lounged around the crackling fire, cleaning their weapons, swapping stories from the day's hunt, and sharing jokes over bites of cured meat and bread. Horns of ale passed between them as the fire burned hot and high, the flames licking the frosty mid-afternoon sky.

In front of them lay the spoils of the day's hunt: a great boar, four fat partridges, and several hares; the beasts laid out in tribute to their morning's success. The scent of wood smoke rose into the air, mingling with the earthy tang of the freshly dressed game. For a few moments, Torvald let himself enjoy the sights and the smells of a successful hunt.

Bringing himself back into the present with a sharp inhale

and a crack of his neck, Torvald caught Bjørn's eye and gave a nod, signaling that he was ready to speak. Bjørn, who was showing the boy how to sharpen the new seax he'd been given, nodded in acknowledgment, then gave a whistle to assemble the men, sending the boy off to the river's edge with a spear to practice his aim on the unsuspecting fish.

"Brothers," yelled Bjørn, "Gather around the fire! Jarl wishes to speak!"

The men settled in, shifting closer to the flames with their ale horns in hand. Torvald rose to his feet, his broad shoulders silhouetted against the firelight.

"Most of you already know," Torvald began, his voice steady and deep, "it is not chance that brings you here today."

He let his gaze sweep over the gathering, the faces of his men illuminated by the flickering firelight as they listened attentively to their chieftain, his deep voice set to the music of the crunch of earth beneath his feet and the Thames softly flowing in the background.

"You have been asked to join this hunt because you have proven yourselves to be men of strength."

"But the strength required for the hunt—or even the battlefield—that is only one weapon in the arsenal of a true warrior, and more often than you think, it is not the best weapon for the fight."

Torvald watched as the men exchanged glances, some nodding thoughtfully while others leaned forward, frowning and listening intently.

"I believe you all might guess where this is going," Torvald continued with a sly smile. "You've seen it yourselves—missing goods, fewer barrels of grain, whispers of trouble from the Saxons. And of course, you've all heard the tales of my *weakness*."

He raised an eyebrow, letting the wry smile sit on his lips a while longer, which drew a chuckle from some of the men, although perhaps not as many as Torvald would have liked.

He stood and began to stroll in front of the fire as he spoke.

"But these whispers, the tensions they create—they too are not born of chance. They are the work of one man." He paused, his tone hardening as he leaned forward slightly.

"The Christian bishop, Æthelwod."

The name hung in the air like smoke, the men growing still as they listened to their chieftain name their target.

Æthelwod," Torvald said, his voice rising slightly, "wears the robes of a Christian bishop, but do not be fooled—he acts like no servant of any God that you've ever heard of. This so-called holy man feeds his greed with coin taken from his people, and from disrupting the trade with us—all while using his influence to stoke fear, hatred, and violence—even against his own."

A murmur rippled through the gathering, nods of agreement spreading among the men.

"Why?" Torvald asked, his voice sharpening. "He desires to see Saxon and Norse once again set against one another; to create a divide so bitter he can justify raising the Saxon fyrd to drive us from our camp, seize our trading routes, and further enrich himself. All in the name of the Christian God, of course."

As he often did, Torvald let silence do the work while the men erupted in protest at the revelation, a tide of anger washing over them. He allowed them a moment before holding up his hand for silence.

"This scheme is more than rumor," he continued calmly. "Lord Osric, the Saxon thegn, delivered evidence of this to me personally. As strange as it sits with us, who have been fighting these Saxons since we were young men, this time, it seems we are fated to be allies. The Saxon thegn is a man with much to lose, yet he has lent his strength and wisdom in shaping a course of action that serves us all.

He paused in his tracks, looking directly at the men.

"I tell you now—I know how odd this must sound to you, that the Saxons are our allies in this fight."

Torvald had fully expected the ripple of unease that ran through the group. One man finally put to words what they were all thinking and called out, "Jarl Torvald! Why not just kill Æthelwod and be done with it?"

Torvald grinned. "Já, it would be easy, wouldn't it? We were all warriors first, and our swords have helped us resolve many problems.

"Let us say we slay a Saxon bishop of rank. What then? Do Æthelwod's lies die with him? Or do they grow, whispered louder by the fools he's already poisoned? In killing Æthelwod, do we not also remove any doubt of the whispers that we plot against them?"

Another murmur ran through the group.

"This is a different fight, brothers," Torvald said, his tone earnest. "The bold strokes of the battlefield spread a ripple like Thor's hammer—it reaches outward, unsettling all around it."

Torvald unpinned the ornate silver brooch from his cloak, removing the garment and letting the heavy wool fall over a nearby log. He held up the silver piece—a finely wrought Norse dragon glinting in the firelight.

"Look at this. This is Fáfnir." His voice carried through the gathering, firm and deliberate. "You all know the tale—Fáfnir, twisted by greed, kills his father for a cursed hoard of gold. He conceals the hoard deep in a cave and sits atop it. Over time, greed corrupts his soul and transforms him into a fearsome dragon. A cautionary tale—greed and an unchecked thirst for power ultimately lead to a man's ruin."

The chieftain passed the brooch to the men, wordlessly gesturing to them to pass it around.

"Æthelwod picks this fight with us not as a man, but as a man becoming a dragon, sitting atop a pile of riches. The Christian bishop wants us to lash out, to become the lies he tells. He wants us to give him the war he craves—for our actions to send that ripple throughout the region, so that he might justify himself."

He paused for a moment, taking a step closer to the men, his voice firm.

"But we will not give him the satisfaction.

"This is a fight won not with blades, but minds. Do not mistake restraint for weakness. Real strength—lasting strength—comes from knowing when to fight and when to hold. We will defeat this dragon in his very own cave, while he sits atop his hoard, and he will never have seen us coming."

The men sat quietly, a few even paused with food still in their mouths as the firelight cast sharp shadows across their faces. Torvald could almost feel their resolve hardening as he scanned the group, now fixed upon his every move.

"This type of quiet strength," Torvald said, his voice steady and deliberate, "this is the true agent of change. This is the strength needed to slay a dragon. It belongs to the man who waits, watches, and strikes—"

Suddenly, without breaking stride, Torvald turned sharply. In one fluid motion, he hurled his axe with a speed and precision that caught even the most seasoned warriors off guard. The weapon whistled through the frosty air, burying itself deep into the center of the trunk of a nearby tree with a resonant *thwack*.

"—he strikes *only* when the time is right."

The men sat in stunned silence for a moment, their eyes darting between the axe buried deeply in the tree and their chieftain, whose calm expression and stance had not faltered. A slow grin tugged at Torvald's lips as he surveyed their reactions.

"Prepare yourselves, brothers," he continued, his voice carrying the same steady confidence as before. "The strength we'll need is not in how fast we can draw our swords, but in how well we choose our moment. And *we* will create that moment. So pass my cloak pin around. Look at it well. Remember what it means, because the next time you see me and Svend wearing Fáfnir, you can consider it a silent call to action. You will have a job to do."

He turned back to the fire momentarily, warming his hands before making a final appeal to the men.

"Before we go any further," he began, his voice calm but firm, "every one of you must understand that we speak of here—what Bjørn and I are about to share with you—it does not leave this clearing. Not a word of it."

He paused, his eyes scanning the faces of the men one last time, the firelight flickering across their expressions.

"If a single whisper of this plan reaches the wrong ears, it won't just be our efforts that are undone. It will be our people who pay the price."

"Now," he said, his tone lighter but no less firm, "grab your horns and gather near. Bjørn and I will lay out the plan. And none of you sticky-handed bastards better leave here with my cloak pin either."

Laughing, the men sprang to their feet, anticipation crackling in the air like the sparks from the fire as they moved in closer.

Torvald strode towards the tree, gripping the axe handle and releasing the blade from the tree with a satisfying crack.

27

Wintanceaster ✕ Winchester

"By order of crown and church, do not come any closer until you have declared yourselves! Archers stand at the ready!"

Osric tightened his grip on the reins, his jaw set as he looked up at the wall, then over at his party. *Eálá*[xv], he thought grimly, *our appearance at the moment will do little to inspire trust!*

And their party was indeed a sight to behold: two Saxon thegns, a towering Northman, a badly injured member of the King's Guard hunched and bloodied in his saddle, and a dead guardsman and an unconscious prisoner—both draped over their mounts.

Just as Wulfric had predicted, they had found the two unfortunate guardsmen a small distance up the road from where the three of them had camped, both tied to trees, only one left alive, the sword missing from the dead man's side. It had taken a fair amount of time and energy to secure the horses the guardsmen had brought with them and hoist the massive unconscious prisoner atop one of them, and the threat of him waking once again was very much on every one of their minds. They were more than ready to turn him over to his captors.

From his saddle, the wounded guardsman lifted his voice. "Elwyn! It's Ulferth! King's Guard!" He gestured weakly toward the unconscious prisoner with a nod of his head. "Wynhelm and I were transporting this prisoner when he attacked. Wynhelm's dead, and I'm struck through and bleeding! With me are the thegns of Wōdenlēah and Beornwic, and the Northman is their trading partner! They have urgent business with the king!"

The guard was silent, his skepticism tangible even from a distance.

The guardsman tried again, louder this time, urgency creeping into his tone. "Elwyn! Come on, man! I'm bleeding out here! They came to our aid—too late for Wynhelm, but without them, this lunatic would be free and I'd be dead! They've subdued him, but you'd best send more men out before the giant awakens!"

There was a pause, the weight of the moment pressing down on the group like the winter chill. Then, the guard addressed Osric directly.

"You're the thegn of where?"

"I'm Osric, thegn of Wōdenléah," Osric called back, his tone calm but commanding. He gestured to his companion. "This is Wulfric, thegn of Beornwic, and this is Svend, overseer of trade at the Wōdenléah trading camp. We three have ridden through the night to reach the king with news of an urgent matter."

The guard seemed to consider this, narrowing his eyes before murmuring something to the man beside him. That man turned and disappeared into the palace grounds.

"We're sending word to Lord King Alfred of your arrival. I'll send some men down to you now. Hold where you are."

"Thank you, Elwyn!" The guardsman shouted back, "These men had best hurry—he's stirring."

Osric, Svend, and Wulfric all snapped their heads toward the prisoner. Sure enough, the giant moved, his groans rising to low, guttural growls. The ropes creaked under the strain as he shifted, his robust frame struggling against his bindings. The horse beneath him strained, snorted, and tossed its head, growing more ill at ease with each passing second.

"We might need to cut that rope before the horse—" Wulfric began, but his words were drowned out by the piercing whine of the horse as it pulled back, its reins taut, its eyes wide with panic.

Svend was already moving. He dismounted in a single, swift motion, his seax gleaming as he unsheathed it. He pulled the tail of the quick-release knot that tied the prisoner's horse to his own, and tossed the rope to Osric.

"Hold this!" Svend barked, advancing carefully toward the thrashing prisoner.

Osric dismounted, handing his reins to Wulfric. "Wulf, get the horses clear!" he shouted, tightening his grip on the agitated horse's lead and grabbing Svend's mount as Wulfric maneuvered away from the fray, joining the injured guardsman at a safe distance.

The prisoner let out a low, bestial growl, his legs kicking wildly as he fought to free himself. The horse beneath him reared, causing the weight of the tethered, flailing man to shift to one side, unbalancing the load for the horse and intensifying its panic.

Much to everyone's relief, the gates suddenly burst open, and five men spilled out with swords drawn. They rushed toward the chaos, but their arrival only intensified the poor horse's panic. It reared again, but this time, Svend was able to lunge in and cut the rope that held the combative prisoner to its back. The man slid from its back, landing in a heap on the cold ground with a heavy thud.

The horse immediately took a few quick steps away from the man, then instantly quieted once it realized the man was no longer on its back. The giant man, however, was not finished yet. He staggered to his feet, woozy and swaying like a drunk, his immense size making the guards hesitate for a split second—a hesitation that provided the man with an opportunity. He swung his arms wildly, knocking one man to the ground before two others got a hold of him.

Osric watched with a growing sense of urgency as another guard joined the fray, then another. Even five against one, the giant man was nearly too much for them. He fought like a cornered beast, his guttural roars filling the air, until finally, one of the guards was able to connect the hilt of his sword with the man's head.

The behemoth prisoner crumpled to the ground, unconscious once more.

The guards stepped back, their breath ragged and faces a mixture of relief and disbelief as they hoisted the man off the ground by his underarms and dragged him through the gate, the giant's feet scraping two generously sized squiggly trails across the hardened ground.

A few more guards emerged and helped the injured guardsman off his horse and in through the gates—the man briefly turning his head towards Osric and nodding with gratitude as his comrades helped him inside.

Only then did Osric release the slow breath he hadn't even realized he'd been holding. He walked over to his horse, pausing as he stole a final glance up at the guard tower before pulling himself back into the saddle. Behind him, Svend also mounted, the leather of the saddle squeaking under his weight.

The three men sat for a moment, allowing the charged energy of the moment to dissipate, until Wulfric finally broke the silence.

"Well," he said, his voice dry and nonplussed as he urged his horse into a slow walk toward the palisade gate, "it is possible, men, that it may be too late for us to slip in unseen."

A grin tugged at Osric's lips, spreading wider as he fought back laughter. He shook his head, spurring his horse forward to follow Wulfric, the tension in his chest finally easing with the utter ridiculousness of the situation. It was not the quiet, clandestine arrival they had hoped for.

From behind, Osric could hear the deep sound of Svend's laughter breaking through.

Osric glanced over his shoulder at the Northman, whose broad grin was unmistakable, even at a distance. The sound of Svend's amusement was contagious, and despite everything—the unfortunate guardsman, the chaos, the weight of what lay

HEART OF THE WILD GODS

ahead—all three of them chuckling as they rode through the gates of Wintanceaster.

* * *

"My lords, good morning!"

The voice reverberated through the stone corridor that led towards the king's hall. The group soon saw that the voice belonged to Lord Odda of Devon[xvi], who nearly collided with them as they rounded the corner.

"I was just on my way to greet you," Odda boomed. "By God, is that Lord Wulfric? It's been many winters, Lord! Tell me, is your father well?"

"He is quite well, Lord Odda, thank you!" Wulfric said, and the two men embraced like warriors.

"Aah, and of course you are Lord Osric of Wōdenléah, I recall you well," Odda said, clasping forearms with Osric, "and I was very sorry to hear about the passing of your wife Leofwynn."

Osric barely disguised his surprise that Lord Odda—the hero of the Battle of the Arx Cynuit over Ubba, the son of the legendary Ragnar Lothbrok—that this man should not only remember him, but knew of Leofwyn's death. He'd met Odda only once, but he supposed that level of savvy was the mark of a man truly seasoned in the politics of Wintanceaster's highest counsel.

"You have my thanks, Lord Odda," Osric said as smoothly as he could manage, "it's good to see you again. This is Svend, overseer of trade at the camp outside of Wōdenléah."

"Svend," Odda greeted Svend with a nod, "welcome to Wintanceaster. You serve Jarl Torvald Ironsight, do you not?"

"I do, Lord."

"I've met your Jarl a few times, both on and off the battlefield—a shrewd negotiator and a formidable man. You must send him my regards."

"I will do, Lord."

Addressing Osric once again, Odda continued, "Lord King Alfred has sent me to convey his appreciation for your efforts in your night's ride, and also for your taking of the escaped prisoner—I imagine that was not an easy man to subdue." Odda chuckled, "King Alfred wishes to extend his hospitality to dine with him this evening, and invites you to pass the night here at the palace."

"That is a most generous offer, and we are honored to accept." Osric replied, "And please relay my gratitude to Lord King Alfred, as well as my apologies for arriving unannounced. The nature of our business has made such tactics necessary."

"Ah, think no more upon it," Odda said, waving off Osric's apology. "I daresay our King secretly enjoys a break in the palace routine, Lord Osric," grinned Odda.

"Ah, here's Mildreth now—Mildreth, please show our guests to their chambers! Lords, I look forward to getting caught up over dinner this evening."

With that, Odda dipped his head and departed as the group all turned to look at the tall, willowy girl with the jet black hair who had floated soundlessly up behind the group.

"If my lords would follow me," the servant Mildredth said softly, her eyes downcast as she floated down the corridor towards their accommodation.

They left the large, fortified stone building that housed the king's hall and walked for several minutes, traversing a beautiful courtyard and entering another building that housed their accommodation. Mildredth stopped in front of the first of three consecutive large wooden doors.

"Lord Osric," she said as she opened the door, "this is the largest of the three chambers—Lord Odda bade me to give this one to you."

"Thank you," Osric replied, although Mildredth had already turned away and moved on to the next door. Osric looked past her at his companions and made a gloating face, taunting them at the mention of having the largest chamber, then headed inside.

This will serve well enough, Osric thought as he entered the spacious and richly decorated room. A small hearth at the far end of the room was already lit, casting its warm glow while keeping the chill at bay. The rich, woodsy smell of wood smoke filled the air, and several tapestries lined the walls, each depicting a different battle scene. A large brazier stood next to an oversized wooden bed, piled high with furs, and Osric immediately began fighting the urge to launch himself into it with a running start.

A metal basin and jug of water had been set out on a small table under a shuttered window, and Osric had already kicked off his boots and was refreshing himself when he heard a rap at the door.

Smiling to himself, he thought, *That'll be Wulf, no doubt—always appearing just when I've set hand to something.*

"What now, Wulf?" Osric called out as he strode to the door, "Come to marvel at how much grander my chamber is than you—"

As Osric swung the door open, it was not Wulfric that stood before him.

It was Alfred. King of Wessex.

"Lord King Alfred," Osric said, his cheeks reddening as he fell to one knee, "forgive me, I thought you were—"

"Lord Wulfric. Yes, I know. I heard." Alfred said, a flash of amusement flaring behind his eyes as he gestured for Osric to stand with his palm open, "Please, Lord Osric, rise. I hoped we might have a private word before dinner. There are far fewer ears pressed against doors here than on the other side of the courtyard."

"By all means, Lord King," Osric said, stepping aside. "Please, enter."

Alfred[xvii] was of average height, slight of build, and had sandy brown hair, a neatly trimmed beard, and penetrating, hyper-intelligent grey eyes that radiated both authority and compassion. He swept past Osric wearing a modest tunic made of fine embroidered red wool and a simple circlet crown. To Osric, he seemed the very embodiment of the understated yet commanding presence for which he was so known.

Mildredth suddenly appeared from behind the door frame, carrying a jug of ale and four cups.

"By the hearth, Mildredth, thank you," Alfred said, standing and waiting patiently while Mildredth quickly set up a small table and two chairs before pouring the ale for them.

"Shall we sit?" Alfred said, gesturing to the chair across from him as he sat down.

"Lord King, shall I summon the other men?" Osric asked.

"In a moment," Alfred said. "First, I would speak with you privately, Lord Osric."

Osric sat across from the king and drew a deep and steady breath, bracing himself for what he was about to do.

"Before you tell me that which you have traveled under the cloak of darkness to discuss, let me say this—I already hold a notion of your purpose." Alfred began, his tone somehow both soothing and penetrating. "You are here today because of the Bishop Æthelwod," the king said flatly, pausing to lift his eyes to look at Osric while sipping his ale. "Am I right?"

"Lord King...yes, I am—you are!" stammered Osric, momentarily caught off guard.

"Trust me, Lord Osric, one need not be a soothsayer to see the Bishop Æthelwod for what he is," Alfred chuckled bitterly and took another sip of ale, "one needs only to spend a moment in his presence to get the full measure of him." Alfred paused again, looking thoughtfully at a distant point in the room before

HEART OF THE WILD GODS

returning his sharp gaze to Osric.

"Granted, I obviously do not yet know the particulars, but I simply want to reassure you that one could say in many ways, Lord Osric, I have long expected you."

"That eases my mind more than you know, Lord King," Osric said, feeling the dread drain from him. "It is no easy matter speaking ill of the man responsible for elevating me to my position," Osric admitted, lifting his ale cup and taking a much smaller sip than he desired.

"Well, yes and no, Lord Osric," the king said, his expression softening. "Yes—Bishop Æthelwod indeed had a hand in your rise, but you forget, Lord, that you earned it—you have shown yourself a true leader of men, and of course we mustn't forget that it was because of you and the sacrifice made by your men that the bishop is even here at all!" Alfred paused, a wry glint behind his eyes. "In retrospect, any regret one might feel about that action is another matter entirely." For a moment, a wry smile tugged at the corner of the king's mouth. "Ah, but this is blasphemy—perhaps I speak too freely now, forgive me," he said, raising his cup to his mouth to suppress the grin.

"Lord Osric, know this," Alfred continued, leaning back in his chair. "I have long believed that it was Æthelwod's hand guiding the ruination of your predecessor. We simply could never come up with the proof. Certainly not with the kingdom at war."

As relieved as he was to hear the king openly expressing his unadorned opinion of Æthelwod, Osric couldn't help but feel that he was being given his first real lesson on the political craft in play in Wessex, something he silently vowed never again to underestimate.

"Æthelwod wanted you as thegn because he saw in you an honorable man who leads with his sense of duty—that same sense of duty he thought might be predictable enough to shape to his own ends. That is his way. He may wear the clothing of a divine emissary, but his misdeeds are no more than the most predictable failings of the weakest of men."

"I beg your leave, Lord King," Osric said cautiously, "this question may be over-bold, but why keep such a man in such a position of power?"

Alfred paused, his grey gaze fixing on Osric, "It's an excellent question, Lord Osric. Hard though it is to believe, it is often better to have a wolf at the door in plain view, rather than lurking in the shadows."

"A watched hand does not strike unseen," Osric said.

"Just so." The king smiled. "I agreed to your appointment for the same reasons Æthelwod did. I, too, believe you to be honorable—yet I believe Æthelwod has vastly underestimated you. I believe that you are not someone to let such a man gain moral purchase. I fear the bishop believes that an honorable man cannot possess a strategic mind and not use it for some bent design. And unless you have come before me to prove me wrong," Alfred continued, becoming slightly more animated, "I shall hold that my judgment on this was sound." The king drank again, a look of plain satisfaction on his face as he waited for Osric to respond.

"Sound as ever, Lord King," Osric said, his relief palpable.

"Good," the king said as he set his cup down. "Now, let's set two more cups, get your men in, and I'll hear the whole tale."

* * *

The sun had already set by the time Osric finally stepped out of his chamber and into the corridor, where Wulfric stood waiting.

"God's mercy, whatever that is they've been cooking, it smells fit for royalty, right enough," he said. "The scent of it drifted straight across the courtyard—I swear I caught it through the stone walls—it pulled me from my sleep!"

HEART OF THE WILD GODS

Wulfric nodded. "My growling stomach would surely have roused us otherwise—the sound of it is actually quite deafening," He grinned, casting his eye down the corridor toward Svend's door. "We may need to wake our friend from the north—he was the one keeping watch through the night."

Osric agreed. Hours had passed since their sudden audience with the king. Osric had called the men in to them and taken the lead as he guided King Alfred through the tangled events unfolding in Wōdenléah.

He had begun candidly with his association with Æfre, Æthelwod's venomous campaign against her, and gone on through the forced betrothal, the vanished trade goods, and the witnessed meeting with the cloaked Northman that revealed deeper conspiracies. No aspect of Æthelwod's dealings in Wōdenléah was left untouched.

Together they had laid forth their plan—to turn an uprising to their advantage, and each man spoke to his part in it. King Alfred listened, studying each man with a keen eye as he spoke, yet his preternatural calm gave little away. Soon enough, Osric thought, they would know whether the king had found their plan worthy.

The two thegns approached Svend's door, but just as Osric raised his hand to knock, it flung open to reveal a refreshed Svend in a deep blue tunic, cup of ale in hand.

Each man had wisely brought a change of clothes and had swapped his travel attire for freshly washed and combed hair, a trimmed beard, and a clean tunic. Svend had even braided his prolific red beard and added a heavy silver chain around his neck, making him look every bit the prosperous Norse trader that he was.

"Ah, friends! I have kept you waiting, I am sorry," Svend said as he tipped back his cup, draining it. "I'll set this down, and we will feast!" He disappeared momentarily back into the room, leaving the door ajar.

As they stood waiting, the door began to slowly ease open on its hinges, allowing the two thegns to catch a glimpse of a hearth similar to the ones they each had in their own chambers, then a table, and then a chest at the foot of the bed.

As the door continued to creak open, they saw it.

A woman, lying on her side, asleep in the bed.

Her back was to them, the furs tumbled down about her waist. The porcelain skin of her back and long raven hair spread across the pillow seemed to glow as the light from the hearth danced across her.

Osric and Wulfric both stood struck dumb, their mouths agape, staring, until Svend reappeared.

Seeing their wide eyes, Svend cast a glance over his shoulder, smiled, and shrugged—utterly nonplussed.

"Svend... how!?" Wulfric sputtered, his voice straining into a half-whisper. "We've been here but hours and you've... it's..."

Svend cast one last look inside, then carefully drew the door shut, careful not to wake the woman as the dull thunk of the door latch resonated down the corridor.

The two thegns stood staring expectantly at Svend, who only grinned.

"What?" He shrugged, eyes twinkling. "Think you Saxons are the only ones with friends in Wintanceaster?" He slapped Wulfric's shoulder with a laugh. "Come—my belly howls. I could eat a whole ox."

Turning, he strode down the corridor.

Wulfric and Osric stood looking at each other for a moment. Wulfric broke away first, his curiosity getting the better of him as he jogged after Svend like an attention-starved puppy, peppering the Northman with questions. Osric followed at his own pace, quietly chuckling as they made their way to the hall.

HEART OF THE WILD GODS

* * *

"Ah, our esteemed guests from Wōdenléah!" Lord Odda called from the doorway to the hall. "Right on time! Lord King Alfred has just arrived and awaits you at the table."

The hall was cast in the warm glow of firelight, both from the hearth and the torches lining the walls. The flickering light cast shapes and shadows onto the carved wood pillars and stone floor, and the scent of roasted meat and freshly baked bread wafted through the air, mingling with the hall's pervasive scent of wood smoke and tallow.

Several long tables with benches ran the length of the hall, and at the far end, upon a raised dais, stood the king's high seat. Around it were other chairs for family and trusted advisors, with richly embroidered tapestries adorning the wall behind them. Just in front of the dais, a thick oak table was laid for a smaller, more intimate gathering.

King Alfred crouched near the head of the table, speaking quietly to a small, sandy-haired boy.

"Ah, my lords, welcome!" The king stood and addressed the group warmly, "Here beside me is the Lady Ealhswith, along with our eldest son, Edward."

Ealhswith sat at the table next to where Alfred stood while seven-year-old Edward, the heir to the throne, pulled at her skirts, curiously studying the three men.

The men bowed their heads in respect.

"You'll forgive me, Lords, for not rising to greet you," Ealhswith smiled, indicating her young son's restless antics, "The king and I would have young Edward grow accustomed to the duties of a king."

"And of course you already know the Ealdorman Lord Odda," Alfred said, nodding his head towards Odda. "We've kept the gathering intimate tonight, appreciating that you must depart before the sun." Alfred gestured to the table. "Pray, be seated. I hope you've brought your appetites with you."

The men took their seats at the long oak table, already set for a feast. Osric found himself seated across from Lady Ealhswith, her keen eyes observing him with a mixture of curiosity and caution. Servants bustled about, laying out platters of steaming food and filling goblets with rich, amber mead.

King Alfred took his place at the head of the table and raised his goblet, his voice carrying across the table. "To our guests from Wōdenléah, Beornwic and beyond, and to the prosperity of Wessex."

The clink of their goblets resonated through the hall just as the food arrived, and almost instantly the hall descended into a quieter hum of conversation.

It wasn't until Osric bit into his food that he realized the full extent of just how hollow his belly had become. The flavors of the roasted meat—venison, as it turned out to be—exploded in his mouth, each bite bursting with juices rich with honey, herbs, and the smokiness of the fire, served with beautifully caramelized root vegetables.

Osric looked with amusement down the table at his travel companions, each in turn closing his eyes in bliss as they dove into their meals, savoring each mouthful like starving men.

The feast was generous and the conversation easy, yet unpretentious. Osric couldn't help but think of it as a reflection of Wessex itself—strong, prosperous, yet measured. The King told stories from Edington that they had never heard told, and Osric had been so drawn into the tales he'd barely noticed when his plate became bare.

After a while, Osric leaned back, his goblet now only half full, the weight of the meal settling comfortably. He had eaten well—more than well—and the rich venison lingered on his tongue, mingling with the sweetness of the mead. Soon, he was resisting the warm hand of sleep as it began to pull at him.

Across the great oak table, Lady Ealhswith had carried on with an effortless grace while also keeping the very active young Edward in hand. When the young boy had eaten his fill, Ealhswith summoned a nursemaid to take him from the hall, and only then did she return her attention to her own meal.

"You must forgive my scattered attention, Lord Osric," she said, dragging Osric back from his reverie, "The King and I seek to give young Edward as much normalcy as we can in these surroundings." She smiled and ate a bit more of her own neglected dinner before continuing. "I dare say, Lord, you eat with the appetite of a man who has traveled far. Tell me, does Wōdenléah feast so well in winter?"

"Lady Ealhswith," Osric replied, a sheepish grin forming at the corners of his mouth for having his voracious appetite marked, "we eat well enough when the harvest is kind and the hunt plentiful, although I must admit, this venison eclipses any I've tasted before."

"Perhaps we ought to have a word with your cook," Lady Ealhswith replied with an amused arch of her brow. "A prosperous kingdom relies as much on full stomachs as it does on skilled warriors, would you not agree?"

"I do my lady," Osric replied, "though I believe Wessex thrives no less from its sharp minds," Osric replied with a glance towards King Alfred.

"And sharp eyes, Lord Osric," Lady Ealhswith replied. "A keen observation indeed. Tell me then, what else have you observed in your short time here?"

Sitting back, Osric drew a breath while he considered the question. "At first glance," he began, "flawless hospitality, excellent food, fine company, and the kind of warmth that one normally only finds among kin." He paused, allowing the sounds of the hall to fill the void while he considered his surroundings.

"And yet?" Ealhswith pressed him further.

"And yet—an unmistakable undercurrent of tension," Osric said, almost wistfully. "Born perhaps of a shared understanding that the peace we currently enjoy may not be so easily kept." Osric paused again in thought, then continued in earnest, leaning forward and looking Lady Ealhswith directly as he spoke.

"One thing I truly believe, my lady, is that wisdom shapes our future as strongly as our swords have defended it. And, I believe that this may yet prove to be our most difficult transition. Those we feast with today might very well be found on the other side of the shield wall tomorrow, making it all the more vital that we remember not only our victories, but also our mistakes."

"Indeed, Lord Osric." Ealhswith sat back, her expression softening, satisfied with his response, "You speak well, my lord. And yes, I agree the sword is but one means by which the future of a kingdom is forged."

"I must confess," Osric admitted, "In the hours we have been here, I feel that I have received a year's mentoring, the value of which I could never repay if I lived a thousand lifetimes." Osric inclined his head in gratitude.

Lady Ealhswith was about to speak when the king set his goblet down and called the table to attention, glancing briefly at his wife, who gave him a subtle nod of approval as all eyes turned to King Alfred.

"My lords," began the king, "I know you have all been awaiting my response, and so now you shall have it—Wessex will stand behind Wōdenléah," the king said decisively. "I have this very afternoon sent a messenger to Bishop Æthelwod, bidding that once our Yule festivities are past, he—or a man of his choosing—bring this court word of our trade dealings in Wōdenléah. In keeping with your plan, I am confident that he will name you, Lord Osric, at which point this court will ensure that you, Lord Wulfric, stand in his stead. Beyond this, Wintanceaster will place no further hand, nor hindrance, to your design."

Osric inclined his head, "Lord King, I am grateful."

King Alfred held up his hand, "There is, however, one matter that I wish to make plain to all. This matter *must* remain closed. This action must not, under any circumstances, be allowed to spill over into something greater. A larger conflict could well bring this kingdom to its knees. Our current treaty that binds us," the king looked at Svend, "it must not be rendered an empty token."

"Understood, Lord King," Osric replied.

"Equally, Lord Odda and I also understand that sometimes, in the heat of battle, if we might be so bold as to call it that, things can go amiss. As men of honor, I have no doubt that you will deliver the Bishop Æthelwod to Wintanceaster to answer for his treachery. You've shown us as much with your actions today."

"Indeed, Lord King."

"As you have seen yourselves, ill fate can often find a prisoner or his keeper along the road to Wintanceaster. It can be quite a hard road, rife with hazards. Therefore, you have the sure word of this court, that if some such misfortune were to befall the bishop that prevents his delivery, neither you nor your men shall bear the blame for such an unfortunate turn of events."

"I understand, Lord King." Osric felt the air leave his lungs at the king's swift and brutal maneuvering.

"The only people in Wintanceaster who know of this, Lord Osric," the king continued, "they are right here in this room, and that is how it shall stay."

Osric felt the weight of King Alfred's words settle into the very cracks of the room, and for a moment, the crackling of the hearth was the only thing breaking the silence.

"My lords," said the king, "we shall leave you now to reflect. This has been a long day for you, and no doubt there is much to ponder." Lady Ealhswith inclined her head towards Osric with quiet grace before leaving the room, a children's maidservant waiting just outside the door with young Edward.

"Lord Osric," the king said, pausing at the doors to the hall, "if we might speak for a moment in the corridor."

"Of course, Lord King," Osric replied, rising from his chair and following the king out into the corridor.

"Lord Osric," the king said, after waiting to be sure they were alone, "As much as I do not wish to add to your growing list of concerns, there is one further matter that I wish for you to consider."

"Lord King?"

"As I was considering what you told me earlier—regarding your betrothal—I couldn't help but set to the conclusion that it might be wise for you to consider the match," Alfred stated plainly, his penetrating but kind gaze fixed on Osric. "Though it is not the place of even a king to tell a man the contents of his own heart, the fact of the matter is, there is much to be said for Aldhem, which is both strong of name and rich in resources. Such a match would certainly strengthen the realm with so trusted an ally." The king allowed a faint smile to tug at his lips as he continued, "Such an ally, I daresay, might find that his influence carries further in this court."

"I understand, Lord King." Osric inclined his head towards his king.

So there it was, as difficult to miss as an arrow to the chest.

The dangled carrot of a rise in station—a literal boost into the light of the king's favor. It was a promise of a future laid out before him—an incentive, meant to warm him to the idea, yet it left him feeling cold and sorrowful.

"I will consider your counsel, Lord King," Osric replied, his voice steady, though he couldn't help but feel that he did not do well enough to conceal the sadness behind his words.

"Good," Alfred said as he rose, placing a hand briefly on Osric's shoulder, the weight of it both reassuring and heavy. "Consider it well, my lord. Matters of the heart are fleeting, but the decisions made for the heart of a kingdom endure." The king's expression softened as he turned to leave before turning back briefly to address Osric once more. "Rest you well, Lord Osric, and may you and your men fare safely tomorrow," King Alfred said, inclining his head towards Osric and smiling faintly before sweeping down the corridor, his long tunic sweeping behind him as he disappeared around the bend.

"Good night, Lord King," Osric replied evenly.

Osric stood a minute in the corridor, his head reeling, before taking a deep breath and slowly walking back into the hall. He sat heavily in the chair next to Odda before reaching out to pour himself another goblet of mead, gaze fixed on the table.

Svend sat back in his chair, arms crossed, his sharp eyes flicking between Osric and the others. Wulfric leaned forward slightly, his fingers drumming against the wooden surface. Odda, seated across from Osric, exhaled slowly, his expression unreadable.

After a moment of quiet, Odda spoke, his tone measured. "It's a good plan, Lord Osric—clever. I commend you for that. But Lord, once you set this in motion, there's no turning back. You'll carry the consequences of this, for better or worse."

Osric raised his eyebrows, feeling the full weight of the future of Wōdenléah pressing down on him. "Then let us make certain it is for the better," he said, raising his goblet.

"What other choice is there?" Wulfric asked, raising his own goblet.

Odda cracked a faint smile as he raised his own goblet. "To quiet strength, then, the only choice."

Svend smiled and silently raised his glass, joining in the toast.

The warmth of the mead spread through Osric as he drank deeply, though it did little to ease the knot coiled in his chest. The plan was set, the king's approval secured, yet from where he sat, the path forward appeared to be narrowing perilously in front of him.

28

Þæc ✕ Thatch

"Håkon! Hvar er hamarr minn!? *[Håkon, where is my hammer!?]*," a man's voice bellowed in Norse from outside Æfre's covered window, followed by a burst of hearty laughter.

Æfre smiled as she stretched out on top of her bed, resting her healing injuries after a morning of barn chores, listening to the lively entertainment unfolding on the roof of her shed.

"What!?" The same voice snapped, now tinged with irritation, prompting even louder laughter.

"*What!?*" A pause.

"By my frosty balls! I tucked it under my armpit!" The voice cracked with sheepish amusement, setting off another round of guffaws.

Æfre laughed out loud, then quickly clapped her hand over her mouth to stifle the laugh, causing an audible snort, and a chain reaction ensued. Her shoulders shook as she fought to keep the sound of her laughter contained, which then caused her to wince at the reminder of her residual injuries.

So far, the men from the camp hadn't realized she understood every word they said—Jarl Torvald had obviously kept her ability to himself, and in doing so offered her a small but amusing gift in the rare glimpse into the genuine and unfiltered world of men when they think nobody is listening.

It was the second day she'd had the three men on her roof—two tasked with the repair, and the third, a guard the Jarl insisted on stationing on the road that led down to her hut.

At first, Æfre had bristled at the idea of constant supervision. She'd protested the night the Jarl mentioned it, both of them sitting by her hearth with cups of ale after her shelter roof had collapsed so spectacularly. But the Jarl was clear that there would be no negotiation on the matter, and quite frankly, she'd been too tired and sore to put up much of a fight.

Ultimately, Æfre was glad for their presence. In the past two days, she had heard the distant echoes of their vigilance several times—the clamor of hooves, shouts, and drawn steel had sent several would-be vandals, or worse, fleeing on horseback. Her gratitude was tempered, however, by the uneasy knowledge that their presence might ultimately make matters worse for her, once word began to spread.

The work on the roof had progressed quickly. One of the men, Harald, was a skilled woodcarver. When he saw her vandalized front door, he applied his craft, transforming it in a mere afternoon with a decorative accent of a thick, intricately braided pattern in the Danish style she recognized as similar to the renderings of intertwined, gripping beasts her father used to draw in his journals. Now, it looked as if it had always belonged there.

With a sigh, Æfre hoisted herself off the bed and padded to the hearth. The partridge stew was simmering in the cauldron suspended over the fire, its savory, comforting aroma welcoming her as she lifted the lid to check it. Earlier that morning, she'd started it with leeks, turnips, sage, and a healthy pour of mead.

The previous day, Cwenhild had dropped by with the bird, a jug of Yule mead, and her usual good-natured gossip. They'd shared a quick cup of ale by the hearth, but Æfre knew that Cwenhild had come for more than just a quick refreshment and an exchange of news—she was genuinely worried about Æfre, it was evident in her eyes from the moment she'd opened the door. There had been a sadness to her, one that remained unspoken, and one that perhaps mirrored Æfre's own regret at the way so many in the burh were turning their backs on her.

Æfre stirred the pot, inhaling the rich scent. The partridge wasn't ready yet, but it was coming along nicely. A pile of dried apples sat waiting to be added when the meat fell from the bone. Her stomach growled in anticipation, and it reminded her that the men atop her shed were likely just as hungry as she was.

She retrieved a loaf of unleavened bread and placed it on the cauldron lid to warm, the scent of it rising faintly as it heated. Turning back to the hearth, she carefully removed several warming stones, their heat radiating through her fingers even through the iron tongs. She wrapped the stones snugly in wool and lined an earthen pot with a soft cloth before carefully layering its contents. Butter, slices of dried meat, and wedges of cheese went in first, followed by a small, well-worn knife. Finally, she sliced the now-warmed bread, wrapping it securely before tucking it into the pot alongside the stones, ensuring the meal would stay warm and ready to eat.

A jug of ale and three horns went into a basket, balanced carefully on her arm as she balanced both items, pushing open the door with her hip, wincing when it pressed into an errant bruise that until that moment, she had not even realized was there.

Outside, she made her way to the shed and stopped at the base of the ladder propped against the roof.

"Hello!" she called up to the men, "I have warm food and ale for you!"

The hammering and rustling of thatch stopped abruptly. Two bearded faces peered over the edge, grinning.

"That is very kind!" said Harald, the elder of the two, his features marked by the calm assurance of experience. "This is Håkon," he added, nodding toward the second man.

"Harald, hvat!? *[What!?]*," a familiar voice shouted from the far side of the roof.

"And that," Harald said dryly, "is Geir." He turned his head towards the voice and shouted. "Geir! Matr! *[Food!]*"

There was a brief pause, followed by the unmistakable sound of someone scrambling with haste across the thatch. A third face popped into view, grinning sheepishly.

Geir—who misplaced his hammer in his own armpit. Æfre smiled, then bit her lip to keep from laughing.

"Would you like me to pass it up," she asked, "or would you prefer to come down?"

The men conferred briefly before Harald answered. "We'll eat up here, it's a fine day, not too cold, and Geir can better keep watch from up here."

"Of course," Æfre replied, handing the earthen pot up the ladder. "There are warming stones inside for your hands, too. But pray come inside if you need the fire—you're welcome anytime."

"Thank you for your kindness," Harald said with a warm smile, passing the pot and basket back to the others. The men settled themselves atop Epona's adjacent paddock shelter, their backs resting against the slant of the thatched roof.

Æfre smiled. "I'm truly grateful for the work you've done here. Please also send my gratitude to Jarl Torvald."

"I think you can tell him yourself," Harald said, grinning as he glanced past her shoulder, raising his arm in a greeting.

Æfre turned, startled to see Torvald Ironsight riding towards her, his gaze fixed directly on her. He sat astride a massive black horse, its coat gleaming like polished onyx in the sun. Everything about him radiated power—an aura of command always seemed to surround him like an ethereal mist. At his side rode a lanky boy on a smaller gelding, his wide, curious eyes drinking in the scene, a bow and quiver slung across his back.

Æfre felt a rush of heat creep up her neck at the memory of unleashing her sharp tongue and even sharper arrow at him the last time she'd seen him.

"Jarl Torvald," Æfre said, reflexively smoothing her hair and walking towards him as she squinted into the sun that shone directly behind the chieftain, making him appear even larger and more imposing in silhouette.

"Oh dear, more Saxon hospitality," Torvald said wryly, returning Harald's wave before turning his attention to Æfre. "You appear to be unarmed, that is a good start," he paused, studying her. "You look better," he said sincerely, "You're healing well?"

"Well enough, yes." Æfre felt heat rise to her cheeks as she avoided meeting Torvald's eyes, still self-conscious of her bruised and battered appearance. Every time in the last few days she'd caught her own reflection, she felt she looked like she'd taken on the Battle of Edington singlehandedly—and lost.

Moving her gaze to the boy who had ridden in beside the Jarl, Æfre was struck with the sudden realization that she knew the boy.

"Eadgar!?" She said incredulously, "Is that Eadgar!?" She moved closer to the boy to get a better look.

"Yes, Æfre it's me," Eadgar said softly, furrowing his brow as he studied Æfre's bruised face.

"By the Gods, Eadgar, I'm so happy to see you!" Æfre cried, her voice bright with genuine delight. "You've grown so much! I thought you'd gone off to the monastery in Wintanceaster." She looked questioningly at Torvald.

"I ran away," Eadgar said, his tone matter-of-fact, even boastful. "I never wanted to be a monk or a priest."

Æfre's mouth twitched as she suppressed another grin. She looked again at Torvald and shrugged, her expression saying plainly, *Can you blame him?*

Torvald chuckled.

No, I can not.

"Eadgar has been living with us at the camp for a while now," Torvald said as he swung down from his horse and set about removing the saddle. "For months, we never heard him speak—not even his name—until a few weeks ago, and now it seems we cannot shut him up. This week, he has made it clear to us that he wishes to become a warrior."

"A dangerous job," Æfre said, looking at Eadgar with wide eyes.

"Exactly what I said." Torvald replied. "It's a lot more than just battles and glory." His gaze flicked meaningfully to Eadgar, though the boy looked unbothered.

Torvald gestured to Eadgar to dismount. "We're starting with the basics," he said, handing the saddlebags off to the boy as he tied the two horses to the paddock fence. "We were up with the sun today observing the men, but it came to light that Eadgar has never held a bow, and I thought... perhaps... if your injuries allow it, you might show him."

Æfre blinked, caught off guard. "Me?" she asked, incredulous. "Surely you have archers in camp who are better suited for—"

"Æfre." Torvald's voice dropped slightly, and he glanced at the men on the roof to ensure they were out of earshot. His expression softened, sincerity glinting beneath his usual commanding demeanor. "Between what you did to your attacker and that warning shot I witnessed the other night, you're by far one of the finest archers I've seen."

And of course, there was that day at the river when I watched from afar as you expertly dispatched that hare with one clean shot, he thought, although there was absolutely no danger he was going to utter that out loud to anyone, least of all her.

"I...um..." A stunned Æfre faltered for a moment under the weight of his compliment before answering, "...very well—yes. I'm still a bit sore, but we can start now. I'll just check the stew on the fire and grab my bow...and maybe a shawl." She smiled shyly, then paused, glancing back at the pair as a thought struck her. "Are the two of you hungry?"

Torvald shrugged in the ambivalent way that Æfre knew men

to do when they really mean *yes*.

"Come with me," Æfre said, motioning for them to follow as she headed inside. Torvald and Eadgar followed, the scuff of their boots close behind her.

Inside the hut, as Æfre moved to the hearth, she couldn't shake the palpable closeness of Torvald's presence just behind her, even though he was several paces away. His energy seemed to fill every space he occupied, pressing in on her senses as much as his physical frame dominated the room.

"By the Gods, Æfre, what is that you're cooking!?" Torvald exclaimed, suddenly more animated than she'd ever seen him, as he crossed the threshold of her hut, taking a deep, exaggerated sniff of the air over where she was cooking. "This smell would drag Odin from Valhalla! What is it?"

"Partridge," Æfre replied, laughing at his enthusiasm. "It's just a stew." She glanced over her shoulder at Eadgar, whose eyes were bulging and fixed on the cauldron. Clearly, the two of them were hungry. "I'm not sure what I'll do with all of it, to be honest, there's easily enough for several—it'll be ready soon, I'll make sure the two of you get some before you go," she said.

Torvald tilted his head, his tone shifting as he asked, "You're not expecting anyone?"

There was something in the way he said it that made Æfre stop mid-motion and turn to face him. His eyes met hers, steady and unwavering, and for a moment, she felt unmoored. He knew. He knew about Osric.

The thought struck her like a lightning bolt, and a wave of heat crept up her neck. Wōdenléah's thegn had clearly met with the Jarl, and he must have been painfully forthcoming.

Perhaps a bit too forthcoming, she thought, cringing inwardly as she tried not to dwell on what the chieftain might be thinking.

Æfre swallowed, feeling an overwhelming desire to shrink

back, perhaps slither under the bed to escape his gaze, but instead, she forced herself to meet his eyes. "I honestly cannot say," she said at last, offering him a weak smile and the unadorned truth—there was little point in doing otherwise, Æfre didn't take the chieftain for a man to be lied to.

Torvald studied her for a moment, his expression unreadable, then gave a slight nod. Æfre wasn't sure if it was a nod of satisfaction or if he was distracted by another thought, but either way, he didn't say more.

The resulting silence between them felt thick with what had been left unspoken, leaving her hyper-aware of every movement she made as she turned back to the hearth. Her ears burned as she sliced the bread, buttering it and layering it with meat and cheese. She wrapped each portion neatly in cloth, hands working methodically to keep herself grounded.

"I'll take those," Torvald said the moment she turned to face them again, stepping forward and reaching for the food. His tone was neutral, but the faint tug at the corner of his lips betrayed his amusement. "Eadgar, you'll get yours when the lesson is over," he added, casting a knowing look at the boy.

"Jarl, he's a growing boy!" Æfre protested.

"Already today, he eats as much as three warriors." Torvald shot a wry look at Eadgar, "You cannot be hungry already. You ate before we left!"

Refusing to let the chieftain leave the boy with nothing, Æfre reached behind her without missing a beat and produced a large slice of cheese. She kept her gaze on Torvald as she handed it to Eadgar, who grinned triumphantly as he stuffed it into his mouth.

Still not breaking eye contact with Torvald, she reached back again, her expression a challenge, and produced another slice. She handed it to Eadgar with a raised eyebrow, as if to dare the imposing chieftain—a leader accustomed to barked orders and ready obedience—to say something.

Torvald stared at her, then at Eadgar, back again, and Æfre could see his face threatening to crack into a grin. Finally, he rolled his eyes, a huff of bemused exasperation escaping as he turned towards the door, shaking his head.

Æfre allowed herself a small, shared look of victory with Eadgar before she suddenly remembered the ale. "Jarl, wait," she called after him.

Grabbing an ale horn from the shelf, she filled it from the rapidly dwindling jug near the hearth and pressed it into his free hand. Torvald raised a single eyebrow, his lips quirking into that familiar, wry smile before he inclined his head in silent thanks and stepped outside.

As the door swung shut behind him, Æfre felt the calm of the room settle back into place. She exhaled slowly, then glanced at Eadgar, who gave her a conspiratorial grin, his cheeks still bulging with cheese.

* * *

"Slide over, men! Jarl's coming up!" Harald shouted as the men all hastily gathered their food and scooted along the roof to make room for one more.

"Good afternoon!" Torvald said brightly as he expertly climbed the ladder without spilling a drop of ale, plopping himself down next to Harald.

"Jarl Torvald," Harald greeted with a broad grin. "Good to see you on such a fine day!"

"A fine craft you've done on that door, Harald," Torvald said, taking a hearty draught of his ale. "It's fit for a hall."

Harald's chest puffed slightly. "Thank you, Jarl. Couldn't leave it as it was."

"No." Torvald nodded approvingly.

Below them, movement caught Torvald's eye. Æfre emerged from the hut, still limping slightly, carrying her bow with the ease of someone who was no stranger to its use. Beside her trailed Eadgar, his lanky form awkwardly clutching his own bow. Æfre moved to the paddock, caught Epona, and led her to her stall, away from the area where, soon, arrows would be in flight. She returned moments later with a large sack painted with a simple target, striding to the far end of the paddock to tack it up beneath a shade tree.

Torvald chuckled as he noticed the men on the roof watching her with unmasked interest, their heads swiveling in unison to follow her every move.

"Careful, men," Torvald said with a smirk, leaning back on one elbow. "Keep swiveling your heads like that and you'll fall off the roof."

The men chuckled sheepishly but didn't look away.

They all watched as Æfre began instructing Eadgar on the basics: stance, grip, and finger positioning. She demonstrated with patience and ease, then stood back to observe as the boy practiced.

"Jarl Torvald," Geir teased, "are our archers really in such a state that you need a Saxon woman to step in? Or—" He raised a brow, "is there another reason?"

Håkon half-laughed, half-recoiled at the boldness of the comment, while Harald snorted through his nose, trying to stifle his laugh.

Torvald allowed the comment to roll off him, letting out a deep, hearty chuckle instead. He tore into his bread and butter, speaking through a mouthful. "Keep watching, warrior—you might accidentally learn something, perhaps stop being such a drain on camp resources."

Håkon and Harald laughed heartily while Geir grunted, laughing as he raised his ale horn in good-natured defeat.

HEART OF THE WILD GODS

"Hey," Håkon said, swatting Geir's arm. "She's shooting, watch."

Torvald turned his gaze back to the paddock as Æfre scraped a line in the earth with her heel, marking the distance. She spoke to Eadgar as she worked, then, almost casually, stepped to the line, notched an arrow, and loosed it in one fluid motion. The arrow struck the center of the target with effortless precision.

"Já, good!" Harald exclaimed, scooting closer to the roof's edge to get a better view.

"Meh," Geir sniffed with his mouth full, between bites of dried meat. "She's standing close."

Torvald grinned, amused by Geir's stubbornness, but his attention shifted to Eadgar. The boy squared up and took his first shot. It went wide, but Torvald admired the way Eadgar handled the miss—no frustration, no sulking. He simply looked to Æfre for guidance, listened well, then tried again.

Torvald marveled at the boy's quiet determination, doubting he'd had that kind of patience at Eadgar's age.

"Håkon," Torvald said over Harald's shoulder, "switch with me. I need a word with Geir."

Håkon stuffed his remaining bread and cheese into his mouth, and the two men clambered over each other. As Torvald took his place, a cheer erupted from the men. Below, Eadgar had landed his first shot on the target, and Æfre was celebrating with a fist in the air.

"Jarl Torvald, I meant no disrespect—" Geir began as Torvald plonked himself down next to him.

Torvald waved him off before he could dig himself into a deeper hole. "Save your breath, Geir. It's fine." He paused, leaning back slightly as his eyes returned to the paddock. "But tell me—how are things with the watch? Any unwanted guests?"

Geir exhaled heavily. "Jarl, there have been a few."

Torvald looked down at the lesson happening below them. Æfre again had her fist in the air in celebration. There was an arrow close to the center of the target, and Eadgar was grinning ear to ear. Æfre walked several paces back and drew another line in the earth with her heel.

"That is what I was afraid you might say," Torvald said, not taking his eyes off the activity below.

In the paddock, Æfre loosed an arrow, again landing it dead center. Harald and Håkon cheered and raised their ale horns, thoroughly enjoying the show.

Æfre, hearing the commotion, looked up at the roof, smiled and nodded demurely, then stuck out her tongue and made a face.

"When they come," Geir continued, "they are prepared for destruction. Last night, they brought torches and arrows dipped in pitch."

Torvald silently nodded but said nothing.

"Jarl, we can keep chasing them, but they are determined. It's only a matter of time—"

"I know," Torvald said, as he watched Æfre land another shot, then continued explaining something to Eadgar.

Geir turned back towards the action below.

"We don't want to start another war with the Saxons over this," Geir said quietly."

"No. We do not."

Below, Æfre was still explaining something to Eadgar while walking back several paces. She turned suddenly, drawing her bow as she did, and took another shot, nailing the target once again. The three men cheered her on, now fully invested, ale horns in the air.

"Whoa. That's some shot." Geir relented, "Very well, Jarl, I see it now."

Æfre glanced up at the men on the roof and laughed, her smile wide and genuine as their cheers rang out. Torvald's eyes lingered on her, taking in the way her confidence seemed to radiate effortlessly, even as she still nursed her injuries. He smiled back, though it didn't ease the ache in his chest.

Torvald knew that whatever solace she found here now likely had a finite lifespan. This place was her family home, but trouble was circling, drawing closer with every passing day, and for whatever reason, the thought of this woman he barely knew losing this sanctuary made his heart feel unbearably heavy as he smiled back at her.

29

Hām ✕ Home

It's good to be home, Osric thought as the hunting party rode through the gates of the burh. He rode at the fore of the party, having joined them straight off the road from Wintanceaster via a cut through the forest, taking him to a clearing where Cenric had already gathered the rest of the party, awaiting his arrival.

Now, he scanned the familiar crowd that spilled from their huts and onto the green—all come to meet the hunting party. The burh had come out in numbers with offerings and traditional Yule blessings. The mead flowed freely, and the scent of roasting meat drifted from the hall through the crisp air.

Over the years, the return of the hunting party had almost become its own celebration, an unofficial gathering on the day before the Yule feast. The mood was jubilant as the entire burh seemed to relax in commemoration of the yearly tradition. Children darted in and out of the crowd, and jovial laughter curled into the cold air, rising like wisps of smoke unraveling into the fading light of the day.

Osric's gaze suddenly came to rest on Bishop Æthelwod, standing like a vulture among the Yule revelers. From a distance, his looming, hunch-shouldered presence seemed almost out of place in the otherwise welcoming scene.

Osric reined in the gelding and positioned himself as far from the bishop as possible while still maintaining some pretense of courtesy. It was a futile effort.

"Lord Osric, at last," Æthelwod called, his voice dripping with false welcome as he pushed his way through the crowd. His smile was wide and warm, and anyone unfamiliar with the bishop would have thought it genuine.

"Bishop Æthelwod," Osric greeted the bishop evenly, dismounting the gelding.

"The hunt must have been a fine one to keep you so occupied!" Æthelwod said, his voice carrying the weight of accusation beneath the warmth and pleasantry. "I had cause to seek you out on your return yestereve, yet you were nowhere to be found."

Osric met the bishop's gaze and smiled, mirroring the man's own disingenuous politeness.

"As is often the case when one is about one's duties, Lord Bishop," he replied smoothly. "I spent the evening with Svend. I was hoping to mend any lingering grievances over the missing trade goods—those that were so curiously discovered in our agricultural shed. I also plan to meet with Jarl Torvald soon to ensure there are no lasting ill feelings. Best to smooth the road before it turns to mire."

Æthelwod sniffed, feigning disinterest. "A noble effort, though one might say such a matter ought to have been left to rest."

Osric tilted his head, affecting a look of quiet contemplation. "One might say that, yes." He said, taking a deliberate, slow pause. "Stolen goods, simply hidden away... a rather unworthy effort, wouldn't you agree?"

Osric busied himself removing his saddlebags and tack, forcing himself to appear at ease, though he longed to watch Æthelwod's reaction as he continued.

"Although I suppose a would-be thief can only do so much with poor hands and limited abilities. After all, what use is a theft that serves no one, least of all the thief?"

Osric heard the bishop lightly clear his throat and shift his stance. Satisfied, he continued, trying to keep his voice light.

"In the end, all that the lazy, bungled effort accomplished was to breed a bit of resentment. And perhaps that was the point of such a weak showing. But ill feeling, as you say, ought to be set to rest."

Osric finally allowed himself to turn around, tack, and saddlebag in his arms. He marked that Æthelwod's expression barely flickered, yet Osric could clearly see the rising shadow of offense in his eyes.

"Ill feeling is indeed a shame." Æthelwod clipped. "Just as it seems a shame when folk cannot see their place and walk rightly in it."

Ah, finally, Osric thought, hoping the bishop had dropped the pretense of idle chatter and was moving directly to the heart of what he wanted to say.

"A well-ordered burh," Æthelwod continued smoothly, "is much like a well-kept flock—each sheep knowing where it belongs, under the guidance of a firm hand."

Osric exhaled slowly, fighting through his fatigue while a storm of irritation rose within him.

"Losing one's sense of place is a terrible shame, without question, Lord Bishop," Osric said, his tone rich with faux gravitas. "Worse still is when good folk are led there—pulled, even, by those who would use them for their own ends."

Osric let his words settle between them like a dense fog while he shifted his saddle and slung the bridle over his shoulder, pausing just a bit longer to allow the bishop to stew in the weight of his remark.

"What is the saying…" Osric continued, "A shepherd who fattens his flock too readily soon finds himself confronted by wolves."

Osric had no idea if that was an actual piece of wisdom that he'd heard somewhere or if he had just invented it on the spot, but it sounded right, and he could tell from the way Æthelwod's expression faltered that it had landed.

Seeing the expression on the bishop's face made Osric realize that his fatigue was perhaps driving his tongue a bit too enthusiastically, and he stood down, allowing caution to reign for however much longer he was forced to endure the interaction.

A few paces away, Cenric stood loitering, listening to every word, not even attempting to mask his enjoyment in what he was hearing. His gaze flicked between Osric and Æthelwod, his eyes glowing with amusement, yet he made no move to intervene.

Æthelwod, predictably, was keen to recover the upper hand. "Speaking of order," he pivoted, "Yule is upon us. A time of unity and good Christian fellowship. A gathering of all those who belong."

Here it comes. Osric nearly sighed aloud at the bishop's predictability. The man couldn't let a conversation pass without some veiled slight against Æfre or a grandiose jab at "the heathens".

"Naturally, my lord," Osric replied smoothly. "The bishop's blessing should be spoken over those meant to receive it."

Æthelwod's lips curved slightly. "Just so. And of course, those who do not belong… well. It would be best if they kept to their own hearths. The Yule feast must be a place of peace, after all—no need to invite discord."

The audacity of this wretch. Osric forced himself to keep his face impassive.

"A wise sentiment, Lord Bishop," he said, "and yet, it seems peace is already strained in some quarters. It is odd how certain folk have grown bold of late. Almost as if they feel protected, perhaps even encouraged."

Osric let the words hang in the air, realizing he'd already broken his vow from not two minutes past to be less confrontational. Yet he marked how Æthelwod's mask of smug superiority faltered again for just a fleeting moment—perhaps it wasn't for nothing.

"Well!" Æthelwod cleared his throat, clearly ready to retreat from the conversation. "I trust you shall enjoy tomorrow's feast,

Lord Osric. We all have much to be grateful for."

He turned without waiting for a response, stalking off with a stiffness that betrayed his irritation.

Osric smirked, smiling lightly as he watched the bishop walk away.

"That we do, Lord Bishop," he muttered under his breath, not bothering to look after him.

From nearby, Cenric gave a low chuckle. "By God Almighty, Lord Osric, that was an absolute delight to witness."

Osric let out a slow breath, shaking his head as he fought back the grin tugging at the corner of his mouth. "Come, Cenric. Let's see to the game and the horses, I'll tell you what you need to know—then, I'd say it's well past time we made a serious study of the bottom of a couple of ale cups."

30

Géola ✕ Yule

"Eadlin!" Wynnflæd of Aldhem's voice cut through the morning quiet of Aldhem's hall, her tone as sharp as a drawn blade. "We must leave for Wōdenléah now! Make haste! There is much to be done!"

Eadlin drew a steadying breath, smoothing the skirt of her favorite dress—an embroidered teal wool that accentuated her auburn hair and brown eyes. She adjusted her belt, pinched color into her cheeks, and ignored the flicker of heat that pulsed beneath her skin—whether it was fever or nerves, she dared not dwell on it.

Her mother had been climbing the walls with anticipation of the feast for the past two days; the woman had finally managed to irritate the last remaining servants she had not yet offended in her daily life with her outrageous demands and constant criticisms. As a result, every moment Eadlin wasn't overseeing the baking of the loaves, she was soothing the nerves of crying serving girls and repairing the bruised sensibilities of irritated ceorls—apologizing profusely to any and all on her mother's behalf.

Wynnflaed, worried about wagging tongues, summoned a healer from Swaffham—a burh to the west of Aldhem, bordering the marshlands that were hours away by wagon. A long way to go for secrecy, but Eadlin understood her mother's fear of gossip and the consequences it could have on a woman trying to navigate her place in society without a husband. Even so, she did not want to think about how much silver her mother had spent to keep her affliction quiet.

The healer had taken one look at the wound on her upper thigh and drawn a sharp breath. "Eadlin, this has festered mightily." A cool hand pressed against her burning forehead. "Oh dear, you are indeed on fire."

She had known—she'd felt the creeping fever, the way the dull ache had grown into a relentless throb, but hearing it spoken aloud had made it real in a way she wished it wasn't.

The healer had wasted no time—mashing garlic and yarrow into a bitter infusion for drinking, pressing poultices of marshmallow root, plantain, and sage against the angry purple lump that had swelled well beyond its original pinpoint size. Her mother had gone pale at the sight of it; Eadlin suspected she had not entirely believed her when she'd told her she had been suffering from an injury. But true to form, the concern in her eyes quickly dissolved into a veil of exasperation—as if Eadlin had let herself become ill simply to inconvenience her and potentially derail the festivities.

"An injury like this that has festered could take your life within days if you are not vigilant."

The healer's words of warning hung in Eadlin's ears like the ringing of a bell before a storm. No one, not even her mother, had argued when the woman insisted on staying an additional day to ensure the treatment was working.

It had been two days of poultices every four hours, of choking down infusion after pungent, acrid infusion, until her stomach rebelled at the very thought. And the stench—Lord Almighty, the stench. The lingering scent of garlic and herbs had seeped into her skin, hair, and clothes, clinging to her like a penance. Her mother had not been shy in voicing her displeasure on that front either, even if she wasn't entirely wrong. Eadlin knew it was hardly ideal for a betrothed woman to attend a feast reeking like a compost heap, especially when she was to be seated beside Osric—her soon-to-be husband.

Still, the treatment worked. The swelling was down, the fever had broken, and the wound, though still tender, started to shrink and drain itself of its poison. It was working.

And then she had stopped.

Not entirely, of course. Eadlin had bathed, then wrapped the wound in a clean, snug bandage, but she had skipped the infusions and poultices the moment the healer left to give herself a chance to clear the stench from her pores. It had been twelve hours now, and already the stench of garlic and herbs had stopped coming off of her like a protective ward.

But she could also feel the pain creeping back; a dull, insistent pulse beneath the bandage. She knew she was taking a dangerous risk, but how could she possibly sit beside Osric swathed in a rancid cloud of garlic and bitter herbs? What if he leaned in to speak to her? *What if he wished to kiss her?*

Her face burned with the thought. No, she would endure it. One day without treatment would not kill her. She would resume the infusions and poultices immediately after the festivities.

With this silent vow, she fastened a sachet of lavender to her belt and draped a strand of amber beads around her neck—a gift from her father, long ago—hoping the warm hue would lend some color to her pallid face. Finally, she secured a bronze comb in her hair before calling back, "I'm coming! Just gathering the last of the baskets!"

The moment she bent to lift the basket of wrapped loaves, a fresh throb of pain darted up her leg, settling in her pelvis. She clenched her teeth, breathing through the wave of discomfort, and stood up slowly.

One foot in front of the other, she thought as she stepped through the hall doors, the chill air biting her fever-warmed skin as she made her way to the wagon.

***

Æfre awoke late on Yule morning to the sound of a dull thump. It was as if something hit the ground just outside her door, followed by the soft, familiar sound of Epona's low nickering. *That will be Torvald's man,* she thought, thinking the sound to be the Northmen whom she would occasionally encounter walking the perimeter of her homestead. While her instinct was to pull the coverlet back up over her head, curiosity finally got the better of her and drove her to force herself upright. She had been planning for a quiet, restful Yule, but the truth was her barn chores came first, so she was just as well to get them done.

It had been easier lately to keep the barn in order. It was quieter with no chickens to scatter in panic at every slight movement she made. But truth be told, she missed those silly birds. There had once been something comforting about their incessant clucking, their chaotic flurry of wings and feathers at even the slightest noise. But now, with only Epona remaining, the barn felt nearly abandoned. Yet she didn't want to risk replacing the chickens, not with tensions with the burh still simmering. The thought of acquiring new birds only for them to disappear, or worse, meet a swift, senseless end—she couldn't bring herself to do it.

As she slid into her underdress and shift, the morning chill seeped through the thin walls of her hut, and she walked to the hearth to stoke the fire. Her hair fell untamed over her shoulders, and she swiftly braided it into a loose plait to avert another fire-related disaster. Belting her seax at her hip, she slipped into her boots and draped an old shawl over her shoulders. It wasn't enough to ward off the morning cold, but a few minutes working in the dust and mud of the paddock would warm her through.

As she opened the door, the light from the rising sun hit her face, and she paused for a moment to take in the clear, cold winter sunlight and admire the fine work Harald had done on the door. As she stepped out, something heavy thudded against her boot. Looking down, she saw a folded fabric parcel resting at her feet.

HEART OF THE WILD GODS

That must have been the sound I heard, she mused, picking up the parcel. The bundle was a thick, muted moss-green wool, and there was fur poking out from between the folds. It was tied with an ornate braided silk cord, to which a small wooden disc was secured—a thin cross-section cut from a young birch tree, beautifully carved with a gebo rune.

Gebo. A gift.

Her curiosity piqued, she stepped back into the warmth of the hut, clutching the parcel. As she untied the silk cord that held it together, the wool unfolded, and her breath caught in her throat.

It was a cloak. A beautiful new cloak.

Torvald Ironsight, she thought, smiling as she regarded the beautiful garment that unfolded in front of her. They had spoken of her burnt cloak the night he'd come to discuss the attack, *right before the roof came down on our heads,* she thought with a wry smile. A garment like this could only have arrived in such a short time from someone with influence and access to textiles.

Someone who runs a trading camp.

It had to be him.

Æfre smoothed the fine wool fabric as she spread the garment open on top of her bed. It was softer than any she had ever touched before—much finer than the scratchy garments she was used to. This cloak felt smooth and luxurious, like something spun by the gods themselves. The moss-green color was perfect—it reminded her of the quiet of the woods, of the enduring strength of the Earth. Intentionally or not, it was also a hue that was a near exact match to her eyes.

The cloak had a creamy beige fur lining along the hood, the feel of it silken and thick under her fingers. She had never owned a garment so fine. She giggled at the thought of the stoic Jarl, perhaps tiptoeing just outside her hut in cold morning hours, sneakily leaving this clandestine gift while she slept just on the other side of the wall.

It was more likely that the guard had dropped it off, but the thought of it, especially since she had only seen him yesterday and he hadn't mentioned a thing, made her chuckle.

Æfre stepped into the cloak, letting the soft, warm fabric settle around her shoulders. The hemline brushed just below her knee—it was perfect for riding, practical but also elegant. She admired the feel of it, the way it fit her, how it seemed to mold to her shape—it felt as if it had been made just for her.

She twirled, allowing the cloak to swish around her and marveled at how something so simple could so instantly transform the way she felt.

As she fussed with the folds, smoothing the edges, something heavy caught her attention—something she hadn't noticed. Pinned to the inside front of the cloak, nestled against the wool, was a beautiful silver pennanular brooch.

Æfre's fingers brushed over the smooth, cool surface, tracing its curve. It was simple and understated—a sleek elegance with the unmistakable weight of silver.

I must thank him properly, she thought, vowing to ride out to the camp after Yule to express her gratitude in person for such a generous gesture.

Still buzzing from the delight of such a beautiful gift, she shrugged the cloak off once again and placed it on her bed, smoothing it out before putting her old shawl back on. There was absolutely no chance she would be doing barn chores today in a garment so fine.

Æfre headed back outside, moving efficiently through her daily routine, a skill set honed by the necessity of solitary living. She tidied Epona's paddock, mucked out the stall, then haltered the mare and led her into the low winter sunlight, tethering her to the paddock fence. The horse, shaggy with her thick winter coat, was in desperate need of a thorough grooming.

From a small wooden chest beside Epona's stall, Æfre retrieved a bound twig brush and an antler pick her mother had given her long ago. She worked methodically, brushing and untangling from nose to tail as Epona stood contentedly, munching hay, basking in the attention.

Æfre was nearly finished picking the mare's hooves when she heard a soft crunch on frost-hardened earth just behind her. She had been so immersed in her work that she hadn't marked the rider approaching.

"A good morning, and joyous Yule to you," came a warm, familiar voice, "You're looking well." Æfre straightened, smiling as she turned, her eyes settling on a grinning Osric who sat astride Leo, his favorite gelding. She hadn't allowed herself to dwell on how much she missed him, but now, seeing him before her, the weight of his absence settled over her like a blanket of snow.

"Osric," she said, unable to keep from smiling, "a joyous Yule to you as well—and yes. I'm healing well." Æfre felt her entire body relax at the sight of him.

He kicked a leg over the gelding and slid from the saddle, landing with a plop directly in front of her with a small, overly dramatic bow, making her snort with laughter.

"Such noble behavior!"

Osric grinned. "If it pleases you, lady…" He took the pick from her fingers with exaggerated grace and crouched beside Epona, lifting her hoof and setting to work.

Æfre leaned against the paddock fence, shaking her head. "It's so like a man to show up when the work is nearly done and make such a grand display of helping."

Osric gasped in mock offense. "Ah! You're giving away our greatest secret! But yes—I've been crouching in the trees, waiting for you to get to these last few hooves before making my entrance."

"Just so. I knew it."

He chuckled, working through the final hooves with efficient strokes. When he straightened at last, he moved towards her, closing the distance between them until Æfre was backed right up against the fence and going no further.

"I miss you," she admitted softly, as if saying it too loudly might sever the last brittle ties that bound them.

Osric lifted a hand, brushing his fingers against her cheek, tracing the curve of her jaw as if memorizing it. Then, with a quiet kind of reverence, he kissed her like a man trying to stop time.

"I can't stay," he whispered against her lips. "The feast tonight—Æthelwod is hovering like a buzzard over a kill, and poor Cwenhild is losing her mind."

"Of course she is." Æfre huffed a soft laugh. "It feels strange not being there to help."

Osric wrapped his arms around her then, pressing his lips to her forehead. She let herself sink into his warmth, her hands lightly gripping the fabric of his cloak, as if they were both holding each other in place.

"Come," he murmured, lips brushing her skin. "Let's go inside and talk."

She exhaled slowly, eyes flickering up to meet his, and saw a sorrowful look of resignation she recognized too well.

"Give me just a moment to put up this great beast next to us." She stroked his face with her hand.

Æfre untied Epona's halter, giving the mare a gentle pat before letting her loose in the paddock and storing the grooming tools.

When she rejoined him, he draped an arm over her shoulders, pressing another lingering kiss to her forehead before they walked together to her hut—towards whatever words needed to be said.

Back inside the hut, Æfre tended the hearth, stoking the fire as Osric settled into a nearby chair—*his* chair. The sight of him there, in a space so intimately theirs, sent a deep ache through her chest. How many evenings had they spent just like this? And yet, everything had changed.

Osric broke the silence first. "I see your door was repaired beautifully."

"Yes." Æfre pulled a chair close to his by the hearth. "I have your friend the Jarl to thank for that."

"Torvald Ironsight?"

She nodded. "The Jarl paid a visit the day after the attack."

She told Osric everything that had happened since she last saw him—the story of how she shot an arrow at his groin made him laugh out loud, as she'd known it would. She told him about Eadgar, how he'd taken refuge in the Norse camp, and how the Jarl had asked her to teach him to use a bow.

She was keenly aware of how Osric watched her as she spoke. So much had happened so quickly—it seemed like months had passed instead of days, and trying to put it all into words left her feeling as if she might come undone.

"Æfre, there is something you need to know." Osric suddenly leaned forward, a solemn expression in his eyes.

He told her everything—of his journey to Wintanceaster, of standing before King Alfred, and how the king voiced support for their plan to thwart Æthelwod's scheme, and finally how King Alfred himself had pressed him toward the match with Aldhem with barely veiled promises of alliance and influence.

"I am telling you this because we believe Æthelwod will make his move soon," Osric said. "We will be prepared for it. If all goes as planned, we will contain the threat—and use it to our advantage to better the future of Wōdenléah."

"By ridding the burh of Æthelwod," Æfre said bluntly, a gleam in her eye.

"Perhaps—yes." Osric met her gaze. "But Æfre, you must not

speak of this to anyone. I am telling you this because he has been so determined—"

A sudden knock rattled the door, and they both startled.

Æfre looked at Osric, her mind searching for who could possibly be calling upon her so unexpectedly.

"No one is expected." She frowned as she moved towards the door. Easing the door open, she found Geir, the guard from the trading camp. Over his shoulder, Æfre could see Wynn, the thatcher's wife.

"Forgive me, húsfreyja,—this woman asks for you," Geir said.

"Wynn!" Æfre exclaimed, "Is all well? Is little Godhild well?"

"Yes, Æfre. Sweet Godhild is well. Her arm is well mended now. Cwenhild watches her—it is you I've come to see."

"Please, come inside." Æfre turned to Geir, "Thank you, Geir. All is well here." Geir nodded briskly and strode back towards the road.

"Come, Wynn, warm yourself by the hearth."

Wynn swept inside and began to remove her cloak, then froze as she spotted Osric.

"Oh! Lord Osric! Forgive me! I didn't know you had a visitor, Æfre."

"It's no bother, Wynn, you're ever welcome," Æfre said.

"I can step out so that you women might speak privately," Osric offered, rising from his chair.

"No, my lord," Wynn said, her voice tinged with urgency.

"It's better you both hear what I have to say. I cannot stay long and...Honestly, I know not what to do."

Wynn burst into tears.

"Wynn!" Æfre ushered the crying woman into her chair by the hearth, then scavenged an empty cup from her shelf, filling it with ale and handing it to her.

"Thank you." Wynn took a sip of the ale and steadied herself.

"I'm sorry, Æfre."

"What is it, Wynn?" Æfre kneeled next to Wynn's chair.

"It's Aelf." She sniffed.

Osric sat forward in his chair at the mention of the thatcher's name, attention piqued.

"Æfre...I know how difficult things have become for you, and I am so sorry for my part in it. I never wished anyone harm. But the bishop—"

Wynn again dissolved into a flood of tears.

Osric began to say something, but Æfre shot him a look.

Let her tell it in her own way.

Osric settled back into his chair.

"Lord Osric, you've heard the things the bishop has been saying in the services—about the heathens. But it doesn't end there. The bishop..."

Æfre's glance flicked over to Osric. He kept a neutral expression, though she could sense the storm under the surface.

"Aelf and others have been meeting with him. They're making plans."

"What plans, Wynn?" Osric asked.

"I know not," Wynn cried, "Aelf will tell me naught but how things will be better once the heathens are driven out."

Æfre and Osric exchanged looks.

"Æfre, since that day you were attacked, I knew I must speak on this. I'm so sorry!"

"Wynn, what happened to me was no doing of yours! I saw the man who attacked me, a Northman. This is not your fault!"

"Mayhap," Wynn said, "yet when I spoke to Aelf of it, he was not surprised. Said it should be expected by those who have not accepted the one true God, and that more is coming. When I pressed him on it, he would say no more. I scarce know him Æfre! The bishop has him in some sort of bewilderment, and he is no longer himself!"

"Wynn, are you and Godhild safe?" Æfre asked.

"Oh yes, Aelf would never—" she trailed off, then looked at Osric. "I'm so sorry, Lord. I know how pressed you are, and it's Yule—"

"You need not ask forgiveness, Wynn. You may always come to me with such matters." Osric said gently.

"I...I really must return. I only wished to warn you, and I would tell you more if I knew it. But please, take care Æfre." Wynn set her unfinished cup of ale down.

"Wynn," Osric said, rising from his chair, "let me ride back to the burh with you. We can speak more on this—if you wish."

"Yes, Lord. Thank you."

Osric met Æfre's gaze, an unspoken apology passing between them.

She answered with a silent nod. He was right—they would have to let the matter rest at least for now.

She walked them to the door and stood watching as they readied the horses, then rode up the path towards the road above.

Once the door closed behind her, Æfre let out a long sigh and leaned against it, Wynn's words pressing down on her. Everything was changing—her safety, his duty, their happiness—all of it poisoned by Æthelwod's schemes.

Æfre looked around the hut, once their private refuge, now a reminder of the truth she could no longer ignore—for them, love, duty, and security could not walk the same road together.

HEART OF THE WILD GODS

31

Symbel ⚔ Feast

"Let it never be said that we fail to honor our guests, nor the Lord God Almighty, with a feast befitting His divine providence!" Bishop Æthelwod proclaimed to no one in particular, preening and idle amidst a centrifuge of women setting places, hauling extra benches into the hall, and making last-minute adjustments. He, of course, took no part in the labor, merely observing the preparations with a critical eye, as if his very presence sanctified the preparations.

"The high table!" he called out, extending a dramatic hand as he glided, preening through the hall like a man already victorious. "The high table must be served only the finest cuts! No mistakes! Time is pressing on, and we would not dare offend those whom the Lord has seen fit to place in such favorable positions. And we certainly would not wish them to wait overlong."

Everything is falling into place, Æthelwod thought, his hawkish gaze sweeping over the high table as he placed a small gold crucifix at the center place setting, the most prominent position at the table, claiming it as his own. *A new era begins tonight,* he thought. This was to be the era of his ascendancy, beginning with that place setting, he would start as he meant to continue by taking what was rightfully his.

Satisfied, he moved around the table, muttering under his breath as he rehearsed his Yule address, gesturing grandly as if already delivering it before an enraptured hall.

He was interrupted by Cwenhild, who trudged in, burdened with a basket of wooden serving platters, the young server Gytha struggling behind her.

"Forgive us if you will, Bishop", Cwenhild said as the two tried to edge past him to get to the tables, but he stood firm, blocking their path with the air of a man oblivious to the concept of moving aside for lesser creatures.

"May the Lord strike me down where I stand if he isn't testing the last of my patience today," Cwenhild muttered to Gytha, once they were finally able to move past him, her tone thick with exasperation.

Gytha tried to stifle a laugh, but was unsuccessful, and it resulted in an audible snort, which she then attempted to disguise as a cough, which only made everything worse.

Æthelwod's head snapped toward them.

"There, there now, girl," Cwenhild said, patting Gytha on the back with exaggerated care as she met Æthelwod's gaze. "It's an exciting day for us all—best not let the Lord's abundant blessings overcome you before time."

Æthelwod raised a sharp brow, then nodded approvingly at Cwenhild's sufficiently pious proclamation, and turned back to his private performance.

The two women exchanged conspiratorial looks before scurrying away, tittering, their suppressed laughter leaving a quiet wake behind them.

The sound of a wagon outside drew Æthelwod to the door. He swept towards the entrance like a sylph and peered out, his expression morphing into an unctuous smile as he spotted Wynnflæd and Eadlin of Aldhem arriving.

"Ah! Aldhem has arrived!" he declared, moving towards them with outstretched arms, his voice saccharine to the point of melting. "And if I may say, Lady Wynnflæd, you have never looked more radiant! Eadlin, you are positively glowing in that color. Lord Osric will be left utterly speechless at the sight of you."

Eadlin blushed and offered a thin smile in Æthelwod's direction before turning her attention to the loaves stacked in the wagon.

HEART OF THE WILD GODS

"Oh, my dear, allow me to call for assistance!" Æthelwod fussed, already turning toward the hall. "Cwenhild! Cwenhild, Aldhem is here!"

"Bishop, really, there's no need," Eadlin said quickly. "I can manage perfectly well." Eadlin walked stiffly towards the back of the wagon, wincing briefly before transforming her expression to a smile.

"Nonsense, my dear! A woman of your standing need not trouble herself with such menial tasks." He snapped his fingers sharply in the air. "Cwenhild! Quickly, now! These loaves will not carry themselves! The Lord's blessings are not bestowed upon the idle."

A long pause followed, until finally Cwenhild emerged from the hall wearing a face like thunder.

"Ah, there you are," Æthelwod clapped his hands thrice. "You really must make haste. We feared we might perish of old age waiting for you to do your duty."

Cwenhild's face darkened to the shade of a boiled beet. She stomped toward the wagon and began gathering the loaves with enough force to make the baskets creak. Then, at last, she spotted Eadlin.

"Oh, Eadlin, my dear!" she gushed, her tone changing instantly. "I was so preoccupied I didn't even realize it was you! You look lovely, my girl! Are you well?"

"Well enough," Eadlin said with a strained smile, lifting a basket. "Come, let's make our escape and get these loaves inside."

"My dear, those were my exact thoughts," Cwenhild murmured, casting Æthelwod a glare cold enough to freeze a man solid.

With that, she, Gytha, and Eadlin made a swift retreat, leaving Lady Wynnflæd alone with Æthelwod.

The bishop turned to the matriarch of Aldhem, his smile

tightening. "Lady Wynnflæd, I see that Eadlin is healing well from her injury of late." His tone was smooth, but his eyes were sharp, watching her reaction closely.

"Indeed, Bishop," Lady Wynnflæd said lightly, brushing a speck of dust from her sleeve. "She is on the mend."

"And did you summon the healing woman, Æfre, after all?" His words were carefully measured.

"Oh, goodness, no," Wynnflæd scoffed, waving a delicate hand. "I brought in a healer from Swaffham—one recommended to me some years ago."

"Swaffham?" Æthelwod arched a brow. "That is quite a distance."

"Indeed," she replied, her voice dripping with measured disinterest. "It was no small torment, to be frank. The treatment was dreadful—the smell of it! Some awful concoction of herbs and poultices—quite a trial for a mother to endure, I assure you."

"Good gracious," Æthelwod murmured. "The wound—was it worse than you had at first held it to be?"

Wynnflæd gave a dismissive sniff. "Not too severe, Lord Bishop, but one must take every precaution, especially with such important matters on the horizon. The healer was quite thorough, perhaps even over strong, but it is done, and she is recovering."

Her tone left no room for further questioning, so naturally, Æthelwod pressed on.

"Indeed," he said smoothly. "It would be most unfortunate if such an incident were to cloud the bright future ahead—the holy union between Aldhem and Wōdenléah."

Wynnflæd smiled—a polished, practiced thing, sweet on the surface but with the reflection of a sharp blade rippling just beneath.

"Of course, Lord Bishop," she replied. "We have everything under control."

HEART OF THE WILD GODS

And with that, she turned, sweeping into the hall, leaving Æthelwod standing in the doorway, his fingers tightening around the crucifix he wore around his neck.

* * *

The guests were already beginning to file into the hall when Osric emerged from his quarters, freshly bathed and clad in a deep blue tunic with embroidery at the cuffs and collar. The air bit at his damp hair, but he barely noticed—his mind was still turning over his visit to Æfre and Wynn's warning of the bishop's plans.

Unfortunately, his ride ride back to the burh with Wynn hadn't provided him with anything useful about Æthelwod's scheme—Wynn really didn't know anything specific about what her husband was up to. It left him feeling on edge, like he was missing something.

As he made his way towards the main part of the hall, he heard the unmistakable bloviating of Æthelwod's voice, smug and self-important. Osric paused, his stomach tightening as he recognized a second voice and realized exactly who the bishop had cornered—*Eadlin*.

He couldn't quite make out what was being said, but he knew instinctively that she would likely appreciate an intervention. He considered stepping in immediately, but instead moved a bit closer to their conversation, lingering just out of sight, taking a moment to steel himself before having the interaction. It was going to be a long night, and he would need every last drop of patience he could muster.

That, and a few generous cups of ale.

"My dear child," Æthelwod was saying, his voice dripping with feigned paternalism, "do not let your nerves overtake you! Our Lord Osric is a fine man, and together, you and he shall restore the rightful order of things in Wōdenléah!"

The rightful order? Osric almost laughed aloud.

"The rightful order?" Eadlin echoed, her attempt at soft politeness doing little to mask her incredulity.

Leaning against the wall just beyond view, Osric grinned.

"My dear, you have been most fortunate in this match," Æthelwod pressed on, "a good, Christian match, and you shall make a most graceful wife to our Lord Osric."

The odd familiarity coming from Æthelwod made Osric shudder.

"Now, my dear, tonight is a night to show strength," Æthelwod continued pompously, "for strength in duty is a woman's greatest virtue."

"Indeed, Bishop," Eadlin replied, sounding utterly exhausted.

The resignation in her voice was what did it. Osric sighed, rolling his shoulders back and steeling his patience. Æthelwod, like the lingering smell of boiled cabbage over a hearth fire, rarely went away on his own—one had to put in a bit of effort. It was time to step in.

Osric rounded the partition and declared, "A joyous Yule to you both!" as he moved towards them.

Eadlin turned to face him, and he nearly burst out laughing—the look on her face was clear—*Thank God you're here. Help me.*

"Ah! Lord Osric! There you are!" Æthelwod crowed, spreading his arms as if greeting a long-lost brother. "Just the man I was searching for when I happened upon the radiant Eadlin!"

Osric inclined his head in greeting. "Bishop Æthelwod. Eadlin." He met Eadlin's gaze with a quick look that said, *I'll take care of it.*

Æthelwod swept a hand toward Osric in an exaggerated flourish. "If I might have a word with you, Lord Osric?" Then, with a perfunctory glance at Eadlin, "Eadlin, you don't mind if I steal your betrothed for a moment?"

"Not at all, Bishop, please." Eadlin's response was so instantaneous that again Osric had to stifle a laugh. Eadlin was already inching towards the hall, her escape route clear.

"I'll see you presently, Eadlin," Osric said pleasantly, ensuring Æthelwod was turned away before he silently mouthed, *RUN!*

Eadlin stifled her giggle with a demure nod, then limped swiftly inside, leaving Osric alone with the bishop.

"Ah, Lord Osric," Æthelwod said, clasping his hands with a sigh. "It pleases me to see that you are a man who is beginning to recognize that his path has been divinely chosen."

Osric kept his expression neutral. "Bishop?"

Here we go.

"Some of us are made to serve not just our own interests, but the greater well-being of our people," Æthelwod continued smoothly, his tone rich with self-importance.

"Indeed, Lord Bishop."

"Such is the burden that men like us must bear," Æthelwod said with a solemn nod. "Although, of course, credit must also be given to the men of steadfast loyalty among us."

"Always, Lord Bishop," Osric replied tightly.

At that moment, Osric saw movement from the hall. It was Cenric, standing near the entrance, trying to catch his eye, as if having been summoned by the bishop's mention of steadfast loyalty. But then, Cenric always had a way of materializing when Æthelwod was making a pest of himself, and Osric was always grateful for it. Osric looked at Cenric, who lifted his hand in an obvious gesture, miming the shape of an ale cup.

Osric nodded emphatically.

Yes, please.

"And yet," Æthelwod droned on, oblivious, "it falls to our leaders to bear burdens that others cannot."

"Such has always been the duty of leadership, Lord Bishop,"

Osric replied evenly. "But tell me, have you a specific burden in mind that you should bring this up?"

At that exact moment, Cenric appeared at his side and pressed a full ale cup into his hand. Osric accepted it with a nod of gratitude, resisting the urge to down it in one go.

Cenric, meanwhile, shot Æthelwod a sideways look and a smile that didn't quite reach his eyes before turning on his heel and slipping back into the hall.

"Ah, but I am getting ahead of myself!" Æthelwod said, smiling indulgently. "I know well that when the time comes, you will serve with all the diligence and grace expected of a man in your position—as you have always done in the past."

Osric took a slow sip of ale. "And specifically what service is it that you refer to, Lord Bishop?"

Æthelwod clapped a hand over his heart, shaking his head. "Ah, I'm afraid I am getting ahead of myself yet again! But suffice it to say, Lord Osric—history remembers those who act. You'll have to excuse me, Lord, I must attend to the guests."

This is going to be a very long night, Osric thought as he watched Æthelwod glide away towards the arriving guests.

He drained the last of the ale from his cup and strode to the back of the hall, intent on a refill. The bishop was setting him up for something—of that, Osric had no doubt. Æthelwod always liked to play with his prey before pouncing, and tonight was no exception. But whatever design the bishop thought he had for the evening, Osric was ready. They all were.

As he made his way through the hall, Osric spotted Eadlin seated, tucked away at the side, her head resting against the wall, her eyes closed. Something felt off. She looked drained. Even in the dim light of the torches and hearth fire, he could see she was pale—too pale. He'd noticed earlier that the usual brightness in her eyes was dulled, and her posture seemed stiff as though she were bracing against some unseen pain.

Pulling a chair alongside hers, he sat and leaned his head back in a similar fashion, exhaling heavily. "It's already been an eternally long day, has it not?" He took a deep draught of ale, turning his head slightly to watch her. He was determined not to make this interaction awkward, as he had been guilty of so many times before.

"Mmm." Eadlin's eyes fluttered open, and she inhaled deeply. "Oh, Osric. I was really and truly away there for a moment." She let out a quiet laugh, but it lacked her usual warmth.

Something was wrong. Osric studied her more closely—her breathing was shallow, and dark circles cast a shadow beneath her eyes.

"Eadlin, are you unwell? What is it?" He reached out instinctively, brushing the back of his hand against her cheek. She felt like she was burning.

"Eadlin, you're fevered!" His voice was low but laced with concern.

"I'm fine, Osric." She gave him a weak smile that didn't quite reach her eyes. "I've been a bit afflicted of late, but I'll endure tonight. After, there will be nothing but time to rest and heal."

"Heal?" Osric narrowed his eyes. "Eadlin, what ails you? This will not do—you should be lying down."

"Osric," she reached for his hand, squeezing lightly. "All will be well. We both need to get through this night. We will smile, we will feast, and afterwards, we can attend to other matters."

He wasn't convinced. Eadlin needed a warm bed, not a night of feasting and politics. He opened his mouth to protest once more, but the moment was once again shattered by Bishop Æthelwod, who seemingly materialized out of nowhere.

"Ah, Lord Osric! There you are!"

Osric forced a neutral expression, his eyes not leaving Eadlin as he answered, "Here I am, Bishop Æthelwod."

Æthelwod's voice was thick with self-satisfaction. "The guests have all arrived. I believe it is time to begin the proceedings. If you would do the honor of striking the shield and having our guests be seated?"

"Of course, Lord Bishop," he said evenly, casting a final worried glance at Eadlin, who gave him a smile and a nod.

"I'll just see Eadlin to her seat, and then we'll begin."

Æthelwod, satisfied, nodded briskly and swept off towards the high table in a flutter of robes.

Osric turned back to Eadlin. "You're certain you have the strength for this?" He offered her his arm, "If you want to lie down—"

"Osric." Her voice was gentle but firm. She smiled as she stood, stiff and controlled. He saw the briefest wince before she masked it. "Let's feast."

He didn't like it, but arguing would only cost her more energy and draw unwanted attention. Saying nothing, he supported her as they moved towards the high table.

As Eadlin settled into her seat, Osric turned to retrieve the ceremonial shield and spear. As he lifted them from the wall, he caught sight of Cwenhild passing by. Without hesitation, he beckoned her over.

"Cwenhild, I'm worried about Eadlin," he murmured. "She's unwell, but she's stubborn. She insists on staying and doing her duty tonight."

Cwenhild's face darkened. "Lord, I hadn't said anything, but I noticed it earlier." Her gaze flickered toward Eadlin, who sat unnaturally still, her eyes fixed on some distant point, as if willing herself to stay upright. "She's not herself."

"She's fevered," Osric said, his tone grim. "Might I ask you to help keep an eye on her if I'm caught up—" he glanced toward the high table, where Lady Wynnflæd was deep in conspiratorial conversation with Æthelwod and Gerēfa Wilfred, the old reeve from Aldhem, an ancient, ruddy-faced man already several cups of mead down and well on his way to being as legless as a fallen oak. "Her mother seems otherwise engaged this evening."

Cwenhild followed his gaze, pursing her lips before nodding. "Ġēa, Lord Osric. I'll watch over her."

Osric nodded gratefully, then turned back to the hall. He raised the spear and brought it down hard against the shield several times. The loud clack echoed throughout the hall, silencing the hum of conversation.

"Come, friends!" Osric cried, using his command voice to ensure it carried over the gathered crowd. "Fill your cups and take your seats! Let us feast together this night!"

The rustling of feet and scrape of benches and chairs filled the hall as the guests took their places. Æthelwod, as confident as ever, sat preening front and center at the high table. To his left, Osric and Eadlin. To his right, Lady Wynnflæd and Gerēfa Wilfred.

As the final murmurs died down, Osric stepped forward.

"Friends, for my part, I shall keep my prattle short. By now, the delicious scent of the roast has reached every corner of this hall, and I know many of you well enough to understand the peril I put myself in by standing between you and a plate of food."

Laughter rippled through the crowd, several of his men chuckling knowingly.

"We have much to be grateful for this Yule night. We've weathered some trials, but here we stand, three winters past Edington, not only at peace but blessed with one of the most prosperous harvests Wōdenléah has known."

A cheer went up, cups lifted in gratitude. Osric allowed the people of the burh their celebration and let the hall settle before continuing.

"Our trade is strong, our defenses steadfast, and our people thrive."

Before he could continue, a voice from the back—emboldened by mead—shouted out, "My lord! When are you going to tell us about the wedding?"

The hall roared with laughter.

Osric smirked. "Ah, cutting straight to the marrow then... Alaric, is it?" He squinted toward the back of the hall.

"Ġēa, Lord!" the voice called back.

Osric chuckled. "Alaric, I'll remember this when next we spar during exercises." The crowd laughed again, and Æthelwod's expression shifted to a beady-eyed scowl, his patience wearing thin.

Still grinning, Osric lifted a hand for quiet. "Very well. I was going to save it for later, but since you insist." He glanced at Eadlin, who gave the slightest nod of permission. Her smile was fixed, but her hands trembled slightly in her lap.

"In case Eadlin's presence at the high table had not made it obvious, let me settle the matter now. Eadlin and I are betrothed, and we will be married in the spring."

Cheers erupted, and Osric stooped, gently pulling Eadlin to her feet. The moment she rose, he felt her sway, her body shaky and unnaturally warm against his. He tightened his grip, slipping his arm around her waist to steady her. The firelight flickered across her face, but beneath the polite smile, she was pale as death.

They stood there, smiling for the crowd, playing their parts. The betrothed lord and lady. The perfect match. He who was hopelessly in love with another woman, and she who might collapse with fever at any moment. *What a sorry pair we make this night*, Osric thought.

Osric held Eadlin close, smiling broadly even as the cold weight of the finality of his announcement settled deep in his gut. Whatever hope he had clung to that somehow he might find a way forward with Æfre—however fantastical that notion may have been—it was put to death in that moment, and by his own hand. They were now locked into the path set before them, and he felt a bit stunned.

When the revelry settled once more and Osric had guided Eadlin safely back into her seat, he forced down the cold knot in his stomach. His mind raced with the weight of what had just transpired, but there was no room for hesitation now. He squared his shoulders, swallowed hard, and addressed the hall once again.

"Friends," he began, his voice carrying through the great hall, steady despite the turmoil within him, "I know your bellies are eager, and I won't stand between you and the feast much longer. But before we begin, let me honor each of you here gathered." His gaze swept the room, meeting the faces of the warriors, farmers, traders, and elders who had bled, toiled, and nurtured the community alongside him.

"The prosperity we share tonight was not won by one man's actions, nor was it granted by fate alone. It is by your strength, toil, and dedication that we thrive. Through victory and hardship, to the brittle peace we now enjoy—you all have stood steadfast, and for that, I owe you my thanks." He lifted his cup. "So, let us drink this Yule not only to the return of the light, but also to the bond we share, to the work we have done, and to the future we will carve together—for Wōdenléah and for greater Wessex!"

A roar of approval echoed through the hall as cups and drinking horns were raised in unison. "To this noble people—may our harmony be a lasting one!" Osric declared, his voice rising above the clamor.

Laughter and cheer surged once more, and when Osric glanced down, Eadlin was smiling up at him, exhausted but present. He gave her a slight wink and a nod before turning back to the gathered crowd.

"Now—" he continued, a knowing glint in his eye, "I believe

Bishop Æthelwod would next like to offer the blessing, Lord Bishop?"

Osric turned to Æthelwod with an expression of well-practiced courtesy, though he knew full well the bishop would seize this moment with the fervor of a man who loved the sound of his own voice. As the bishop rose, robes shifting like a ruffled bird, Osric sat and took a measured sip of his ale, bracing himself for whatever might come.

Bishop Æthelwod stood and smoothed his robes ceremoniously, giving an exaggerated, grandiose nod to Osric.

"My most faithful friends, before we ask for the blessing of our Lord Almighty for this most gracious Yule feast, I wish to take a moment to recognize our Lord Osric—a true servant of Wōdenléah by both his leadership and his sword."

The bishop let the words hang, allowing them to settle over the hall like an embroidered mantle of righteousness. Osric merely inclined his head, careful to keep his expression neutral. He took a long draught from his ale cup, more for something to do with his hands than out of any real thirst.

"As you have just witnessed by his most humble address to you, Lord Osric is a man of unyielding resolve when it comes to the prosperity and well-being of his people. Why, it was by his own sword that my own life was saved on the battlefield at Edington!"

Osric barely stifled a smirk. That was certainly one way to tell it. The truth was that Æthelwod had blundered too close to the fray during the invocation and had required rescue, an act that had cost the lives of two of Osric's men. Æthelwod had not been "on" the battlefield so much as he was trying to flee it.

"Yet," Æthelwod's voice sharpened, shifting gears, "there are those who dwell within our borders who do not share the same dedication to this land!"

Here it comes, Osric thought.

HEART OF THE WILD GODS

"The Northmen traders," he declared, voice thick with scorn, "reap the bounty of our soil, their purses swollen with coin, yet what do they give in return? A mere pittance!"

Osric tightened his grip on his cup, his knuckles whitening. He kept his face blank as murmurs rippled through the crowd, eyes flicking between Æthelwod and Osric, waiting for some indication of agreement—or defiance.

"It is time," Æthelwod pressed on, voice gathering force, "for these heathens who grow fat off the wealth of Wōdenléah to offer fair tribute! And who better to act as our emissary in this just endeavor than the man seated at my right? A man whose heart beats for this land, whose very soul is bound to Christendom!"

A slow, hot boil of anger began to spread through Osric's chest, but he took a deep breath—slow and steady, measured to the point of imperceptibility. He stared into the emptiness of his drained cup, forcing himself not to react as he gripped the arm of his chair. Beside him, without a word, Eadlin's pale hand slipped atop his hand. A small, silent acknowledgment. A steadying touch.

Æthelwod's voice swelled with triumph. "And so, my friends, Lord Osric—ever a man of duty—will depart for Wintanceaster in two days' time to stand for us all. He will see to it that the heathens are brought to account, and he shall petition our wise and just King Alfred to ensure that we, the true people of this land, are not burdened further by those who take more from the trade than they give!"

A hush fell. Every eye in the hall was on Osric.

Osric forced a smile, one carefully shaped to reveal nothing. He inclined his head, offering a nod of deference. His stomach churned, and the cold grip of realization tightened around his gut. This was it. Æthelwod had made his move.

Across the room, he caught Cenric's gaze. A brief but knowing exchange passed between them.

This is it.

"Lord Osric," Æthelwod purred with satisfaction, "I need not tell you what a great honor this is. A task fit for a man of your talent and standing. I have no doubt that, as ever, you will serve as a righteous hand in this matter."

Osric lifted his empty cup. "Thank you, Lord Bishop."

Æthelwod's lips tightened into his version of a smile. "And now, my friends," he declared, turning back to the hall, "let us stand and give thanks to the Lord Almighty, whose grace sustains us this night."

Osric exhaled slowly as he rose. He slipped an arm around Eadlin's waist, steadying her—or perhaps allowing her to steady him. She was swaying from fever, he was swaying from fury, but in that moment, he guessed neither could say which of them was holding the other up.

* * *

Eadlin's stomach lurched as the great platter of roasted meat was set before her, the rich aroma turning her insides. With Osric's help, she had managed to stay upright through the invocation, but there was no chance she'd manage more than a few bites of food tonight—she could barely stand to look at it. Keeping up appearances, she reached for a thick slice of bread, placing it on her plate as a pretense of participation—at least she would be seen with something on her plate.

She inhaled slowly, forcing the nausea into a fragile submission, then took the tiniest sip of ale—even that made her stomach recoil. Her head and wounded leg pounded in time with her heartbeat, her vision wavering in and out of focus. Her body felt like a battlefield, like she was fighting some unseen enemy with every labored breath.

Next to her, Osric was tearing into his portion of venison with a warrior's appetite, but his attention kept flickering to her. Every time he noticed her lack of food, his brow creased in concern. She mustered what she hoped was a reassuring smile, but judging by his expression, it had done little to ease his worry.

Eadlin turned her focus outward, scanning the hall, weighing her options. If she began to feel any worse, she would have no choice but to excuse herself. The thought of walking past the entire gathering, of every pair of eyes following her struggle, made the heat rise up the back of her neck. She traced the quickest path in her mind—the back entrance by the thegn's quarters. A more obstacle-laden route, to be sure, but at least she would be spared the scrutiny of the entire hall's complement if she didn't have to limp through the whole length of the hall.

"Eadlin," Osric leaned in and spoke in low tones, "I can see you're struggling. Go lie down in my quarters if you need to. I'll handle any questions."

"Thank you, Osric," Eadlin said, realizing that it was unlikely she'd make it through the night in her current state, "I'll likely do just that. I think I'll just step outside and get some air for a moment, then return and try to eat something first—I don't want to waste the opportunity to enjoy the spoils of the hunt!"

Osric's expression remained doubtful. "I'll go with you—"

She cut him off before he could rise. "Don't be silly, Osric. Stay and enjoy your meal. I won't be long."

Osric looked dubious but did not press her further. When he helped her to her feet, his assistance appeared to anyone who might have been watching like an intimacy shared between a betrothed couple.

Eadlin moved carefully along the back of the hall, keeping close to the high table. The floor seemed to shift beneath her, and her step faltered. She reached for the wall, fingers pressing against one of the embedded wooden beams as she steadied herself. Squaring her shoulders, she forced herself upright and continued, disappearing behind the partition leading to the back exit.

Out of sight at last, she let her guard slip. Her body sagged against the wall, using it for support as she dragged herself along, making her way to the door.

At the high table, Osric had not stopped watching. When his eyes met Cwenhild's across the hall, he saw that she, too, had been observing. He gave her a slight nod in Eadlin's direction, but the gesture was unnecessary—Cwenhild was already rising, weaving through the crowded hall to follow.

The cold night air hit Eadlin like a slap to the face as she exited the hall. Her vision blurred, the world tipping strangely beneath her feet as though she were walking at an angle. She took a few steps, gripping the outside wall for balance, drawing in deep lungfuls of the frozen air in a futile attempt to steady herself.

Her stomach twisted violently. She barely had time to turn before she retched, spilling what little she had eaten onto the frost-hardened ground. Wave after wave of nausea wracked her, leaving her shaking, gasping, and weak. Even when there was nothing left, her body still heaved, draining her of what little reserve she had.

Lightheaded, her fingers tingling, she clung to the wall. The pain in her wounded leg had worsened, a dull, heavy weight dragging at her thigh, each step sending fresh bolts of agony shooting up into her groin.

Another wave of dizziness struck. The world tilted.

She stumbled again, her body sagging sideways, and she slumped against the side of the hall. The unyielding cold, hard surface of the wall was the last thing she felt as it broke her fall and she collapsed, slipping into the deep, dark abyss of unconsciousness.

32

Sēocness ✕ Sickness

Æfre startled at the sudden pounding on her door, her quill slipping from her fingers and landing with a soft pat against the parchment of her leechbook. The wooden table she was sitting at rocked with the vibration, causing the candle on the table to cast chaotic shadows on the walls of the hut. She'd been so engrossed in her writing that she hadn't even heard the rider.

The pounding came again, more insistent this time, once again rattling the wooden door on its hinges. Her pulse quickened. Someone calling at this hour, with such urgency—it likely wasn't anything good, but whoever it was, had gotten past Torvald's guard, so surely it had to be someone either known or who was in urgent need of a healer.

Æfre hesitated, glancing at her bow that sat across the room, instead picking up her seax as she rose from the table.

"Æfre!" A familiar voice called from behind the door, slightly muffled by the thick wood.

Cenric.

"I'm sorry, Æfre," he continued, punctuating his words with another urgent knock. "I'm afraid it's an urgent matter."

Æfre barely had the door open before Cenric stepped forward and into her hut. His expression was grave, and her stomach tightened.

"What's happened?" she asked, stepping aside.

"It's Eadlin," Cenric said, his voice low and grim. "She collapsed outside the Yule feast."

"Collapsed!?"

"She's very unwell."

Æfre's mind sharpened at once; hesitation, doubts, and any

other personal feelings were instantly pushed aside as she fell naturally into her duties. "And they need me to attend?" she asked, already moving, her hands reaching instinctively for her satchel.

"Yes—please, Æfre." Cenric exhaled, "I know this is—"

"Cenric," Æfre cut him off mid-sentence, "If someone in the burh is in trouble and I have the means to help, that is all that matters." She grabbed her bag and began pulling jars from her shelves, carefully selecting and decanting herbs into smaller containers. "Tell me everything you know. Anything could be useful."

"I don't know much," Cenric admitted. "Her mother said she was injured just under a week ago. Another healer treated her, and she seemed to be on the mend—until tonight."

That was enough to send a cold ripple of concern through Æfre. An unhealed injury was one of many dangerous possibilities. She paused and took a steadying breath, trying to consider every possibility.

She reached for a small bundle of tools, knives for lancing, linen for binding, a set of iron tweezers, and her mortar and pestle. She began to take stock of additional herbs she thought might be required: dried feverfew, willow bark, and a measure of honeycomb for poultices. The worry of having enough of the right materials soon had her overfilling her bag.

"I'll take Epona," she said over her shoulder, securing the seals on her clay jars and bundling them into her satchel. "That way, I can carry more of my supplies."

"I'll tack her up while you finish," Cenric offered, already striding toward the barn.

"Thank you, Cenric," Æfre said as she fastened the buckle on her saddle bag. She could already feel the night pressing in around her—she was about to embark on a ride that would take her straight into the heart of a situation both she and Osric had not wanted to face. It was unavoidable that attending Eadlin would be awkward; yet, through her experience, Æfre knew that if Eadlin was as sick as Cenric suggested, there would likely be nobody there with any desire for conflict. Eadlin's well-being took precedence over everything else.

She smoothed a hand over her cloak, securing it with the fine silver pennanular brooch. *Such a beautiful cloak*, she thought as she felt the moss-green wool thick and warm against her skin. *Funny that the first time I should wear such a lovely thing is in an unhappy situation like this.*

By the time she stepped outside, Cenric was waiting with Epona, the mare already saddled. The air was sharp with cold, their breath curling in the frosty air like apparitions floating up into the night sky.

"We'll have to take it slower than I'd like," Cenric said as he mounted his horse. "The road's treacherous in this dark."

Æfre swung up into her saddle, adjusting her reins and cloak. "I understand," she said, "but if this situation is as dire as you suggest, we must try to make haste—Eadlin may not have time to spare."

Cenric gave a firm nod, then turned his horse uphill to meet the road to Wōdenléah. Together, they rode into the night, hooves pounding against the frozen earth, riding as quickly as they dared towards the burh.

The night favored them—the clouds had parted just enough to allow the moonlight to spill over the frostbitten landscape, granting them the speed of a canter for most of the short journey. Now, as they reined in through the palisade gate, Æfre could hear the sounds of merriment drifting from the feast in the great hall, and could smell roast wafting out into the frigid night air, rich with spice and fire.

Cenric led them straight to his and Cwenhild's hut, both of them dismounting with swift efficiency.

"I'll take Epona into the stable with me," Cenric offered as Æfre retrieved the last of her supplies, "you go ahead on in."

"Thank you," Æfre said, slinging the heavier of her saddlebags over her shoulder before making her way to the door.

She had barely taken a step when the door swung open and Osric emerged, his head bowed, his posture heavy with exhaustion and worry. He took a few steps forward before glancing up—and stopped dead in his tracks.

"Æfre," he startled, his voice barely more than a breath. A mixture of relief, worry, and weariness was etched onto his face, as if the weight of the world had settled there, stubbornly refusing to shift.

"I'm here," she breathed. "You know I'll always go where I'm needed."

"I know Æfre, it's just—" Osric hesitated for a moment, instinctively reaching up to cup her cheek before remembering where he was and letting his hand fall to her upper arm, "this feels...unjust."

"Osric, that is of no account just now," Æfre said, shaking her head.

He exhaled sharply, trying to gather himself. "I know. I —" He glanced over his shoulder, ensuring they were alone before leaning in, his voice dropping so low it barely stirred the air between them, his face so close his beard tickled her cheek.

"Much has happened. Æthelwod has dispatched me to Wintanceaster in two days. He's making his move."

Æfre stiffened, her breath catching. "So soon."

"He announced it just this night," Osric continued. "He sought to take me by surprise. And I suppose he did."

"Osric, forgive me, I really must make haste—"

"Æfre, of course. Forgive me, of course you must." Osric rubbed his hand over his beard. "I should get back, at least for a while," he said reluctantly, giving her arm a squeeze and looking at her one last time before heading back to the hall.

"You'll find me later?" Æfre asked over her shoulder, "I'll not be leaving here until this is settled. It could be some days."

"I will," Osric said, before disappearing into the night.

Æfre lingered for only a moment before steeling herself with a deep breath and turning towards the hut, bracing against what she might find within.

As she pushed the door open, she was immediately struck by the oppressive heaviness of the sickroom—the kind of hushed, breath-holding silence that clings to a place of illness. The air was thick with the scents of damp wool, hearth smoke, and sickness.

Eadlin was laid on the bed, her face as pale as death despite the soft, flickering glow of the hearth candlelight that illuminated the hut. Her eyes were closed, and even from across the room, Æfre could see her chest rising and falling in quick, shallow breaths. The sight sent a jolt of fear through her—she knew that look well. Eadlin was on the precipice. Afflicted people who looked like that were often only mere hours from slipping beyond reach.

"Oh, Æfre, thank God!" Cwenhild exclaimed, "I'm afraid Eadlin is very poorly."

Æfre's gaze flickered to Wynnflæd, who was seated stiffly on the other side of the bed. The older woman met her eyes—not with hostility, nor with welcome, but with the brittle and fearful composure of a mother holding herself together by sheer force of will. Without a word, she looked down again at her daughter.

Æfre wasted no time, stepping swiftly to the bedside and kneeling beside Eadlin. "I understand she has been suffering from an injury?" she asked, addressing Wynnflæd.

"Her right leg—her upper thigh," Wynnflæd replied, her voice taut. "She never told me exactly what happened, only that she had been injured at the loom."

"The loom!?" Cwenhild exclaimed, eyes widening. "Oh, Lady Wynnflæd, why did you not say? I believe I was there when it happened! Perhaps a week has passed! Eadlin dropped a freshly sharpened bone pin beater—it struck her deeply, right into her thigh! She laughed it off, insisted she was fine—" Cwenhild broke off, turning stricken eyes toward Æfre. "Could that be the cause of all this?"

Both older women looked at Æfre,

"It certainly could be," Æfre answered, while holding Eadlin's wrist between her fingers, feeling her pulse. *Too fast. Too weak.* A sure sign of sickness that had spread beyond the wound.

"She was treated earlier this week?" Æfre asked, keeping her voice steady.

Lady Wynnflæd nodded stiffly. "Yes. I brought in a healer from Swaffham. She applied poultices four times a day and had Eadlin drink herbal infusions."

"And they helped?"

"They were working." A flicker of helplessness crossed Wynnflæd's face. "Until today. It was some combination of garlic and other herbs, though the stench was dreadful, poor girl. Still, she was improving."

"That is of great use, thank you," Æfre said, as she met Wynnflæd's gaze. "I need to see the wound. Do you wish to stay?"

The noblewoman hesitated. Æfre softened her tone. "I ask not because I wish to send you away, but because the initial treatment will likely be painful. Even with every measure I can take to ease her suffering."

Wynnflæd swallowed, her face rigid with grief and resolve. "I shall stay—for a while, at least. Though I do not have a strong constitution for such things."

"I understand."

Without needing instruction, Cwenhild was already at

work—removing Eadlin's shoes and loosening her belt with the anticipatory knowledge of a woman who had stood at Æfre's side through many such nights.

Æfre leaned in, her fingers brushing Eadlin's cheek. Her skin was clammy. "Eadlin," she said firmly. "Will you let me see your eyes?"

A faint flicker of movement. Eadlin's eyelids trembled but did not fully open.

"That's good," Æfre murmured. "Keep talking to her," she said to Wynnflæd, "she hears you."

Cwenhild and Wynnflæd worked to remove Eadlin's overdress, carefully peeling it away from her chemise underlayer. As they did, Æfre's eyes swept over Eadlin's body, searching for further signs of sickness or injury. Her breath caught. A rash. She pressed her finger gently to the rash.

The rash did not blanch as she pressed, and in fact it appeared to be spreading. It began at the top of her right foot and crept up her calf, with a smattering also around her upper thigh. It was not a good sign—it was the rash of poisoned blood. Æfre knew that once the poisoning had taken hold to the point of a rash, it was often difficult to convince it to let go.

Moving her eyes up Eadlin's body, Æfre could see that the bandage on her thigh was stretched tight, and redness was swelling tracked upwards past its top margin.

"I'm going to remove the bandage now, Eadlin," Æfre warned softly.

Slowly, carefully, she unwound the cloth, revealing the wound beneath.

A thick, angry mass of swelling had risen at the site of injury, its center barely open but glistening with infection. The surrounding skin was hot and taut, streaked with spreading lines of red that crept ominously towards her groin.

"Oh dear Lord, the poor girl," Cwenhild said softly, "This is about where she dropped the pin beater, Æfre."

Wynnflæd's hands clenched into fists. "It has gotten worse," she whispered, as if only now allowing herself to see the truth. "It was not this large before. And that redness above it—" she swallowed hard. "That was not there."

Æfre pressed gently at the edges, feeling the rigidity of the swollen tissue, hot and rigid to the touch. Eadlin moaned softly, instinctively trying to pull her leg away from the touch.

"I'm sorry, Eadlin," Æfre murmured, rubbing a soothing hand over her shin. "I know it hurts. I will be as quick and gentle as I can." But even as she comforted, the truth unsettled her gut—the infection had burrowed deep. Perhaps even to the bone—a concern she did not share with the others in the hut in that moment.

Æfre sat back for a moment in thoughtful consideration of what her next step might be.

"Lady Wynnflæd," she began, "I'm sorry we must be here tonight."

Wynnflæd's throat bobbed. "The healer said the poultices were drawing the sickness out."

"They likely were," Æfre said, choosing her words carefully. "But my fear is that some of the sickness has remained trapped inside, and that it has continued to fester."

Panic flickered across Wynnflæd's face. "But, if the sickness was leaving, how can it have worsened?"

"Sometimes," Æfre said gently, "a wound that closes too soon or does not fully drain traps sickness within, causing it to fester." Æfre hesitated, giving Wynnflæd time to process what she was saying. "And now... I'm afraid that the sickness has entered her blood and is poisoning her. My lady, we are working against time here."

Wynnflæd blanched, words caught in her throat. "You mean—" Her hands trembled. "You mean I might lose her?"

HEART OF THE WILD GODS

"For Eadlin to have the best chance, I need to drain this wound. That will mean making a cut and cleaning out the wound, which will be painful. Eadlin is very weak right now, and because of this, I dare not give her henbane or nightshade before I cut—"

Æfre reached across the bed and took the elder woman's hand in hers.

"My lady... I will do everything in my power. But we must act now."

Wynnflæd let out a gasping sob as she looked down at Eadlin, fought to regain control, then straightened.

"Yes," she whispered to Æfre in earnest, allowing herself a rare moment of unfiltered vulnerability. "Yes. Do whatever you must. Please—please, save my daughter."

Cwenhild wiped her own tears with the corner of her apron, then turned to the fire, already boiling water, unrolling linen, and setting out Æfre's tools.

Æfre squeezed Wynnflæd's hand once more, then turned to the task at hand.

"Cwenhild, have you any strong ale?" Æfre asked. "Just a single horn will do."

"I do."

Cwenhild fetched a jug of strong ale and a drinking horn, setting them down beside Æfre's supplies.

"Thank you, Cwenhild, and if you could cut a few of those linens into long strips, about the width of your thumb, and put them to boil."

Cwenhild nodded and got to work while Æfre readied her tools. She reached for a small, tightly sealed jar—her reliable wound salve[xviii]. Within was a blend of mashed garlic, leek, wine, and bovine bile, aged nine days in a bronze vessel, then sealed and stored. She had little to spare, and every drop counted.

"We'll need to position her so the afflicted leg is on top and the wound can drain."

They moved swiftly, propping Eadlin with pillows, adjusting her until she lay as comfortably as possible.

"Lady Wynnflæd, will you take your leave, or do you wish to stay?"

"I'll stay."

"Good. It will help if you speak to Eadlin, reassure her—hold her hand if she allows it."

Wynnflæd didn't hesitate, taking her daughter's limp hand between her own and drawing her chair closer to the bed.

Æfre tucked a clean cloth beneath Eadlin's wounded leg, then poured some ale from the horn generously over the wound, saturating the torn flesh. The sharp scent of fermented grain mingled with the damp warmth of the hut.

She selected a small iron knife and moved to the hearth, holding the blade steadily over the flames, the metal darkening as it heated. Once satisfied, she withdrew it and doused it in ale—the sizzle echoed through the hut like rain spitting on the embers of a dying campfire.

"I'm ready to begin."

Cwenhild, without needing to be asked, moved to the far side of the bed, bracing Eadlin's leg.

Æfre took a slow breath and met Eadlin's glassy eyes. "Eadlin, I must make a cut now. You shall feel it, and I am sorry for it, but I will be swift."

Eadlin barely stirred. Æfre turned to Cwenhild, who gave a single, firm nod. *Ready.*

Æfre steadied her grip and drew her knife across the infected mass with an even amount of pressure.

Eadlin jerked violently, a strangled cry tearing from her throat as she tried to kick out. Cwenhild leaned down with all her weight, pinning Eadlin's leg, while Wynnflæd clutched her daughter's

HEART OF THE WILD GODS

shoulders, murmuring desperate reassurances as Eadlin thrashed against the pain and wailed.

The wound split like an overripe fruit, and thick, purulent pus pressed out through the incision like a rancid half-set jelly, its stench choking the air.

"Forgive me, Eadlin," Æfre murmured as she worked, voice calm but urgent. "I know it pains you, but I must cleanse it well."

She seized one of the boiled linen strips that Cwehild had prepared and hung, and gently pressed around the wound, coaxing out the infection.

Eadlin moaned, her body arching against the pain. Cwenhild and Wynnflæd fought to keep her still, their own faces strained with exertion.

Æfre remained focused—her hands working away as she muttered softly under her breath while she worked.

"...out of the marrow and into the bone,
from the bone into the flesh,
out from the flesh into the hide..."

Her voice wove through the tension in the hut, steady and unbroken. She continued pressing, clearing, working as fast as she dared.

"What is she saying?" Wynnflæd asked Cwenhild softly, not daring to interrupt Æfre's process.

"It's the Uuurmsegen[xix] healing charm," Cwenhild replied, just as Eadlin let out another heartbreaking wail.

"How much longer?" Wynnflæd's voice was raw, desperate.

Æfre didn't look up.

"...out from the hide and into this arrow,
Woden, let it be so."

At last, Æfre sat back, exhaling deeply, allowing Eadlin a moment of respite as the silence settled around them like a blanket.

"The wound is clean." She wiped her brow with her shoulder

and glanced at Cwenhild. "Let's give her a moment's peace before dressing it."

Eadlin lay limp, brow glistening, chest rising and falling in shallow pants. Æfre reached for her hand and gave it a light but purposeful squeeze. A moment passed—then, weakly, Eadlin squeezed back.

Relief uncoiled slightly in Æfre's chest with Eadlin's response—as weak as it was, she was still fighting. Æfre turned to Wynnflæd and allowed herself a small smile. "She's still with us."

Wynnflæd exhaled, voice shaking. "Thank God."

Cwenhild stretched, rolling her shoulders. "Anything else I can do?"

"Cwenhild, you've done plenty," Æfre assured her. "Rest a few moments—I'll need you again for the dressing."

For a few minutes, the three women sat unmoving in the taut silence of the hut, each lost in her own thoughts until Æfre broke their vigil by retrieving her iron tongs from her supplies. She passed the instrument through the hearth's fire, then doused it in ale and used it to lift one of the boiled linen strips.

Dipping the linen strip into her precious healing mixture, she swirled it, watching as the fabric absorbed the pungent mix.

"The dressing is ready." Æfre said Once the linen was saturated, let's finish this so she can rest."

Once more, Cwenhild and Wynnflæd took their places, steadying Eadlin as Æfre worked.

"Eadlin, deep breaths now."

With gentle movements, Æfre laid the sodden linen into the wound cavity, gently packing it in with iron tweezers. Eadlin shuddered and whimpered at the touch, but the better part of her strength was already spent.

Æfre finished swiftly, wrapping the leg in clean, dry linen, securing the dressing in place.

HEART OF THE WILD GODS

"It's done," she said quietly. Then, louder, "Eadlin, I've finished. That's the worst of it behind you now."

No response. Only the soft rise and fall of her chest.

Æfre turned to Wynnflæd, the fatigue and strain in her voice finally betraying her calm exterior. "The dressing will be changed twice a day. I will tend it myself to monitor the wound until I am satisfied that it is healing well." Æfre pulled a long, deep, steadying breath before continuing. "Eadlin has fought well—but, my lady, she is not yet out of danger. Her blood is still poisoned; all I have done is remove the source. Now, her body must take over the fight."

Wynnflæd swallowed hard. "How long until we might know?"

"It's difficult to say." Æfre softened her tone. "The most important thing is supporting her through it. I'll prepare an herbal infusion, and we must keep her drinking, whatever she can manage, even if only from a damp cloth."

Wynnflæd nodded, her exhaustion plain.

Æfre hesitated, then added gently, "Lady Wynnflæd, it's late. Eadlin will rest for a while now. You should return home to rest. Fetch some things that you know will bring her comfort: a clean shift, a favorite pillow—I will remain here."

Cwenhild touched Wynnflæd's arm. "Eadlin is safe here. Come, Cenric can take you."

For a long moment, Wynnflæd said nothing, locked in place, looking at Eadlin. Then, finally, she gave a stiff nod and got up.

As the two women gathered their cloaks and stepped out into the night, the hut fell into a hollow silence.

Æfre took a long, slow, unsteady breath, turning her gaze once again back to Eadlin.

She peeled back the woolen blanket, checking the dressing one last time—securely in place.

Dipping a cloth into the boiled water, she pressed a few drops into Eadlin's dry lips. She stirred, her throat working to swallow.

A favorable sign.

It would be a long night. But at least for this moment, the most painful part had passed.

Æfre got up and stirred the embers in the hearth, coaxing the fire before pulling a few chairs together, close to the bedside. With a quiet sigh, she settled beside Eadlin, readying herself for a long night of watchful vigil.

33

Ærende ⚔ Message

Cenric pressed onward—turning the wagon onto the road to the trading camp, charged with doing his lord's bidding.

With the Yule festivities continuing on into the small hours, Osric had seized the opportunity to deliver not only Wynnflæd back to Aldhem for the night to rest, but the opportunity to get a message to Torvald Ironsight. Cenric had agreed to the task without hesitation.

While the scop[xx] enthralled the hall with heroic lays of past battles, Osric and Cenric had slipped unnoticed into the back of the hall and quietly gathered several wooden boxes' worth of jugs of the Bishop's prized Yule mead. Æthelwod was certainly too preoccupied with bending the ear of any in the burh willing to hear his grievances about the heathen traders and their supposed lack of contribution, and the two were able to load the wagon at the back entrance, in plain sight of the hall, without interruption.

Now, Cenric guided the wagon along the quiet road, the horses' steady plodding and the grinding of the dirt road beneath them the only sounds that cut through the crisp night air. He had nearly reached the turnoff leading down to the valley, towards Æfre's hut, before encountering another soul.

A lone figure sat watchfully on a stump at the roadside, practically invisible to anyone unfamiliar with the landscape. Clothed in Norse attire, the man wore a charcoal-hued woolen cloak and a fur mantle to ward off the cold. Cenric recognized him instantly as one of Torvald Ironsight's guards, the same man he had passed earlier when fetching Æfre.

The guard had already spotted him and was rising to his feet, readying himself. Cenric reined in the horses as he approached.

"Joyous Yule!" he called, lifting a hand in greeting.

"Glaðligr Jól [*Joyous Yule*]!" The guard, recognizing him, waved back, visibly relaxing at the prospect of not having to chase off an intruder.

"Æfre, the healer, won't be returning tonight," Cenric informed him. "Likely not for several days. The girl she was called to attend is gravely ill."

"Ah, but I stay here regardless," the guard said, "it seems your healer has many who would destroy her home."

"Ġēa," Cenric sighed, "it wasn't always that way…" his gaze drifting to Æfre's family homestead. He lost himself in thought for a moment, then started suddenly, as if remembering something. Reaching under the wagon seat, Cenric pulled out a small jug of Æthelwod's Yule mead. "A token of appreciation from the thegn of Wōdenléah."

The guard's eyes lit up, and he reached eagerly for the jug. "Ah! Very generous!"

Cenric chuckled, holding the jug just out of reach, "Now—do *not* go drinking yourself legless on watch! If your Jarl comes down on you, we have never met!"

The guard laughed, accepting the jug. "Understood!" He fished a drinking horn from beneath his cloak and poured a generous measure of mead. Then, holding up the jug, he gestured toward Cenric, eyebrows raised.

Cenric smirked, "I see you came prepared," he said, waiting a beat before reaching under his own cloak and producing his own drinking horn. The two men shared a laugh as the guard filled Cenric's horn.

"It's Yule." Cenric shrugged.

"Glaðligr Jól!" the guard toasted.

"Wes hál[xxi]!" Cenric countered.

Both men took a deep drink, and a blanket of silence fell upon them as the guard eyed Cenric thoughtfully. "You're out late."

Cenric's gut tightened slightly at the observation, but he kept his tone light. "The crisis that sent me after the healer set everything back. I'm only now making my rounds—Yule gifts from the thegn to our partners and neighbors." Cenric held up his drinking horn and indicated the blanket-covered boxes in the back of the wagon.

The guard nodded, seemingly satisfied, and said no more on the matter. The two men drank in silence for another few minutes before Cenric broke the spell.

"Run anyone off today?" Cenric asked.

"Já. Just once." The guard met his gaze and drained his drinking horn.

Cenric exhaled slowly.

"The Jarl put us here to keep your healer safe, but we can't fight them." The guard poured himself another modest measure of mead, then offered some to Cenric, who declined with a wave of his hand. "They now begin to understand we don't mean to fight. We cannot start war—another war."

Cenric chuckled internally at the guard's little touch of self-awareness. "Certainly not."

"Já so—the pretty healer, I think she will have trouble."

Cenric's jaw tightened. "My friend, it pains me to say we've all reached the same conclusion." He drained his mead and tucked the drinking horn away. "I'd best be on my way. Stay safe, stay warm—and mind the mead!" He winked. "Good night, friend."

"You too, my friend." Cenric urged the horse on, soon arriving at the gate to the trading camp.

"Joyous Yule!" Cenric called to the guard at the gate. "Apologies for the late hour I come on behalf of the thegn of Wōdenléah, bearing a Yule gift—a token of our appreciation of our continued good relations."

"A Gift?" The guard approached, running a weathered hand over his salt-and-pepper beard as he eyed the wagon.

Cenric reached behind him and yanked a corner of the blanket off the stacked boxes of mead.

"Ah! Now, I see!" A grin stretching ear to ear spread across the guard's face.

Cenric mirrored his grin, pulling two jugs from the top box and handing them over. "Tell me, friend, have I arrived too late to speak with Svend or your Jarl?"

"They're in the hall," said a familiar voice, coming from the direction of the guardhouse. Eadgar stepped into the night from behind the older guard.

"Eadgar!" Cenric bellowed. "I heard you were staying out here!"

"Hi, Cenric! Joyous Yule."

"A Joyous Yule to you, too! My God, boy, you've grown!" Cenric laughed. "What are they feeding you?"

"This one eats anything not nailed to the table," the guard chuckled, cuffing the boy playfully on the back of his head. Eadgar's ears burned red.

"Eadgar," the guard said, "run and see if Svend or the Jarl is in any shape to speak with our guest."

Eadgar jogged off toward the hall.

"You can pull the wagon up to the front of the hall," the guard offered. "Easier to unload."

"I appreciate that." Cenric clucked to the horse and flicked the reins, guiding the wagon forward.

Each time the longhouse door opened, music and laughter spilled into the cold night, the revelry showing no signs of slowing. Cenric jumped down from the wagon just as the door swung wide again. Jarl Torvald strode out, drinking horn in hand, Eadgar trailing behind. Despite the late hour, the Jarl looked steady—more than could be said for many of the men and women who were staggering about outside the hall.

"A Joyous Yule to you, Jarl Torvald. I'm Cenric, I—"

"One of Lord Osric's most trusted men—I know who you are."

Impressed, Cenric inclined his head. "The thegn sends a token of his appreciation. I apologize for the late hour."

Torvald waved off the apology and moved closer to the wagon.

"Lord Osric sends a gift of the bishop's special reserve mead," Cenric said, beckoning the Jarl closer as he lifted the blanket covering the stacked boxes. Then, lowering his voice, "Bishop Æthelwod announced tonight that he'll send Osric to Wintanceaster in two days."

Torvald met Cenric's gaze, saying nothing, then pulled back the blanket to inspect the cargo.

"Very generous of the thegn," he said.

"As you know, Lord Wulfric will be summoned," Cenric continued in a hushed tone. "He'll arrive in a few days' time. Lord Osric plans to make camp at a woodcutter's shed in the forest—not far from here. Æfre can get the information to you."

Torvald's brow lifted. "Æfre is aware of our plan?"

"She is, Jarl. Osric thought it best to tell her. She's in the burh now, tending to Lord Osric's betrothed—she's taken ill."

Torvald let out a sharp exhale. "The guard mentioned she was sent for—I did not realize for whom." He paused, contemplating the situation. "The thegn and I must speak soon."

Torvald reached into the wagon, yanked a jug free, and uncorked it with his teeth. He swirled the jug, sniffed, and his eyes lit up with pleasant surprise. Flicking the dregs from his drinking horn, he poured himself a fresh serving.

Cenric grinned. For the second time that evening, he reached under his cloak and produced his own drinking horn.

Torvald's face instantly split into a smile. Chuckling, he filled

Cenric's horn.

"Glaðligr Jól." Torvald raised his drink.

"Joyous Yule, Jarl."

They drank.

Torvald grinned, mouth still full, savoring the golden liquid to the fullest before swallowing it. "It's quite good."

Cenric took a deep draught from his horn. "It'll taste even finer, Jarl, when you hear that Osric and I lifted it from Æthelwod's hoard, unbidden."

Torvald threw back his head in laughter. "More stolen property, then."

"Indeed."

"Well, this stolen property is delicious," Torvald said before turning and barking at two loitering men. "Erik! Ivar! Help us get these boxes inside!"

Before they could reach the wagon, Torvald grabbed two large jugs for himself. "These are mine." He grinned.

Cenric grinned back.

Eadgar, hovering near the doorway, stepped forward to help, but Torvald clapped a firm hand on his shoulder.

"Not you. Sun will be up soon. To bed."

Eadgar's face fell, but the Jarl's tone left no room for argument.

"Cenric, will you say hello to Cwenhild for me?" Eadgar asked.

"I will." Cenric thought a moment, then added, "Say, if we sent for you on a day the bishop was away, would you come?"

"Yes."

"Good. Cwenhild will be pleased to hear it." Cenric clapped him on the back. "Now, listen to the Jarl. Off with you."

"Good night, Cenric. Joyous Yule."

"Joyous Yule."

Eadgar jogged toward the gatehouse.

Torvald's men had stacked all they could carry and brought

the first load into the hall. Cenric and Torvald stood in silence, drinking Æthelwod's stolen mead under the frosty Yule sky.

"Tell Lord Osric we'll move forward with our part of the plan tomorrow," Torvald said. "It will take root quickly—we'll be ready. And we stick to the plan, já? All of us."

"We stick to the plan."

The two men drank in silence, contemplating the days ahead as sounds of merriment rose and fell with each opening and closing of the hall's door.

34
Æfter ⚔ After

Torvald awoke with a start the morning after Yule, still dressed in his clothes from the night before. While unlike most of the men, he hadn't drunk himself into a complete stupor, the last thing he remembered was reclining back on his bed, his mind tangled in the next steps of their plan. Æfre's troubles with the burh and a thousand other nagging thoughts all seemed to worm their way into his head every time he'd tried to close his eyes. He'd been certain sleep would evade him.

Not so.

Torvald chuckled, rubbing the sleep from his eyes and yawning as he glanced over at the thin sliver of sunlight spilling onto the floor outside his quarters—light sneaking in through the hall door left ajar.

He hoisted himself up, rolling the stiffness from his shoulders, and shuffled through the partition to his accommodation that led to the main hall. Food first. Then, hot water to bathe.

He stepped out of his quarters and into a scene that might have passed for the aftermath of an actual battle. Bodies sprawled across benches, cloaks pulled over faces. Others slumped in chairs, heads thrown back, mouths open in drunken snores. Some had collapsed where they sat, one young guard even using a half-eaten plate of food as a pillow.

There will be some sore heads in this camp today, he thought as he moved to the hearth, stirring the embers back to life before filling a bronze pot with water to heat. He rummaged for bread and cheese, tearing a chunk free just as the door slammed wide open.

Sunlight flooded in, drawing groans and curses from the miserable wrecks strewn about the hall. In the doorway stood

Svend, his silhouette filling the door frame. His shadow stretched unnaturally long across the earthen floor—casting an outline like that of a giant.

"Góðan morgin!" Svend bellowed, his voice crashing over the hall like a war horn. Groans and curses rippled through the half-conscious men as they stirred, shielding their eyes from the morning light. "You lazy drunkards, on your feet! Ingrid and Bodil are outside, waiting to clean up your mess, but they're too polite to wake your sorry hides!"

He booted a bench out from under the legs of a groggy trader, sending the man sprawling with a grunt.

Torvald sat at the back of the hall, perched on the edge of a table, grinning as he tore off a hunk of bread and paired it with cured meat, watching the scene unfolding before him.

"Whose friend is this!?" Svend grabbed the passed-out young warrior by the hair, lifting his head like a battle trophy. Bits of congealed meat clung to the young man's face, his eyes fluttering but failing to fully open. "Who claims this rancid whelp!?"

A voice called from the back. "I've got him, Svend!"

"Come get your friend!" Svend barked. "The ladies need to work, and the Jarl and I need a private word!"

Two men appeared, looking more than a bit worse for wear. Each man grabbed the unconscious warrior under an arm, and together they hauled him off like a sack of grain. Awakened by the commotion, the others slowly roused, muttering curses as they collected boots, cloaks, and whatever shreds of dignity they might have had remaining.

When the clamor finally subsided and the last of the overstayers had filed out of the hall and into the crisp morning air, Svend walked to the hall's door and pushed it open.

"Ladies, it's clear. Come in."

Ingrid and Bodil hurried inside, the cold coloring their cheeks as they carried buckets, brooms, and bundles of dried herbs to freshen the air.

Torvald swallowed the last of his meal and stood, stretching. "Ingrid, Bodil—I did not know you were out there waiting. I'll see to it you're compensated for the extra trouble."

The women smiled. "Thank you, Jarl Torvald," they said almost in unison.

Bodil suddenly seemed to remember something. She turned back to her supplies, retrieving a small cloth bundle tied with a cord. "Your washed clothes, Jarl."

"Ah! Thank you." He gave them a quick nod and a smile.

"Have you anything else for washing?"

"I will shortly, Bodil," Torvald said. "I'll bundle it and leave it here with something extra for you both."

"Thank you," Bodil replied, handing him a bundle of dried lavender. "For your quarters."

"Thank you, Bodil, that is exactly what's needed in here!" Torvald turned to Svend. "Grab some food, old friend, prop that door open a bit, and meet me in my quarters. This hall smells like an ale-soaked boot, and I want to wash the stink off."

He lifted the pot of warmed water from the hearth and strode back to his quarters.

Stripping off his slept-in clothing, he tossed it onto the washing pile, washed up quickly, and pulled on a fresh tunic and trousers. He yanked the linen undersheets from his bed and bundled them up, tying everything together with the cord from his clean laundry.

At his carved bedside table, he grabbed his grooming kit, combed through his hair with an ornate bone comb, and trimmed his beard with a small pair of scissors.

Long overdue, he thought as he studied his reflection in the polished bronze mirror, running a hand over his jaw.

"You do smell better now," Svend called from the doorway,

finishing off a thick slice of bread topped with some cheese.

"I do, don't I?" Torvald laughed. "Sadly, the same can't be said for some of the wretches you chased out of here."

"Indeed not. The folly of young blood." Svend smirked, still chewing.

Torvald fastened his belt, sheathed his seax, and counted out a few coins from the leather pouch at his waist. "We need to talk about how we do this."

"We do."

Torvald smirked. "You want to actually take a swing at me in front of the men?"

Svend chuckled. "Old friend, I've thought about taking a swing at you many times over the years—but for this, I don't think we need the theatrics."

Torvald laughed, "Good. Whispers have already started. With the thegn sent away, getting the rat bishop to act on our timeline should be a seed easily planted."

"Agreed. And a well-placed, *loud* argument between the two of us, that should be more than enough to get tongues wagging about internal struggles. Hopefully it will inspire him to act." Svend chuckled, "Bjørn offered to play peacemaker if we did actually want to fight."

Torvald laughed, then shrugged. "Could be useful—the men will go to him afterwards for details more easily than they would us. It could be a better way to move this thing along."

"True, Jarl."

"Let's bring him in then, why not?" Torvald chuckled as he pinned his cloak at the shoulder with his Fáfnir brooch. "You've got yours?"

Svend tapped his own silver brooch, its intricate dragon carving catching the firelight. "Of course."

"Well, then." Torvald grinned, eyebrows raised as he gathered

HEART OF THE WILD GODS

his bundle of washing, looking directly at Svend. "Let us go spread stories of our crumbling leadership."

As they left the hall, Torvald dropped the washing bundle and coins on the table in passing. He spoke in a hushed tone. "We should split up this morning—cover more ground so everyone sees."

Svend nodded. "Agreed, Jarl."

"Besides, you always make me laugh, and we're supposed to be fighting."

Svend snorted, barely stifling his own laughter as they stepped into the morning light, each heading in opposite directions.

35

Horsern ⚔ Stable

"Cwenhild, you have my sincere thanks!" Æfre exclaimed, tearing into the stew made with the remnants of the previous night's feast. With the long, grueling night behind them, it was only now that Æfre allowed herself the luxury of looking away from Eadlin long enough to eat, and she was beyond ravenous. "When I'm tending someone, I think little of my own keeping," she admitted through a mouthful of stew.

Cwenhild set a cup of small ale down next to her. "No sense in having two of you falling into infirmity, is there?" She scoffed gently, "We'd have to scoot poor Eadlin over in that bed to make room for the both of you."

Æfre let out a snort of laughter—her first in what felt like ages. Exhaustion was beginning to blur the edges of time; she would have struggled to say what day it was, or even what year.

The night had been long and unrelenting. Eadlin had been delirious, far weaker than Æfre had hoped. Her heartbeat fluttered like a butterfly's wing, her skin was clammy and cold, her breath rapid, shallow, and ragged. More than once, Æfre feared she might just slip away, but Eadlin had held on.

She had used every method she knew to drag Eadlin back from the brink. She warmed the bed with hearth stones, wrapped her in heavy blankets, and sat a constant vigil, speaking to her and pressing a soaked cloth to her lips, coaxing her to take in water and herbal infusions. It had been slow and painstaking—Eadlin barely responsive at times, slipping in and out of awareness—but as the first slivers of sunlight crept through the window coverings, Eadlin had finally sipped from a cup on her own. Her fever still raged, but her breathing had steadied, and her heartbeat was stronger and steadier. She had turned a vital corner, and relief had flooded through Æfre so thoroughly that she did not even realize she had tears running down her cheeks until Cwenhild had quietly pressed a cloth into her hands.

Osric arrived not long after sunrise with Wynnflæd in tow. Aldhem's matriarch made a beeline for Eadlin's bedside and remained there, hanging on to her daughter's hand like a drowning victim grasping at driftwood. As Æfre prepared the medicines for Eadlin's dressing change, she felt Osric's worried gaze linger on her—she thought he was likely alarmed by her exhausted appearance, but he said nothing.

Osric stayed long enough to pay his respects before duty pulled him away. Æfre could almost feel the words they both wanted to say to each other as he stood in such close proximity in the hut; it lingered heavily in the air between them, but it was neither the time nor the place. Instead, they settled for a few stolen glances from afar, and he bid them farewell.

Æfre did get some of her willow bark infusion into Eadlin, enough to break her fever for a time and take the edge off of her pain. When she, Wynnflæd, and Cwenhild changed the dressing again, they found the wound much calmer—less purulent, less angry. The rank fetor of the previous night had faded—the wound appeared to be responding favorably.

They changed Eadlin's underdress, freshened the bedding, and Wynnflæd brushed out her auburn hair and braided it. Finally, as morning stretched into afternoon, Eadlin found true rest.

Æthelwod arrived briefly, unusually restrained and somber, his usual air of self-importance appropriately subdued. He inquired about Eadlin's condition but spoke only to Wynnflæd, as though Æfre and Cwenhild were no more than shadows in the room. They all stood in respectful silence as the bishop murmured a swift and impersonal prayer over the sickbed. With the final amen, he turned on his heel, spoke a few hushed words to Wynnflæd once more, and was gone, never once sparing Æfre a glance.

Wynnflæd stayed on a bit longer until she was satisfied that Eadlin would rest comfortably, then took her leave to go up to the church to pray.

Now, from across the hut, Cwenhild sat astonished as Æfre scraped the last of the venison stew from her bowl with a giant hunk of bread. "Æfre, I can bring you more, if you like," she said, eyes wide. "By my troth, I'm always in awe of the way you set about your food. You've the appetite of a starved hound."

Æfre let out a short laugh. "It's an art, Cwenhild—wrought by years of diligent practice."

Cwenhild chuckled and shook her head. "Where you put it all baffles me, it's as if you have a hollow leg! But now you should rest, my dear. Lord Osric has offered his quarters if you'd like."

"Thank you, Cwenhild, but I'm not ready to leave her just yet," Æfre said. "She'll be stronger soon if she keeps on in this manner, but she was so unwell last night I'd rather bide here should she take a turn. But you should take the quarters. I can pull these chairs together and rest while she's settled."

"So be it," Cwenhild said, collecting the empty bowls. "I'll be back soon, and we can judge the state of things then."

As the door closed behind Cwenhild, silence settled over the hut—a rare and welcome thing.

Æfre arranged two wooden chairs together and reclined, wrapping herself in her new cloak. In the bed next to her, Eadlin slept, her breathing reassuringly deep and steady. For the first time since she'd arrived, Æfre let her mind drift.

Strange, how little time had passed since the attack on her at her homestead. She startled awake some nights, the memories of it raw as an open wound, the bruises still fading on her skin. And now, in some cruel twist of fate, she sat in the very chair Osric had occupied that night as he sat with her—only now it was she who was watching over the woman he would likely marry.

She exhaled slowly, pushing the thought aside. Eadlin was an innocent in all of this. Æfre would not see her suffer. If she had the skill to give Eadlin the best chance of recovery, then it was her duty to see it done.

Everything else—the emotions, the tangled web of expectations and regrets—all of that would just have to wait.

Outside, the muted hum of burh life drifted through the walls, lulling Æfre into a fitful sleep beside her charge.

* * *

"You were dreaming," said the soothing voice, "I was just about to wake you."

Æfre had jolted awake, her heart hammering so violently she was certain it could be heard from one end of the burh to the other. Disoriented, she blinked against the dim light, struggling to place her surroundings. One lone candle, nearly spent, cast distorted shadows across the walls as the last muted amber tendrils of sunlight reached through the window coverings.

"She began to stir not long ago," the voice—Cwenhild's, she realized—continued. "I hadn't the heart to wake you—well, not until it was clear you were trapped in a nightmare."

Cwenhild's keen gaze pierced through the dimness of the hut, searching Æfre's face.

Æfre exhaled sharply, rubbing her eyes. "I'm sorry, I didn't mean to rest so long."

"Nonsense," Cwenhild dismissed, "you've more cause than any of us to rest—if anything, you should do so more often. Besides, she's quite settled. She only stirred a short while ago."

Relief spread through Æfre's chest, along with a twinge of regret at having made her nightmares known. Since the attack, they had been relentless—always the same, always dragging her back to that night. The Northman in the dark cloak pinning her down, tearing at her dress, his fingers crushing her throat. Sometimes in the dream, she fought, but her arm remained trapped, useless. Other times, she broke free, only to find her seax missing, her hand finding only the empty sheath. Every night, a different variation, a new way for her mind to whisper, *what if...?*

But this too would have to wait. Shaking the remnants of the dream from her thoughts, Æfre swung her legs off the chairs and straightened. Leaning in, she pressed the back of her hand to Eadlin's forehead. "The fever's returned," she murmured, "but that's expected this early on. I'll warm more willow bark infusion—see if she can manage a few sips."

In the evening quiet of the hut, Æfre set the pot back on the hearth, and together, she and Cwenhild silently worked to prop Eadlin upright.

"I'm cold," Eadlin rasped, her voice papery-thin after a day of silence.

Cwenhild's smile brightened the dim room. "Ah! She speaks! Worry not, my dear, we'll fetch more blankets."

"And I wanted to wear the yellow dress..." Eadlin's words trailed into incoherent muttering.

Cwenhild shot Æfre a glance.

Æfre nodded. "She's still a bit delirious. It's common after such an illness. It will pass as the body heals and she regains her strength." She swirled the infusion in the pot, watching the dark liquid catch the firelight. "This has had ample time to seethe—it should be even more effective now."

Pouring half a cup, she cooled it with a splash of water before settling beside Eadlin once more.

"Eadlin, I have herbs for you. Can you swallow some for me?"

A sluggish nod. "Yes. Very well."

"Small sips." Æfre tipped the cup gently.

Eadlin took a drink, then wrinkled her nose. "Eew. Yuck. Bitter."

Cwenhild stifled a laugh, and Æfre felt a smile tug at her lips. "Well done, Eadlin."

Eadlin continued to mumble between sips—disjointed fragments about midday meals, dresses, duty—then her tone became intensely earnest and she looked at Æfre.

"The midday meal." Her voice dropped to a conspiratorial whisper. "He didn't remember it, you know."

Æfre smiled again, humoring Eadlin's fevered delusions as though she were a child spinning a fantastical tale. "The midday meal?" she echoed, tilting the cup for Eadlin to drink once more.

"He fell asleep at the midday meal, and her name was on his lips." Eadlin swallowed more of the infusion and grimaced. "Yuck.... 'Don't cry,' he said...he said 'don't cry, Æfre, my love. I cannot bear it,' but he was asleep."

The smile faded instantly from Æfre's face as the cup of infusion trembled in her hand. She felt the breath leave her lungs as if struck.

"He doesn't love me, Mother." Eadlin slurred, her voice fading and eyelids drooping. "He loves the healer." Her eyelids drooped, exhaustion overtaking her once more. "I'm tired now."

Eadlin rolled over, and sleep once again claimed her.

Æfre however, sat frozen. The cup still poised in her grip, one hand still on Eadlin's shoulder as her vision blurred as a surge of unstoppable tears welled.

The door swung open, and Wynnflæd swept inside in a rush of cold air. "Forgive me, I was caught up with the Bishop! That man is certainly fond of the sound of his own—" She stopped short at the sight of her daughter asleep, but sitting upright for the first time. The mask of composure shattered, and she rushed to Eadlin's side.

HEART OF THE WILD GODS

Cwenhild moved swiftly. She gently pried the cup from Æfre's unsteady fingers. "My lady," she smoothly addressed Lady Wynnflæd, "Eadlin has improved this afternoon. She is still somewhat delirious, in and out of fevers, which Æfre assures me is to be expected, but she's taken her infusions well and is resting soundly."

Wynnflæd sagged with relief. "Oh, thank the Lord Almighty."

Her sharp gaze flickered toward Æfre, who remained stiff, silent, as pale as death itself.

Cwenhild intervened again, her voice as warm as it was firm. "Æfre was just about to take a much-needed break now that Eadlin is faring better." Her eyes bore into Æfre's, speaking the words she dared not say aloud.

Æfre blinked, forcing herself back to the present. "I—yes," she croaked. "Yes, I was."

Cwenhild nodded approvingly. "Take as long as you need. We're here."

"Thank you." Æfre rose on unsteady legs, "You must forgive my manner," she said to Wynnflæd, "I'm simply overtired," she said as she moved toward the door, without once glancing back. The tears had already begun to fall.

Æfre shoved open the hut's door harder than she meant to, wincing as it slammed against the frame. The cold air bit at her overheated skin—she'd forgotten to grab her cloak, but she wasn't about to go back.

Her breath came in shallow bursts as she forced herself to walk instead of run. People still milled about, visiting friends and neighbors, still on a high after the previous night's festivities. She didn't want anyone to see her like this. In fact, she didn't want anyone to see her at all—barely holding herself together. She needed to find somewhere to come apart beyond the watchful gazes of the burh.

Her eyes suddenly landed on the stable. It was close. Epona was there. If anyone did discover her, she'd have a reason.

She moved quickly, every step a battle against the storm of emotion building inside of her, threatening to break free. If she could just make it inside, just reach the shadows, she could fall apart in peace.

Æfre was so focused on getting to the stable that she didn't notice Osric and Cenric standing nearby, deep in quiet conversation. She didn't see the way they noticed her distress and stiffened at her approach, their gazes following her hurried steps as she disappeared into the stable.

Cenric caught sight of something approaching from the direction she had just come from and straightened. "Go to her, Lord," he said under his breath. "I'll deal with what's coming up behind her."

Osric turned and saw Æthelwod making his way towards them, his stride purposeful, his eyes searching.

Without hesitation, Cenric stepped forward, intercepting the Bishop before he could draw any closer. Osric hesitated just long enough to see them in discussion before they disappeared into Cenric and Cwenhild's hut—redirected!

Osric paused a moment, then turned and headed for the stable door.

* * *

As Æfre slipped into the dim quiet of the stable, the thick, familiar scents of hay, horses, and damp aged wood filled the air. Bridles and halters hung on hooks next to the stalls, which stood empty, their occupants turned out to the paddock—yet the quiet that was left in their absence did little to quell the turmoil of her mind.

She quickly scanned the empty stable, her gaze landing on the stack of wooden boxes against the far wall. Beyond the boxes, a mound of hay slumped in a dim corner, its shape oddly foreboding in the dim light.

She remembered sitting on those boxes with Cwenhild the last time she had ridden in for a visit, just days ago. That had also been the day she truly learned what they were up against. And of course that had also been the day of the attack—the day everything seemed to spin out of control.

Her breath was now coming too fast, too shallow, and she reached out, gripping the rough edge of a box for support. She leaned over, desperate to slow her breathing and get hold of herself, but the grief surged, too powerful to contain. A sob wrenched free from her throat, raw and unbidden. She clamped a hand over her mouth, muffling the sound in case someone passing by outside might hear. But the dam had broken. Frustration, anger, sorrow, exhaustion—every emotion she had forced down finally broke free, sweeping away the last of her strength as she unraveled in the quiet stillness of the stable.

"Æfre."

The deep voice came from the shadows. Æfre gasped, jerking upright as a figure stepped forward, emerging from the gloom.

"Osric," she rasped, barely able to form the name.

In two strides, he was before her, his arms wrapping around her, pulling her tight against him. His lips pressed to her temple, warm and grounding.

"Osric, I'm sorry," she sobbed. "I'm just so tired."

"Æfre, you have nothing to be sorry for." His hands cradled her tear-stained face. "What you're doing would be overwhelming for anyone."

She put a hand over her eyes, as if to shield herself, struggling to make sense of the storm inside her. "Eadlin was delirious, and she said..."

"Æfre, listen to me," he said softly

"I don't know why it struck me as it did, but when—"

"Æfre!" His voice was firm, steady, anchoring her. He gave her a gentle shake, forcing her to meet his gaze. "It doesn't matter what she said."

He kissed her forehead, lingering. "It doesn't matter."

He kissed her cheek, then the other, each touch light yet reverent. "What matters is that we have failed you. This community—none of us have supported you—honored you as we should."

His voice dropped lower, thick with regret. "*I* have not honored you."

His lips met hers, fierce and insistent. Æfre felt him pouring every unspoken word, very regret into the kiss. When he pulled back, it was only for a moment, searching her face before claiming her mouth again, deeper, more urgently.

Æfre felt something deep within her core stir at the urgency of his kiss, and she kissed him back passionately—frantically.

Before she knew it, she was moving backwards, Osric's hand supporting her lower back as he used his own momentum and body weight to push her across the floor until she was pinned up against the timber wall of the darkest corner of the stable.

Æfre's breath quickened into ragged gasps as the two of them frantically clung to each other between kisses like two drowning souls caught in a current. She felt the deep ache of her longing building within her as they hungrily devoured each other—his desire pressing insistently against her thigh.

She hastily unfastened his belt, and it fell to the ground with a dull clank, the weight of his seax and coin purse causing a plume of hay dust to rise, thickening the hazy stillness of the air around them.

She craved having him close to her again—his familiar touch, his smell—she wanted to cling to these things and let them carry her off, as they had so many times before. She pressed her forehead against his as he unfastened her belt, removing it in a single motion and casting it aside and into the haystack, where it landed with a soft rustle.

Reaching under his tunic, Æfre could feel his hardening bulge straining against the fabric of his trousers, and she loosened them, then raised her own skirts to her knees. Osric slipped his hand under her skirts, quickly finding her familiar, most sensitive place, causing Æfre to let out an audible gasp, which Osric stifled with a passionate kiss as he continued to gently move his hand under her skirt.

Her breath was coming in rapid, rhythmic sighs as he reached under his tunic and freed himself from the ever-tightening constraint of his trousers and braies, letting them fall around his calves.

Æfre slid her thigh up along his, curling a single leg around him as he entered her, anchoring them both in the heat between them. She clung to him, whispering his name into his ear as he thrust deeply into her again and again. They were uncontrolled and reckless, yet familiar in a way that felt grounding and steady to her. The feel of him moving inside her, the way her back pressed up against the cold, prickly dullness of the timber wall—it all felt like a refuge at a time when everything else in her world was unraveling.

She drew him deeper into her with her leg, and a moan caught in the back of her throat—she was already near her release, and he leaned back slightly, his head tilted at an angle that she knew allowed him to watch her, as he always loved to do.

Æfre shook with climax a moment later, quickly covering her own mouth with her hand to prevent her cries from being heard beyond the stable. The look and feel of her taking her release drove Osric to his, and burying his face in the nape of her neck, he climaxed in several deep, shuddering thrusts, her arms coiled around him, each clinging to the other until they both finally became still.

For a long while they sat in silence, leaning entwined against the stable wall. They stayed as long as they dared, but the rising scent of the evening meal wafting in from the hall signaled that soon, Osric would need to take his leave. Æfre, too, felt the pull to return to Eadlin. If she kept to her careful routine and stayed diligent, perhaps by tomorrow she could turn Eadlin over to her mother's care. One more day, possibly less.

They stood, buckling their belts in silence, the warmth of Osric's body still lingering against hers. They took turns brushing dust and bits of hay from each other's clothes, their fingers lingering longer than necessary.

"You should take your leave first," Æfre murmured. "I'll wait a while before heading back."

Osric hesitated. "If you're sure—"

"I'm sure."

Osric looked to the door, then remembered himself, and turned back to Æfre. "I leave tomorrow. Æthelwod believes he's sending me to Wintanceaster. I'll be out of sight until it happens—I plan to make camp in the woodcutter's shelter."

"I remember it."

"Wulfric will be here, but... promise me you'll keep out of sight, during this— whatever happens next. No trips to the shelter, we cannot risk it."

"I understand, Osric. You needn't worry."

He simply nodded, now out of excuses to stay any longer. He stepped in close to Æfre and took her in his arms, pouring himself into one last kiss before turning and leaving the stable.

Once again, Æfre was alone, surrounded by the still, hazy quiet of the stable.

36

Ġeflit ✕ Argument

"Svend! If you wish to challenge this decision, speak plainly! Make your case or step aside!" Torvald Ironsight's voice boomed from within his quarters, rattling the rafters and disrupting the evening meal to the extent that every corner of the crowded hall fell silent. Bjørn swept his gaze across the room. Conversations had died, drinking horns halted mid-air. Warriors and traders who had been laughing moments before now leaned in, eyes sharp, ears pricked and receptive. From within the Jarl's quarters, Svend's voice rang out, equally heated.

"Torvald, we have known each other far too many winters for me to bite my tongue! I am telling you—stop letting this slide! Those missing shipments are only the beginning. You must see it! Why do you let these Saxons walk all over us!?"

"And yet there you stand," Torvald shouted back, "you've grown rich—fed and clothed by the coin earned from trade with them! We have never been so prosperous as now! Yet you would bite the hand that feeds you for the sake of a few sacks of grain and some weapons!? We do not have any proof that this is more than an isolated opportunist!"

"Come now, Tor! How can you be so blind!? Perhaps the tales of your growing weakness are not so exaggerated after all."

A murmur rippled through the hall. Bold words. Bjørn's spine straightened as he scanned the faces of the men once more. The tension was so thick it could be cut.

Near the hearth, Leif lounged with three others, feigning disinterest—but his eyes betrayed the truth. He was listening. They all were.

Satisfied that their performance had taken root, Bjørn pushed to his feet and strode toward the back of the hall, slipping behind the partition.

"Jarl Torvald! Svend!" He yelled, louder than necessary. "Come, Svend. Let us walk together. The night air will clear our heads."

Bjørn stepped inside the Jarl's quarters, just as an almighty crash rang out—the sharp shatter of pottery breaking.

"Best you remember whose hall this is when you speak to me in here, Svend." Torvald roared.

"*Hæ*! Jarl Torvald! Svend! Enough!" Bjørn barked, scanning the room—only to find both men lounging in chairs, grinning like foxes. Each held a drinking horn of ale, utterly at ease.

Torvald twirled a small grain sack in his hand, its contents shifting with the unmistakable sound of broken clay pottery.

He smashed it inside a sack. To make cleanup easier. Bjørn swallowed his laughter and pressed on with the plan. "Svend." He thundered, "Come. Let's go."

Svend downed the rest of his drinking horn and nodded affably to a grinning Torvald. "This isn't over, Tor!" He said, grinning, yet in a voice uncharacteristically laden with threat.

"Svend!" Bjørn yelled as Svend stood and handed his empty horn to Torvald, who nodded graciously and shook out the last drops of residual ale. "Let's go!" Bjørn seized Svend's arm and half-shoved, half-dragged him toward the door.

The instant they crossed the threshold into the hall, Svend's entire demeanor shifted. Amusement vanished, replaced by a coiled, quiet rage.

He played the part perfectly.

Bjørn hustled him towards the door, all the eyes in the hall boring into their backs with such intensity that he half-expected the two of them might burst into flames.

Outside, they kept up the act, striding down the row of tents and makeshift shelters along the main road. Bjørn still muttered about cooling off, manhandling Svend as though he were an out of control rabid dog.

When they reached Svend's turf-roofed hut near the market stalls, Bjørn delivered the grand finale of his performance—he kicked the door open and shoved Svend inside, following him in and slamming the door shut behind them.

For a moment, they stood in silence, the dim glow of the neglected hearth fire barely illuminating the small space. A heavy silence after so much activity settled between them. Finally, Svend exhaled and broke the quiet.

"Drink?"

"Já."

Svend chuckled, fumbling in the dark before striking a flame to a candle. He set out two cups and a jug of ale, pouring generously.

"Was it enough?" Bjørn asked.

Svend handed him a cup. "We did exactly the right amount. Leif and his lot were paying close attention, and the men will all be talking. By tomorrow, I think we'll find that things will start to move." He took a deep draught of his drink.

The hut fell silent again as they both drank and turned over the possibilities of what might come next.

"There may be others," Bjørn said at last. "Men following Leif's lead—some we don't even know about."

Svend nodded. "Without a doubt. But they won't stay hidden for long, and now we must put our trust in the men we know to be ours." Svend drank deeply from his cup, draining it before pouring himself another. "Everyone saw you step in to break the fight. They are aware that you work closely with me and Jarl Torvald. They'll want to know where you stand if the leadership of this camp is challenged." He leaned back, swirling his ale. "And those outside our plan... they'll be looking for a side to choose."

"So I have to pick one? Or...pretend to?"

Svend gave him a knowing look. "Bjørn, I don't think it'll matter. When the time comes, they won't ask—they'll act. Torvald, me, and probably you as well—I imagine we will become hostages."

Bjørn frowned; the thought hadn't even occurred to him. "What's stopping them from just killing us?"

Svend let out a dry laugh. "Nothing, if that's what they really wanted. But Jarl Torvald is certain that's not the game we're playing." He took another sip, then leaned in. "Remember who's truly behind this. Æthelwod doesn't want Northmen fighting Northmen. He doesn't want a change in our leadership structure; he wants us gone. Æthelwod needs the unrest to look like a threat to the Saxons, and he can't get that simply from a bit of infighting. He'll fan the flames until they march in as the 'solution' to a problem he created."

Bjørn exhaled. "So, when the men ask me where I stand?"

Svend tilted his head. "If the fight tonight had been real, how would you have answered that question?"

Bjørn didn't hesitate. "I'd have said Jarl Torvald has never wavered in his duty to this camp."

Svend grinned. "Then there's your answer."

37

Wrecca ⚔ Banish

"Can I please have some water?" The voice, small and distant, pulled Æfre from her bedside slumber.

Her eyes fluttered open, and she jerked upright, a jolt of panic surging through her as she realized the early morning light was seeping into the hut. Once again, she hadn't meant to fall asleep.

"Eadlin, you're awake!" Æfre breathed, relief mixing with her panic. "I'm sorry—I dozed off. Are you in pain?"

Eadlin's voice came hoarse but steady. "No, I... I'd just like some water, if I could."

"Of course!" Æfre grabbed the jug and poured water into two cups. "I think I'll join you."

Eadlin managed a weak smile as she reached for her cup.

"Slowly," Æfre cautioned, observing her. "You've had nothing but small sips for days. Your body needs time to adjust."

Eadlin took a few tentative sips, then let out a soft groan. "My Lord, I'm so thirsty! Why am I so thirsty?"

"You've had a fever for days." Æfre reached out instinctively. "May I?"

Eadlin gave a slight nod, and Æfre pressed the back of her hand to her forehead—cooler. A rush of relief filled her.

"It seems your fever has broken," she said, unable to keep the happiness from her voice.

"I awoke in a sweat," Eadlin murmured.

Æfre gave a reassuring smile. "Believe it or not, that's a good thing. Your body is fighting back stronger now."

Eadlin nodded, but didn't say anything.

"Would you like to refresh yourself? I would like to have a look at your wound and change the dressing if you're agreeable."

"Yes, please."

Having laid out the dressing change supplies in advance, Æfre worked swiftly to assess Eadlin's wound, which had healed considerably since the previous dressing change. For a while, the quiet of the hut was punctuated only by the sounds of Æfre at the tools of her craft, until she broke the spell.

"Eadlin, this healing wound is a fine sight." She said, "I'm pleased with your progress. In a few more days, we won't need the strips inside anymore. I'm not hurting you, am I?"

"No, it's tolerable now."

"That's good. You're mending well—I'm about finished. Do you want to try to stand while I change the bedding?"

"That would be good."

Æfre helped Eadlin to her feet for the first time in days, steadying her as she reacquainted herself with the sensation of being upright.

"Go slow now...there. Well done. How does that feel?" Æfre asked, sliding the chair at the bedside closer to Eadlin so she could steady herself, then swiftly changing the bedding.

"Strange—but not in a bad way. My legs feel like a baby deer."

Both women giggled.

"I'm just so unusually weak."

"It's to be expected." Æfre said, "Your body has been through a battle, but every day you'll see improvement. It's important to move now. Bild your strength back." Æfre gave the clean bed linen a final flick and laid it over the straw mattress. "There. This is finished. Do you want to get back in, or would you rather sit for a while?"

"I think I'll get back in bed—that's quite enough excitement for one morning. But it's nice to know I can still stand. I honestly wasn't sure." Both women giggled again as Æfre helped Eadlin back into the bed.

Back in bed, Eadlin sagged against the pillows, exhausted but jubilant at her small victory. "How long have I been here?" She asked, her expression turning thoughtful.

"Just under three days," Æfre told her. "Since Yule, when you collapsed. You'll probably recognize this hut as Cenric and Cwenhild's. Osr...Lord Osric has kindly given them use of his quarters until you're recovered. He leaves for Wintanceaster today."

Eadlin frowned. "I remember Osric being sent to Wintanceaster. Bishop Æthelwod announced it at the feast. But after that... It's all hazy, as if in a dream." She looked expectantly at Æfre.

Æfre hesitated. She hadn't been there on the night—was it her place to tell Eadlin what had happened? But Lady Wynnflæd and Cwenhild were both absent, and Eadlin deserved to know.

"Cwenhild told me you left the hall as the meal began. Apparently, Osric asked her to follow you and make sure you were safe—she found you collapsed."

Eadlin exhaled sharply, covering her face with her hands. "This is all my fault." She groaned, the sound muffled by her hands.

"Eadlin, of course, this isn't your fault."

"No, it is, Æfre." She lowered her hands, eyes filled with regret. "I was getting better, but the treatments were so strong—they made me nauseous, and I absolutely reeked—as my mother would oft remind me—multiple times a day! Apparently, I left a lingering scent everywhere I went!" She let out a bitter laugh. "But it was vanity, pure vanity. I stopped the treatments the day before the feast to give myself time to get it out of my system. I meant to start again immediately after...I just didn't want to be so utterly disgusting while seated so near to my future husb—"

She cut herself off, looking at Æfre. "Sorry."

Æfre swallowed hard, forcing a smile and taking Eadlin's hand. "Don't be sorry, Eadlin. I'm just glad you're better. That's what matters."

An awkward silence settled between them. Eadlin studied her as if she wanted to say more.

"Æfre?"

"Yes?"

"Nobody has said so, but I feel like perhaps you may have saved my life."

Æfre averted her eyes and immediately started tidying her supplies, putting everything back into her bags—a desperate attempt to distract herself from her current predicament.

"Perhaps."

She fought to steady herself, swallowing tears before they could form as the previous night's tryst in the stable with Osric flashed through her mind. She forced the turmoil rising within her down.

"Æfre, thank you," Eadlin said, the unmistakable ring of sincerity warming her voice, only making the situation feel that much worse.

"You're welcome, Eadlin. Truly." Æfre managed to say without bursting into tears.

Eadlin gave Æfre a faint smile before her eyes drifted shut. Within moments, she was asleep, and Æfre was once again alone with her thoughts.

She scooted her chair back so she could rest her head against the wall and sat still for a while. She felt a coldness that seemed to be coming from her gut and spreading through her. Æfre felt powerless, like she was being shown a preview of the future that stretched out before her if things were to stay exactly as they were.

She closed her eyes for a moment to let the sensation pass, taking several deep breaths as a single tear escaped her eye.

She'd meant to stay awake, but she was helpless against the multiple days' worth of exhaustion that she'd built up. Before she could stop herself, she too succumbed to sleep, still sitting in the bedside chair.

HEART OF THE WILD GODS

* * *

"Æfre... Æfre!"

A firm shake jolted her.

"Æfre, dear, wake up." Cwenhild's voice was gentle but urgent.

Æfre's eyes fluttered open to find Cwenhild and Wynnflæd standing over her. Just behind them, Bishop Æthelwod loomed like a spectre, his expression unreadable.

"Cwenhild... I'm sorry. We fell asleep."

"Don't fret, dear. All is as it should be," Cwenhild assured her. "Lady Wynnflæd has come to see Eadlin with the Bishop, and I was hoping for your assistance in the hall while they visit."

Even in her sleep-deprived state, Æfre sensed something in Cwenhild's tone—something that told her she should agree without hesitation.

"Of course. I'll just get my cloak." She rose groggily, glancing at Eadlin, who still slept soundly. Turning to Wynnflæd, she offered a weary smile.

"Her fever broke in the night. She was awake this morning, speaking with me. The wound is healing well—she even stood for a short time." Æfre's words trailed off as she took in the heavy silence that followed.

Something had shifted overnight. She could feel it. The air in the room felt thick, weighted with unspoken tension. Æfre glanced from face to face, searching for an answer, but pressed on. "With continued care and rest, she should make a full recovery."

Again, silence. Cold. Unwelcoming.

Æfre pulled her cloak around her shoulders, preparing to follow Cwenhild.

"Æfre."

Wynnflæd's voice stopped her at the threshold of the hut.

A long pause stretched between them before Lady Wynnflæd

finally spoke.

"Thank you."

She didn't meet Æfre's eyes.

Æfre dipped her head. "You're most welcome, Lady Wynnflæd."

A quick glance at Æthelwod confirmed what she already knew—he was purposefully avoiding her gaze, looking anywhere but at her.

Perplexed and increasingly suspicious, Æfre stepped outside, the hut's door swinging shut behind her.

"Cwenhild, what is happening?" Æfre asked as soon as they'd put enough distance between themselves and the hut.

Cwenhild sighed, shaking her head. "Æfre, dear, I'm not entirely sure. Those two have been as close as hounds on the hunt today. And knowing the bishop, whatever it is will come to light soon enough—undoubtedly in some grandiose fashion."

"That's what worries me," Æfre said.

"Now, come." Cwenhild ushered her into the hall. "I need a small favor—this way."

She led Æfre toward the back of the hall, pausing outside the thegn's quarters where she and Cenric had been staying. "Oh! Where is my mind? My dear, there's a basket on the table inside the quarters—could you fetch it for me?"

"Of course."

Æfre stepped around the partition and into the quarters. She spotted the basket on the table, and just as she reached for it, a familiar voice startled her.

"You know, by the laws of this land, a thief caught in the act of stealing personal property in broad daylight must repay the value of the item up to threefold, or lose a hand."

Æfre spun around to find Osric, a smug grin on his face; the unmistakable shuffle of his accomplice Cwenhild's retreating footsteps could be heard just on the other side of the partition.

"Æfre, you look exhausted."

Æfre scoffed. "Why, thank you, Lord. What an extraordinarily kind observation. You're no fresh-faced lad yourself, you know."

Osric chuckled, stepping closer. "That came out entirely wrong."

"I should hope so, *my lord*." She smirked.

He sighed, shaking his head. "I'm sorry, Æfre. Exhausted or not, you're beautiful." Pulling her to him, he kissed her.

When he pulled away, his expression turned serious. "And now I need to be ill-mannered once more."

"Oh?"

"It's this." He held up a folded piece of parchment. "I need you to get it to Jarl Torvald."

Æfre took it, turning it over in her hands. "That should be easy enough—the man has a way of materializing out of thin air. Am I allowed to know what this is?"

"A simple rendering. The location of the woodcutter's shelter. Æfre, I need you to deliver it yourself. No messengers. Straight into his hands. It's best that we meet there tomorrow, after the sunrise."

She nodded. "Of course."

Warmth flickered in his eyes. "Good." He kissed her again, cradling her face between his hands. For a moment, he just looked at her, studying every contour of her face. Then he kissed her once more—deeper, lingering.

Æfre was the first to pull away. "Osric, don't start—"

"Just one more—"

"Osric!" She giggled, stepping back. "It's time for you to be on the road to *Wintanceaster*, Lord." With exaggerated flourish, she tucked the folded parchment into the sleeve of her overdress.

He sighed, conceding with a smile—his eyes glinting in that way that always made her knees weak. "Stay safe. This will be over in a few days. After that, we'll figure out what's next."

Æfre held his gaze, unable to move. Then, without thinking, she rushed forward, kissing him one last time—a wordless confession of her fear that she was losing him.

Just as quickly, she pulled away, turned, and headed for the exit.

"Æfre." His voice stopped her at the threshold. She turned.

"Don't forget Cwenhild's basket."

* * *

"Are those...my bags? My supplies?" Æfre asked as she and Cwenhild returned to the hut. "Why would they be outside?" The two women looked at each other, and dread spread like spilled ink through Æfre's chest. *What could it possibly be now!?*

Æfre picked up her bags, opening them to inspect their contents. Everything was there—someone had haphazardly packed everything away, and Æfre was certain she knew who.

"Ah, Cwenhild, there you are." Bishop Æthelwod declared as the door to the hut suddenly swung open, as if on cue. The wraithlike clergyman stepped out into the cold daylight like a shadow slipping from beyond the veil. "I wanted to tell you, Cwenhild, that Æfre's presence will no longer be required at Eadlin's bedside."

"I'm sorry, Bishop, I don't understand," Æfre said.

Æthelwod flatly ignored Æfre, addressing only Cwenhild, "It is the duty of all of us, Cwenhild, to ensure that Wōdenléah does not stray from the one true faith. I would hope that you might be able to help your friend see our perspective."

"Your perspective, bishop. And I daresay you could help her see it yourself, seeing as she's standing right in front of you." Cwenhild spat.

"Cwenhild," Æthelwod's tone was disingenuously saccharine, as if he were speaking to a small child. "Æfre's presence here may seem like a harmless family legacy, but the simple truth is, if we allow even a modicum of heathen influence into our midst, we invite peril upon our souls."

"Peril upon our souls!?" Cwenhild snorted, growing increasingly incredulous, pointing an accusatory finger inside the hut, "Æfre saved that girl's life!"

"Cwenhild." Æfre said softly, trying to gently discourage her friend from taking any more swipes at the bishop, "All is well."

"No Æfre, all is most certainly not well," Cwenhild shouted. Several passers-by had now stopped to stare.

"Cwenhild, I know you and Æfre are close." Æthelwod oozed insincerity.

"This is not about *me*, bishop!"

"My dear Cwenhild, you must understand that the very presence of any heathen, even one as particularly skilled as Æfre, imperils not only Eadlin's soul, but the souls of all those who might seek her out for healing. It simply must stand that only those who walk in the light of the one true God attend our sick and wounded."

"Cwenhild, please. Let us take our leave!"Æfre said, nervously eyeing the growing crowd of onlookers that continued to gather near the hut, drawn by the spellbinding drama being played out. "I can instruct you in private on Eadlin's care."

"Please, Cwenhild," Æthelwod cooed, "take no offense at this decision. Even your heathen friend here seems to understand when to yield."

"It is not your decision that offends me, Bishop." Cwenhild roared, puffing out her chest, and moving closer to Æthelwod with a look in her eye—a hawk's glower that Æfre had never before seen from her friend.

"It's the fact that both you and I know that you don't really believe it," Cwenhild said coldly. Accusingly. "We both know that you—"

"Cwenhild! It has been days since any of us slept properly." Æfre said, holding Cwenhild by the arm as she began to drag her away from the hut, heading in the direction of the stable. "We shall take our leave now. Cwenhild, come."

Without acknowledging Æfre, Bishop Æthelwod simply inclined his head and slithered back into the dimness of the hut like a viper under a rock, leaving an indignant and sputtering Cwenhild to contend with her rage.

"What are all of you looking at!?" Cwenhild raged at the gathered crowd. "Is it that you enjoy a bit of cruelty for sport!? Is this what is meant by your Christian charity!? Go home! Why do you stand here like witless fools!? Be gone!"

"Cwenhild!" Æfre pulled Cwenhild along until they were out of the thick of the gathered crowd. As the two women stood facing each other in front of the stable, Cwenhild burst into tears.

Embracing her friend, Æfre whispered in her ear, "Cwenhild, all will be well. You know well enough how to help Eadlin, and I can show you what you need to know. All will be well."

"It's not just about Eadlin, though, is it, Æfre?" Cwenhild sobbed.

Cenric emerged from the stable, having heard the shouting, and behind him strode Osric, leading his favorite gelding, tacked up for his journey. The confused men looked at Æfre, then at Cwenhild, then back at Æfre.

"It's been a really long few days," Æfre said, still embracing Cwenhild. "We're all tired."

Over Cwenhild's shoulder, Æfre caught Osric's penetrating, inquisitive gaze. *Æthelwod*, she mouthed to him.

"Cenric," Æfre said, still acutely aware that there was a lingering group of people watching them. Is Epona still in the paddock? I believe I need to take my leave fairly soon."

"Yes, Æfre, I can tack her for—" Cenric looked worriedly at his wife, still in Æfre's arms.

"No, Cenric, I'll do it myself. Why don't you see to your wife—she can tell you both what's just happened.

"Æfre," Osric began.

"Lord Osric," Æfre said, addressing him formally in front of the onlookers, "it really is better if I take my leave now," she said insistently, "and quickly." She added softly, already moving towards the stable. "I will go straight home—you need not worry. It's for the best."

Adjusting her bags over her shoulder, Æfre disappeared into the stable, emerging what felt only like moments later with Epona, fully tacked.

Cenric, Osric, and Cwenhild were all standing in a tight circle, with Cwenhild holding court, gesturing wildly as she spoke.

Æfre mounted, catching Osric's eye as she did. They exchanged one long, last look before Æfre urged Epona on, and horse and rider disappeared out the front palisade gate.

38
Eode ᛉ Travelled

"Jarl Torvald!" Håkon called, stepping briskly from his makeshift post as Torvald and Eadgar approached on horseback. "She's not long back."

Torvald reined in his stallion, his gaze flicking past Håkon's shoulder, sweeping the distant road and the dark fringe of the forest beyond. He exhaled slowly. "Any more since we last spoke?"

"None today, not since she returned from the burh." Håkon hesitated, shifting on his feet. "But there were quite a few nosing around while she was gone."

"Does she know?"

The guard nodded. "Já. She asked me outright, Jarl—I couldn't lie to her."

Torvald studied him for a moment, then gave a curt nod. "You did the right thing, Håkon."

Relief softened the man's face.

Torvald tightened his grip on the reins. "This can't go on. "I'm working on a solution, but this..." Without waiting for a response, Torvald urged his stallion on, and they rode down towards Æfre's homestead.

"Wait outside with the horses, Eadgar," Torvald instructed as they both dismounted, handing his reins to the boy, "I won't be long."

Eadgar nodded, already tying the animals to the paddock fence as Torvald strode toward the hut.

The door swung open before he could knock. A weary but smiling Æfre stood just inside the threshold, holding a pile of kindling.

"Jarl Torvald. I had a feeling I'd see you today." She stepped aside, waving him in. "I heard you coming. Come in—though I warn you, it's cold. I've only just returned, and the hearth's gone out."

Torvald stepped inside, his gaze catching on the moss-green cloak draped over her shoulders—the one he had given her. It suited her.

"It looks good on you," he said before he could stop himself, hoping that his voice didn't betray the fact that seeing her wearing the cloak he'd had made for her made him feel like a shy, lovesick adolescent boy.

Æfre blinked, then glanced down as if only just remembering she was wearing the cloak he'd gifted her. She set the kindling down next to the hearth, brushed herself off, and gave a little twirl, laughing. "It's truly the most thoughtful and lovely gift, Jarl Torvald. And as you already knew, it was very much needed. It has been placed straight into service."

"It is good I could fix at least one unfortunate thing," Torvald said evenly.

"I had meant to ride out to you to thank you in person the day after Yule, but of course they sent for me from the burh," Æfre said.

"Leave the fire to me." He stooped and picked up the kindling, then pulled his flint and steel out of the pouch at his belt and, with a few practiced strikes, ignited a spark.

Æfre sighed and collapsed into a chair. "Thank you, Jarl. I'm exhausted. I haven't slept properly in days. I didn't feel I could leave Eadlin at first—" she paused, watching him. "I assume you know who I was tending to?"

Torvald tossed a fresh log onto the fledgling flames, careful to avoid her gaze—as much to grant her a bit of privacy as to steady his own nerves.

"I do."

The hut was silent for a moment as the hearth fire began to

crackle.

"And did everything come to good in the burh?"

Æfre exhaled, rubbing her temples. "If by that you mean, will Eadlin recover? Yes. In that way, it came to good."

Torvald heard the unspoken words.

"And yet?" He turned, watching her.

Æfre met his gaze, and he saw something hard behind her exhaustion. "And yet—I fear it might be me who does not recover."

Torvald said nothing, but let out his own long, slow exhale. The hearth fire was burning well now, and he pulled up a chair to sit across from Æfre, the wooden legs scraping against the packed earth floor of the hut. Silence settled between them, thick and woolen, until at last, she spoke again.

"Æthelwod convinced Wynnflæd of Aldhem to dismiss me this morning."

The fire crackled, filling the space where neither of them spoke.

Æfre huffed a bitter laugh. "You'll be able to guess why, of course. According to our friend the Bishop Æthelwod, only 'those who walk in the light of the one true God' are fit to tend Wōdenléah's sick and wounded. The likes of me would imperil their souls."

Torvald rolled his eyes. "That stale old kenning is rolled out like a battering ram whenever the Christians need to exert power."

"Exactly so."

Torvald seized the moment. "That's why I'm here—"

"You're here to speak of the ongoing threat to my well-being." Æfre interrupted, her resignation made plain.

"I am."

She fell quiet, staring into the fire. The flames cast dancing shadows across her face.

At last, she broke the silence, "It's only this last day that it's begun to feel real."

Torvald frowned. "What is?"

She looked up, her eyes unreadable. "That everything I know—everything I have ever known here—that it may cease to be."

Torvald sat back, sensing there was more she had yet to say. He waited, but she did not offer more.

"Why not just become a Christian? Even in name only?" he asked at last, his tone even.

A smirk tugged at the corner of her mouth. "You mean like Guthrum[xxii] did? Yes, perhaps I might also declare myself queen of Wōdenléah."

Torvald let out a hearty laugh.

Æfre chuckled, "I think you understand well, Jarl, that the concessions afforded to men and kings do not extend to the likes of me."

Torvald nodded. "No, I don't suppose they do."

"Osric asked the same of me not long ago," she mused. "And my answer remains unchanged."

Torvald leaned forward. "I want you to know—I did not come at Osric's bidding."

Æfre waved a hand. "I know that, Jarl. And I take no offense. It's a fair question. And we both know this isn't really about faith. It's about power."

She sat up suddenly. "Would you like some ale? Pardon my lack of manners, but by the Gods, I could use a cup of ale."

Torvald laughed. "Yes, please Æfre."

As she busied herself filling the cups, she continued, "The women in my family have always lived freely. We tend to the sick, we help bring forth the babes, we make medicine, and we hunt. Surely, there have always been those who distrust or scorn us for adhering to the old ways, but it has always been our way, and we have always served the community. For me to give up living freely, as my family always has, as is *the only way I know*—I suppose it would feel to me a lot like death."

Torvald listened, stroking his beard in thought. "Have you considered leaving?" He took a deep draught of ale, observing her response as he drank.

"I have nowhere to go, Jarl Torvald. The only real connections I have are here. How might you imagine things would go if I were to just appear somewhere—a heathen woman alone in a strange village?" She laughed bitterly and swirled the ale in her cup before drinking.

Torvald smiled, looking into his own ale cup in silence for a moment before asking, "And what if you did have somewhere to go?"

She hesitated, studying his face before answering. "I am in no position to refuse help, Jarl. As long as it is, in fact, help—and not another well-disguised form of control." She took another sip. "Know you of an unoccupied cave I might dwell in?"

Torvald chuckled, shaking his head.

Æfre suddenly gasped. "Eálá!, I nearly forgot!" She set down her ale cup and pulled the folded parchment from her sleeve. "From Lord Osric—the location of the woodcutter's shelter. He requests that you all gather tomorrow after the sun rises."

Torvald unfolded it, scanning the drawing before tucking it into his tunic. He leaned back in his chair and drained his ale cup, then sat upright, suddenly seeming to remember something. "I should let poor Eadgar come warm himself."

"You've brought Eadgar with you!?" Æfre asked. "Has he been waiting out in the cold this whole time!?" She chided the chieftain, grinning as she moved towards the door. Casting Torvald a look as she opened the door to the hut, she yelled, "Eadgar! Come warm yourself by the hearth! The Jarl wishes to beg your forgiveness for leaving you outside like a flea-bitten stray!"

Eadgar jogged in, grinning. "Hello Æfre!"

"Hello, Eadgar. Are you hungry?"

"That one is always hungry!" Torvald called from his chair.

"A little, yes," Eadgar said as she scuffed up to the hut and over the threshold.

"Well, I'm not sure what I have on hand, but I'll see what I can scrounge up. Come inside."

"Don't you eat all of Æfre's food!" Torvald could be heard barking at Eadgar as the door to the hut closed.

39
Gield ✕ Tribute

Bishop Æthelwod startled, letting out a shrill, almost girlish yelp that shattered the evening quiet and seemed to bounce from the timber rafters of the church. He hadn't seen Leif sitting alone in the shadows at the back when he walked in, and the shock nearly sent him to meet the Almighty.

"Oh, it's you," Æthelwod snapped, hastily smoothing his robe, irritation replacing the temporary abandonment of his dignity. "What are you doing here at this hour, lurking in the shadows?"

Leif just stared. His voice was flat, edged with the contempt he no longer bothered to hide from the man who paid him. "You told me to come when I had information. I have information."

"Yes, I bade you come, but not like this!" Æthelwod gestured wildly. "You can't just go skulking around, leaping out from behind corners, frightening people!"

Leif stood. "Very well," he said flatly as he turned toward the door, calling Æthelwod's bluff.

"Wait." Æthelwod exhaled sharply as he called out to the man, already exasperated that the evening of quiet contemplation he had envisioned for the end of his day was slipping through his fingers. Without looking at Leif, he muttered, "What do you know?"

"Jarl Torvald and his second-in-command are at odds." Leif paused, his hand on the church door, not turning to face the bishop. "If we're going to act, we should act now. Rumors of the Jarl's weakness are spreading like wildfire through the camp; he has near come to blows with his second in command, and the men are restless, frustrated with his failure to discover whoever is diverting the trade shipments."

Æthelwod's fingers worked the smooth, cold silver of the cross that hung at his neck as he contemplated the information. "You're certain of this?"

"I witnessed it myself! Bjørn practically had to drag Svend out of the hall—things got so heated between him and the Jarl. Cracks are quickly forming in the leadership. That always leads to chaos. The time is right."

Æthelwod narrowed his eyes. "Bjørn—the angry young chieftain's son, yes? Is he ours?"

Leif hesitated. "Hard to say."

Æthelwod turned sharply, his fragile patience thinning. "What does that mean?"

"Bjørn is close to both Jarl Torvald and Svend. He says the right things, but he's from a prominent family. I don't think he would take the risk. And Jarl Torvald is supposedly mentoring him."

Æthelwod scoffed. "Then he's useless to us." He began to pace slowly. "The stolen goods—where does that leave us?"

Leif folded his arms. "Nothing else is changed. The tension in the camp is real, and our numbers are strong. The leadership is crumbling, and those who won't join us have signaled that they won't stand in our way. All we need is a spark."

Æthelwod stilled. "And you can provide this?"

"I can."

"Can you?" Æthelwod snapped, "Because the last time I tasked you to take care of something of a rather specific nature, you came back wearing two arrows. Put there by a woman, no less!"

Leif said nothing, yet his inner thoughts were betrayed by the murderous flash behind his eyes.

Æthelwod turned back to the altar, his eyes darkening with focus. Silence stretched between the two men for a moment as the bishop weighed their next move.

"We'll need just a bit of time, not much." The bishop's voice was measured and calculating. "Lord Osric will be on his way, and I'm told by Wintanceaster that Lord Wulfric of Beornwic will arrive to stand in his place."

Leif frowned. "Is that good or bad for us?"

Æthelwod waved a dismissive hand. "Wulfric is of noble blood, raised in a household that survived Edington. I'm on familiar terms with his father, the ealdorman—managed to hold on to his land after Edington. That tells a story—loyal to the crown, yes, but more significantly—status conscious and politically astute." The bishop's familiar smirk began to form at the corners of his mouth. "A man raised in a politically astute family is, before all, usually able to ascertain whose hearth provides the greatest warmth. I believe he'll fall in line."

Leif remained unconvinced. "Perhaps. But will he go so far as to raise the fyrd?"

Æthelwod's expression darkened. "He will, because I will see that it is done. And you and yours will make it so that he does not have a choice but to do so." The bishop's tone brooked no argument. "I would not have sent Lord Osric to Wintanceaster if I harbored any doubt that the time is close. I'll watch Lord Wulfric when he arrives, ensure the pieces are in place." His fingers continued to fuss over his silver crucifix. "If you don't hear otherwise, we'll go on as planned."

Leif remained by the door, staring at Æthelwod in silence. After a moment, the bishop met his gaze, irritation prickling at his nerves.

"Well?" Æthelwod snapped. "Was there something else?"

Leif didn't answer. He simply stood, expectant and unmoving.

Æthelwod exhaled sharply, muttering under his breath as he reluctantly reached beneath his robes, pulled out a small coin pouch, and tossed it across the nave to Leif.

Leif caught it effortlessly with one hand, wearing the expression of someone trying to locate the source of a bad smell. He gave Æthelwod one last withering look before turning and walking out without another word.

40

Scidd ✕ Shed

At first, it was the sound of approaching hoofbeats cutting through the early morning quiet, then a voice being carried through the frosty air. From inside the woodcutter's shelter, Osric, Svend, and Torvald all heard Wulfric before they saw him, announcing himself proudly like a king returning to reclaim a usurped throne.

"I say!" Wulfric called out, the solid thud of his boots hitting the ground as he swung down from the saddle and stretched his back. "You must forgive me for keeping you waiting, yet you may now rejoice, lords, for I have at last graced you with my presence! Your humble shelter shall now know the glory of my many charms! Tell me, is there any hope for a horn of early morning ale from this fine establishment?"

Osric chuckled and shook his head—Wulfric and his grand entrances.

Wulfric found a spot to tie his horse alongside the others, then rounded to the front of the woodcutter's shelter, adjusting his sword and smoothing his quilted tunic. "I do hope the service is good here, my lords, it's simply—"

He stopped short.

For a moment, Wulfric simply stared into the opening to the shelter at the sight before him, a broad grin spreading across his face until he finally dissolved into a fit of unrestrained laughter. "Now this—this is a sight to behold! The three of you stuffed into this small shelter look like three oxen in a puppy's kennel!"

Osric glanced at Svend and Jarl Torvald Ironsight. Even though they'd all three left their weapons outside, the two giant Northmen and Osric, himself not a small man, were indeed crowded into an awkward tangle of elbows, knees, and boots inside the cramped shelter. From the outside, they must have looked utterly absurd.

Svend laughed heartily, looking at Torvald. "He is not wrong."

"Hello, Svend!" Wulfric said warmly.

"Hello, Lord Wulfric! It is good to see you again!" Svend grinned, unfolding himself with difficulty to clasp arms with the newcomer, ducking his head to keep it from connecting with the low roof. "This is Jarl Torvald Ironsight, our chieftain. Jarl, this is Wulfric, thegn of Beornwic."

Wulfric's easy humor shifted as he showed the Jarl the respect his station commanded. He sidestepped the small fire burning outside the shelter and extended his hand. "Jarl Torvald. Your reputation precedes you."

Torvald clasped his arm firmly, his gaze steady. "Lord Wulfric. Svend tells good tales of you as well."

"And of course the thegn of Wōdenléah," Wulfric said ceremoniously, spinning on his heel and turning his attention to Osric."

"Wulf," Osric laughed, "I won't even try to stand to greet you in here. In fact, I suggest we get to speaking of what must be done before we draw unwanted eyes."

Wulfric agreed, unbuckling his sword belt and propping it against the shed's outer wall. He crouched, awkwardly lowering himself onto the packed earth near the door. The others jostled, laughter rippling through the tight space as they shifted to attempt to make enough space.

"First—you have my thanks for meeting me here," Osric said, still grinning as he watched the men struggle to make room. "The setting is less than ideal, but it allows us to speak plainly. Æthelwod is ready to move, likely very soon. We all have experience enough to know how these things can twist and turn, but if we can steer it right, we can try to leave as little impact as possible on our respective settlements, and as Lord King Alfred has cautioned me directly, avoid the threat of a wider conflict."

Torvald and Svend both nodded. Wulfric listened intently.

"If you're all agreed, I believe it's best we talk this over once more—beginning with location. The location of this action perhaps matters most." Osric continued, "I believe it's best we keep it outside both of our gates."

"Agreed," Torvald said, "not too close to Wōdenléah. We can be heard, but not seen. That way, we remain focused on who's involved."

"Ġēa," Wulfric said.

"Já," Svend nodded.

Osric exhaled. "Very well, in that case, I propose the leftward bend in the road—on the way in to the burh—where it widens before the meeting of the ways."

"Já, we know it," Torvald said.

"A short walk hence from Wōdenléah," Osric continued. "We may be heard, but the forest will give us plenty of cover."

"Good," Torvald agreed. Svend and Wulfric nodded.

"I also propose some trusted men in the trees along the road, watching from the flanks," Osric said.

"An ambush?" Torvald smirked, an eyebrow raised.

Osric chuckled. "Not this time, Jarl, but you know well enough, we need to have eyes all around us when the moment comes."

"It is a good idea." Torvald conceded, "We will take the east side of the road."

"And that leaves us with the west," Osric said.

"What of those we find have planned to act against us?" Wulfric interjected. "Do we have an idea of what numbers we are dealing with? I assume we return them to their settlements for questioning and justice?"

"That's the plan," Osric said, looking at Torvald and Svend. "But remember what Lord King Alfred said to us—regarding

Æthelwod. That bears consideration."

Svend leaned in. Torvald's gaze remained steady.

"As I'm sure Svend told you, King Alfred had words for us before we left Wintanceaster," Osric said to the chieftain. "At the feast's end, he made clear that Wintanceaster was not as surprised by our visit as we might have expected," Osric said. "The matter of our returning Æthelwod to Wintanceaster to face justice came up. I believe his exact words were that if an 'unfortunate incident' were to occur on such a treacherous road while delivering the bishop to Wintanceaster, there would be no consequences."

Silence settled over the shelter.

Torvald broke it first. "The king wants him gone."

"So it seems," Wulfric murmured, exhaling slowly.

A guarantee of immunity. It should have been reassuring, but even after all that had passed, the thought of killing a bishop unsettled Osric. After all, he had once saved the man's life and had sworn to protect church-held lands! True, the bishop had surely repaid his efforts by driving a wedge between him and the woman he loved, endangering her, committing treason…yet, to slay a high-ranking bishop…

"You need not decide this course of action now," Svend said, reading Osric's face.

"He's right," Torvald added. "The answer to this will come soon enough."

The others nodded.

"We know Æthelwod's man in our camp will make a move—likely some false act of Saxon sabotage," Torvald said. "It is also likely that Svend and I, and perhaps even Bjørn—" Torvald glanced at Svend, who nodded, "we anticipate being taken hostage—they will want leadership out of the way. But our men know what to do. However this goes, we will light a fire big enough to be used as a warning to your lookouts."

HEART OF THE WILD GODS

Osric turned to Wulfric. "Then the charge is yours, Wulf. You'll ensure the fyrd is in position, and you'll give the command. Make it plain, so there can be no doubt. We have only one chance."

Svend grinned. "Wulfric, make it something worthy of a boastful telling at a hall feast, já?"

Wulfric smirked. "I wouldn't dream of disappointing you, my lords."

Osric smiled, shaking his head as his gaze swept over the chuckling men. "I've nothing more. Any of you?"

They glanced at one another, but no one spoke.

"Now comes the worst part," Svend muttered. "The waiting."

A few nods, a grunt of agreement.

"If that's all," Wulfric said, bracing himself as he pushed up from the hard floor of the shelter, "I've no doubt Æthelwod awaits me in the burh, basking in a haze of serenity, being a man possessed of such an abundance of patience."

"That, my friend, is far from the truth of it." Osric laughed. "He will be watching you like a hawk."

"I'd expect nothing less." Wulfric straightened with a wince. "And I don't expect I'll be able to send word to any of you, for any reason—not until this is done."

"A wise choice," Torvald agreed, "Æthelwod is a rat, but rats are intelligent creatures." The chieftain shifted awkwardly before reaching out to clasp Wulfric's arm. "Lord Wulfric, you have my thanks."

Wulfric nodded and clasped Torvald's arm before reaching for his belt and sword. "Jarl Torvald. Svend. When next we all meet, I hope to be filling ale horns and discussing trade."

Osric rose stiffly, crouching as he stepped closer. "Wulf, my gratitude is simply beyond measure."

Wulfric gripped his shoulder. "Old friend, it's an honor."

They embraced, then Wulfric turned and made his way out.

Svend followed soon after, giving Wulfric time to gain distance before setting off.

That left Osric and Torvald, stretching out stiff limbs in the newfound space, eyeing each other in silence.

"Lord Osric," Torvald began.

"I know what you're about to say, Jarl." Osric cut in, an exhausted smile pressing at his lips. "We need to speak of Æfre."

"Já. We do."

Osric said nothing. Instead, he reached beneath the bench, drawing out a jug of Æthelwod's mead and two ale horns.

Torvald's expression lightened, and he grinned, "You've kept your hoard well hidden."

"Too early?"

"Never."

Osric chuckled, the beginnings of a smile tugging at his mouth. "The high seat has its comforts, Jarl." He said, gesturing around him at the cramped, dusty shelter they sat in.

"Better a cramped seat than a comfortable grave, Lord Osric."

Osric let out a long exhale and handed Torvald a horn of ale. "I'm listening, Jarl."

41

Nīewe Þegn ⚔ New Thegn

Bishop Æthelwod's patience was wearing thin.

Wulfric, Thegn of Beornwic, should have arrived well before midday. The morning meal had long since passed, and the sun had begun its slow climb toward the height of the day—still no sign of him. There were plans to set in motion, matters to address, and he despised delays.

He paced the floor of the hall with measured steps, each pass becoming more agitated than the last. When finally, he heard the sound of hooves followed by Cenric's booming greeting, he exhaled sharply, more out of impatience than relief or welcome.

Drawing his cloak tight around him, Æthelwod swept through the hall's doors and squinted as he gazed towards the stable. The rider—yes, surely that was Wulfric, that had to be him—the man wore a fine wool cloak, his tunic modestly embroidered, his posture unhurried and upright.

Entirely too self-assured for a man arriving late, Æthelwod thought as he studied the thegn from Beornwic. Wulfric bore the familiar, careless confidence of one born into nobility; the kind Æthelwod himself had never been able to wear comfortably. Such ease came too easily to men like Wulfric, men born into a world surrounded by power.

Some men have to carry the stone uphill, he thought, *while others find it waiting for them at the summit.*

"Ah, there you are," Æthelwod called to the men, striding towards them. "Lord Wulfric, I presume."

Cenric clapped Wulfric on the shoulder and passed a wordless glance to the bishop before leading his horse into the stable.

"Lord Bishop, yes!" Wulfric answered with that same effortless charm. "It's been some time, has it not, my lord! Am I as much as you remembered me to be?"

"I was expecting you hours ago," Æthelwod said, flatly, unsmiling.

"Indeed, and I regret the delay," Wulfric replied smoothly, unfazed, still smiling. "It seems there's no end to the burdens placed on the thegn who dares attempt to serve in more than one place at a time. You have my sincere apologies, my lord." He dipped his head in polite deference. "And I am also charged with bringing you my father's greetings and wishes for your continued good health and fortune."

At the mention of the Ealdorman of Beornwic, a name that carried weight, Æthelwod's expression immediately softened under the spectre of political prudence.

"Indeed," he said, voice suddenly infused with warmth. "How fares the Ealdorman?"

"He is well, Lord Bishop. His mind is sharp and his will strong."

"Good, good. Tell him I was asking after him when next you speak."

"I shall." Wulfric inclined his head again, still wearing that unreadable half-smile.

"Now," Æthelwod said, voice tightening again, "there is the business of the work to be done. A matter of some urgency has arisen—one that will require your presence a few miles outside the burh."

"Oh?" Wulfric adjusted the saddlebag over his shoulder.

"Come inside," Æthelwod said, gesturing toward the hall. "You'll want to see the thegn's quarters, and then we may speak over a cup of mead. I'll tell you all that's required."

"Very well, Lord Bishop," Wulfric said, stepping into stride beside him. "Lead on."

HEART OF THE WILD GODS

* * *

Wulfric sat on the edge of the bed in the thegn's quarters, shaking his head with a grim half-smile. It had taken little more than the mention of his father's name to manipulate the bishop's demeanor—he was like a plough ox with a halter. Some things simply never change.

Still the same pompous cloak fanner who used to frighten us as children, he thought, pulling at the edge of the bedcover. Whether his time in Wōdenléah stretched days or weeks, fetching and carrying for Æthelwod was going to be a spectacular trial of patience.

With a sigh, he forced himself off the inviting feather mattress and exited the thegn's quarters, rounding the partition into the hall.

"Ah, Lord Wulfric. There you are." Æthelwod had planted himself at the high table, a cup of mead before him and another poured at the seat beside him. "Please, Lord. Sit."

Wulfric took the offered seat and raised the cup, taking a draught. His brows lifted despite himself.

"This is... quite good. Elderflower?"

"It is indeed, Lord!" Æthelwod brightened like a newly lit candle, becoming uncharacteristically animated as the conversation veered to brewing. "Though only I know the exact recipe, and so it shall remain. None but I may measure the honey."

Wulfric gave a short laugh, masking his surprise at the bishop's sudden transformation.

"Fair enough," he smiled. "I wouldn't dare press you further on the matter."

"We are drinking what remains from the Yule batch," Æthelwod went on, his pride unchecked. "It was marvelously received. I still wonder how the folk managed to make so many jugs disappear."

Knowing Osric, Wulfric had a fair guess—but he held his tongue.

"Truly, Lord Bishop, it is worthy of the feast hall."

"Indeed." Æthelwod's good cheer then vanished as swiftly as it had appeared. He straightened. "Now, to the day's purpose."

Wulfric set down his cup.

"There is one who lives among us—or near enough. A healer. From a family that has served this land for generations, we've turned to them often in need." Æthelwod paused, his gaze narrowing. "But this healer does not walk in the light of our Lord."

Wulfric stilled. His throat dried.

"A healer?" he said. "A woman, then?"

"Indeed. The woman Æfre." The bishop studied Wulfric, hawk-eyed, watching for any tremor of recognition. "You know the name?"

Wulfric furrowed his brow and took another drink to steady his hand, though it did little to calm him—a cold fist had settled in his gut. *So the bastard means to do it. He means to throw her to the wolves.*

"She must be handled... carefully," Æthelwod continued. He leaned in, voice low.

"Oh?" Wulfric strained to keep his tone level, forcing another swallow.

"She is... *close* to Lord Osric. Has he never mentioned her? You and he were once known to be close."

"No. I've never heard the name spoken." Wulfric let the pause linger, as if considering. "Are you certain of this? Surely Osric would have mentioned it—and the man is betrothed, after all."

Æthelwod's lips tightened. "You may read the summons for yourself." He reached into his sleeve and produced a tightly rolled parchment. "It will, of course, need to bear your seal as acting thegn, though a copy's already gone to Wintanceaster."

"To Wintanceaster?" Wulfric's voice betrayed his disbelief. "You would have her stand before the *witan*?"

Panic surged beneath his skin. He took the scroll, unrolled it, and forced himself to sit as still as a stone while he read the summons as quickly as he dared. Each line confirmed what he feared. *At best, she might hope for punishment or exile. At worst—*

He rolled it up again, hiding the tremor in his fingers.

"Tell me, Lord Bishop," he said lightly, "are such charges so common here in Wōdenléah? I've never seen one in my years, nor have I ever heard my father speak of any."

"Not common, no. But this case is... particular," Æthelwod replied. "One might say we're tending the Lord's garden—clearing weeds where they grow. Since Edington, we've seen the truth—change is the Lord's will. And in times of change, we must guide the flock, must we not?"

"Of course, Lord Bishop." Wulfric set down the cup. The mead now sat like spoiled milk in his belly. "By God's mercy, may He guide us."

"Indeed, Lord Wulfric." Æthelwod's face glowed with the satisfaction of a victorious man who believed himself righteous and rewarded. "Now, if you'll come with me, I believe Cenric has the wagon prepared."

* * *

Everything had come to a grinding halt—an eternity dragging on. At least, that's how it felt to Æfre as she stood next to her hearth, listening to the crackling and hissing of the fire while sipping the cup of ale she carried. It had only been a day since she'd handed Torvald Ironsight Osric's hand-drawn map of the woodcutter's shelter, yet it seemed like a lifetime ago. No word, no movement from the camp—nothing. Even the would-be vandals from the burh had gone silent. It felt as though everyone around her had one foot on the ground and the other in the stirrup—everyone just waiting, breath held, for something to happen.

Cwenhild had managed to send word of Eadlin through a textile trader. The merchant, who frequented the burh, had been plied by Cwenhild with Yule cake and a jug of Æthelwod's mead in exchange for passing along a message via Torvald's guard. According to the messenger, Eadlin was recovering slowly but steadily, and she'd already gone home to Aldhem. Cwenhild had seen to the last dressing change, and Eadlin, now up and moving, albeit with a limp, had watched and helped so that she could tend to it herself at home.

Æfre exhaled slowly, shaking the dregs of her ale into the fire. No sense in dwelling on what she couldn't change. There were greater matters at hand, and little she could control about any of them.

Grabbing a thick shawl, she stepped outside to tend to Epona. The winter day was stunning—crisp air, the ground firm and cold, and the sky clear and bright under the low afternoon sun.

Æfre gave Epona a quick nuzzle, her fingers brushing the horse's neck before she began her slow walk around the paddock, eyes scanning the terrain for any hidden hazards. For the first time in days, she felt unburdened, free from the whispers and the constant scrutiny that had marked her visit to the burh. Here, in her own space, she could breathe again. She surveyed the paddock ground with satisfaction, finding little more than a few stray willow spars from the roof thatching and a broken arrow that lay half-buried, one of her own. She noticed how the fletching had worn away almost entirely, and guessed it had been there for quite some time.

She moved on to Epona's stall, finding it undisturbed since she'd last tended to it. With a couple of passes, she refreshed the straw, hardly breaking a sweat.

As she turned her thoughts to the rest of her afternoon, she carried the large water buckets towards the creek. Kneeling by the water's edge, she filled the buckets, contemplating what she would do with what remained of her afternoon.

My leechbook. The thought struck Æfre suddenly. She still had a few pieces of parchment safely tucked under her bed, and this quiet afternoon would be the perfect time to begin replacing the pages that had been torn out and damaged the night of the attack.

With a quiet blessing to the goddess Eorðe for her gift of water, Æfre stood and made her way back to the barn, the cool breeze lifting the edges of her shawl. As she neared, the sound of wagon wheels grinding against the frozen earth reached her ears—someone was approaching.

Quickly, she finished filling Epona's trough, hung the water buckets back up, and grabbed an armful of hay from the small hayrick, tossing it into the paddock before wiping her hands on her skirt and stepping out to greet her unexpected guest.

Æfre looked up the path at the approaching wagon and froze, her breath catching in her chest.

Æthelwod.

Why was Bishop Æthelwod coming down her path?

He sat stiffly beside a man she did not recognize. The stranger's tunic bore subtle marks of wealth and rank—too fine for a ceorl or even a reeve, yet too plain for an ealdorman.

This must be Wulfric, thegn of Beornwic.

The man's grip on the reins was tight, his expression unreadable as he brought the wagon to a halt. Æthelwod leaned toward him in an attempt to say something, but Wulfric did not wait. He jumped from the wagon, boots striking hard against the ground as he strode straight over to her.

Æfre glanced past him at the bishop, still seated in the wagon, his eyes fixed upon them. Whatever this was, it was not good.

She forced a smile. "Lord Wulfric, I presume?"

"Gēa," His voice was low, hurried. "Æfre, I am sorry to meet you this way—I had no say in this—but you must trust me now..."

Her smile faltered.

"Lord Wulfric!" Æthelwod called from the wagon as he awkwardly climbed down, "You speak so softly—I fear I did not hear!" He smoothed his robes as he awkwardly stepped down from he wagon, his gait heavy with self-importance.

Wulfric did not look away from Æfre. "I was merely introducing myself, Lord Bishop." He raised his voice. "Wulfric, Thegn of Beornwic, acting in Osric's stead."

Æfre gave a slight nod. "It is good to meet you, Lord Wulfric."

"And you. You may *trust me* that I will carry out Osric's affairs with all duty."

She met his gaze. *Understood*.

Æthelwod gave a sharp nod. "Yes, yes. It is well to settle pleasantries, but we have weightier matters at hand." He stepped beside Wulfric with the boldness of a man planting a banner in conquered territory. "Has Æfre been informed of why we are here?"

"Not yet, Lord Bishop," Wulfric said evenly. "I was about to."

Æthelwod needed no invitation. He reached into his sleeve and produced a parchment, clearing his throat before unfurling it and reading in a tone dripping with pomposity.

"In the holy name of Our Lord God Almighty, by the command of Wulfric, Thegn of Beornwic, acting in the stead of Osric, Thegn of Wōdenléah, and by the will of Æthelwod, Bishop of Wōdenléah, the healing woman Æfre is hereby summoned to stand before Church and Crown at the next meeting of the witenagemot[xxiii], there to answer for her use of charms and workings not sanctified by God or law."

HEART OF THE WILD GODS

Æfre recoiled. "A summons!?" She looked from the bishop to Wulfric, whose jaw clenched as he turned slightly away.

Æthelwod pressed on, voice swelling with self-righteousness.

"It has come to our knowledge that the woman Æfre has made use of charms and leechdoms unapproved by the Holy Church. She lays no cross upon the sick, nor calls upon the Lord's mercy in her craft."

Æfre exhaled a sharp exasperation. "Bishop…"

His eyes flashed at the interruption. "Further," he said sharply, "we hold in our possession pages taken from the woman's leechbook—writings and runes not of holy sanction, used by the woman in rites of the old Gods."

A presence stirred at the path's crest. It was Geir, Torvald's guard. He stood, hand resting lightly on the hilt of his sword, his gaze fixed upon them.

Æthelwod, undeterred, bloviated on. "Let it be known that the woman Æfre is accused of heathenry and unlawful practices, for she calls upon powers not of Almighty God. She shall stand before the court and answer plainly the question of whom she does serve."

Æfre gasped, eyes stinging as she turned a pleading gaze to Wulfric.

He returned her gaze with a look that remained steely and calm—a silent command.

Steady.

"Further," Æthelwod continued, voice rich with satisfaction, "the woman Æfre shall stand no longer among free folk until she has answered for her heathenry—that no man nor woman might doubt the judgment that such accursed practice earns. This summons bears the mark of both crown and cross, to which the woman Æfre is bound to answer."

Silence hung thick as he rolled the parchment and tucked it back within his robe's cuff. Then, with a saccharine smile:

"Now, Lord Wulfric—if we might accompany Æfre into her dwelling to collect her leechbook."

42

Ġetacen ⋈ Taken

"Jarl Torvald!"

The doors to the hall slammed open so hard one of them cracked against the timber frame with a sharp smack.

Torvald looked up from the high seat, jaw tightening. He had just settled a tense quarrel between two silver merchants—men whose tempers ran hotter than a knife in the forge—and they'd only just come to terms.

Though he wore the face of a chieftain annoyed by the intrusion, inwardly Torvald actually welcomed the interruption. His stomach had begun growling loudly enough to compete with the merchants' incessant bickering some hours ago.

"Geir, it had better be worth the breath you just knocked from the Gods to come storming in here with the manners of a goat!"

"Jarl—"

Torvald's eyes narrowed. Geir's face—pale, tight, stricken—told him instantly that there was more to the story.

Trouble.

He mumbled an excuse to the merchants and quickly stepped down from the high seat. "Shouldn't you be on duty, Geir?"

The young warrior gave a hasty nod and jerked his head toward the door in silent request. Torvald followed him outside without further discussion.

They stepped outside, the cold wind instantly penetrating their clothes. Geir led him around the side of the longhouse, away from prying ears.

"Jarl Torvald," Geir blurted, breathless, "I'm sorry for the way I—"

"Enough. Speak."

"They've taken Æfre."

The words struck like a blade. Torvald stopped cold.

"What?"

His voice came out low and dangerous, like a wolf's growl before the bite.

"Who took her? Slow your tongue, Geir. I want to hear every word."

Geir nodded, chest heaving. "The Saxon Bishop. Æthelwod. And another man I didn't recognize—noble, by the look of him. They came in a wagon."

Torvald's fists clenched. His voice went preternaturally quiet. "You saw this with your own eyes?"

"Yes. The woman was tending the horse. The noble jumped down first—spoke to her, too low for me to hear. And she was smiling, but seemed wary, but—then the bishop joined them, and everything changed."

"Changed how?"

Torvald realized that he had been pacing and ground to a halt, his gaze bearing down on Geir with the intensity of a hot iron.

"It turned....formal. The bishop read from a scroll. Spoke of the Christian God, of charms not sanctioned by their church. I didn't understand all of it, but it felt like some sort of accusation."

Torvald's heart sank—this was precisely the scenario he'd feared might befall Æfre. And with Æthelwod about to launch his uprising at any moment, he didn't have time to ride out to Osric and confer with him—it left him no time for counsel, only action.

Torvald stood for a moment, willing his mind to quiet before turning back to the young warrior standing in front of him.

"We'll need another man. Someone who knows everything."

"Håkon is in our quarters."

"Good. And we'll need a wagon, and as many empty boxes as you can find."

HEART OF THE WILD GODS

Geir blinked. "Yes, Jarl."

"Go to Svend. Tell him I sent you. Tell him what you need and why. He can man the hall while we're gone. Move quickly—I'll meet you at the gate."

"Yes, Jarl."

"Go, now!"

Geir ran off to do as he was ordered, leaving Torvald in place for a moment, his breath fogging in the cold as rage burned beneath his ribs, heavy and hot. In an effort to calm and focus his mind, he clenched his fists, then slowly loosened them. Again. And again, until he could focus his mind on what came next.

Æthelwod, you limp, greedy, goat-fucked bastard. If any harm comes to this woman, I will carve her name in runes into every one of your bones myself—and you will still be breathing when I do it.

He turned sharply and strode back into the hall to bring a swift end to the merchant dispute, grabbed his cloak, and once again headed out the door.

* * *

The sun had already slipped behind the hills when the three men turned the wagon down the narrow path to Æfre's homestead. Torvald rode at the front beside the driver, his jaw clenched, cloak drawn tight. The two warriors had done well—the grain wagon was loaded with empty wooden boxes and old sacks, enough to look like honest cargo if eyes were to turn their way.

As soon as the wagon halted at Æfre's door, Torvald leapt down, boots crunching against the frosty ground. He wasted no time, throwing off the first crate and barking orders.

"Personal belongings first—clothes, keepsakes, anything that looks like family blood runs through it. And anything to do with healing—herbs, and anything that looks like it's for medicine-making. If it seems like craft or knowledge, take it. Make sure there's nothing left here that *niðingr*[xxiv] Æthelwod might twist into proof of witchery. Work fast—I'll be right back. I'm going to fetch the horse."

"Right away, Jarl," Håkon said, hesitating just a beat. "Do you know something we don't?"

"Only what a lifetime of experience whispers to my gut, Håkon," Torvald said, already turning away. "So far it has served me well."

Epona was grazing in the paddock, enjoying the hay Æfre had put down for her earlier. Torvald clucked twice under his breath, and the mare's ears pricked forward, nostrils flaring.

"Gott kveld *[good evening]*, Epona," Torvald said softly.

Epona bobbed her head and nickered, one of her ears flicking back and forth as she sauntered over to him and nuzzled her nose into his chest, blowing sweet, grainy breath out of her velvet nostrils.

"Hei, já. You're coming with me tonight."

He turned and walked towards the barn, and Epona followed, her hooves thumping dully against the earth as she sauntered behind him like a curious shadow.

Inside, he found her halter and slipped it on, leading her back outside and tethering her to the wagon's rear before returning to the barn. He then gathered every scrap of tack, every grooming tool, and filled grain sacks until the small hayrick was bare.

Might as well, he thought; *it helps nobody if it is left to rot.*

When he stepped back into the cottage, the two warriors had already packed most of Æfre's personal belongings in the hut.

"Nearly finished, Jarl," Geir called. "Still got space in the wagon."

Torvald's eyes swept the room. Everything was humble, practical, and pretty much packed and ready.

Then his gaze stopped on the bed.

HEART OF THE WILD GODS

It stood not far from the hearth, large and cut from heavy oak. Two tall posts marked the head, and were draped with blankets. His gaze caught on the footboard—it had a carved strip he hadn't noticed before. He stepped closer, brushing his fingers over it. Knotwork beasts twisted and grappled along the length of it, each one gripping the next in a tangle of jaws and claws. Wolves, or dragons—hard to say. But the craftsmanship was familiar. It was undeniably Norse.

"Did you see this?" he called, not taking his eyes from the wood.

Geir and Håkon crossed the room and stood beside him, quiet for a moment.

"This is nicer than the bed I sleep in." Torvald mused as he pulled the blanket from one of the posts at the head of the bed. The wood beneath was carved into the head of a dragon, its form curved like the prow of a longship, its teeth bared in a silent snarl.

"This is the bed of a king," Geir said with a short laugh. "Where did it come from?"

"I know her father was a Dane," Torvald murmured. "Perhaps it was his hand that made it."

They stood in silence for a beat longer, all three of them looking.

Then Torvald straightened. "Take it apart. You say we have space? It comes with us." He said, pausing for a moment as he spotted her bow and quiver by the door, just under where she'd hung her moss green cloak, the silver brooch still pinned to its front. He collected both and walked out to the wagon.

Geir and Håkon exchanged a look but got right down to work, pulling at pegs and joints, grunting as they dismantled the frame without splintering the old wood.

Less than an hour later, the wagon rolled away from Æfre's home, piled high with boxes, tack, sacks of hay, and every piece of her life they could carry. Epona trotted lightly behind, her hooves clopping steadily on the winter-hardened road.

Æfre's homestead grew smaller behind them, the hearth fire slowly dying in a home that had been stripped bare of all but the memories that were forever etched into the wood.

43

Cwepan ⚔ Accused

"You'll remain here until the Witan sits," Æthelwod snapped, dragging Æfre by the arm. His grip felt like a vice for a man so spare, and it squeezed tightly on what remained of her injuries. Her leechbook, clutched tightly under his free arm, was pressed like a prize against his ribs.

Wulfric followed a few paces behind, every step bristling with frustration, his mind racing as he tried to conjure a way to get word to Osric—and quickly. That letter the bishop had sent to Wintnaceaster could change everything for Æfre. She stood formally accused, and even though it was likely to go nowhere with the king on their side, it was not something that would be soon forgotten by the increasingly mistrustful population of Wōdenléah.

As they ducked through the heavy wooden doors of Æthelwod's brew hut, the bishop shoved Æfre up against a stack of small wooden casks.

"You'll stay in here in the meantime. I'll have a suitable sleeping arrangement brought in. And, I might add, you do not have leave to help yourself to any of the mead store." He turned, ready to shut the heavy door when Æfre spoke.

"Might I have a moment to visit the hedge before you lock me in here, Bishop?"

"Say again?" Æthelwod asked, irritated and not understanding the question.

"I would be grateful," Æfre said evenly, "if Lord Bishop might allow me a moment to see to my comfort."

"What is this chatter!? Speak plainly, woman! What is it you want!?" Æthelwod barked.

Wulfric, who had been pacing, stopped—his patience worn through. "The privy, Bishop! She is asking if she might visit the privy before you confine her."

"Ah. I see." Æthelwod sniffed, "Well, I suppose..."

"Bishop," Wulfric said, exasperated and struggling to maintain his composure, "perhaps it might be satisfactory if I fetch one of the women who might accompany Æfre, who I daresay will also require an evening meal." He cast a glance at Æfre, who gave a faint smile and nod.

Æthelwod waved a hand, already half turned. "Yes, very well," he clipped, "however, until such time as your escort arrives..."

He pulled on the heavy door to the brew hut. As it was closing, Wulfric shot Æfre a look over Æthelwod's shoulder.

Hold fast, I'm working it through.

The door latched with a heavy chonk.

"I shall be in my quarters when access is again required, Lord Wulfric," Æthelwod said stiffly, slipping a ring of keys back onto his belt, which he concealed under his cloak, vanishing into the shadows and into his quarters.

Wulfric walked quickly towards the hall, though he dared not let the urgency he felt in his chest show. Æthelwod meant to make a spectacle of Wōdenléah's healer, and it was eating him up that he couldn't immediately warn Osric that the woman he loved was in peril.

Rounding the corner of the hall, he nearly collided with Cenric, who was striding up the path in the opposite direction, his cloak flapping behind him in the icy wind.

"Lord Wulfric!" Cenric exclaimed, "I've come for the wagon, but tell me true—what is this I hear of you and the bishop returning with Æfre? They are saying that she's locked within the bishop's brew hut? Surely this is nothing more than the wagging of tongues."

HEART OF THE WILD GODS

"Cenric, I'm afraid you heard true," Wulfric said. "Come, have you eaten? Let's take this inside the hall where it's warm—but we'll have to speak low."

* * *

"The witan!?" Cenric balked. "Eálá! He's gone clean mad," Cenric muttered, trying and failing to keep the volume of his voice low.

Thankfully, the evening meal had already been served, the fire was low, and the room fairly quiet save for a few stragglers murmuring over ale. Across the room, Cwenhild sat at the center of a knot of women. Cenric caught her eye, beckoning her over while Wulfric made for the hearth, filling three bowls with the last of the stew in the pot, and snatching what bread was left.

When he returned, Cwenhild leaned close to her husband, brow furrowed, listening. As she did, her face shifted—first to disbelief, then worry, then to a red-hot, smoldering fury.

"Oh, Lord Wulfric," she hissed, keeping her voice low. "What in the name of the Almighty are we to do now!? That man must be stopped!"

Wulfric took a bite of stew, chewing slowly while he turned over every possibility in his mind.

"There may not be much we can do this night," he said at last. "I would prefer to ride out to Osric myself, yet I fear that whatever Æthelwod has planned might begin at any moment. And it is unsafe for both horses and men in the forest at night..."

He let his thought hang unfinished for a moment, then leaned in, his voice low.

"I know that whatever might befall Æfre, Osric will blame himself. As you all know, he's not the sort to suffer guilt lightly."

Cenric rubbed his temples and added slowly, "Lord, it's not a perfect solution, but we've men on the road already, as you know. Once we have word of movement, any movement, we'll be getting a rider to him so that he knows it has begun—we can inform him then. It may not be swift—as you say, the forest is slow going by night, but it will be sure. And in the meantime... as much as I hate to say it, she's likely safer here in the burh, even confined."

Wulfric sighed and dragged his last hunk of bread through his stew. "A fair point, Cenric. I hope you're right."

Wulfric looked at Cwenhild. "Will you come with me to the bishop's, Cwenhild? I've brought Æfre some food, and she's asked the bishop for a short break to see to her comfort—Æthelwod insists she be accompanied, lest she run off in the middle of the night, by his absurd reasoning."

"Of course, Lord," Cwenhild said, shaking her head. "But he may or may not want my help—he knows we're close. And I'll fetch more food than that. I've seen that woman eat."

She disappeared into the back of the hall, returning with a cloth bundle—bread, a wedge of cheese, and dried meat to add to Wulfric's offering of stew. Without a word, the three of them stepped out into the night.

"I'll go on ahead," Cwenhild said, already rounding the side of the hall. "Poor Æfre's likely half-starved."

"Mind yourself around Æthelwod, sweeting." Cenric warned, "No outbursts—no sense in anyone else getting caught in the man's clutch."

"You have my word, husband."

Cwenhild gave Wulfric a nod, then vanished into the darkness, her footsteps crunching on the frosted earth.

Wulfric and Cenric ambled in the direction of Æthelwod's residence, letting the silence of the night stretch between them as their breath sent miniature dissipating clouds up to the stars.

The two of them had taken no more than five paces when a voice rose from the shadows.

"Lord Wulfric—"

HEART OF THE WILD GODS

Both men turned towards the sound, their hands instinctively reaching for their seaxes.

A tense moment passed before Cenric broke the silence.

"Alaric?" he said, eyes narrowing.

Alaric stepped out of the shadows, cheeks still ruddy from the cold nighttime air. "Ġēa, Cenric," he said, then turned to Wulfric. "My lord, we've had word from the lookout not moments past. A fire is burning."

Wulfric's pulse quickened. "And?"

"No movement yet," Alaric said, "but it's coming. Matter of time now."

Wulfric met Cenric's gaze. This was it.

"How long now?"

"In the time it takes to twice walk from the gate, Lord. Barely that."

Wulfric exhaled slowly, steadying his nerves. "Then I don't know of it. Not yet. I'll return to the thegn's quarters, we'll keep to the rhythm. Fetch me in just enough time for us to meet with the bishop—he needs to appeal to me to raise the fyrd."

Cenric glanced at Alaric, who gave a tight nod. "That's sound, my lord."

"Good." Wulfric drew a deep breath and let it out like a man bracing for a punch to the gut. "Cenric, I trust you can see to it that Osric hears?"

"You have my word, Lord. I'll deliver the news myself."

Wulfric clasped his shoulder briefly, nodded at Alaric, then turned and walked purposefully back to the hall—towards what felt like would be the longest short wait of his life.

44

Styrtan ✕ To Start

"Eldr! Eldr! *[Fire! Fire!]*"

Even through the thick door of the hall, Torvald heard the man's warning cries as if he stood at his shoulder.

The signal horn sounded outside, like the dying cry of some giant, wounded beast, followed by the sound of hurried footsteps.

Torvald stood still in place, listening as intensely as a hunted deer as he began to catch the sharp, acrid scent of the fire as it started to burn his eyes and catch in his throat.

It's started.

As the smell of the fire grew stronger, he was glad he'd insisted they quietly disperse the precious winter food stores—they'd distributed them evenly across different locations throughout the camp. Losing any of their stored goods would be a blow, but this action ensured that such a loss would be survivable.

"Pick up your buckets! Form a chain!" The command rang out, and Torvald recognized the voice immediately. It was Harald, the woodcarver, rallying the men in precisely the manner they had discussed.

Torvald's heart pounded; every instinct urged him to burst from the hall and join the efforts already underway. Yet he forced himself to follow the response as they'd conceived it. He paced the hall until at last, Bjørn burst through the doors, axe in hand.

"Jarl—" Bjørn began.

"Was it the main food stores, Bjørn?" Torvald demanded, his voice tight with urgency.

"Já, Jarl, it—" Bjørn panted.

"Then come!" Torvald grabbed the axe from beside him, not waiting for Bjørn's response as he shoved past him, the two men sprinting towards the fire.

We may still save some of it.

As they approached the blaze, Torvald could see that the firefight was in full swing—a living chain of men and women stretched from the creek to the burning structure, passing buckets and water skins to the men fighting the flames.

Harald barked orders as he organized a second bucket chain as more people arrived. Seeing the chieftain, he approached him, nodding briskly—an acknowledgement of his Jarl's accurate predictions of how the scenario they faced might play out.

"You were right! They hit the main food stores!" Harald shouted over the chaos, "And these winds breathe life into the fire!"

"The elevated floor feeds it from beneath!" Torvald shouted back. This wind was not something that they had planned for. He looked over at what was quickly becoming an engulfed structure, the inside of which was illuminated by a furious orange glow cast by the flames that devoured the thatch and leaped through cracks in the timber.

"We'll lose everything within!" Torvald shouted.

"We will!" Harald agreed, "and the ground is frozen hard, so digging a boundary is slow-going."

"Focus now on keeping everyone safe and preventing this fire from spreading!" Torvald shouted, advancing a few steps towards the inferno, where Bjørn labored alongside Svend and several other men, hacking away at the remaining parts of the unburnt structure in an attempt to remove and scatter the timber and rob the fire of its fuel.

"Jarl Torvald!" Harald's voice rang again, halting Torvald as he turned back to face Harald. "Word has spread—this blaze is no accident. The talk is that this is an act of sabotage by the Saxons, intent on driving us from the camp!" Harald spoke loudly to ensure he was heard by all those around him.

HEART OF THE WILD GODS

Torvald held Harald's gaze for a moment—a look of acknowledgement, followed by a curt nod. As impossible as it seemed in such chaotic and uncertain circumstances, the plan to steer the narrative appeared to be working. "Thank you, Harald," he barked, then plunged back into the fray to join Bjørn and Svend. Their planned rebellion may have been a ruse, but the fire currently consuming what was left inside their main food store was very real.

Torvald braced against the punishing heat of the fire. It singed beards and lashes the instant any of them got close enough to swing an axe, the wind fanning the flames like a blacksmith's bellows, turning fire and ash into a frenzied storm that licked at the night sky and coiled round the rafters like a vengeful serpent.

From within the inferno, there was suddenly a series of loud cracks, and the engulfed structure groaned as if the gates to the underworld had just been pried open.

"It's coming down!" Bjørn roared. "Back! All of you, back!"

He yanked Svend by the belt and dragged him clear just as the remaining structure gave way with a deafening crash, separating Torvald from the rest of the men.

The collapsing timber hurled glowing embers high into the night sky, showering the retreating men as a cascade of splintering wood fell to the ground—scattering like smoldering bones crushed under the foot of an unseen giant. The rubble pile belched out a great plume of smoke that rolled over them like a thunderstorm.

Torvald turned his face away and dove clear of the falling debris, the heat choking him as he landed hard on the packed ground. He rolled over, spat out a lungful of soot, and pushed himself backwards on his elbows, away from the charred and glowing structure as the heat clawed at his skin.

"Svend! Bjørn!" He shouted, unable to see through the suffocating black smoke that shrouded everything nearby. No answer. "Everyone! Take account of each other—we leave nobody lying injured!" He yelled into the blackness, coughing as he struggled to his feet, his voice barely carrying over the chaos of the fire and the shouts of retreating men.

The smoke parted a bit, offering the chieftain a blurry glimpse of the completely burnt structure—small pops still sparking and fizzing within it. No sign of any of the men who were standing closest to the blaze when it collapsed.

He staggered towards the charred rubble, but the heat quickly drove him back. *Another way then.*

He turned quickly to try to approach from another angle, and nearly collided with a group of three men, their faces masked with pieces of torn and dampened linen, the skin around their eyes covered in soot.

A moment passed as Torvald strained to identify the men in front of him. It was only when the hilt of a sword connected with the back of his head that he realized what was happening—he was about to be made a hostage.

So that's how they decided to lay the snare, he thought, as the edges of his vision grew dark and he felt the world slip out from under him.

* * *

Torvald was roused by the sensation of being dragged by the boots. His head was pounding, and he could taste the unmistakable metallic tang of blood in his mouth. He felt the lip of a timber threshold beneath him, then a jarring thump as they let his legs drop onto a cold, earthen floor.

"Still breathing, Jarl?"

Svend.

Torvald pushed himself upright and looked in the direction of the voice, his vision swimming as he braced himself against the floor as if he might slide off the earth at any moment. Svend and

HEART OF THE WILD GODS

Bjørn sat leaning against the far wall of what looked like an empty merchant's storehouse, their faces sooted, eyes alert.

He drew a slow breath, hissed as his fingers found the back of his head. When he withdrew his hand, it was slick with blood.

"Jarl! Catch!"

Bjørn tossed a linen strip he'd brought for smoke cover to Torvald, who caught it and pressed it to the back of his head as nausea curled in his gut.

"þǫkk *[Thanks]*," he muttered through the pain, keeping pressure on the wound. "Já, Svend, I breathe, though I make no promise that I will not vomit in here."

He looked out the open door of the hut and saw Harald in the distance, gesturing towards the hut, amidst a heated argument with one of the masked men.

Torvald pushed himself up on his elbows, straining to see, when another figure appeared in the door frame—another masked man.

The man crouched, hovering over the chieftain, cocking his head like a bird of prey. He leaned in close and spoke low. "Your time here is done, Jarl. A change in order is coming."

He raised a foot to Torvald's chest.

In a flash, the chieftain rolled over and caught the man's leg, yanking and twisting it in a single motion that sent the man sprawling and howling in agony.

Torvald rolled back on his elbows as the pounding in his head overtook him once more.

The masked man scrambled to his feet, seething with rage as he pulled back again to try and land a blow.

"Enough!"

A third masked man rushed in and grabbed the man, yanking him back by his cloak and shoving him out the door. "That is not what we are here to do! Go!"

The man came back into the hut and began pulling the door closed, but hesitated for a moment once the wooden door obscured him from sight—he pulled his linen mask down.

Håkon.

Håkon had managed to secure an inside position in the so-called rebellion.

Håkon said nothing—just nodded to Svend and Bjørn, then met Torvald's gaze, a look of concern spreading across his face as he indicated Torvald's injured head.

"Sorry, Jarl, that should not have happened. I should have been keeping closer watch on the bastard. You whole?"

Torvald gave a sharp nod.

Without speaking, Håkon pulled the linen back over his face, nodded at the men, and stepped back into the night, the heavy door closing behind him.

* * *

Harald's eyes stung from the thick smoke as the sodden wool sail hit the burning debris pile, letting off a feral hiss of steam. The smell of scorched fleece hung heavy in the air as the red striped cloth flattened over the remaining pile of embers like a shroud. The last tongues of flame were finally being dampened into submission beneath the weight of the heavy, soaked fabric.

"Thank you, Inga. We'll see you repaid for this," Harald said, eyes still fixed on the smoldering sailcloth even though his shoulders had already begun to relax now that the threat of a spreading fire no longer seemed imminent.

Old Inga, the camp's eccentric textile merchant, shook the soot off of her blackened hands and snorted. "Bah—the damned thing has been sitting in the corner of my workshop half-torn to rags. Repairing it was going to be more trouble than reward. Dragging it to the creek was the best thing to do with it." She gave a satisfied

HEART OF THE WILD GODS

nod and turned back towards the men and women who had been fighting the fire without waiting for thanks.

Harald clasped her shoulder in passing, offering a wordless nod of respect. Around him, the men and women who had been fighting the blaze were scattered and about, coughing out the soot, pouring water over their faces, and gulping deep from water skins.

Harald spotted Håkon leaning against the rough timber wall of a hut, the dim firelight from nearby torches illuminating the hardened leather vest he now wore over his tunic. His eyes tracked two figures across the camp—Leif and the one called Eirik—the same two who he'd helped capture Svend, Bjørn, and Jarl Torvald. They stood like two crows on a fence, rallying a gathering crowd to their cause.

Harald joined Håkon without a word, leaning against the wall and mirroring his posture, his arms crossed, as he watched the two men. The heavy stink of wet wool and ash still hung close in the cold night air.

"That's Leif, is it?" Harald asked after a pause.

"Já. And the other one is a sword for hire— Eirik—calls himself a merchant. Maybe, maybe not." Håkon shrugged.

Harald said nothing for a while, studying the men. "Is our Jarl still breathing?" He asked quietly, not taking his eyes off the two men across the camp.

Håkon nodded. "Bleeding, but já, still breathing. That blow from Leif—I should've seen that coming." Håkon shook his head, a pained expression on his face.

Harald grunted, gave Håkon's shoulder a firm clasp. "We're in it now. What's done is done. Are these two idiots going to move on the burh or not? We need everyone at the meeting point soon."

"They are," Håkon murmured, "look there—see the way the boy weaves through the crowd? And that brings more swords by the moment—he's quietly spreading the word."

"Is that Eadgar!?" Harald exclaimed, "Jarl Torvald is going to have my hide—he didn't want the boy touched by this."

Håkon laughed, "Since when do any of us have any say over what that boy gets himself into?"

Harald grunted.

"To be honest, he's been more use than half our men." Håkon said, "So few people pay him any notice, he moves through the shadows like a fox. But you're right—this is where it must end for him." He took a deep pull from his water skin. "I'll need to keep a closer watch on Leif—we can't have him hurting anyone else."

"I'll take Eadgar with me when I release Jarl and the men," Harald said. "Give him some other task—make sure he understands he's not to follow us."

They both turned as more warriors joined the gathering throng—armed now, voices rising. Leif stood on a wooden box, his voice cutting through the din of the camp.

> "And what has Jarl Torvald done for us, truly? Our goods disappear, stolen—and he bids us wait! Yet he calls the Saxons guests, who steal from us, who burn our food supply—guests, not foes! But look around you—here we stand, the ruins of our food stores lying in ash, and where is your Jarl now? He is nowhere to be seen! Perhaps he has run to his friends the Saxons!"

"So!" Håkon said, pushing himself off the wall. He unsheathed the sword at his hip, picked up his shield, and cast Harald a quick grin. "To the swords!" he said, winking at Harald before turning and jogging across the camp, striking sword against shield as the rebellion prepared to march towards Wōdenléah.

Harald chuckled. "Fight bravely and your name will be sung!" He yelled after him, smirking sarcastically, "and send that little whelp Eadgar over here!"

45
Gūþ ✗ Battle

"We'll need to be on our way soon, Lord," Cenric said, his hand firm on Osric's shoulder before turning to hoist the last of the saddlebags onto Osric's gelding, giving him a bit more time to process what he'd just been told.

Osric stood rigid outside the shelter, hands braced on his hips, staring into the night. He wore his muted red quilted tunic—still with a layer of travel grime from the road to Wintanceaster—sword and seax at his hip, helmet tucked beneath his arm. He'd dressed for battle, but was hoping for nothing more than some posturing and a few carelessly flung insults.

The smell of ash and fire hung heavily in the air from the blaze at the distant trading camp. He'd been able to see the glow from the fire just beyond the treeline even before someone had been dispatched to retrieve him, and by the time Cenric had arrived, Osric was packed and waiting.

What Osric had not anticipated was the news that Cenric brought with him—a summons for Æfre to appear before the witan—something that as far as Osric could remember, had never happened to anyone accused of anything in Wōdenléah, even those who stood accused of theft or violence.

Heathenry. "Unlawful rites", is what Cenric said he'd called it. Osric clenched his jaw. It was a hollow, ridiculous charge—anyone would see it for what it was in the halls of Wintanceaster, yet it would still have to be answered. And Osric knew that was the point.

There were plenty in Wōdenléah who still burned herbs to ward sickness or whispered charms over a cradle, as generations of their families always had. As his own family had. This summons wasn't about proving Æfre innocent or guilty; it was about alienating her—branding her as an outsider not to be trusted. It was about control, and it was a callous way to repay the efforts of someone whose family had served Wōdenléah for generations.

A white-hot rage rose from the depths of Osric's gut all the way up into the back of his throat until he could practically taste it—guilt and helplessness in equal measure. He remembered Jarl Torvald's warning to him as they drank mead inside the very shelter he stood in front of. The chieftain had warned him that a move like this might come—even suggested a potential way out for Æfre, and Osric had foolishly dismissed it. Even now, Osric realized he was selfishly unwilling to let her go.

He cursed himself as he recalled the conversation. He had been overly confident that Æthelwod wouldn't dare stir the pot now that his betrothal to Aldhem was official, but the bastard had done it. And now Æfre sat behind locked doors, her name irreversibly smeared, and there was not a thing Osric could do about it without igniting an even greater fire. By making the accusation official, Æthelwod had, in a single stroke, killed Æfre's future, complete with ink and wax seal.

"Lord, that's the gelding saddled." Cenric said softly, "It's time we moved."

"Thank you, Cenric," Osric replied without looking at him. He cast one last look into the woods, where the distant blaze at the camp no longer glowed brightly above the black silhouette of the trees. He took an extended inhalation, tasting the cold and the distant smoke—a taste which only slightly masked the bitter taste of his own guilt.

"It'll be slow going in this dark, my lord," Cenric said as both of the men mounted, "but I know the track. Keep close, do as I do. We'll douse the torches before we reach the old road. Just mind you don't set the trees ablaze as we go."

HEART OF THE WILD GODS

* * *

"Over here, Lord," came a voice, quiet and urgent, from just beyond the treeline.

Godwin.

Godwin and Alaric emerged from the darkness of the trees like two shadows and took the horses without a word, guiding them down towards a clearing that served as their staging area.

The path through the forest had been slow going, just as Cenric had warned, but they had made steady progress. The moment they reached the road, their pace quickened. More than once, they'd paused at the sound of the Northmen they could hear behind them—voices raised in song, swords and axes clattering, boots scuffing frozen ground—loud on purpose, just as the plan demanded.

"They're not far off," Alaric said quietly; "Maybe a mile, no more, and we expect the fyrd to appear around the bend any moment."

"Good, then we've timed it well." Cenric said, "Lord Wulfric and Cwenhild will have instructed everyone in the burh to keep to their hearths until they hear otherwi—"

Before Cenric had even gotten the words fully out, they heard it; the steady thump of boots on hard ground. The creak of leather, the whisper of cloaks, and the hollow knock of spear hafts against wooden shields. The fyrd was approaching. Wulfric was right on time.

"Right, this is it." Godwin said, "Alaric, let's fan out within the tree line—find the clearest line of sight you can. Are the horses secure?"

"Hobbled and grazing."

Cenric turned to Osric. "Come, Lord. This way. You can fall in at the rear unseen once they pass."

Osric gave a brief nod. He pulled his helmet down—cheek plates snug against his jaw, the nasal guard shadowing his face—and drew his cloak close over the familiar cut of his war-gear. In the shadows of the night, he could pass for any of the men in helmets.

He and Cenric moved softly, stepping between roots and brush, careful not to rattle their weapons or knock their shields against the trees.

Cenric suddenly raised a hand, and they dropped low.

And there they were.

Osric couldn't help but admire the imposing visual of the Wōdenléah fyrd—he was unused to seeing it from any perspective other than within.

They marched in quiet strength, arranged in a loose column by household and rank, no drum, no chant, just the solemn sound of shuffling weaponry and boots crunching the ground beneath their feet. At the fore, the burh banner swayed in the wind—two outward-facing black boars flanking a proud oak at the center, presented on mustard-gold cloth—a representation of strength, bravery, and ancestral tradition.

Osric scanned the fyrd's ranks, recognizing faces from just about every corner of the burh. These were his people. For years, he'd trained, laughed, and bled beside these people. It heartened him to see them marching united—not against the Northmen, although there were likely more than a few among them who believed that the so-called heathen horde was indeed the enemy—no, this time they were united against an internal foe; against a lie that would continue to oppress and exploit both them and their Norse counterparts if allowed to remain in power.

That lie, Osric thought with grim amusement, was currently splendidly arrayed, chest puffed like a crowned peacock, sitting high in the saddle at the center of the fyrd.

HEART OF THE WILD GODS

True to form, Æthelwod, the man who so detested horses, had claimed his place on horseback, front and center, just a few rows back from the shield wall. Æthelwod undoubtedly would have considered this a prominent position, surrounded by enough skilled retainers to protect him from any real threat.

Wulfric rode to the column's flank, easy in his seat, leaving Æthelwod to bask in what many hoped would be his final grasp at authority over Wōdenléah's fate. Judging by the look on Wulfric's face, he seemed more than happy to take whatever distance between himself and the bishop he could get.

As he studied the bishop, Osric thought about the other clergymen he knew who would give a blessing before a battle. If they dared approach a potential conflict at all, they would typically do so clad in a short cope or tunic more suited to the rough ground and potential hazards of the field. Not Æthelwod. His dramatic, trailing robes caught every gust that blew through the trees, billowing the cloth and snapping it like a ship's sail. The constant flapping was spooking his mount—a skittish young chestnut that danced nervously beneath him as the fyrd moved past where he and Cenric crouched.

Osric watched with narrowed eyes as Æthelwod's horse tossed its head and shied at every clattered spear and rustled cloak. He knew that horse—one of Cenric's youngest stock—an animal not yet sure under saddle. Not fit for any battle, and certainly no mount for an equine-despising bishop whose horsemanship skills were mediocre at best.

A grin pulled at the corners of Osric's mouth. That choice couldn't have been an accident. Cenric had put Æthelwod on the greenest beast in the yard.

Still lying low in the tree line, Osric turned his head, peering through the brush at Cenric, who crouched a few paces off. Cenric was already looking directly back at him—grinning, satisfied, and utterly responsible. Pleased even that Osric had noticed his efforts.

As the tail of the fyrd marched past, Osric seized his moment. He gave Cenric a quick wink and a nod and pulled his helmet as low as it would sit. With the last of the fyrd nearly past, he took a deep breath and stepped silently from the tree line, melting into the back of the formation. To anyone watching, he was just another man returning from a brief comfort break at the side of the road.

Cenric watched him merge into the sea of spears and shields, waited a few more moments, then slipped out of the woods and into the formation, making his way to his usual position in the second line behind the shield wall.

* * *

"How fares it with you, Jarl?" Svend asked, casting a glance sideways at Torvald as they rode towards Wōdenléah under the cold hush of night. Torvald gingerly rolled his neck, then rubbed at his temples with his free hand.

"I'll not die," he muttered, "the pounding is easing off."

Svend nodded and looked back towards the blackness of the road laid out before them. "It's not long now. If the Gods are with us, there will soon be one less reason for anyone to have a headache in Wōdenléah."

Svend's quip earned a dry laugh from Torvald—cut short by a sharp wince as he clutched the back of his head. "Úi! Perhaps don't make me laugh just yet." Torvald said, still chuckling while simultaneously trying not to.

"Sorry, Jarl." Svend grinned, turning his attention back to the road.

Ahead of them, Harald and Bjørn kept their mounts at a steady pace, eyes scanning the shadowed tree line for signs that the meeting point, or trouble, lay near—their silence heavy with readiness.

HEART OF THE WILD GODS

The three of them hadn't been long in the hut they were thrown into as captives; Harald had played his role well since the beginning, feigning loyalty to Leif and whispering just enough treason to win his trust. Once left with the task of securing the camp's leadership, he'd needed to do little more than simply open the door, and Torvald, Svend, and Bjørn had stepped into the night as free men again—no fanfare, no heroics.

Eadgar, sent by Håkon, had been the one to deliver the news that the camp was clear. A few moments later, the four of them mounted up and slipped off into the dark. Before they left, Torvald had crouched beside the boy and fixed him with a hard look.

"You've done well tonight, Eadgar," Torvald said, his voice steady, a hint of pride beneath the weariness. "But you went against what I asked of you—and that can't happen again."

Eadgar looked ready to argue, but Torvald raised a hand to stop him, his gaze steely, and the boy looked down at the ground.

"No harm was done this time—Håkon looked after you well, but tonight this thing ends for you. No more creeping about in the shadows while there is a possibility of steel being drawn. You've done your part, and I'm grateful—but from here, it's no longer your fight."

He rested a hand briefly on the boy's shoulder, firm but not unkind.

"Go on now—get to your bed, or the hall's fire if you're cold or hungry. But not another step behind us. Not tonight."

To everyone's great relief, the boy had obeyed.

"Jarl!" Bjørn's voice broke through his thoughts. He looked up and saw that Bjørn had turned his mount around and was trotting towards him. "We're here. Everyone is in position."

Torvald straightened in his saddle, eyes scanning the treeline just off to his right.

"We should leave the horses here," Torvald said, swinging one leg over and dropping to the earth. He made a point to land lightly, careful not to jar his skull again—the ache in his head had only just begun to ease, and he meant to keep it that way.

The four of them secured their horses and slipped into the woods, moving swiftly and silently, stepping over roots and deadfall, bracing weapons tight against their bodies so no metal would clatter. They crept parallel to the clearing where the men from the camp had gathered. When they drew close enough to see faces, they split—Torvald and Svend keeping to the rear, Harald and Bjørn sliding off to cover the center and far side.

The Northmen from the camp stood fewer in number and looser in formation than the Saxon fyrd—yet they seemed somehow fiercer, as if the fire of past raids still burned in their eyes.

Torvald realized it had been less than three years of peace between their people—if peace was even what you could call the lesser degree of organized violence that currently existed in Wessex. He supposed that most people in the burh had only ever seen his people with steel drawn; the memory of burning halls and murdered kin still fresh in many minds.

If all went to plan, that would not be anyone's fate on this night.

Yet even as Torvald had the thought, the campmen began their old ways. They thumped their weapons against their shields in a rising wall of sound—faces twisted into wolfish grins and eyes blazing with an old, familiar hunger for a fight.

The chieftain strained to read the reactions of the Saxons from the distance he was at. To their credit, they held their ground, though many of the younger ones were gripping their spears with white-knuckled hands.

An unwelcome knot of unease crept into Torvald's chest—this moment was the knife's edge, where all could easily be lost for both sides. If the men on either side were to forget themselves and allow old feelings, fears, and urges to take over, something as banal as a sneeze or a dropped spear could turn this manufactured standoff into a very real slaughter.

Torvald realized he wasn't the only one to sense this danger, because near the fore, Wulfric suddenly swung down from the saddle. He walked the first line of the formation, speaking low to the men, clasping shoulders, nodding to some, offering quick words to others. Here a grin, there a steadying hand.

Torvald watched with grudging admiration.

Wulfric, for all of his seemingly unserious antics, wielded a gift rarer than a fine sword or noble birth—the man was a natural leader with the ability to steady men's hearts. In less than a day's time, he had woven himself into the Wōdenléah ranks like he'd always walked among them. It was no small thing, even for someone who came as a trusted ally of Osric.

As Wulfric moved, Torvald's men grew louder, hammering their shields and raising their voices in a chorus that seemed to rattle the trees. Yet through all of it, Wulfric remained calm, weaving through the line, planting calm where panic threatened to grow—precisely what was needed in that moment.

Wulfric suddenly turned from the Saxon formation, shouldering his way through their shield wall.

"Hold," he yelled—both hands raised over his head, moving deliberately until he reached the center of the open ground between the two forces. With slow, deliberate movements, Wulfric single-handedly unfastened his sword belt, letting it fall, blade and seax clattering to the cold-hardened earth. As his weaponry hit the ground, the road fell into an uneasy silence. Breath rose up into the night in sharp, silent puffs, leaving only the sound of cloaks flapping in the gusting wind.

"I would have words before weapons!" Wulfric shouted. "By right, and before these witnesses, I call for parley!"

The Northmen shifted where they stood, the uneasy scrape of boots on frozen earth and the low clatter of weaponry the only sounds permeating the otherwise taut silence.

Torvald held his breath. This was Wulfric going through the expected motions, yet he quietly cursed the fact that they hadn't spent more time on the small, dangerous details of this particular moment. All the grand planning in the world meant little if a single man lost his nerve now, and there were at least a million different directions this thing might veer off in.

For a heartbeat, nobody spoke—until a shout split the stillness. "No parley!"

A tense moment passed, the Northmen shuffling as they turned their heads to seek the source of the voice.

"There will be no parley!" the voice shouted again, more slowly and deliberately as the formation parted and Leif emerged with Eirik hard at his heels.

Torvald's eyes narrowed as he scanned the formation, catching sight of Håkon and Geir shadowing the flanks, moving slowly, almost imperceptibly in tandem with Leif and Eirik—hands resting easy on their hilts, bodies tight with readiness.

"No parley!" Leif shouted with his whole chest as he strode forward. "We will no longer hear the words you speak in service of lies and theft! You burn our stores by night, and mumble prayers to your Christian God by day, thinking it will wash you clean!"

"I ask you one more time, Northman," Wulfric shouted, unarmed and standing his ground, "do not throw away the welfare of so many so recklessly. Will you not seek to stay the blade while sense might still prevail!?"

Leif spoke no more, but instead slowly drew his sword, the sharp, scraping hiss of steel against scabbard echoing through the trees.

Torvald's hand instinctively closed around the hilt of his own sword, although he was on his belly in shadows and brush, barely daring to breathe. Every man present was a coiled spring—a breath held before a sword falls—both sides thrumming with an unstoppable, mounting energy. The fact that this was not to be a real conflict seemed to be getting pushed further and further into the background.

"Still your hand, Tor," Svend said in a near whisper, nudging Torvald and giving a quick nod towards Torvald's sword hand.

Torvald shot Svend a questioning look—a heartbeat passing before he felt his own hand resting on the hilt of his sword. He glanced down, half in disbelief, finding his fingers clenched tight around the grip and the sword a quarter of the way drawn.

"My sword hand remembers its work," he muttered, shaking his head with a sheepish grin and a long, slow exhalation as he quietly pushed his sword back into the scabbard.

From across the divide, the unmistakable voice of Bishop Æthelwod suddenly rang out like a cracked whip. "Lord Wulfric, you heard the heathen—he refuses the parley! He leaves us no choice but to respond with might!"

"Very well," Wulfric replied, his voice as cool as iron. Without taking his gaze off of Leif, he bent at the knees, slowly and deliberately gathering his sword belt. He buckled the belt back around his waist, the motion calm, unhurried—to Torvald it appeared as though Wulfric thought he had all the time in the world. The Saxon thegn then very calmly withdrew to his place within the ranks, settling at the heart of the second line, just behind the wall of locked shields.

Across the field, Leif mirrored him, striding back to stand at the center of his front line, shoulder to shoulder with Eirik.

Torvald quickly scanned the two formations.

This was it. Everyone was in position.

A deathly quiet descended over the road, the only sounds the rustle of the trees in the biting wind and the occasional shuffle of a foot or dull clunk of a weapon.

"Eyes sharp, Svend," muttered Torvald, "the storm's about to break."

* * *

Wulfric's eyes flicked over the throng of menacing Northmen facing them, their heavy stares fixed, fuelled by the weight of a thousand battles between them. He swallowed hard against the knot that continued to tighten in his gut. Never in his life would he have thought he'd find himself here—voluntarily staring at a wall of formidable warriors, armed with nothing more than a prayer and a plan that hinged entirely on them not doing the very thing that had made them such a fearsome force to begin with. They needed to hold back. Everyone did.

Wulfric's thoughts turned for a fleeting moment to his wife Edrys, pregnant with their first child. When he'd told her of his intention to help Osric, she had vacillated between pride and concern before landing on outright panic. She had begged him to be cautious, to stay away from the madness on the front line—if only he had listened. He had assured her it would never come to blows, and while he would never deny a lifelong friend and brother in arms help when needed, it wasn't until that very moment that he realized he may have underestimated the danger. He sucked in a breath, the tension of the moment settling over him like the weight of a sodden cloak.

"Well, Osric," Wulfric muttered to himself, "we're in it now."

His hand found the grip of his sword, drawing it with a swift, skyward slice, the metallic melody of drawn steel ringing in the trees.

"Men of the fyrd," Wulfric's voice boomed, "you've heard true! If they truly would rather settle this by the sword...if they are in such a hurry to get to their beloved Valhalla, I say we do not keep their Gods waiting a moment longer!"

The Northmen growled like wolves, their swords striking shields, a gathering storm, designed to strike fear in the hearts of all they encountered.

"Ready!" he shouted, his sword raised high. "Shields firm!"

The deep, resounding sound of the shuffling of feet and clatter of weaponry rose from the fyrd, the weight of a burh's worth of shoulders pressing against the shield wall.

"Stand fast," Wulfric continued, his voice firm, low but filled with an undeniable authority. "Steel your hearts, steady your hands!"

Both sides were now coiled, taut like a bowstring, ready to strike. There was no longer any room for doubt, no second-guessing. Wulfric's pulse beat loud in his ears—a feeling that, for a fleeting moment, he thought he could see reflected in the faces of the men facing him from across the divide. But now, the best he could do was hope that they were thinking the same thing that he was as he gave the command.

"With me now! Let no man falter, and leave none standing!"

Both sides erupted in a raw, deafening roar as men on both sides crouched like hungry wolves on the hunt.

"Forward on them!" Wulfric barked, his pulse hammering in his chest.

Across the field, Leif and Eirik were the first to break away—surging forward with swords drawn.

But nobody else moved.

Wulfric saw it instantly. In one swift motion, he pointed the tip of his raised sword to the ground and thrust it into the hard-packed earth before him. The sharpened blade sank deep with a crunch—disarming himself as the sword stood upright like a war banner, pinning his fate to the spot.

To his left, he heard the clang of steel as it fell dully on soil, though he didn't dare risk a glance with Leif and Eirik still bearing down on him.

In front of him, silver flashed across the divide. Another sword clattered down. Then another. One more off to his right. Two more behind. Then the sound spread like metallic rain on an iron roof as weapons fell, metal hitting wood as shield rims, axes, swords, and spears struck the ground—an entire field of men casting their arms aside.

Wulfric could see that one Northman across the divide still clung to his sword, his gaze darting left and right in confusion as he haltingly advanced. Harald suddenly emerged from the treeline like a striking wolf, closing the distance between them in three strides, and wrenching the man's blade away before driving him forward, shoving him to his knees at the center of the divide.

On the Saxon flank, Alaric burst from the tree lines and seized a similarly bewildered fyrdman still clinging to his weapon, stripping the spear from his grasp and dragging him to the center of the divide to join the Northman.

Eirick slowed his pace as he ran at Wulfric, recognizing that something was amiss as he knitted his brow at all the discarded weapons on the ground before him. He'd barely had time to jog to a halt when Bjørn suddenly appeared beside him, punching him squarely across the jaw and sending him stumbling backwards before disarming him and herding him to the front with the others.

But Leif—Leif did not falter. The giant Northman continued to churn forward at full tilt, eyes locked on Wulfric, blade high. Wulfric squared his stance, disarmed and bare-handed, lifting his chin as the giant warrior bore down. In a few heartbeats, he would decorate the man's steel blade as it speared through his chest. He looked at his sword, which stood in the earth in front of him. Retrieving it would most certainly ignite a firestorm of rage from the Northmen and derail their plan, yet not retrieving it, his child would never know his face. His wife's touch, but a memory.

Not enough time. So be it.

Leif was now close enough for Wulfric to feel the wind rushing from his charge.

Seemingly out of nowhere, a large blur slammed into Leif's side. The crack of the impact echoed across the field, toppling both men in a bone-jarring collision that rattled Wulfric's own rib cage. The two men skidded across the ground, the Northman slicing his keg on Wulfric's planted sword as they skidded past.

Leif's sword slipped from his hand and skittered away, clanging end over end before coming to rest at the feet of a young fyrdsman, who instinctively kicked it out of reach.

The tangled Northmen groaned on the ground near Wulfric's feet. Another figure rushed up—another Northman, hair bound in a leather cord. He ignored Wulfric and knelt by the heap.

"Geir! Allt gott?" The man barked in his native tongue.

"Já, Håkon," came a muffled reply, followed by a groan as Geir rolled himself over and stiffly pushed himself up off the ground with a grunt, pausing to inspect the cut on his leg.

Håkon clapped his comrade's shoulder, nodding grimly as Geir limped off. Then he seized Leif by the tunic, hauled him to his knees, and yanked him close, their faces inches apart.

"Hrafnarnir munu hafa þik! [*The ravens will have you!*]" Håkon practically spat in the man's face, then pulled his head back and head-butted him with such a resounding clack, Wulfric was sure he felt his own eyeballs wriggle in their sockets.

Håkon straightened, still holding the now-bloodied and drooping Leif by the tunic, shook his head, and looked squarely at Wulfric. The Northman looked Wulfric up and down.

"You good?"

Wulfric nodded stiffly, breath shallow. "Good. You have my

thanks."

A grunt, a nod—and Håkon hauled Leif away, tossing him into the center of the divide with the other captives.

Wulfric let out a shaky exhale, trying to keep it as quiet as possible as he looked around. The field had quieted, and the aggression that had been so palpable a moment ago had all but dissipated. All of the weaponry still lay on the ground on both sides of the divide. Both sides had also closed ranks, forming a circle around those being held, with the captives kneeling in the center.

It was done—almost. The last of the known traitors knelt before them—with one notable exception.

Wulfric felt any residual adrenaline suddenly drain from his body, and he shifted slightly on his feet, hoping the men on either side of the circle wouldn't notice as his knees wobbled and he fought the urge to vomit.

The moment settled heavily around them as the men on the road once again regarded each other across the divide. For several minutes, it remained quiet as both sides allowed the charged energy to ebb away. So intent were they, nobody marked the lone fyrdsman slip from the flank and disappear into the forest.

46

Unwreoghen ⚔ Revealed

"What is the meaning of this? We must move on them at once! Lord Wulfric! The men must advance!"

Æthelwod's voice split the darkness of the early morning and tore Osric from his battle-vigilant state. He had been utterly fixed on Wulfric, his oldest friend, watching in cold dread as moments before, he'd come perilously close to becoming an adornment at the end of a Northman's blade.

Osric had been forcing his way to the fore, hand on the hilt of his sword, ready to cast aside whatever plan they had for the sake of Wulfric's life—then one of Torvald's men had come crashing in at the last moment.

"Lord Wulfric!" Æthelwod shrilled again. The bishop's mount shied and turned circles beneath him as the bishop's voice grew shrill with rising panic. "This cannot stand! It will not stand!"

Around the circle, Saxon and Norse alike began to shift. The ring of men, drawn tight about the captured men on their knees, loosened in silence. All eyes turned to Æthelwod now, their gazes flat, cold, and accusatory.

"Weapons! Take up your weapons, I say!" Æthelwod spat in Wulfric's direction, his horse dancing and foaming at the bit, nearly unseating him. "What is this? What is this!?"

Osric shouldered his way forward, his jaw set. At the second rank, he caught movement—it was Cenric, quiet as a cat, slipping behind Æthelwod's twitching mount. Without a word, Cenric raised a flat hand and smacked the beast sharply across the right hindquarter.

The horse bolted with a squeal, pitching Æthelwod backwards and sending him crashing into the dirt in a billowing heap of robes.

Freed of its rider, the chestnut calmed instantly and wandered off towards the circle's edge, snuffling for grass.

Raucous laughter broke out from the Northmen—and more than a few of the Saxons—the men roaring as Æthelwod writhed in his tangled robes, blinded and trapped within the fabric, looking like a sack full of angry weasels. The more he struggled, the louder the men laughed.

Osric allowed himself a breath of grim satisfaction—then set it aside. Enough.

"Fyrd! To me!" His command voice cracked sharply over the din.

The men fell silent immediately, their heads snapping around at the sound of the familiar voice of their thegn. The Northmen, catching the shift, quieted—still chortling and wiping their eyes.

"Hear me, warriors!" Osric barked, stepping clear of the ranks as they parted for him, his voice steady. "This ends now."

He strode into the ring just as Æthelwod tore the robe from his face, squinting against the darkness in the direction of the voice. A deafening hush fell over the circle.

"Bishop Æthelwod," Osric said, unfastening his helmet and removing it, shaking out his hair, and tucking the helmet under his arm. His tone was low, measured. "This ends now."

He crossed to Wulfric, looking his friend in the eyes while clasping him by the shoulders and giving him a firm shake. His friend's eyes, though steady, were shadowed by the near miss. Seeing it sank a slow-burning rage deep in Osric's belly.

He turned back to Æthelwod, his eyes ablaze.

"The grip you've laid on these people—the fear, the greed, the broken oaths and heavy-handed dealings—it ends here, tonight."

The color drained from Æthelwod's face. He scrambled backwards towards the other men kneeling in the circle, propelled by his elbows and heels, his usual confident pomposity abandoning

HEART OF THE WILD GODS

him at the sight of Osric's cold stare.

"Lord Osric—you should be in Wintanceaster! You have duties—grave duties that you have forsaken! This is dereliction! Many men—great men—will be displeased, deeply displeased..."

The bishop tried to stand and caught his foot in his robe, sending himself sprawling face-first onto the ground. Another chorus of laughter erupted from the men.

Osric stood stone still and allowed it. Æthelwod's reckoning had been long in coming.

After a few moments, a deep voice resonated through the laughter.

"Nǫgr! [*Enough!*]"

The circle momentarily stilled, then the Northmen parted cleanly down the middle. Through the gap strode Torvald Ironsight, with Svend and Bjørn close at his heels.

The Norse chieftain barked a sharp translation of Osric's call to his men, his voice carrying clear in the cold morning air. Without pause, he crossed to Osric; the two clasped forearms, warrior to warrior, before turning together to face Æthelwod.

What little remained of the bishop's mask of confident self-righteousness melted like thin ice. The sight of the Saxon thegn and Norse chieftain greeting as allies shattered whatever restraint he had left, and his face twisted bitterly.

"Lord Osric! How could you?" Æthelwod's voice broke into a keening wail. "You—a man of faith—you would cast aside your own people for these godless heathens?"

Beside Osric, Torvald grinned, teeth flashing in the half-light, and let out a low, incredulous chuckle and shook his head.

Osric echoed Torvald's sentiments with an exasperated shake of the head. The bishop flailed at their feet, ensnared in the very trap he'd set, robes tangled, dignity long fled—and still he clawed for the moral high ground.

Osric stepped forward, planting his feet wide, his voice cutting through the gathered men.

"I will remind the Bishop," he said, turning slowly so all could hear him—pausing as Torvald echoed his words in Norse, "and any man here who needs hearing, that the men and women of the trading camp stand here lawfully under the Treaty of Alfred and Guthrum. They are guests of the Kingdom of Wessex. Wōdenléah is a named trading port. I, together with Svend, whom you know, and Jarl Torvald Ironsight, work hand in hand to ensure fair dealing under that treaty."

He let the weight of those words hang a moment before continuing, voice steady and rising.

"Make no mistake, my Saxon brothers. I know too well the pain many of you carry from the raids of past years. Over half my body bears the scar of a Northman's blade—one that near ended my life. And it is entirely possible that some day soon we may once again be on opposite sides of the battlefield. But if we are to endure, if this land and her people are to outlive this violence, we must step beyond old wounds."

He turned to the Northmen, Torvald translating close at hand.

"To you, our trading partners, there is no Saxon plot to steal your goods. There never was any such plot. What you have seen at work is one man's hand stirring discord among you. Jarl Torvald will speak for that truth.

"And to my Saxon brethren, there is no threat to your hearths from any who do not pray to the Christian God. That, too, is falsehood, sown by the same hand. This is plot spun for power and land. A plot which dishonors both our treaty and the will of our Lord King Alfred. Put plainly, it is treason."

He let his unflinching gaze settle back on Æthelwod.

"It grieves me to say these things as a man of faith. But the root of it stands before you now. Therefore, Bishop Æthelwod is stripped of office as of this moment. He will answer in Wintanceaster to King Alfred himself.

"Now—Jarl Torvald and I have matters yet to settle," Osric called out, his voice carrying steady and sure. "So we bid you good morning—for now. Return to your hearths. To your families. And I give our trading partners this promise—the next time we stand across from one another, it will be over a platter of roasted meat and jugs of ale."

A ripple of nods moved through both camps. A few cheers rose, light and genuine. Osric glanced at Torvald, who gave a sharp nod of approval.

Torvald turned to Svend and Bjørn. "Put these two in the wagon," he ordered, pointing to Eirik and a younger man who'd not thrown down his weapon—a new face, not long in the camp. "Question them hard. Find out if the young one even belongs here. He may have been swept up by the wrong wind. The thegn and I will bring Leif with the Saxon bishop to the Wōdenléah."

Torvald started away, but after a few strides, he turned back, planting his feet square. His voice rang clear. "Men, you handled yourselves cleanly." The chieftain flashed a rare but genuine smile and turned again to Osric.

"Lord Osric, come. We've things to discuss."

* * *

Æfre startled awake as the brew hut door groaned open, her heart hammering against her ribs. She dragged the thin blanket tighter about her shoulders and narrowed her eyes as she squinted into the torchlight spilling from outside.

"Who's there?" She asked.

"Æfre."

A warm, familiar voice.

Osric.

She rose stiffly from the hard, earthen floor and crossed the hut. When she reached him, her hands gripped his tunic tight as they locked in a hard embrace. Osric pushed the door open wide, letting the cold night air flood into the hut.

"Is it over?" she asked, brushing dust from her skirts and running her fingers through tangled hair. "I was asleep."

Osric suddenly paused and cupped her face, tilting it gently. His jaw clenched as he saw a fresh red mark across her cheek and a split in her lip.

"Who did this?" His voice dropped low, dangerous. His eyes darkened and snapped towards Cenric and Wulfric, who had just appeared at the door, herding Æthelwod and Leif into the hut.

"Your heathen friend has a sharp tongue, Lord Osric—she needs a lesson in respect." Æthelwod spat as Cenric shoved him across the threshold.

Osric's hand shot to the hilt of his sword. Fury flashed in him like flint against steel.

"You *niðing!*" Osric growled and surged forward.

"Osric!" Æfre snapped, catching his arm before steel had a chance to clear the scabbard. Wulfric stepped in fast.

"Steady, old friend," Wulfric muttered. "Breathe, brother. Don't give the snake what it craves."

"Osric," Æfre said more softly now, slipping to his side. She laid her hand on his sleeve and met his eyes. "Leave him. His fate is decided." She looked directly at the bishop. "Leave him to it."

Her gaze wandered off of Æthelwod to the man beside him, causing the bottom to drop from her stomach. It was the man from the attack at her homestead. Her fingers dug hard into Osric's arm.

"Æfre?" Osric followed her stare.

"You." Her voice cut sharply and low.

Leif lifted his head and met her stare. His face stayed empty—resigned, hollowed-out.

HEART OF THE WILD GODS

"You left your cloak in my pasture," she said, ice threading through her words.

"Is this..." Osric began.

"The man who attacked me. Yes."

The shock that had first numbed her suddenly cracked open, and a hot, molten anger poured through her. Her jaw set tight.

"How's the shoulder?" she hissed. "Sore, I imagine. I hope you were paid well for your trouble." She glared at Æthelwod before returning her gaze to Leif. "An injury through the joint like that won't heal without giving you some bother. You may never fully recover. Perhaps you'd like me to put a few arrows in the other one for balance?"

A low chuckle echoed from across the room. Æfre's eyes flicked to the doorway where Torvald Ironsight leaned, shadowed at the edge of the torchlight, leisurely working on eating a hunk of bread.

"Jarl Torvald."

"Æfre."

Hearing the name of the chieftain spoken, Æthelwod swiveled around sharply, panic etched into his face.

Leif, however, sat still, a man already come to grips with the fact that he was standing on the precipice of his own demise.

"I'll have my leechbook back now, Bishop." Æfre turned her gaze back to the bishop.

"I should say *not*." Æthelwod scoffed, "It will be needed before the witan."

Osric scoffed. "Cenric, can you please see if you can retrieve Æfre's leechbook from the bishop's residence?"

Wulfric tossed Cenric the key ring he had taken from Æthelwod.

"Of course, my lord."

"Bishop Æthelwod," Osric continued, "Æfre will not stand before the witan."

Æthelwod barked a bitter laugh. "If that isn't a fool-warrior's boast come to life. Lords Osric and Wulfric—Wintanceaster will hear of your exploits soon enough. I'll see you both stripped of land and name. Mark me."

"Lord Bishop," Osric was growing increasingly exasperated as he addressed Æthelwod. "You seem not to grasp what is unfolding in this hut. Let me speak plainly—your time in Wōdenléah is ended. You hold no sway in Wintanceaster. You've conspired against the King's peace—against the treaty with Guthrum and the Danelaw. You've committed treason, and as such, you'll be treated as a traitor."

"Surely," Æthelwod sputtered, "when Wintanceaster hears of this—"

"It is with the blessing of Wintanceaster that we have unmade your plan this night!" Osric shouted. "They know all!"

The bishop paled, his mouth failing to produce enough sound for a whole sentence. "I... I don't understand..."

"Everything that happened on that road tonight, and everything that will happen in this hut, happens with the blessing of Alfred, King of Wessex."

"What do you mean, what will happen—?"

"Heimskr goði! [*foolish priest!*]" Leif's voice boomed like thunder. "Are you so dim!? What he's saying is we are dead men! Do you see now? We are ghosts!"

A silence fell over the room like a thick fog.

"Surely not!" Æthelwod huffed, his voice now fraying at the edges. "Lord Osric, you wouldn't dare take my life! You couldn't!" Æthelwod gasped, as if to reassure himself.

"Lord Bishop," Osric said after a moment of contemplation, "I once had the grave misfortune of admiring you—before I understood the man you truly are. And yet you are right. I cannot, and will not take your life."

HEART OF THE WILD GODS

Osric put his arm around Æfre and turned towards the door, where Torvald Ironsight stood watching—waiting like a wolf. Osric gave Torvald a quick nod, and Torvald tossed his unfinished heel of bread out the door, then leaned behind him and addressed someone unseen.

"Ertu reiðr!? [*Are you ready!?*]"

Two massive shadows crossed the threshold—Bjørn and Svend, each still wearing battle gear and bearing a bucket of thick, dark pine pitch.

"Bishop," Osric continued as he ushered Æfre out the door, "I am not going to take your life this night—but I cannot rightly say what these men might do. Good night, Bishop."

Osric and Æfre stepped into the cold, early morning darkness, the strong signature of pine pitch wafting faintly behind him. He nodded to Wulfric as the door to the brew hut groaned shut.

The last thing he heard was the zing of a sword leaving its scabbard, followed by the indignant pleadings of a corrupt Bishop.

47

Los ✕ Loss

"Don't fall asleep back there, Æfre," Osric said gently over his shoulder.

They rode tandem on Cenric's great horse—a broad-backed, even-tempered beast obtained for supply runs during the Battle of Edington, and one both Cenric and Osric had taken a liking to when the fighting had come to an end.

The dark, early morning air was sharp and cold, though the first whisperings of dawn now pressed at the horizon.

"I'm awake," Æfre murmured.

"You don't sound it."

"Mmm," Æfre responded, eyes heavy. She felt as though she had no words left to give, as if all the breath to form them had been knocked from her chest.

The ride had started fast with Osric pressing the horse to a canter, putting ground between them and whatever fate was befalling Leif and Bishop Æthelwod.

Æfre didn't know how much time had passed when she felt the pace ease, but once the pace slowed to a walk, Æfre was able to loosen her grip and relax a bit as they continued in silence—the steady thud of hooves against the hard-packed earth the only accompaniment.

Æfre watched the landscape pass slowly, allowing her eyes to unfocus as her cheek smeared with road dirt from Osric's tunic, the horse's rolling gait rocking her gently back and forth.

Earlier, as they'd passed the meeting of the roads, she'd noticed that there was hardly any trace of the confrontation that had occurred there earlier. The mark of some shuffled feet, a bit of trampled grass, and a lone fyrdsman—a straggler—making his way back to the burh at the side of the road, but otherwise there was nothing to see—just the thick, silent, anticipatory stillness of the darkness before daybreak.

As they rode, Æfre noticed there was a change in the air.

"I smell fire," she said, sitting straighter behind the saddle, awakening a bit as the distinct, acrid smell of smoke tweaked her nostrils.

"As do I." Osric replied, "The earlier blaze from the trading camp, no doubt." He said, though Æfre thought that he sounded a million miles away—lost in thought.

As they rode a bit further, Æfre noticed the smell of smoke intensifying—it seemed close.

"Osric, I think it's getting stronger. Do you smell it still?"

"I do, Æfre, hold on." Osric's brow furrowed, and he leaned forward and urged the horse into a canter.

With each stride of the horse beneath them, the smell of smoke grew stronger, and a sense of dread began to take hold in Æfre's gut.

"Osric..."

They rounded the next bend and emerged from the forest to a sight Æfre knew would change her world as soon as she laid eyes on it. The sky beyond the crest of the next hill glowed orange in the dark early morning sky.

Osric urged the horse on up the hill as fast as the beast could carry them. Once they reached the top, he reined in hard, nearly unseating both of them.

Below them, burned Æfre's homestead.

The hut, the livestock shelter, even the paddock fence, and a few of the surrounding trees were all ablaze—they could feel the heat from the massive fire as it radiated up the hillside.

For a moment, neither of them moved as they processed what they were witnessing.

"Osric! My home!"

HEART OF THE WILD GODS

Then suddenly she gasped, "Eorðe protect me—Epona! She was in the paddock!"

Before Osric had a chance to say anything, Æfre launched herself from the back of the horse.

"Æfre, no!"

He twisted around in an attempt to grab her, but she had already hit the ground running and was flying downhill towards the fire.

"Epona!"

"Æfre, stop!"

Osric leapt from the saddle, tossing the reins around a tree branch. He sprinted after her, catching up with her a little more than halfway down the slope. He hooked an arm around her waist and dragged her to the ground.

"Æfre stop! It's not safe!"

"Let me go! Osric, she's in there! Osric!"

Æfre thrashed and fought against him with all of her might, but Osric held fast.

"Æfre! Jarl Torvald has Epona! Æfre stop! Jarl Torvald has her!"

Æfre continued to fight for another moment until what he had said sank in, and she finally went still.

Osric sat up, cradling her shoulders, turning her face to his. "Æfre. Look at me. She's not in there. Jarl Torvald has her. Epona's at the camp. She's safe."

Æfre was ashen-faced, her eyes hollow. She nodded almost imperceptibly, then turned to face the fire.

"What have they done?" she muttered, silent tears streaking her dirt-stained face as she knelt, clutching the earth.

Osric eased his grip, resting one hand on her shoulder. She didn't move a muscle as the fire roared below, devouring thatch, timber planks, and every silent memory within them.

Shouts rang out—Norse. Men scrambled at the edges of the blaze, some hacking down burning wood with their axes, others dashing the flames with water from the creek in whatever they could carry it with. Weapons and shields lay discarded on the ground all around them.

The two of them remained there, rooted to the spot as they watched the last material ties Æfre had to Wōdenléah get consumed by the blaze, the place of her birth reduced to nothing more than embers and ash.

Æfre became aware of a shadow kneeling before her—Harald the woodcarver. His face was smoke-smudged, exhausted. He gave Osric a solemn, knowing nod, then turned to her.

"Æfre," he said, "I am sorry. We saw it from the road, but—"

He stopped, eyes lifting to a point in the distance behind her.

Torvald Ironsight sat atop his black horse on the crest of the hill, the beast foaming at the bit from the run. Behind him rode Bjørn and Svend. The chieftain dismounted, eyes fixed on the burning homestead. A few quick words passed between them before Svend rode on towards the camp. Bjørn followed Torvald down the slope.

Harald glanced again at Osric, giving him a slight nod of the head as he indicated the Jarl approaching them.

Æfre felt as if she were crouching at the end of a long, dark tunnel. The men's voices—Torvald's, Harald's, Osric's—they all drifted past her like a scop's tale told around a hearth. None of it felt real. She clung to the idea that once the story was finished, she might rise and walk away from the spot where she crouched, everything in her world having returned to the way it had been

She stayed still, rooted in place by the memories that dwelt in the places she was watching disappear before her eyes. The creek behind the pasture. The birch she used to climb. The scent of thatch and her herb garden in summer. As long as she didn't move—if he stayed right where she was, motionless and glued to the spot—she could hold the place in her mind, untouched. This last piece of her life in Wōdenléah could not be swept out from under her like an errant feather suddenly freed from underneath a boot.

She did not know how much time had passed when she felt a pair of strong arms under her own.

"Æfre, you must stand. Dawn is near. We must go."

Osric's voice.

Æfre stood, but couldn't turn away.

"Come," he urged gently, "Æfre, please."

She turned and faced Osric, then turned towards Torvald, in turn looking directly at both men without really seeing either one of them. Neither man spoke.

Osric wrapped an arm around her, guiding her gently as the two of them turned and walked slowly back up the hill, toward the great horse, which still stood dutifully where Osric had barely tethered it.

Torvald stepped aside and allowed them to pass, dropping his head respectfully, as one might at a funeral procession, peering up at Æfre as she passed.

Æfre looked at Torvald, and saw a look behind his eyes that she had never seen before—a helplessness that neither sword nor strategy could mend.

Osric guided Æfre back up the hill, with Torvald following them at a respectful distance. At the top, Osric mounted and gave Torvald a nod. The jarl helped Æfre up behind him.

As the three of them rode on towards the trading camp, Æfre looked back a final time at the remains of her homestead, once her entire world, as it sank behind the rise.

48

Aesce ⚔ Ashes

"That's it, Lord Wulfric—we're near done now!"

Wulfric let out a breath and drove his shovel deep into the mound of damp earth before him. His shoulders ached, his tunic clung wet and heavy with sweat and ash, and his arms were streaked with the stinging mix of mud, smoke, and pitch from the fire that had, as was being told, unexpectedly broken out at the bishop's brew hut.

Cenric shouted encouragement to the others, his voice hoarse from the long, arduous night. Around them, the brew hut had dwindled to smoke and hissing embers—little more than a blackened shell—one that contained the remains of the two unfortunate souls who had tragically lost their lives in the blaze.

The tale whispered among the gathering crowd was already beginning to take shape. After the skirmish on the road—a simple misunderstanding that ended on good terms—Bishop Æthelwod had returned to the brew hut where Æfre was being held, intent on checking his most recent batch of mead. He surely must have kicked over his lantern, or perhaps mishandled a torch, trapping himself behind a wall of flame. And of course poor Æfre—the healer locked away, asleep at the far end of the hut—she'd had no chance at all.

At least, that's how Cwenhild spun it as she stood wiping away her tears at the center of the group of onlookers, watching her husband extinguish the last of the flames while she threaded together a tapestry of reality and myth with such practiced expertise it would have been impossible for anyone to find the seam.

Wulfric found himself having to turn his gaze downwards at his tunic several times to mask his awe at Cwenhild's deft retelling of events.

The fire had ignited quickly and burned extremely hot, taking the thatched roof and pitch-coated joints down in mere minutes, just as Jarl Torvald had said it would.

But they had held it. The soil-and-manure mix they'd gathered had smothered it before the resin had a chance to reignite and spread. The church and residence—the nearest structures to the blaze- still stood, as did the many boxes of mead, which had been swiftly relocated, stacked neatly in a corner of the stable.

The plan had been a risky one, but the danger was now behind them. All that was left was the grim task of recovering the departed, what little was likely left of them.

Wulfric noticed that Cenric, too, had paused—his shovel idle in his hand as he surveyed the smoldering ruin. Wulfric stepped closer and spoke low.

"Cenric. It's in hand now. Take yourself to the camp—there's time still. Take Cwenhild with you. Go be with her while you still can."

Cenric stopped in his tracks, gratitude washing over him.

"You're sure, Lord?"

"Of course I'm sure! Fetch Cwenhild and go. Alaric, Godwin, and I will see to the rest." Wulfric smiled and waved him off. "Go! Quickly! The day is already upon us. You can tell Osric and the Jarl how we've fared."

Wulfric watched as Cenric approached his sobbing wife, putting an arm around her and whispering something in her ear before nodding graciously at the gathered crowd and guiding her gently, but swiftly away, towards the stable.

Wulfric looked over at Alaric and Godwin, giving the men a knowing nod before rolling his neck and setting his boot against the shovel again.

HEART OF THE WILD GODS

There was still work to do.

49

Cyre ⚔ Choice

"Is that how they started it?"

The sound of Osric's voice brought Æfre out of the thick fog she had withdrawn into for what remained of the journey, and she slowly opened her eyes to find they had already arrived at the camp and were passing what appeared to be the remains of a burned-out hut. The acrid smell of scorched timber and ash still hung heavily in the air, stinging her eyes as they plodded along..

"It is—" replied Torvald, "one of our food stores."

Osric said nothing further, but Æfre felt his hand reach back and rest on her knee, his thumb gently moving back and forth—like he was making sure she wouldn't disappear.

After the chaos of the fire at her homestead, they were all depleted and had made the rest of the journey at a walk. But this time the horse's rolling gait no longer threatened to lull Æfre to sleep. She remained awake yet distant—stunned and hollow after watching the only home she'd ever known burn to the ground.

"Here," Torvald said, breaking the silence as he gestured to the left. "Epona is here."

Æfre slowly raised her head and looked in the direction the chieftain had indicated. To her left stretched a vast paddock, fenced with stout split-rail timber. A few well-kept horses grazed beneath a sloping shelter. With them stood Epona—her pale dappled coat marking her out immediately among the throng of bay and black coated beasts. The horses all stood around a tall, conical hayrick, tearing themselves mouthfuls and chewing methodically, their ears flicking lazily in the early morning cold.

Torvald whistled lightly as they neared, and Epona's grey head shot up, ears pricked and attentive.

"Æfre," Osric said gently, coaxing her back into the moment. "Look—there's Epona."

He nudged their mount closer to the paddock fence, and Epona came sauntering over, stretching her neck out over the fence and nibbling at Æfre's leg. Through her exhaustion, Æfre felt herself smile at the warmth of the mare's sweet grassy breath on her leg—an equine sigh of relief at a vow kept.

Æfre laid her hand on her mare's forehead, but did not speak.

The other horses suddenly raised their heads, their ears flicking forward like blades as they assessed a threat posed by a new sound.

"Jarl Torvald! Lord Osric!"

Eadgar suddenly appeared from the stalls, his tone urgent. He began running towards them, scattering the horses at the hayrick. Epona startled, widening her stance and snorting like a dragon, but she held her ground.

"Slow down, boy! You're spooking the herd!" Torvald barked.

Eadgar instantly slowed, faltering as he cast a sheepish glance at the horses he'd spooked. He climbed over the fence rail, casting a furtive glance at Æfre, who was still focused on Epona and seemed not to notice him.

"I told you to get to your bed," Torvald said sternly.

"I did." Eadgar insisted, breathless, "I mean I was, but..."

"But, what? If you haven't defied me, you have no reason to worry. Speak plain!"

Eadgar stepped closer and beckoned Torvald to lean down. The jarl did, and the boy whispered into his ear. When he pulled back, Torvald's jaw had set with a stern expression.

"You're sure, Edgar?"

"I am, Jarl Torvald."

"Very well. Finish what you were doing here and get yourself to the hall—you'll speak to the thegn yourself."

Eadgar gave a brief nod, cast a worried glance at Osric, and turned and ran back to the barn. Halfway across the paddock, he remembered himself, and with another sheepish glance at the horses he'd scattered, slowed to a walk.

"He knows who burned Æfre's home," Torvald said as he drew up beside them, still watching Eadgar as he disappeared back into the stalls.

"I think I have a pretty good idea of who that might be," Osric said, his hand tightening on Æfre's leg with a reassuring squeeze as he urged the horse back into a walk.

"Já, well. The boy should tell you himself." Torvald said, "He's nervous—thinks you'll tell the bishop he's here. He doesn't want to go back to an orphanage."

Osric nodded silently, riding on without looking at Torvald. A moment of silence stretched between them before he responded.

"It's unlikely I'll tell the bishop," Osric said flatly, casting a sideways glance at Torvald.

"Já. Unlikely."

Æfre closed her eyes, leaning her head against Osric's back as the men's voices drifted once again—they seemed far off, yet she somehow heard every word.

* * *

Torvald was glad to see Svend had already cleared the camp's hall of its occupants by the time the three of them clamored in, their footsteps thick with fatigue, crunching the soot-stained rushes spread across the earthen floor as they shuffled over to the hearth.

Osric and Æfre collapsed onto the bench closest to the hearth, both of them dirt-streaked and exhausted. Æfre laid her head on Osric's shoulder, closed her eyes, pulled her knees in close, and drew her arms around herself as if trying to make herself small enough to disappear entirely.

Osric shifted slightly on the bench, throwing a protective arm around her and murmuring something into her ear before pressing his lips against her forehead.

Torvald watched them as he pulled up another bench across from them, feeling like he was invading their privacy, even though they were all sitting in *his* hall, mere feet from his own quarters. His gut tightened at the thought of the harsh finality of the conversation the two of them were about to have, and he paused for a moment, allowing the silence of the hall to remain unbroken for just a bit longer.

"Jarl," Svend said softly behind him.

Torvald turned to see Svend with three horns of ale.

"Þakk, Svend." Torvald passed two of the ale horns over to Osric.

"Æfre," Osric said softly, gently displacing her as he reached for the ale horns.

Æfre sat up, blinking her eyes and shaking her head as if trying to see clearly through a thick fog.

"Jarl Torvald, I'm sorry. Thank you." She took the ale horn from Osric and sat up, taking a deep draught, closing her eyes as she swallowed and taking a deep breath—steeling herself for whatever might come next.

"You owe no apology, Æfre." Torvald said, "All that has happened to lead us here—none of it is your fault." Torvald gazed at Æfre intently, wanting to be certain she was taking in what he was saying. The woman had been through a great deal in a relatively short period, and she appeared to be nearing her limit. It felt like a gut punch to Torvald to have to potentially deal her the final blow.

"It is you, Æfre, who has suffered the most in all of this," Torvald said plainly.

Osric nodded silently, took a deep breath, and closed his eyes, letting his head drop.

Torvald marked Osric's reaction—the thegn was visibly feeling

HEART OF THE WILD GODS

the full weight of responsibility for his part in the doomed relationship—for inadvertently providing Æthelwod the leverage he needed, and perhaps a multitude of other reasons that may or may not have contributed to the situation they now found themselves in. Torvald didn't know Osric well, but he knew enough to know that it would be impossible for him to ignore the part he'd played in all that had transpired.

"Æfre," Torvald continued gently, "everyone here has been concerned for your safety for some time now. Tonight was a great loss, and we are truly sorry."

"Thank you," Æfre said in a near-whisper, though she didn't, perhaps couldn't, look directly at him.

"Æfre," Osric added gently, "Æthelwod may no longer be able to strangle the burh with his schemes, but the lies he planted about you—those lies have only grown with time. They continue to live on in many of these people."

"Yes," Æfre said softly, tears now brimming.

"Æfre," Torvald said gently, "I believe I can help you."

After a moment, Æfre finally raised a tear-streaked face to the chieftain, but said nothing.

"There is a settlement in Styrvik, in Danelaw East Anglia, where the Thames meets the sea." Torvald paused, trying to read her reaction before continuing, "It's where I was before I took over this camp."

Torvald paused again, glancing over at Osric, who met his gaze before turning his attention back to Æfre, his hand absentmindedly running up and down the back of her arm—both men anxious about how she might respond.

"I still have a small homestead in Styrvik, and I can offer that home to you, Æfre, for as long as you need or wish to stay." Torvald paused, and when no response came, continued. The settlement would welcome a healer of your experience, and there, you would be safe—you would be under my protection."

Æfre shut her eyes and took a deep breath, wiping the tears that had spilled down her cheeks with her sleeve and leaving a dirty streak across her face. She looked at Osric, who returned her gaze with a fixed, earnest look as he gently reached out and rubbed the new dirt from her face with his thumb.

"What I'm saying, Æfre," Torvald continued, "is that in Styrvik, you could live freely—as you once did here. I would ensure that"

"I don't see that I really have much of a choice now," Æfre said softly, as if to herself.

"We will not compel you to do anything against your will, Æfre," Osric said gently.

"Osric is right," Torvald said. "It is entirely your choice. But whatever you choose, it must happen tonight. There is a supply run leaving very soon, and this time of year we keep a strict timeline to meet estuary tides."

Torvald watched Æfre intently as Osric whispered something in her ear, and she nodded. "I can give the two of you a moment," the chieftain said. He moved to stand, but faltered as the sudden movement caused the thumping pain in his head to return.

Æfre's head snapped around, her healer's instincts once piqued, bringing her back fully into the present.

"Jarl, you must let me see to that wound."

"The wound will be fine, Æfre, it can wait." He waved her off dismissively and swallowed hard against a surge of nausea, rubbing his eyes and breathing deeply as he willed it to pass.

Æfre narrowed her eyes, studying him for a moment, then huffed—rising from the bench, she handed her ale horn to Osric and walked over to Torvald, positioning herself behind him as she looked down at his wound.

"This is not the type of wound you put off, Jarl Torvald. Men have lost their lives from lesser injuries allowed to fester."

Æfre tilted her head and wiped what remained of the tears that had been streaming down her face onto the upper part of her sleeve, then placed a hand lightly on either side of Torvald's head, her thumbs resting on his cheeks as she gently angled his head to get a better look.

"Tilt your head down, Jarl," Æfre said in a voice that brooked no argument.

Torvald, unaccustomed to being touched without invitation, instinctively recoiled from Æfre's touch, unsure whether it was an act of disrespect, intimacy, or impertinence.

"Please," Æfre said more softly, feeling his resistance.

Torvald furrowed his brow and looked over at Osric for help, who met his gaze with his eyes wide and brows raised—his look a clear, unspoken message.

It'll be much easier if you just do what she says, my friend.

"þrályndr [*obstinate*]," Torvald mumbled under his breath, dropping his chin with a groan and pinching the bridge of his nose as he felt another surge of pain and nausea wash over him.

"I heard that, Jarl." Æfre shot back smoothly in Norse.

Osric suppressed a grin and shook his head slowly at Torvald.

Let it happen. It's out of your hands.

Torvald was conscious of the time—they really needed to leave soon to make their supply timeline, and equally, he wanted to get Æfre out of Wōdenléah under as little scrutiny as possible. But in his current state, the idea of a four or five-day journey made his stomach churn, and he told himself that giving the woman a minute to work her craft wouldn't completely derail them.

"Right there—good, thank you," Æfre said, examining the wound. "This is quite deep—it will require cleaning and a stitch or two. You're having headaches?"

"Já."

She moved around to face him and lifted his chin with two fingers, looking directly into his eyes. Her emerald gaze was intense, and it made Torvald feel as though she could see directly into the inner workings of his mind — perhaps even read his thoughts.

"Are the headaches constant? Or does the pain come and go?" She used her thumbs to gently lift both of his eyelids.

"It... comes and goes," Torald said, now fully resigned to whatever process was currently underway.

"Do you feel unsteady? Is your stomach unwell?"

"Já, a little."

"Osric, would you put a pot of water on the hearth to boil, and I—" Æfre trailed off.

"Pots are kept in back, Lord Osric, behind the partition—on the left." Svend chimed in from his seat a few benches back.

"What is it, Æfre?" Osric asked, returning from the back of the hall with a few mid-sized pots.

"I've forgotten—I...I have no supplies." Æfre said softly, "No herbs, no tools...the fire, I—"

"Ah." Torvald interrupted, looking up from holding his head in his hands.

"I've got it, Jarl," Svend said, popping up from the bench he'd settled on. "You stay where you are. Æfre, will you follow me outside for a moment, please? There's something you should see."

"Svend, I'm afraid I really must—"

"Æfre, Osric interrupted, "go with Svend. It'll take but a moment."

Confused, Æfre cast one last worried glance at Torvald but followed.

"Thank you, Æfre," Svend said as he held the door to the hall open for her, "this will be quick, I promise you. Follow me."

* * *

HEART OF THE WILD GODS

Outside the hall, Svend took a sharp right just outside the door and walked along the side of the hall until they came to a wagon, hidden in the shadows towards the back end of the hall.

"Come, Æfre," he said as he pulled back the heavy woolen cover that was concealing the wagon's contents. "You will surely find something of use in here."

Confused at what they were doing out there, Æfre nonetheless stepped forward, hugging herself against the cold as she peered into the wagon.

"What am I meant to be looking for?" she asked, not fully processing what she was looking at. Svend waited patiently as she continued to scan the contents of the wagon—and suddenly, items began to look familiar. It wasn't, however, until Æfre laid eyes on the neatly folded moss green cloak with the silver brooch pinned to it that it registered—she was looking at all of her own belongings."

"Is this—" her gaze snapped over to Svend.

"Your belongings, Æfre, yes." Svend replied with a gentle smile, "Well, most of them."

Æfre felt herself overcome with emotion at seeing all of the material things she had assumed were lost—each of them a representation of an aspect of the life she thought she had just witnessed go up in flames.

She covered her mouth and stifled a sob while she looked upon what remained of her life in Wōdenléah, all packed into the back of the same supply wagon that she'd watched pass her homestead every day.

"How?" She rasped, looking at Svend incredulously, fresh tears streaking her face as she ran her hand against the carved headboard of the bed her father had made for her mother.

"Jarl Torvald," Svend said softly. "He took a few of the men and emptied your hut not long after we heard you were taken."

"He knew?" Æfre asked.

"No Æfre," Svend mused, "None of us really knew what was coming, only that it was clear something was bound to happen at some point. Jarl Torvald's intuition is a peculiar riddle that even the Gods themselves choose to stay silent on. But I'm afraid now we must make haste." Svend climbed up onto the wagon.

"Tell me what you need," he said. "Describe it if you must, and I'll help find it."

Æfre quickly pointed out her bag of supplies and described her seax to Svend, who searched for it while she rummaged through a wooden box filled with her clay jars of dried herbs, plucking out a few essentials. Svend finally found the sheathed seax in one of the boxes, admiring its carved handle before handing it over to Æfre.

"That's it, Svend, thank you." She said, reattaching it to her belt and reaching into the wagon and picking up her cloak before the two of them headed back inside.

* * *

Torvald and Osric sat huddled together, immersed in deep, quiet conversation, when Æfre and Svend returned to the hall. Eadgar had joined them too—he was sitting at the end of his own bench, happily working on a piece of flatbread piled high with dried fish and cheese.

"Jarl Torvald," Æfre said softly, still drying her eyes with her sleeve. She stopped beside Osric, the disbelief still raw on her face. "I have no words strong enough to express my gratitude for retrieving my belongings."

Torvald met her gaze with a stoic nod, and she felt his eyes, as well as Osric's, press against her, weighing whether to ask if she'd made a decision yet.

Looked from one man to the other, her eyes coming to rest on Eadgar.

"It was the thatcher, Aelf, wasn't it? I thought I saw him at the side of the road. It was he who burned my home?"

"Yes," Osric said, his expression pained. "He must have slipped from the formation. We never knew he didn't return with us. I will ensure that his actions do not go unanswered, Æfre, I promise you."

Æfre gave a single nod but said nothing further, instead turning to her herbs. The pot of water that Osric had set over the hearth steamed furiously, and she scavenged a few jugs and ladled some of the boiling water into them. A handful of dried leaves hissed as they hit the surface, and the sharp, bitter scent of feverfew mixed with the sweetness of chamomile and yarrow quickly filled the hall. She moved in silence, preparing her tools.

No one spoke—the quiet hanging low above them like the sag of old thatch threatening collapse.

Æfre retrieved her ale horn from Osric and drained the dregs from it, rinsing the horn with boiled water. She poured a measure of the steeping infusion into the horn, then paused for a moment before turning back to face the men.

She crossed to Torvald. The Jarl sat with his elbows resting on his knees, eyes closed, fingers pinching the bridge of his nose as though he was afraid that releasing it would cause all of his thoughts to spill out upon the earthen floor.

"Jarl Torvald," she said.

He opened his eyes and straightened.

"Drink this," she said, offering the horn. "It will ease the pain in your head and settle your stomach. I must clean that wound."

Torvald glanced at the horn, then at her, searching her face for an answer, but she kept herself hidden. No promise. No hint.

Æfre reached down, took the ale horn from Torvald's hand, and replaced it with the horn full of herbal infusion.

"This will serve you better than ale in this moment."

Without waiting for a reply, she turned briskly and walked toward the hearth, draining the last of his ale in one pull as she moved.

"I can feel the pair of you looking at me," she said after a pause, her voice low—matter-of-fact. "You want an answer. Well, now you shall have it."

"Jarl Torvald," she said, turning to face him. "I accept your generous offer. I will go to Styrvik."

A breath left Osric like a man struck in the chest. He bowed his head, shoulders heavy with something more than weariness. Æfre looked over at him and saw relief—and the profound grief beneath it. They both knew this to be the final nail in a door that they would not be able to reopen.

"That gladdens me," said Torvald. "But we must leave very soon."

Torvald glanced up and subtly nodded toward Svend, who had already risen and was securing his cloak, moving towards the door with silent purpose.

Æfre gathered her supplies and settled herself behind the jarl's bench. "Then we'd best see to that wound," she said, threading her bone stitching needle.

"This will be uncomfortable, it's been given a chance to start closing," she warned, " and I do not wish to risk giving you herbs that dull the mind while this injury is not yet a day old."

"I've endured worse," Torvald said.

"Very well," she murmured, "I'll work quickly."

Æfre cleaned the wound swiftly, her fingers moving with purpose even as a mounting dread coiled in her chest—the impending timeline of the journey she'd just agreed to hanging above them like a burgeoning storm. Every action she completed, every stitch she placed brought her closer to departure, closer to the moment she would leave Osric—leave everything else he'd ever known.

She fought a futile battle against the tears that stung her eyes, and they began to spill down her cheeks as she leaned over the chieftain. Every time she glanced up, she found Osric watching her. He was silent, unmoving as he leaned forward on the edge of his bench, elbow on his knee, chin in his hand. His thumb stroked the edge of his beard absently, the half-full ale horn dangling forgotten in his other hand. The look in his eyes pierced straight through her like a hot iron—it was as if he was trying to memorize her every feature.

She felt Torvald tense beneath her hands as she began to stitch the deeper part of his wound. His jaw tightened, his breath caught—yet he said nothing.

"Forgive me," she muttered quietly in Norse, her voice a barely audible croak over the crackle of the hearth. She turned her head and wiped her cheek against her shoulder. "Nearly done, Jarl."

She glanced up at Osric again, and again he instantly locked eyes with her. He wore a faint smile—a wistful one that glinted with a grief that mirrored her own.

This cannot be how we were meant to part.

A fresh bout of tears began to flow, and she lowered her face to her shoulder again so they wouldn't fall onto Torvald's wounded head.

"Last one," Æfre rasped, as she looped the final stitch, her hand shaking.

"I'll give the two of you a few moments after this," Torvald said gently, expertly reading the room.

Osric gave a slight nod in return, eyes closing briefly in silent gratitude.

"Finished," Æfre said shakily, cutting the tail of the final stitch. She reached for the herbs she had prepared earlier, her fingers unsteady as she folded them into clean linen to create a poultice.

"Jarl, your hand—" she said softly, and pressed the bundle into Torvald's offered hand, then guided him to hold it against the stitched wound while she wrapped a clean strip of cloth around his head to keep it in place.

"This can come off in a day," she said as she busied herself cleaning and repacking her tools, "once the wound has had time to settle."

Torvald stood and faced her, but she could not look at him for fear she would lose what little remained of her frayed composure.

"I'll wait outside. Take a few moments," he mumbled.

Æfre nodded, but still did not look at him.

Torvald looked over at Osric and nodded, then stepped toward the door, pausing at the threshold.

"Thank you, Æfre," he said without turning.

Then, he disappeared through the door into the pale light of morning.

As soon as Torvald was gone, Osric was on his feet, moving towards Æfre. He flung the dregs of his ale into the hearth where they hissed and spat, the horn falling to the rush-strewn floor. He crossed the room in long, unsteady strides and scooped up Æfre in his arms before she could turn to face him.

Æfre had been standing stiffly, distracting herself with her tools and herbs, but the moment she felt Osric's embrace, her remaining resolve abandoned her. Like a waterskin slashed by a careless blade, she felt as if all that had been holding her together suddenly spilled out onto the floor and was immediately lost.

Her knees buckled beneath her, and together they sank—slowly, heavily, to the floor; a single branch finally bent beyond recovery by the weight of a shared burden they could no longer bear.

Osric buried his face into the crook of her neck as she sobbed—her sorrow finally overtaking her.

"May God forgive me, Æfre," he muttered desperately, "I have utterly failed you—I did not stop it, and I should have. I should have done so much more, fought harder..."

Osric cupped her face in his hands the way he had so many times before—a familiar and reverent ritual. He kissed her, a deep and sorrowful kiss, trying desperately to anchor himself to her—lingering as if it might somehow stop time.

A moment passed. Or perhaps it was several—Æfre couldn't tell which. She was desperate to cling to every aspect of this moment. She wanted to memorize the smell of hearth smoke mixed with the grassy freshness of the rushes covering the floor that crunched underfoot. She tried to memorize the rustle of wool against linen that always accompanied their closeness—the way the dust collected in the quilted seams of his tunic, the striking, azure blue of his eyes, and the way his beard was a shade lighter at its center and adorably flecked with grey at the sides.

When at last they separated, it was Æfre who broke the silence.

"Æthelwod was determined," she said quietly, "he was never going to stop."

"No," Osric replied flatly, his expression stricken. He shifted gently so Æfre could rest her head against his chest, just as they had the night he had found her wandering the forest.

"You will always have a place here," he whispered in her ear. "Your family land, your homestead—it will always be yours to claim. I will ensure that it stays so."

Æfre said nothing but pressed in closer to him, allowing the sounds of the hearth to fill the room until the sound of shuffling feet could be heard outside the door to the hall, breaking the spell.

They were out of time.

50

Langscip ⚔ Longship

Æfre felt the grinding of the wagon's wheels deep in her belly as they rumbled down the sloping road, disturbing the early morning quiet with each jostle and jolt of the wooden frame. Svend swayed in the driver's seat as he guided the team along the well-worn track towards the camp's port. The scent of smoke and oakum drifted up, mingling with the damp smell of the Thames, familiar things that seemed suddenly foreign on this morning.

She sat pressed against Osric, his arm firm around her shoulders as if protecting her against the grim silence that seemed to underscore the impending permanence of their separation.

They crested the hill and began the final descent to the port below. It was alive with activity—a stark contrast to the camp's relative stillness after the so-called rebellion.

Men hauled bundles of textiles onto the longships as the wind snapped and tore at the tent set up to keep the cargo dry. Nearby, a handful of guards warmed themselves over a fire while they shared a stack of flatbread.

Æfre pulled her cloak tighter, her fingers going white with the cold. Her gaze fell upon two great longships that bobbed gently with the motion of the Thames, their carved, snarling prows staring into the endless grey of the flat, winter sky.

The sight of those fantastic carved beasts stirred memories of her father's tools, which had rendered many such creatures, the exact figures that featured in the tales he told her as a child about the ship that bore him across the sea to a new, promising land. Yet, those same snarling beasts had also adorned the ships that had brought with them an endless stream of violence, destruction, and heartbreak. And now, such a ship was supposedly to be her salvation.

She did not entirely believe it.

"Æfre." Osric's voice was raw, drew her gently back into the moment.

The wagon had stopped. He was no longer seated beside her. He stood on the ground, reaching up with one outstretched hand to help her down.

For as long as the gods willed, this would be the last time her feet touched Wessex soil.

A feeling of panic surged through her as images flashed in her mind—her favorite hunting and fishing spots along the river, the cold creek behind the ashes of her home. Osric's smile by her hearthlight. His arms. His voice.

Her panic surged until she felt like she couldn't breathe or move.

She looked down at Wōdenléah's thegn and saw the grief written plainly on his face—the recognition of her panic.

Osric's expression shifted, clearly recognizing the rising storm within her. His voice dropped to little more than a whisper.

"Come."

Æfre looked up to the wagon's front, where Svend had turned in his seat, his expression one of pure compassion.

"Our paths will cross again, Æfre," he said, giving her hand a firm squeeze. "That, I promise you. Go now, and go safe. Jarl Torvald will see to it."

Æfre could not answer, but nodded, squeezed Svend's hand once, then turned back to Osric, whose hand was still extended.

She took it, climbing down, her legs trembling beneath her. Once on the ground, she fell into his arms, and he planted a firm, lingering kiss on her forehead as she clung to him like a woman drowning. With his arm around her shoulders, they began the slow walk towards the longship.

HEART OF THE WILD GODS

As they stepped onto the pier, Torvald appeared, seemingly materializing from out of nowhere, and stepped onto the longship. He was bundled against the cold, in a cloak with a fur mantle and a woolen cap pulled down over his bandaged head, obscuring his injury. He extended a hand to Æfre to help her aboard when the sounds of a commotion from just up the hill interrupted them.

"Wait!!" A woman's voice shrieked, cutting through the sounds of the port. "Æfre! Osric! Wait!"

A wagon barreled down the hill, approaching quickly.

Jarl Torvald's head snapped towards the sound, and the warriors that had been warming themselves by the fire were instantly on their feet, shields lifted and steel drawn as they moved to intercept the interloper.

Osric squinted at the approaching wagon that was now completely blocked by Torvald's warriors.

"It's Cenric," he said under his breath before realizing he needed to make their identity known before one of the warriors got a blade into one of them.

"Jarl Torvald! It's Cenric. Cenric and his wife Cwenhild—they've come to say farewell to Æfre!"

Torvald looked at Osric suspiciously for a moment, then saw for himself as he recognized Cenric.

"Hold your swords!" Torvald bellowed.

The warriors faltered, but remained standing with weapons at the ready.

"Hold your swords, let them pass!" Torvald repeated, and the warriors parted, re-sheathing their swords as they retreated.

The moment there was an opening, Cwenhild burst through, practically pushing the massive warriors out of the way, her skirts gathered in her fist as she huffed and puffed onto the pier, her face flushed with exertion and emotion.

"Æfre!" she cried, her voice cracking. "Oh, Æfre—merciful

God, we made it in time!"

Æfre broke from Osric and ran to meet her, and the two women embraced tightly at the end of the pier. Cwenhild immediately burst into tears.

"Oh Æfre!" Cwenhild sobbed; "I'll miss you more than words can hold, but we're both just so glad that you will be safe, dear girl—away from all that has befallen you!"

Æfre, overcome, managed only to nod and hold on tighter.

"Now, dear girl," Cwenhild whispered earnestly into her ear, "all will be well. You'll see. It must be." Cwenhild said, as if willing it to be so.

I always said, Æfre," came Cenric's voice as he approached the pair, "you are, and shall ever be one of our own."

Æfre and Cwenhild drew Cenric into their embrace, and the three of them huddled together one last time.

"Lord Osric has already given his word—he will help us write you, so this is not a farewell, Æfre. Not truly." Cwenhild said.

The three of them huddled together a few moments longer, whispering to each other in these final moments until Æfre heard the sound of Osric gently clearing his throat behind them. She looked up, and both Osric and Torvald were looking at her. Waiting

It was time to leave.

She squeezed the hands of Cenric and Cwenhild, then rejoined Osric. He slid his arm around her shoulders once more and walked her all the way to the side of the longship, where Torvald stood waiting.

Torvald gave Osric a look, then turned away slightly, offering them a moment.

Osric did not waste the offer—he grabbed Æfre and pulled her in, kissing her with such soul-scarring intensity that for a moment, the whole world fell silent.

HEART OF THE WILD GODS

In that moment, it was just the two of them alone. There was no longship, so bitter winter wind, no pressing timeline—just the quiet airlessness of unspoken truths, much like that night she'd sought refuge in the barn.

Æfre dared not move, striving to hold on to the kiss indefinitely. She wanted it to brand her soul so it would never fade. She willed every detail of the moment into her heart; every warmth, smell, and texture preserved and imprinted within her that she might always have this inner sanctuary to retreat to.

Behind them, the warriors clambered aboard the longship, some grinning, curious, and elbowing one another at the spectacle—until a cold, steely glance from their chieftain struck them silent.

Osric finally stepped back, still holding Æfre's face in his hands.

"Remember," he said, voice low. "Your homestead. It's your land. It always will be."

Torvald turned back to face the pair of them, and their time was up.

Still holding Æfre's face, Osric pressed his forehead against hers for the last time.

"I will always love you, Æfre," he murmured.

"I love you, Osric," Æfre whispered, forcing herself to turn from him as she faced Torvald, who stood waiting, hand outstretched.

She took the chieftain's hand and stepped aboard the longship.

Torvald guided her to a cleared spot near the prow—little more than a pile of furs lashed down with cord—but said nothing when she chose instead to stand at the ship's side, unblinking, never taking her eyes off of Osric.

"To the oars!" Torvald barked.

At once, warriors and traders moved to settle into their places.

The oars rose, shafts held upright as the bitter wind cut across the deck, tinged with the smell of damp. From somewhere ashore, the sorrowful signal horn sounded, rolling over the mist and water in an aching lament.

"Cast off the ropes!"

As the ropes fell away, Æfre felt the longship shift beneath her as it caught the first tugs of current in the Thames.

"Push off!"

The horn sounded again as the oars on the landward side of the longship were used to push away from the pier. Æfre felt the knot in her stomach tighten as they drifted away from the camp.

"Ready to row!" Torvald commanded, his voice sounded closer to her this time, and she felt his broad hand glance reassuringly against her shoulder as he passed behind where she stood, pausing briefly to peer over the side at the longship's hull before draping a blanket over her shoulders.

Æfre never moved, nor did she take her eyes off the spot where Osric stood as the longship moved smoothly away. The signal horn sounded again, and she strained hard against the flat winter light. She was desperate to keep him in her sights, yet with every breath she took, he grew smaller—first he was the man she loved, then a familiar blurred shadow, then just a small russet speck standing on a faraway pier.

The water swished with the rhythm of the oars as the longship began to round the first bend in the river. What remained of the camp—the shouts of men, the scent of smoke and oakum—it had all but disappeared now, yet Æfre stood, fixed to the spot as she watched her small russet speck disappear behind the curve of the bleak winter shoreline.

* * *

Epilogue

Upon this last day of December, in the year of our Lord 881, Osric, Thegn of Wōdenléah, sends greeting to Lord Alfred, King of the Saxons, and to his trusted counsellor, Lord Odda of Devon. With this pledge of service and friendship, I pray that Our Lord grant you both health and prosperity in the years to come.

I must first bid you tidings of a grave misunderstanding that befell some nights past between Bishop Æthelwod of Wōdenléah and the leaders of the trading camp of Jarl Torvald Ironsight.

By the mispassing of false word regarding the course of trade goods, tempers flared betwixt men of Wōdenléah and in the camp. Believing it to be an uprising, Bishop Æthelwod did raise the fyrd to arms.

In short time, the truth was made plain, and no blood was shed, nor lasting ill will borne on either side.

Yet mischance did swiftly follow on. That same night, upon returning to his residence, Bishop Æthelwod entered his mead-store, where it is thought he mishandled his lantern, as flames did quickly take hold, tragically trapping the bishop within. This very day we have gathered his remains, along with a second set of remains belonging to the unfortunate healing-woman Æfre, who at the hour of the fire was confined there whilst she awaited the witenagemot. Both shall be laid to rest and given due honor in keeping with their station.

It is with thanks to Almighty God that we pray this kingdom and all in it may pass through this, and any such further trials in peace and unity, as one people.

In all humility, ever your servant in Christ and in arms,

Osric, thegn of Wōdenléah

* * *

The flickering hearth light cast restless shadows across King Alfred's face as they stood in the echoing magnificence of the hall. The king allowed his arm to fall, still holding the letter, before turning to Odda, his expression unreadable.

"I trust my lord has read this?"

"I have, Lord King," Odda replied with a brisk nod.

"Good." The King replied, moving towards the hearth, where he held the parchment over the flame until it caught, then held it at arm's length while both men watched it slowly blacken and curl. "We must inform Archbishop Æthelred[xxv]. Let him go to Wōdenléah for the rites. He and the thegn can discuss which priest of fresher wisdom and broader vision might be suitable for Wōdenléah's changing age."

"It shall be done, Lord King. I'll send a man at once." Odda bowed deferentially and left the hall.

King Alfred turned back towards the hearth, dropping the last, unburnt piece of the parchment into the fire, watching as it turned to ash.

A (Ridiculously Brief) Note About History

In the late 9th century, much of what we now know as England was under Viking control. The country had endured years of summertime Viking raids, eventually leading to a massive influx of emboldened invaders.

One such large influx landed on the shores of England in around 865 AD. They were a formidable force that came to be known as the Great Heathen Army. Numbering in the tens of thousands, they swiftly dismantled Saxon kingdoms and claimed the land as their own.

The once-powerful Saxon kingdoms of Mercia, East Anglia and Northumbria were eventually forced to cede their territory, resulting in a Viking stronghold stretching from north of present day York all the way to London. By 877, only the Kingdom of Wessex, the south and southwestern portion of England, remained under Saxon rule. The success of Wessex in repelling the Viking invaders was in no small part due to a determined resistance led by King Alfred (now often referred to as Alfred the Great), making Wessex the last unconquered Saxon kingdom.

However, in 878, the Danish Viking leader Guthrum's army struck Wessex. The Vikings overran much of the kingdom, and defeat appeared imminent. King Alfred sought refuge in the marshes of Athelney, in western England, near present-day Somerset. Within the protection of these wetlands, King Alfred regrouped, rallied his forces, and ultimately launched a decisive counterattack at the Battle of Edington. This Saxon victory compelled Guthrum and his forces to enter negotiations, marking a pivotal turning point in Alfred's resistance.

Negotiations led to an informal agreement known as the

Treaty of Wedmore, in which Guthrum agreed to be baptized as a Christian and begin withdrawing his army from Wessex, back to East Anglia where he would pronounce himself king.

This informal treaty was followed-up by the more established written agreement called the Treaty of Alfred and Guthrum, which defined borders between Viking and Saxon lands and laid the groundwork for coexistence between the two. Though sporadic uprisings still erupted, the treaty did create a temporary peace.

This marked the official recognition of The Danelaw; a Viking-governed region within England. While this treaty did not bring about the end of Saxon and Viking conflict, it drew a line that would shape the land for generations to come.

The Treaty of Alfred and Guthrum also ushered in a new era of trade in England, and Great Britain as a whole. In addition to formally recognizing The Danelaw, the treaty enabled the expansion of affluent trade networks between the Saxon and Viking regions, with a wide array of products such as textiles, exotic spices and agricultural products regularly changing hands. Trade routes along the rivers were especially significant; the shallow-bottom longships used by the Vikings were able to navigate far into the rivers to move large quantities of goods.

The legacy of Viking invasions in Britain is etched into the landscape, language, and culture even today. Ancient place names like York (from the Norse *Jorvik*), fire festivals in Shetland, and the continued uncovering of archaeological finds like burial ships and hoards of silver all pay homage to a time when Viking longships ruled the seas and their warriors shaped the course of British history.

HEART OF THE WILD GODS

Author's Notes

[i] A *leechbook* is a type of medical text from the Anglo Saxon period. The name stems from the Old English term *lǣ ċe,* meaning healer. Healers were also called "cunning folk" in the vernacular.

[ii] *Hǫrðaland* was a county located in the west of Norway, near Bergen. Today, that area is called the county of Vestland.

[iii] *Eorðe* (pron: ertha) is an ancient Goddess of the Earth and mother of all things, often invoked in old medieval English charms involving matters of fertility, particularly in agricultural communities where abundance was a matter of survival.

[iv] This chant is from passage CLXI of The Lacnunga, referred to as "For Delayed Childbirth." The Lacnunga is a collection of Saxon charms and remedies that were recorded by monks around the late 10th to 11th Century. This is the earliest written account of such charms, many of which date back to pre-Christian Saxon beliefs and therefore many that appear in text were the later, modified versions post-Christianization.

"For Delayed Childbirth" is perhaps a misleading title by modern standards; it originally referred to a woman struggling to conceive and carry a child to term. It has therefore been used slightly out of context here - mostly as a means of recognizing it as one of the very few Saxon charms that was written for and meant to be spoken by women.

[v] In the 9th Century, a *trencher* referred to a serving plate on which meals were served. The earliest versions of trenchers most likely used during this time period by laypeople were often hardened, day-old bread discs with food piled on top.

[vi] A *hare form* is a small depression in the grass where the hare rests during the day.

[vii] In 9th Century Norse culture, a *völva* was a female seer or shaman who usually also functioned as a community's healer. The Völva quite often lived

apart from social norms, and was considered the link between the physical and spiritual realms. She was well respected, and sometimes even feared by those in the community.

[viii] 9th Century *small ale* referred to a low alcohol beer that was meant to refresh and not intoxicate. it was often served in place of water, which was untreated and often unsafe to consume.

[ix] The *Vulgate* is the late 4th Century translation of the Bible that was widely in use in 9th century Saxon England. It was commissioned by Pope Damascus in 382, and its translation is attributed mainly to Saint Jerome.

[x] A *draugr* is a malevolent "undead" being with roots in Norse mythology (yep—zombies!), often associated with the guarding of burial mounds. Although there are varying depictions in various sagas, they often possess supernatural powers.

[xi] Skaði [*Skadi*] is a Norse Goddess associated with winter.

[xii] *Wicce* is an Old English word meaning "to practice sorcery", which eventually evolved into the word witch.

[xiii] A *pin beater* is a long, sharp tool (looks like an extra large needle) used in textile making on a loom. It is used to press the weft of the textile firmly into place while weaving.

[xiv] Bjørn's Saxon riddle is the famously ribald Riddle 44, an actual Anglo Saxon riddle borrowed from the Book of Exeter—a tenth-century manuscript collection of Old English poetry and riddles, named for its home in the Exeter Cathedral. While the book itself came into being a century after our story is set, the riddle likely predates the book it is from and it has been included here as it is a perfect example of the rich oral Saxon tradition of poems and riddles. Plus, it's hilarious. So, there's that.

Exeter Book Riddles. http://penelope.uchicago.edu/~grout/encyclopaedia_romana/britannia/anglo-saxon/flowers/enigmata.html

[xv] *Eálá* is an Old English expression that best translates to the modern

HEART OF THE WILD GODS

"oh!" or "alas!"

[xvi] Lord Odda was an Ealdorman from Devon known for his victory at the Battle of Cynwit in 878, over Ubba, the son of the legendary Ragnar Lothbrok.

[xvii] *Alfred* (often referred to as Alfred the Great) was King of the Saxon Kingdom of Wessex from 871 - 886, and after the establishment of the Danelaw, remained the Anglo Saxon King in Wessex, the only surviving Saxon kingdom in England.

[xviii] The recipe for Æfre's wound salve is an actual remedy from the 10th Century Old English medical book *Bald's Leechbook*. Originally created as an eye salve, a 2015 research collaboration at the University of Nottigham found that the ancient concoction actually had highly effective broad-spectrum efficacy against the modern superbug MRSA (Methicillin-resistant Staphylococcus aureus)!

https://pmc.ncbi.nlm.nih.gov/articles/PMC6261618/

[xix] The Saxons often used traditional metrical healing charms in their medical practices. These charms often took the form of incantations chanted while performing a specific action, and were meant to heal afflictions from a spiritual approach.

Below is the entirety of the 9th Century old Saxon *Uuurmsegen*, which translates closest as a charm "against worms"—although the "worm" in this instance could be any affliction from an actual parasite or infection to something more vague. The reference to "Drohtin" used here translates loosely to "Lord", which would have been the term used in post-Christianized Saxon England. Prior to Christianization, the reference would have likely been to the pagan-Germanic God Woden.

"*Go out worm, with nine wormlings, out of the marrow and into the bone, from that bone into the flesh, out from the flesh into the hide, out from the hide into this arrow. Drohtin! Let it be so.*"

[xx] A Saxon *scop* was a poet, storyteller or bard, a highly-respected member of society whose role was that of a keeper of cultural tales, telling historical stories and myths in village halls and royal courts. It is a societal position similar

to that of the Norse *scald*.

[xxi] *Wes hál* is an Old English expression meaning "be thou healthy" or in a modern context, "be in good health". It is the origin of the later term "wassail."

[xxii] *Guthrum* was a Danish leader of Viking forces, defeated by Alfred the Great at the Battle of Edington in May of 878. After his defeat, he was forced to negotiate with King Alfred and driven from Wessex. Per the terms of the agreement with King Alfred, Guthrum was baptized as a Christian before declaring himself King of East Anglia, a Viking-controlled region of England that was part of what eventually became the Danelaw.

[xxiii] The *witenagemot,* often referred to as simply the witan, literally translates to "meeting if wise men", and refers to the Anglo Saxon royal assembly, consisting of thegns, ealdormen, bishops and of course the king.

[xxiv] In 9th century Old English / Old Norse a *níðing /níðingr* was considered the worst imaginable insult. It referred to a coward or villain who had lost all honor.

[xxv] *Æthelred* served as the Archbishop of Canterbury from approximately 870 to 888.

Don't miss out!

Visit the website below and you can sign up to receive emails whenever Kendall Brooks publishes a new book. There's no charge and no obligation.

https://books2read.com/r/B-A-OVEPE-KQPCH

BOOKS 2 READ

Connecting independent readers to independent writers.

www.ingramcontent.com/pod-product-compliance
Ingram Content Group UK Ltd.
Pitfield, Milton Keynes, MK11 3LW, UK
UKHW040611060326